A Bond of Venom and Magic

The Goddess and the Guardians
Book One

Karen Tomlinson

Cover art by Jonas Jodicke
https://www.facebook.com/JojoesArt/
Map by Gregory Shipp
https://www.facebook.com/gregoryshippmapmaking/
Map illustration by Kevin Heasman at
https://www.facebook.com/dynamodoodles/
Edited by Monica Wanat

For Annie and Abbie, our beautiful girls.
May you blaze your own trail across this world!
This book is for you with all my love.

The Eight Kingdoms

A Bond of Venom and Magic

Part One

The Forest

Chapter One

Silence swept through the forest, deafening to Arades Gillon's fae ears. In the act of shoving a freshly felled tree further onto the ancient cart, he froze, his gut twisting with fear. The fresh scent of pine sap tickled his nose as he ignored the woodcutters bantering across the small clearing.

He pushed his bulk upright. Sweat beaded between his shoulder blades and trickled down his spine. Arades sucked in a deep breath, desperately reaching for the cold, calculating calm that had kept him alive for so many years.

It wasn't there. His heart raced, pounding against his ribs; for the first time in his life, Arades readied himself to flee from his enemy. His breath became shallow and fast, his keen eyes searching out the nightmarish shadow that lurked in the gloom of the old forest. It wouldn't be alone.

A guttural growl rippled through the trees, sinking deep into his bones. A violent shudder racked his body. For seventeen years that sound had been blissfully absent from his life; there was no mistaking it. The creature fixed its yellow, predatory gaze on one of the other woodcutters.

Arades had to run. Now.

Spinning on his heel, he burst into motion.

The Seeker snarled. Drool ran from its gaping jaws as it leaped from the dark shadows.

Yelling a warning to his friends would achieve nothing. They were as good as dead. Wild snarling filled the air as more Seekers burst from the forest. Petrified screams were cut short as human throats were slashed open by razor sharp claws.

Arades did not look back. Experience told him what he would see, and he did not wish to see his friends die such violent deaths. Terror squeezed his heart as yet more screams were abruptly silenced.

He would not—could not—fail. Panicked, Arades increased his effort and sprinted toward the town, its people and his beloved daughter.

The Seekers tore at the warm flesh and blood of the dead men, splintering and gnawing on their bones. Cranach gorged himself quickly and efficiently. He growled long and low; that small amount of warm human flesh did not sate his blood lust. If anything, he craved more. His pack had travelled for weeks without stopping to hunt, bypassing settlements where fresh fae and human flesh lived. On and on they had run, focused only on surviving and reaching their prey.

Relenting for one moment Cranach watched his brothers feast with an almost paternal relish, giving his starving pack time to drink the blood that would make them strong again. Minutes later, when only blood and ragged remains soiled the ground, Cranach snarled. The pack reacted instantly.

Their prey was so close; he could almost taste her filthy, mixed blood. She would not escape now. Besides failure would mean having his body broken slowly and painfully into pieces by his lord. His clawed fingers curled tightly around a small scrap of cloth. Snarling in distaste, he raised it to his nostrils, inhaling the sickly sweet scent that clung to it. This girl was more than the usual mix of human and fae, she was something he had never encountered before. The ancient power in her stench burned his sensitive nose, causing him to snort mucus into the air in an effort to expel it.

Revolted, he bared his teeth, stretched his body to its full height and howled. The pack instantly followed Cranach's order. The muscles of their back legs bunched and rippled under their thick, greenish-brown hair as they burst into movement. Sweat glistened across their filthy, humanoid torsos, and their gore-covered jaws snapped menacingly at each other.

With shoulders hunched and heads thrust forward, the Seekers ducked between the branches of the dense trees.

Cranach growled, snapping a tree branch out of his way with one gigantic claw. Running upright was impossible in this forest. He howled once. His brothers immediately complied with his order. Without breaking stride, the Seekers fell on to all four limbs and increased their speed. Their black claws churned up the forest floor as they charged towards their prey and the unsuspecting trade town nearby.

Arades pumped his arms and legs until they burned, crashing through the forest, forgoing stealth. Wind rushed by his ears as he forced himself to go faster. Vaulting a rotten, moss covered tree trunk, his hands slipped and he stumbled over exposed slimy tree roots as he landed. Years of training and instinct kicked in and he righted himself immediately.

The forest was so thick around the northern trade town of Berriesford that taking to the sky was impossible. Arades needed at least ten feet of clear space around him to spread his wings and fly. His lungs burned, sweat running down his forehead into his eyes. Feral snarling and crashing permeated the dark damp shadows behind him as the beasts gave chase, but he dare not look back lest he stumble and fall.

Brambles clutched at his boots, branches catching his clothes and legs—but he pushed on resolutely, his long legs devouring the uneven ground.

He broke from the forest into the arable land surrounding the town. Arades roared as he launched himself upwards into the sky. He snapped out his wings and beat against the air, faster and with more vigour than he had used for years. Thousands of tiny feathers covered the strong membranes, catching the invisible strength of the breeze.

Gods, he had been so stupid! As a warrior he should have flown more, armoured more.... "Complacent idiot!" he berated himself.

His wings were weak from underuse. Arades clenched his jaw, forcing the armoured particles out from between his feathers, shifting them with his fae magic until they completely covered the whole of his wing span. Within seconds a burnished, golden metal coated his wings, tattooed with his own unique pattern of glowing markings.

The stone town of Berriesford nestled in gently rolling farmland two miles in the distance. Even from here he could see the busy trade roads leading into the town. Arades swallowed his fear for all those people, feeling the malevolent presence of the Seekers behind him. With all his strength, he drove himself onward using the wind to help him soar towards his daughter.

Curious faces looked up. Berriesford folk were unaccustomed to seeing armoured fae warriors in their skies. Trouble was scarce in these parts since the treaty with the Ice Witches nearly one hundred years earlier.

Arades ignored their surprised exclamations and gazed anxiously toward the roof of his own small house. Landing solidly on the dirt track outside his home, Arades sprinted to his front door. He nearly knocked the door off its hinges. The shelves he had put up the month before rattled enough to knock down the small statue of Lunaria, the goddess of creation. It smashed into pieces on the floor. Arades grimaced, hoping that was not a bad omen.

"Diamond! *Diamond! Where are you*!" he bellowed.

He belatedly remembered she was working in the school house. He had promised Tanelle, Diamond's mother, he would educate their daughter and that is what he had done. Now she was on the other side of town, the side nearest to the beasts that hunted her. Growling with frustration at his stupid mistake, he grabbed his two Silverbore swords from beside the fireplace, turned and ran back outside.

The stooped form of General Edo came limping around the corner of the house. To the people of Berriesford this man had only ever been seen as a scruffy forest dweller—a loner, who lived in a small hut in the forest and spent his time gathering and selling the sweet yellow berries that grew among its vast emerald depths.

"Arades! What's going on?" General Edo shouted, narrowing his steely grey eyes and scrutinising Arades' armoured wings and urgent movements.

"They're here! They're here for her. We have to get her away from this town. *Now!*" shouted Arades, his brown eyes full of anxiety.

His friend nodded and immediately shook off his tattered cloak. General Edo straightened his shoulders and spine to expand his wings, transforming into a fae as tall and broad as Arades. Metal shimmered across the general's wings. Grim-faced and determined, both fae warriors bent their knees, spread their golden wings and launched in to the sky.

Chapter Two

Diamond hummed a gentle tune as she walked between the neat rows of wooden school desks. The pile of slate boards balanced precariously in her arms rattled. Offering to clean the schoolroom and lock up today was completely selfish. She liked the peace and quiet of the old school house after the children had gone home.

Leaning on the wall, Diamond glanced through the window at the trees and shuddered. It wasn't that she was scared of the eerie wood that led to the old temple grounds, it just seemed more sinister than usual today.

A sharp gust of wind tugged leaves from the wildly swaying branches, sending them dancing into the air. A sudden colourful cacophony of greens and golds whirled until the leaves settled like a beautiful carpet on the ground. She frowned, deliberately shrugging away the heavy unease that had plagued her since she had said a curt goodbye to her father this morning.

Diamond mentally kicked herself; arguing with her dad would not change her life. She was seventeen and acknowledged that he only worried for her safety. It was hard to admit he was right. The war and her heritage made travelling a dangerous prospect; besides, much as she wanted to find work in one of Avalonia's more southern cities, she did not want to leave her dad behind.

Diamond tried to feel grateful. She was lucky compared to other half-bloods. Her father had taught her reading and writing and had helped her secure a paid job, paltry though her income was. She huffed despondently. The thought of being an assistant teacher in this tiny schoolhouse until she was old and grey was truly depressing.

Stop feeling sorry for yourself, she admonished herself, knowing other half-blood girls her age were either married off or put to work in one of the inns or pleasure houses that crowded the Dregs. On the north side of Berriesford, it was a warren of dirty small streets, pleasure houses and a haven for shady, underhand deals. She was lucky—really she was. At least her father loved her enough to educate her and wanted her to stay safe.

Besides, Berriesford wasn't that bad. It was sort of safe here, not like the southern borders of Avalonia where the war with the Wraith Lord raged on. Some of the stories she heard from the bedraggled refugees who arrived, starving and desperate, made her blood curdle. It spoke volumes that they had braved months of exhaustion and hunger to travel through the endless forest to get as far north as Berriesford.

Her fingers absentmindedly brushed some chalk dust off a slate. At least her father wasn't trying to find a fae mate for her among the male newcomers or trying to marry her off to some local tradesman. Diamond snorted. She had absolutely no desire to saddle herself with a mate or a husband.

Besides, most men—of either race—considered her looks unnatural and her mixed blood offensive. It was clear she was considered the lowest possible marriage candidate for anyone. Her top lip curled in a snarl. Respectable boys avoided her—until their parents weren't watching, then it became fun to torment her. And passing traders who were too drunk or desperate to care often caused her problems, considering a young half-blood an easy target, especially when they cornered her alone.

Diamond's hands turned sweaty, and she thrust thoughts of being cornered out of her head.

Her unique looks were a curse. Her father said she was beautiful and stood out, but she didn't want to be noticed; she just wanted to feel normal. Even other half-bloods ridiculed her appearance. That was because most of them could pass for either fae or human and were generally accepted into their chosen society. Diamond was simultaneously too fae and too human; her up-tilted, vivid eyes and delicately pointed ears declared her fae heritage, and her average height and lack of wings revealed her human legacy.

Diamond's nostrils flared as the deep-seated pain of rejection raised its ugly head. In a trading town like Berriesford people were supposed to be more open-minded, especially with so many hunters, traders, miners and refugees venturing into town. But it did not matter, such deep-seated and ancient prejudices against bloodlines were not easily set aside, even in a town so vastly removed from the southern and eastern cities of Avalonia.

That was one of the reasons her father had wanted her to stay at home. The bigger cities were more devout in their religious beliefs and laws, and ever since she was small, Diamond's life had been a mix of insults and fights to defend herself. Her father had fought many times over the years, sometimes viciously, to protect her from the intolerant attention of others. But he could not be there all the time. If it hadn't been for her gangly best friend Tom, she would have gone mad from loneliness years ago.

A pair of misfits together, she chuckled, picturing her friend's floppy brown hair and light brown eyes. Being skinny and weak, Tom had been tormented nearly as much as Diamond.

She clenched and unclenched her fingers at the thought of all the dark alleys she had run down and hidden in over the years. Controlling her panic, she breathed deeply until the feeling settled. Together they had become experts at hiding from the gangs of kids the crime syndicates used to steal and pick pockets of the drunk and unsuspecting. When he had turned fifteen, Tom shot up to over six feet; although still skinny, he had begun fighting back.

Smiling, Diamond began cleaning the slates with a soft cloth that sent motes of chalk dust swirling into the air. Coughing and waving her hand in front of her face, she stood and placed the slates neatly on an old wooden shelf with a glance out of the window as she did so. A movement in the small copse of trees behind the yard made her squint. She wiped her hands down the skirt of her grey woollen dress and stifled a groan.

Mr Stenson's goats must have escaped again. Irritated by the old man's forgetfulness, Diamond grimaced. For the third time this week she was going to have to round them up and lock them back in their pen, or they would be stolen. Racing out of the front doors and down the steps, she careened around the back of the old stone school house.

A chill wind eddied over her bare arms, making her shiver. She rubbed them as she ran into the gloom between the trees, trying to ignore her unease.

An ancient, round stone structure with a domed roof stood in the shadows. A temple to the goddess of creation. Its crumbling walls and lichen-covered roof always saddened Diamond. People this far north didn't care much for religion—of any kind. The state of the temple was a testament to such apathy. Nevertheless it remained standing. The clearing around it, scarred with fire pits, served as a burning ground for the impoverished dead. None but the moneyed traders and wealthy business people could afford the burning tax the sheriff imposed for the larger, more prestigious crematorium across town.

As she neared the temple, Diamond's footsteps stilled. She paused under the thick branches of a large, red Lyca tree and listened intently. The wind blew the leaves so wildly it was difficult to hear anything above the din. Sudden snuffling from the undergrowth made her jump, then she giggled as a goat came trotting up.

"There you are, you naughty goat! Why do you keep on running away? Hmm? Now, where's your friend?" she asked the goat sternly.

The goat just looked at Diamond patiently and carried on grinding her jaws. Diamond could almost sense its lazy amusement. After a few more minutes she found the goat's companion chewing the leaves off a thorny, yellow berry bush. Diamond swallowed her annoyance. It wasn't Mr Stenson's fault. He was elderly and not really able to cope on his own anymore. By the time Diamond dragged the two stubborn goats out of the trees and past the school grounds to their pen, she seethed with frustration.

Grabbing the slats of the old gate, she heaved it off the ground and propped it across the entrance to the pen. Diamond wedged one end of a branch tightly under the gate and kicked the other end firmly into the soft soil, repeating the action several times until the gate was solid. Surveying her work with satisfaction, Diamond rubbed her hands briskly down her skirt.

I'll get Dad to come and fix this, she decided, hastening back through the woods, knowing Mr Stenson would never do it by himself.

Diamond trotted up the steps to the school house then froze, her scream sticking in her throat.

"Run!!" roared Arades as he saw Diamond in the doorway, her silver hair flying wildly in the wind.

The creature snarled at her from the far end of the room. Saliva dripped from its fangs as it launched itself forwards with a blood-curdling growl, its yellow eyes narrowing. A piercing scream escaped her. Stumbling backwards, Diamond lost her footing and went toppling down the steps. The world tilted and she fell heavily on to the last two steps. Pain shot through her ribs as her breath whooshed from her lungs.

"Dad!" she shrieked, lifting her head to see.

But Arades could not answer. He stood facing the charging creature, his feet planted firmly, his knees bent in a solid, defensive stance. Diamond had never seen him look so fierce. In his hand he clutched one of the ornate Silverbore swords that normally was propped beside their fire place. Gasping, Diamond registered her father's golden covered wings just as he swung the blade forward to meet the charging beast.

His wings had never looked metallic before, but she knew what that armour meant, even as her mind grappled with her understanding. Her father was a warrior! Only warrior fae could protect their wings in such a way.

"Diamond! In the name of the goddess—*run!*" Arades bellowed over his shoulder, already swiping a back-handed blow at the creature.

The note of desperation in his voice made her stomach lurch. She scrabbled up. "Dad!" she screamed again. She had to help him! As her foot hit the first step, solid muscle grabbed her from behind. She squealed as the world tumbled, and did not stop until her spine slammed into a fallen tree trunk. Pain shot across her shoulders, a cry escaping her lungs as her head cracked against solid wood.

Diamond forced her eyelids open. Blood dripped down the back of her neck, fear clutching at her belly. One of the hideous creatures had thrown her. Snarling, it jumped in the air and landed about six feet away. Her eyes widened. All she could see were the stringy bits of flesh that hung from its yellowed fangs. She screamed again, terror paralysing her limbs. It stomped towards her, sharp claws digging up the earth, its muscles rippling and shifting. Malformed hands reached out for her throat. Diamond cowered but the tree trunk at her bruised back stopped her retreat.

It was difficult to grasp any sensible thought. Violent pain throbbed through her skull. Forcing her limbs to move, she patted the leaf-strewn ground for a weapon of some kind. Her fingers closed tightly around the end of a branch. Diamond swung at the creature's head with all her might. It connected and snapped in two like a twig, the separate pieces flying in opposite directions.

The creature hesitated, shook itself, then roared in outrage, covering her in a spray of stinking saliva and blood. Suddenly the ear-splitting roar was cut off. It looked down at the long Silverbore sword that protruded through the muscles of its abdomen. The blade disappeared with a grotesque sucking sound. Another flash of metal; and whoever wielded the sword embedded it with terrific force in the creature's neck. Diamond squealed as warm blood sprayed over her face, chest and arms. She stared in horrified fascination as the creature fell sideways, making a dull thud as it hit the ground. Blood bubbled out between its sharp teeth and pumped from the large gash in its neck.

Diamond couldn't drag her gaze from the carcass. Sightless eyes stared back at her. Dizziness threatened to overwhelm Diamond as thick, dark blood seeped onto the grass, running up against her legs in a warm pool. The rotten stench from its insides hit her nostrils. It was too much. She gagged, saliva rushing her mouth. Never had she smelled anything so foul.

"Get up," growled a gruff voice.

"Uncle Amsal?" whispered Diamond disbelievingly, trying to swallow the gags that rippled from her stomach right up through her throat.

"Yes. Get up. Now!" he barked sharply.

Diamond tried to push herself up, stunned to see her father's best friend with armoured wings framing his silhouette. *What in the name of Chaos was going on?*

He yanked her hard to her feet. "Now, Diamond!" he barked, reaching for her shoulder.

"No. We have to help Dad!" she managed to cry, and pulled herself away from his grasp. Before Amsal Edo could catch her, Diamond was running full pelt towards the door of the school house.

A chorus of frightened shouts and screams of agony filled the air. The answering guttural roars from the creatures made her stumble, but she reached the doors and took the steps at a leap, wailing for her father. The hellish creature snarled at her as she skidded to a halt outside the open door. A loud scream bubbled up her throat. Arades hung limp and deathly pale in Cranach's grip, blood pumping from a deep gash in his chest. A rip in his thigh splattered ruby red blood onto the old wooden floor. The creature bared his sharp fangs in a grin, his eyes glowing with malice.

"Dad? No!" she cried, tears blurring her vision even as her father's pain-filled eyes found her own. A strong arm encircled her waist.

"Diamond!" yelled Amsal, then his head twisted to behold his friend. "Oh gods, Arades...." His voice turned hoarse with grief. He thrust his golden wings out from his back, but before he could take to the skies, another creature came charging around the side of the school house and leaped. Diamond screamed as the hairy, stinking body slammed into Amsal Edo, catapulting them both from the steps and across the ground. Loose stones ripped at her clothes, scraping the skin off her exposed skin. Barely functioning, Diamond could only watch as the creature loomed over Amsal's inert body, opening its jaws to rip out his throat.

"*No!*" she shrieked and picked up a large stone, throwing it with all her might at the creature's head. It bounced off his shoulder but gained his attention. Breathing heavily Diamond scrabbled to her feet, grabbing the nearest fallen branch as a make-shift weapon. Immediately the creature left the general and stalked toward Diamond.

The snarling became louder. Panicked, pain-filled screams echoed through the air as the nightmarish beasts tore into the townspeople. Diamond managed to keep from collapsing with fear. Her heart hammered in her chest, needles of pain shooting across the wounds on her hands as she tightened her grip on her pathetic weapon. Pitiful and small, Diamond stood facing the approaching beast, her silver hair blowing wildly around her head. Her violet eyes widened with terror. The creature stopped ten feet from her. Straightening his grotesque body he bared his rotting teeth. Bravely Diamond clutched the branch.

Fixing her with his cold hunter's eyes, he snarled but did not attack, instead he stretched his neck, took a breath and released a spine tingling screech. The sound froze Diamond's blood. It was a summons.

Fear unlike any she had experienced before stole her breath. Diamond spun on her heel, watching as more of the hideous beasts prowled out from the dark shadows between the trees. One by one they surrounded her, devouring her with their hungry eyes. Her very bones shook as she noticed the fresh blood dripping from their jaws and coating their upper bodies in dark red.

Why didn't they attack? Diamond gulped, her mouth so dry now it was impossible to swallow. Frozen to the spot, her knees shook so hard they threatened to collapse. They were waiting for something. A bead of sweat trickled down her temple, mixing with the blood leaking from her head wound.

With a shaking hand she swiped it away just as the flash of a greenish pelt blurred the corner of her vision. She whirled. The monstrous creature was emerging from the school house. Bigger than all of the others, he leaped from the steps and landed heavily nearby. The growl he emitted was long and low, his eyes now alight with triumph.

Her bladder threatened to void. This creature had killed her father; it was her father's blood that soiled this creature's face, her father's blood that dripped from his mouth. Her face crumpled, a loud sob escaping her. Clawed feet churned up the dirt as he stalked forwards, baring his fangs. Instinctively Diamond swung the branch at his head, but her arms were weak with terror. A large clawed hand caught her feeble weapon and yanked it from her grasp. Giving a growling chuckle, her attacker tossed the branch over her head. It landed with a distant thud.

Diamond could only whimper as sharp claws curled around her slim neck, squeezing just hard enough to make it impossible to scream. Heat seared her insides, a singular instinct to survive overwhelming her. She curled her hands into fists, hitting and tearing desperately at his hairy arms and sweaty body with her fingernails. Sweeping her from the ground, he dangled her in one claw like a rag doll before pulling her right up to his jaws. He chuckled at her pathetic efforts to cause him harm.

Diamond could not turn away from his foul breath. Triumph sparked in the creature's yellow eyes. Leisurely cutting off her air supply, he tightened his grip and lifted a scrap of cloth to his nose with his other clawed hand to inhale deeply. Tipping her head slightly to one side with a twitch of his thumb, he pulled her close. She didn't even have enough air to squeak as his tongue flicked out and tasted her blood.

Anger and disgust sparked heat in her belly. This demon had killed her father! Realising she did not stand a chance of survival, Diamond swung her heavy arms over his muscled shoulders. Fighting to stay conscious she locked her fingers around his hairy head and shoved her thumbs hard into his eye balls, grinding her teeth and snarling. She would cause this vile creature as much pain as possible before she died. Warm liquid exploded over her thumbs, running in blood-stained rivulets down her wrists. With all the breath squeezed out of her she couldn't even cry out in agony as he roared, piercing his claws through the soft skin of her neck.

May the goddess save my soul, Diamond prayed, feeling as if her head was going to explode. With one last concerted effort, she thrust her thumbs further into the demon's eye sockets. It gave an ear-splitting bellow and slammed her into the ground, almost throwing himself on top of her. Her head struck stone and stars exploded behind her eyes. Suddenly heavy, her arms fell away from him. Mercifully the creature released her neck and stumbled sideways, falling to its knees. She valiantly fought the darkness, but her eyes rolled skywards as she began to lose consciousness. Diamond blinked in disbelief. Winged figures hurtled towards her, too fast for her blurred eyes to follow.

Chapter Three

The creatures shifted into a circle around Diamond and their injured pack leader. Baring their fangs and tensing their bodies, they quivered in anticipation of more killing. The winged figures dived closer and the creatures leaped upwards with their clawed fingers extended like spears. With infinite grace, the diving figure closest to Diamond somersaulted, easily evading the attack and landed nearby. With his large metallic wings he knocked the nearest creature off balance before driving a sword into another.

One creature vaulted to straddle Diamond's body, a clawed foot landing on either side of her chest. A scream exploded from her as it reached for her ravaged throat. Once again her survival instinct kicked in, and her insides began to burn. She would not just lay here and wait to have her throat ripped out! Ignoring the sightless beast kneeling nearby, Diamond bent her knees and lifted both feet. Grunting, she shoved them hard into her assailant's lower belly and sent him toppling backwards. He roared with rage; but before he could recover, the large figure cut the creature down with his two Silverbore swords. Warm blood splattered over Diamond's face. She pushed herself up, her arms shaking, gagging. Her eyes darted around. She had no weapons, nothing with which to defend herself.

"Here," barked a gruff voice, and she found the cold metal of a dagger pressed into her slick palm.

Diamond did a double take. Dark wings flashed a deep, rich blue as they pulsed behind him, their silver markings shimmering with light. A fae warrior. Diamond looked at him stupidly, her eyes huge and round. Never in her life had she seen such beautiful sapphire blue wings. They were stunning. She staggered as long dirty claws slashed out. The warrior's gloved hand shot out and steadied her as he spun himself between her dazed form and the creature. Blood welled from the deep slash wounds now marking the side of his throat.

"Fight!" he growled down at her before attacking at full speed, driving the creature back so fast he became a blur of armoured wings and flashing blades.

Diamond screamed as another creature lunged for her. The dagger almost fell from her trembling fingers as she slashed backwards and forwards ineffectually. Agilely the warrior leaped back in front of her. In two swipes of his blades, her attacker was dead, a foul stench filling the air as his guts spilled out. Diamond swallowed her disgust and stumbled away from the carcass.

She watched wide-eyed as Amsal Edo, only a few feet away, swung his sword with obvious skill. Other fae warriors landed around her, forming a protective circle. With cold efficiency they killed all the remaining creatures. It was over in seconds. The only beast that still lived was the huge leader who had killed her father. Without hesitation, the blue-winged warrior slashed the tendons of its deformed ankles, incapacitating it. It roared its fury and pain but could do nothing. Kneeling blindly a few feet from Diamond, it sniffed the air. She swallowed her disgust. Despite no longer holding the piece of rag it was scenting her again.

"Diamond! Diamond, are you hurt?" shouted Amsal Edo urgently. He ran towards her, his normally icy grey eyes wide.

She shook her head, beginning to tremble from head to toe; cuts and bruises did not count. The ground ran thick with dark, almost black blood; guts and gore spilled all around her. Never had she seen such a gruesome sight. The animal stink and metallic odour of blood made her stomach clench. Swallowing didn't do much good but she persevered, not wanting to throw up in front of these hard-faced warriors. Her blue-winged saviour raised his large Silverbore sword to end her father's killer.

Silverbore, the highly prized metal of the fae race. Strong, yet malleable for any gifted fae metal-smith. It was also iron-free and therefore would not burn the fae who were notoriously sensitive to the cheaper, lighter iron weapons favoured by humans.

His blade glinted as he slashed down.

"Wait!" she cried.

With spectacular skill and precision, he stayed his hand, his blade halting a hairsbreadth from the creature's throat. Glancing sideways at the warrior, she took careful and deliberate steps toward the creature. Clutching the dagger in her shaking fingers, Diamond steeled herself not to run when the creature pulled his lips back from his teeth in a defiant snarl. The warrior growled in warning and pushed the sharp edge of his sword against the creature's hairy throat, drawing blood.

"Still yourself," he warned it. "Do not come any closer, girl. This Seeker wants to end you," he warned with a scowl.

She walked closer anyway and answered, "I know."

An overpowering chill seeped into her bones. Her father had told her tales of the dark creatures that lived in the far off Barren Waste Lands. A land wreathed in mist and home to monsters ruled by the Wraith Lord. An immortal being, he had been imprisoned in the Barren Wastes and had waged a war on the lands of the mortal Oden dynasty for nearly two thousand years.

It seemed the Wraith Lord was not content after finally overthrowing King Oden of Rhodainia and escaping. He was pushing his forces into Avalonia. All the monsters she had read about, heard stories about, had seemed so far away as to be imaginary; but this creature was very real, and so was the blood staining her clothes and drying upon her skin. Diamond knew the Seeker was still deadly even with the edge of a sword pressed against his throat, but she needed answers.

"Why are you here?" she asked, keeping her voice strong and steady whilst staring at the mess that had once been its eyes. No remorse flickered in her soul, only a grim satisfaction that she had caused it harm and suffering, at least a little bit, before it died.

The fae warrior laughed grimly at her efforts. "It cannot talk or understand, girl. There is no point in asking it questions. It just hunts and kills."

Diamond narrowed her eyes, tilting her head to study the creature. "Yes, you can, can't you?" she said to it. "You can understand me very clearly and talk to me."

It was a statement not a question, and she knew without a doubt it was true. She could feel its intelligence, its absolute killing focus oozing from its soul. The warrior raised his eyebrows, looking at her like she was mad, but she ignored him.

The Seeker rumbled a harsh laugh, making her and everyone else tense. She gasped as its growling voice resounded in her head. It was both an intimate and disgusting sensation. In response Diamond found her hand gripping tighter to the dagger.

'You are our prey, you ignorant half-breed. Our master, Ragor—Lord of Wraiths—wants your blood extinguished from this world. He wants you dead so your womb may not quicken with foul-blooded offspring, and he wants that trinket you carry between those teats of yours.' It growled another insulting laugh. *'And I will still take it from*

you.'

Diamond's breath hitched. *My necklace? How does the Wraith Lord know of my mother's dragon crystal?*

The fae warriors watched the silent exchange suspiciously. Amsal Edo put a firm hand on her shoulder, making her jump.

"Come, child. I don't know what lies it's telling you, but let these men kill it before it harms you or poisons your mind," he urged her.

"Wait!" she cried as the warrior's muscles tensed. She wasn't done yet. "Why did you kill my father if it's me you want?" she asked, her voice shaking with grief. It was so hard to suppress the unfamiliar rage that burned in her belly as another vicious laugh rumbled from the creature's chest.

The warrior watched her intently. His eyes narrowed, he kept his blade firmly in place even as the creature pressed his neck against the razor-like edge. Blood welled.

'He was in my way, and I wanted you to see him die, to know you were next. I would have let you hear him beg for your life but you ran away.' It huffed a growl. *'It did not stop him, though. He screamed your name before he died. But I was hungry and fae blood tastes far better than human when it is laced with fear and hate.'* Another throaty chuckle rocked his hairy shoulders. Clearly he was not in the least bit bothered about his impending death. *'Your father's screams were like sweet music to my ears as I gutted him and drank him dry.'*

His chuckle turned to a snarl and suddenly he lurched forwards, but Diamond had been waiting, the dagger burning a hole in her hand. With all her strength she thrust it up through his deformed ribs and pierced his heart at the same time as the warrior sliced its throat.

"For my father!" she hissed into its lupine ear as blood spurted hotly over her face and hand, and his weight sagged onto her arm. The warrior jerked her backwards, letting the lifeless body sag to the ground. He spun her around by her arm giving her a hard stare.

"It could have killed you," he stated sharply.

Diamond glared back as defiantly as possible, trying to ignore the large scar that stretched from the corner of the warrior's mouth, up across his cheek to the corner of his eye, into his hairline. It curled the side of his mouth into a parody of a smile, giving him a vicious appearance as it cut through the heavy growth of black beard. Wanting to run in the opposite direction was childish, he had defended her after all.

"But it didn't," she countered, wishing her voice sounded less afraid.

Silence hung between them before he said in a deep voice, "We should go."

Diamond held the sticky dagger out to him.

"Keep it," he said, staring down at her steadily as he stepped closer and curled her fingers back around the dagger hilt. Tilting her head back to look up at him, she blinked. Gods, he stood even taller than her father, at least another four inches. Diamond was only average height, and standing this close to him made her feel more insignificant and out of place than ever. Stunning dark blue eyes regarded her impatiently. She studied the rest of his face, or rather, what she could see under the thick growth of black beard.

His skin looked a deep golden brown. It was not the pale skin of most Avalonian fae. Covered in blood and beard, she found it impossible to guess his age. Even the blue iridescent hues in his black hair were like nothing Diamond had encountered before. Five small braids ran across his scalp from his wide strong brow to the nape of his neck where they were fixed tightly with a beaded leather string and hung down to just below his shoulders. His nose was straight, if slightly too large. Diamond frowned. His eyelashes were strangely pure white, completely at odds with....

Dark eyebrows raised at her scrutiny. Immediately her face flushed, heat rushing into her cheeks. She dropped her eyes, thankful he chose to turn his attention to Amsal Edo. No longer fuelled by fear and a need to survive, Diamond's body trembled with exhaustion and shock. Arades Gillon had been her rock, the one person who had grounded her and given her the ability to deal with the taunts and hate that often came her way. The world seemed suddenly vast and empty. Like long-lost kin being welcomed home, she allowed panic to bloom through her brain; all the tricks, all the well-practised ways her father had taught her to hold it back crumbled in the face of such grief. Her knees threatened to give way at the same time her body began to shiver violently.

Diamond was only vaguely aware of the warrior speaking in clipped and efficient tones. Rubbing her arms Diamond tried to take control of herself.

Focus on something else, she told herself as she forced her breathing to calm. The warrior was in her direct line of sight so she concentrated on him. It was obvious he was in command.

Studying his clothes, she tried to work out where he and his men had materialised from. His three-quarter length, plain leather jerkin was lightly armoured, and an assortment of evil-looking blades were sheathed on baldrics that criss-crossed his broad chest. Large daggers nestled in scabbards at his waist and he held two Silverbore swords in his big hands. The blades were relatively sleek for a warrior as large as him. They were far heavier than any Diamond could ever hope to lift.

Diamond glanced around at the other fae warriors. All fae were tall and broad in shoulder, and these were no different; however, they did not have the look of Avalonia. Their skin was more olive, their hair the darker brown she had come to associate with the refugee fae from Rhodainia...and her father. All of these warriors wore similar garb, although none had so many weapons and were not as tall or broad as their commander.

Emblazoned across their leather chest plates was the outline of a gold dragon. Warriors of Prince Oden. *What in the lost gods and goddesses are such a band of warriors doing so far north? Are they hunting me too?* With shaking fingers she touched the place between her breasts where her necklace lay. *What is so important about it—or me—that the Wraith Lord hunts us down?* But no, she would consider these questions later. Diamond glanced back at the fae warrior.

A serpent curled across the broad expanse of his chest. Her throat constricted. A Queen's elite guard, sworn to protect and serve the immortal monarch of Avalonia. Diamond's heart sped up. The nameless fae Queen, Diamond's queen, had brutally defended her lands, and ruled her people ruthlessly for over one thousand years.

Diamond knew the hate and fear she had suffered as a child was because the Queen abhorred half-bloods. Diamond tensed, she had been right to fear this warrior. He was one of the most highly skilled warriors on this continent and would view her of little import when he realised what she was.

The other warriors cleaned their weapons in a cursory fashion and extended their golden wings, ready to fly.

It was hard not to stare at the guard's blue wings. They were truly stunning. Far more beautiful than anything she had ever imagined. And astonishingly, he had managed to survive to adulthood in a kingdom owned by a ruler intolerant to any other than gold-winged fae.

Without exception, all the warrior's wings were covered in a unique swirling pattern that shimmered. Thick beards covered their faces too. They must have been out in this forest for weeks, months even, if they had come from as far away as Valentia, Avalonia's capital city.

Diamond looked at the ground and took a shaky breath. The school house loomed at the edge of her vision, a nightmarish shadow. Grief tore at her heart as she took a step toward it.

"Don't!" uttered Amsal, his hand shooting out to grip her arm. Blood covered his fingers. "Don't let your last memory of him be what's left in that school house."

"But we can't just leave him!" Diamond choked out, unable to hold back her sobs.

"Yes, we can. We must. Diamond, we have to leave. There are still...more of these beasts. And it seems they are searching for you," he gasped, his skin sweaty and pale. It was then she noticed the blood saturating his shirt sleeve and dripping to the ground.

The warrior stepped up to Amsal Edo. "Who are you?" he asked coldly, his hands grasping his gory swords. "You have a warrior's wings and fight with experience and skill."

Amsal looked down sideways at Diamond and kept a tight hold on her arm. "My name is Amsal Edo, and I am—or was—Primary General in the Combined Army of Rhodainia."

Diamond gasped. *General? In the Combined Army?* The Combined Army was the biggest army in the known kingdoms! It had been formed thousands of years ago when Lunaria had imprisoned Ragor in the Barren Waste Lands. An ancient pledge signed with blood and magic had decreed all rulers, whether human or fae, were required to conscript soldiers to bolster the army. Only over the past few years, since King Oden had disappeared and his generals had been killed in battle, had many conscripts deserted. Rumour was rife among the refugees that many soldiers had returned to their own lands because they had no faith in their young prince. It had always been the Combined Army that had kept Ragor's creatures from escaping the borders of the Barren Waste Lands, and it was the Combined Army that had failed....

Diamond's eyes widened as Amsal Edo continued.

"I answer only to King Oden of Stormguaard, and since he is dead that now makes the deposed prince my monarch and these warrior's mine to command." General Edo's voice was hard and strong. He straightened his body and looked directly at the warrior. "I am going to take Diamond south east to Valentia. She will be safe on the island city. We both know Ragor cannot get through the shield that protects it. You heard as well as I did that these creatures are hunting her. Whatever the reason, they will not stop. The man who lies dead in that school house was General Arades Gillon, Diamond's father. I promised him I would care for her and get her to safety if anything happened to him...."

A general? A warrior? My father?

Just as the bottom of Diamond's world dropped out, his explanation was interrupted by a high pitched panicked shout. She vaguely recognised the yelling voice.

"Hey! Diamond! Diamond! Wait. It's me!" shouted the tall, skinny young man as he raced up to her.

"Tom?" exclaimed Diamond shakily.

The general glared at Tom and swore under his breath.

Tom skidded to a halt in front of Diamond, looking at her blood-stained face and clothes in horror. Panting, his eyes widened and he ogled General Edo and the other warriors.

"Who are you?" the warrior asked, regarding Tom coldly.

"I'm Diamond's friend. Who are you?" Tom snapped back, paling under the ice in the warrior's glare.

Diamond feared for her friend and stepped between them. "Tom. It's okay. They saved me." She grasped his hand, fighting to keep her voice even. "Tom, Dad's dead. One of these...monsters killed him."

Tom encircled her with his bony arms. "I'm so sorry, Diamond," he whispered, "Mum is dead too.... One of those things went into our house and I heard her scream. I-I ran away," he whispered, his voice breaking with self-disgust.

Nearby, more feral roars filled the air. Diamond pulled away from Tom, her head snapping toward General Edo. The warrior sheathed his swords. "General Edo, sir, we need to go—now," he said with authority.

"So be it. I know of a cave three hours by wing from here. It is up a sheer cliff face and should be safe to rest in for tonight. Diamond, stand still for a moment," the general instructed.

Diamond stood mute as General Edo leaned forwards and cut strips off her skirts, instructing her to bind his arm, which she could only do with Tom's help as her fingers were shaking.

"I will carry you to the cave," the general said, but he sounded tired, his body listing as he leaned heavily on his sword.

The warrior stepped in decisively with no emotion in his voice. "Sir, you are exhausted. I will take the girl."

The general raised his eyebrows, his brow furrowed in a frown, but he nodded reluctantly and took a step back. Diamond's heart beat against her ribs, her eyes shifting back and forth from the warrior to the school house. Her body tensed—ready to bolt—but he stepped in front of her, his broad-shouldered bulk blocking her path. His beautiful sapphire and silver eyes narrowed and held hers, as if he knew exactly what she was thinking.

Chapter Four

Danger and impatience pulsed off him in warm waves. It was a strange, almost tangible sensation that rippled over Diamond's exposed skin, startling her. Instinctively she stepped back, rubbing her arms. Fearful of him, she looked to General Edo for guidance. His mouth a tight line, General Edo nodded. But the school house....

The Queen's guard took in her blood-covered, grief-stricken face, his eyes dropping to the wounds on her neck. Unaware, Diamond's gaze stayed focused on the school house.

It was impossible to just leave. Her father deserved better than to be abandoned. He had died to save her. All this—all this screaming and death and bloodshed was her fault. Diamond's face crumpled, tears dripping down her cheeks.

"Can't we at least take him to the temple? His soul will not enter Eternity if we don't release it with fire," she sobbed, not caring what any of them thought.

A new wave of terrified screams saturated the air. The warriors shifted uncomfortably, moving to face outward with swords drawn.

"No. We cannot stay. It's too dangerous. Any remaining Seekers will hunt you until they can no longer scent you. The only way to escape them is to fly you somewhere distant from here." The Queen's guard held his arms out expectantly.

Diamond stared at him. Before she knew what she was doing, Diamond launched herself into a run, screaming for her father at the top of her voice. *He is not dead.* He could not be—because she did not know what to do without him. Tears blurred her vision as she sprinted. He could still be alive....

It only took seconds before the Queen's guard caught up with her. Wordlessly he grabbed her waist and hoisted her up. Diamond had no choice but to latch her fingers onto him. The roughness of his touch shocked her out of the madness that had taken her. Choking on gut-wrenching sobs, she closed her eyes. He extended his wings in one swift, powerful movement, then launched up into the sky.

Wind roared in her ears as those startling feathered membranes turned to metal and picked up speed, thudding solidly against the air. Weeping, she curled her fingers into his leather-clad shoulders, grief ripping at her heart as the school house and everything she knew grew smaller, disappearing until even the haunting screams of the dying faded. Her handsome, loving father was truly gone—and it was all her fault....

Oblivious to time or the cold wind against her skin, Diamond cried herself dry. Eventually her sobs settled into hiccoughs. As awareness returned, it was an effort to lift her heavy head from the elite guard's chest. At least they had rescued Tom. Guilt stabbed at her. She hadn't even thought of him since the guard had snatched her up. Her friend was clutched in the arms of another warrior, looking pale and stunned.

Diamond's insides felt like they had been ripped out, leaving her hollow and numb, yet her heart ached with a fierceness that threatened to tip her over the edge of reason. Her father was gone forever; never again would she feel his love or forgiveness or hear the anger in his voice when she pushed him too far. Blind panic stole her breath. She would never see him again.

"Slow your breathing before you pass out," the guard advised unemotionally. Diamond ignored his tone and tightly gripped his solid shoulders, using his bulk as a lifeline. She didn't care what he thought of her. She needed something, anything, to keep her anchored before she lost her mind completely. Keeping her eyes closed and her cheek against his chest, Diamond concentrated on the shift of the guard's shoulder and back muscles. They moved powerfully under her fingers as his wings beat a steady rhythm. After a while the tingle of panic in her fingers and lips abated.

The queen's guard ordered a brief stop to collect their packs, which had been left many miles from the town, but he did not land himself. With apparent ease he hovered above his men to keep a look out. That task completed, the warriors followed General Edo. Several times the high winds forced them to change direction. Invisible eddies wildly blew through Diamond's bloodied silver hair. Hissing with impatience, the guard moved his chin to trap her hair out of the way. She might have apologised or grabbed it in her hand—if she could have brought herself to care. The cold eventually numbed her hands to the point where her grip on his shoulders slipped. Alarmed, her eyes flew open. The ground was a frighteningly long way down.

She gasped, her eyes anxiously finding his. Heights had never been easy for her to deal with.

"I will not drop you. You can let go if you wish," he said brusquely, hitching her higher. For a moment his sapphire eyes flicked to hers. It was easier to close her eyes and drop her head back on his shoulder than even consider meeting that icy regard. She must appear so weak and feeble to someone like him.

It felt like hours passed before General Edo shouted, "Here!"

Bracing her hands on the guard's shoulders, she twisted her head to see where they were going. A cave materialised from behind some spiky bushes that clung tenuously to the sheer cliff face. General Edo landed first, followed by the others one by one.

The guard hovered, watching them and ignoring her. When the ledge was clear he glided in, landing with light-footed grace. Inside was gloomy but large enough for all twelve of them to fit. Only the Queen's guard had to bend his head to keep from banging it on the roof. Absentmindedly he lowered her to the ground and turned to the general.

"General Edo, it would be best if you rest here and take some time to clean and re-bind your wounds. We will be back with food and water soon, and tomorrow we have far to go. Karl! Zane! Finn! With me. We will hunt due west. The rest of you go east. Be back here by dusk," he told them. "We will rest here tonight and re-join Prince Oden tomorrow."

They all saluted smartly and chorused, "Yes, sir."

"Karl. Give the general your salve and clean bindings for his wound."

"Yes, sir," Karl replied and delved in his pack, passing the items to General Edo. The general nodded his thanks.

Without so much as a glance in her direction, the guard turned to leave.

"Wait!" uttered Diamond reaching out to touch his arm before the inappropriateness of that action caught up with her brain. He turned back, eyeing her hand coldly. Her eyes widened at the sharp stab of pain in her fingers. Wincing she dropped her hand immediately. It felt like something had bitten her.

"Yes?" he replied coldly.

"Err...what's your name?" she asked, suddenly feeling inadequate and foolish.

He cocked his head, weighing her up, deciding if she was worth an answer. She squirmed under the weight of that midnight gaze.

"Commander Casimir," he replied after a few seconds.

"Oh. Is that it? Don't you have a first name?" she blurted before it occurred to her sluggish brain that being on first name terms with a Queen's guard was absurd, especially for a half-blood.

"Yes. I do," he answered, annoyance colouring his tone. "You are not in the military and clearly neither are you a full-blooded human or fae, so how you address me—by my first name, which is Hugo or Commander Casimir—is of no importance to me." He looked her up and down, a shadow of distaste curling his mouth. "I can see why your father kept you in the northern forest. Someone like you will not fare well in the southern cities." He looked to General Edo, who stood stoic and silent, before looking back at her again. "Valentia may be safer than the forest, but you will have no rights there, especially as an obvious half-blood. Is that still the course of action you wish to take, general? You could appeal to the prince to keep her with his people in the valley."

"No," interrupted the general sharply.

Diamond almost missed the exchange about her future safety, she was too busy trying to ignore the hurt his words caused her. Of course she was of no importance to him—to anyone. Shrinking within herself, the consuming numbness of grief and inadequacy threatened to devour her, but manners, the manners her father had instilled upon her, won out. She squared her shoulders and forced herself to form words and speak. "I will do whatever Uncle—I mean General Edo—thinks best. I—err, just wanted to thank you, commander f-for s-saving me," she stammered even as she lifted her chin. "Despite my unimportance."

His face was severe enough she found it difficult to look at him. Surprise flickered in his eyes, warming them for an instant before ice settled once again. He dipped his head silently, an acknowledgment of her gratitude before launching himself elegantly out of the cave after the others.

Chapter Five

Diamond awoke with a start, sweat running down her spine and between her breasts. The floor underneath her was hard and cold. Panting, she tried to get her bearings. The pounding in her head made it so hard to think. Cracking her eyelids open she swiped the dampness from her cheeks and tried to pull herself together. For a moment confusion fogged her brain. *Where am I?*

Then everything came flooding back. The Seekers, her father—her nightmare. A horrible place in her mind, plagued by dragons and fire and blood and monsters. Diamond stifled a sob and pushed herself upright. Focusing on anything else but those dark thoughts, she cast her eyes around the cave.

The warriors had all returned. General Edo and Tom sat near the cave entrance, silhouetted against the firelight. A small boar sizzled and dripped juices into the flames, releasing a mouth-watering aroma that, despite her lack of appetite, made Diamond's stomach grumble loudly. Warmth filled the cave, the glowing orange flames casting her into a veil of shadow.

Seeing the others eating did nothing for her. Despite the emptiness that filled her, Diamond's limbs were shaking too much to get up and venture across the cave. Trying to control her trembling body and addled mind, she inhaled and pushed her back up against the cave wall. Absorbing the solid strength of it, Diamond closed her eyes and forced the disturbing dream into the recesses of her mind. Concentrating on the pain from her bruises helped distract her and, after a few minutes, her breathing settled and the shaking lessened.

Feeling a little stronger, she opened her eyes to find Hugo sitting in the blackest shadows opposite watching her closely. Obscured in the gloom of the cave his eyes only glinted, but she had no inclination to look at him. Instead she cast her eyes at the spit over the fire and pushed a hand against her aching belly. Not knowing if she was hungry or just sick with grief, she closed her eyes again. Memories of her father's gentle voice filled her mind.

"Daddy, why did all the warriors have gold wings in that faery tale? I don't like gold, blue is my favourite colour. I want to see a warrior with blue wings...."

Her father chuckled. "Blue wings don't exist; fae only ever have red, gold, green and pearlescent wings, or pearls as we call them. But remember only golden-winged warriors live in Avalonia now—just like the story tells you."

"Did the bad lady kill the fae with pretty wings just because she didn't like their colours?"

"No, my little jewel, she killed them all because their magic can make her stronger." Her father looked and sounded so sad. "Fae magic that was once mighty in this kingdom now dwindles so low that only the strongest fae can be taught to use it."

"Where did magic come from, Daddy?"

"Long ago Lunaria, the goddess of creation, gifted the fae with magic. She gave us four levels: red to wield fire and heat." He settled her into bed. "And just like fire, red-winged fae are powerful and not to be trifled with. Their temper is as quick to blaze as the fire and heat they command. Green is the colour of fae who can create and control flora. They can encourage life to flourish and make excellent healers. Then there are gold-winged fae, who just love the gleam of metals—any metals. In my home in Rhodainia they were by far the most common fae but not the only ones. Some could even pinpoint metallic ore through the ground. In Avalonia fae can only force the metallic elements of their magic to armour their wings. Then there is the weakest and gentlest of our race, the 'pearls', who have very little magic of their own. It is said that as soon as the wicked queen took the throne of Avalonia she ordered any child born with magic above gold killed at birth."

"Oh." That answer had been far too long and Diamond had lost interest. "When will I grow wings? I want red magic, or maybe pretty gold magic, then I can be special and strong like you, Daddy."

He had smiled and pulled the bedclothes around her, tucking them in tightly.

"Diamond, you do not need magic to make you special, you already are. And you do not need wings to fly because jewels like you can soar right across the sky all by yourself. Have you ever seen a shooting star?"

"Yes, Daddy," she replied gravely.

"Well, you are just like them. One day, when you are grown up, you will soar right across this world and leave a blazing trail behind you...and you will not need wings to do it, my sweet girl."

"Really...." she gasped, snuggling down into the warmth of her familiar bed.

"Here," said Hugo, pushing a bit of bark piled with meat toward her folded hands. Diamond jumped. "You need to eat," he said tersely.

Her mouth dropped open before she took the offering and placed it on the ground beside her. A Queen's guard did not serve a half-blood food. Diamond swallowed nervously, not used to being near someone so heavily armed—or so big and imposing. Another surprise, he lowered his bulk next to her and stared at the meat, then her. A silent command. Sighing, she picked it up again. His shoulder rested only inches from hers, making her fully aware of his proximity. A strange warmth bloomed inside her, as if her body were reacting to the closeness of his. Feeling smothered, she shuffled sideways.

"What did that vile creature tell you? Why is the lord of the Barren Waste Lands hunting you?" Hugo asked, keeping his gaze forward.

"I don't know," she lied, not taking her eyes off the succulent pile of meat. Lying had never been her strength, and the food was a good excuse not to look at him. Her father had always been able to sense any lie she uttered, so she was not well-practised in the art of deception. Besides, this warrior was in servitude to a wicked and cruel ruler. *Can I trust him?*

Despite the delicious aroma, Diamond really did not feel like eating. Instead she dared a sideways glance. Her eyes alighted on the jagged white scar that marred Hugo's face. It caught and held her attention. Something told her changing the subject away from her lie would be safer. If one immortal ruler wanted her necklace, maybe his Queen would too.

"Would you tell me about Valentia?" she ventured nervously. He had seemed so cold earlier—but for a reason Diamond was at a loss to understand, he had brought her food and now sat inches from her half-blood body. Maybe he was feeling benevolent and would be willing to answer her questions.

"General Edo thinks the island city will be safer for me than this forest, but you don't. It's where you're from, isn't it?" She made her voice sound in control and steady, even though asking this emotionally shutdown warrior a personal question felt awkward and unnatural. Then again, she didn't know what else to say to distract a killer whose blades gleamed with every small movement he made, a male who was sitting so close she could feel the heat radiating from his body.

Hugo leaned his forearms on his bent knees, his leather armour creaking as it strained against the expanding muscles of his back and shoulders. He turned, angling his head slightly, surprise flickering in his eyes. Diamond absently noticed he had dressed the wound on his neck.

"Yes." He hesitated, clearly deciding whether or not to continue.

Diamond wondered how often he was asked to speak about himself. Probably never, she surmised, attempting an encouraging smile. It seemed neither of them was socially practised.

Hugo turned his attention back to the flames. "I was raised in the guard's quarters in the palace, so Valentia is my home. The general is right in a way. The island city will be safer for you than the forest. But, like every town and city, there are monsters and demons of a different sort lurking in its shadows." He looked at her.

She gulped at the warning in his eyes. "Why hasn't Ragor attacked the city?" Diamond asked quietly.

"Oh, I think there are many reasons. For one, the size of his army is too big to travel swiftly. They also seem intent on attacking every town and village in their path. Any souls who have not fled are being hunted down by the Wraith Lord's troops. It seems Ragor wants to kill as many as possible and possess their dead bodies to swell his ranks. He consumes their souls, then turns them into monsters."

A ripple of disgust shuddered through her body. "But what can he want with so many souls?" she whispered.

"Devouring the energy of a soul is like a drug to Ragor, especially when they die fighting and screaming."

Diamond trembled at his words. "But surely even Ragor can only feast upon so many souls before he will glut himself and explode from the inside out?" she asked with a grimace.

Hugo huffed, an unexpected smile twitching his lips and twisting his scar into something hideous that even the gloom of the cave could not hide. "Now wouldn't that solve all our problems?" he muttered, glancing at her. The smile slipped away as if it had never been when he registered where her eyes rested. "Consuming the energy of a soul is his sustenance. It makes him stronger—but only for a short time, then he needs more."

He faced forward again. Silence fell between them but Diamond stayed quiet; somehow she knew he was not done speaking yet.

"When Ragor escaped the wards holding him inside the Barren Waste Lands he fought to reach Stormguaard. King Oden battled him for years on the borders between Rhodainia and the Barren Waste Lands. But then the king disappeared. That left Prince Oden alone to rule. One by one his generals were assassinated or ambushed, and Jack's army slowly disintegrated around him until he had only young and untried commanders. I was sent there by my Queen with several fae legions to help him. But I think we all realized it was too late. Jack, Prince Oden, was only fifteen when Ragor attacked. It didn't end well, as you know. Saving as many people from Rhodainia as possible became the prince's priority."

His eyes took on a distant look. "Ragor's army of the dead moved faster than anything I had ever seen before. They travelled as if moved by the wind. The grasslands of Rhodainia are dry and dusty in the summer months, and although we had prepared, it made no difference. Each of Ragor's dead soldiers used the dusty ground to transform into a swirling column of dirt, into Dust Devils. Even the most experienced soldiers struggled to fight them."

Does he mean himself? she wondered. It didn't seem appropriate to prompt him, so she sat quietly—waiting.

"Dust Devils are impossible to kill—until they reform back into the husk of the man or fae they once were." His head twisted and he looked at her.

She wondered why he was telling her this—telling her anything at all—after what he had said earlier.

"The farther north the Wraith Lord invades, the damper the ground becomes. When grasslands turn to forest, Dust Devils can no longer transform. That and the combined forces of Jack and the Queen have slowed Ragor down. But even that hasn't been enough to stop him. The prince has withdrawn his troops to concentrate on defending the Rift Valley wall, whilst the Queen continues to destroy his forces in smaller campaigns. Survivors are escaping wherever they can; many are going north thinking they will avoid the conflict, but the Rift Valley and Valentia are still nearly full to bursting. So many souls will only continue to entice Ragor. I expect he will attack the city this winter."

Diamond stared at the pile of meat in her hand, dread tightening her belly. Nowhere was truly safe.

"Don't worry, Valentia's ancient magic shield will slow Ragor and his army down. He will not break through easily," Hugo informed her in a mildly condescending and irritating tone.

She nodded but wasn't naive enough to be convinced. Ragor was as ancient as that shield—it would not stop him forever. "I know about the shield," she answered, her voice sharper than she intended. "I am not completely ignorant just because I'm a half-blood. I can read and write and everything," she bit out, then took a breath. His prejudices were not entirely his fault; besides, his assumption she would be illiterate was hardly unique.

" My...father," she nearly choked on that word, "told me tales of Valentia and the Queen, though I am not sure what was true and what he made up to entertain me as a child. What will happen when Ragor reaches the Rift Valley wall? Surely he will put siege to the city and starve everyone to death. It would be far less effort for him than a war, wouldn't it?"

Hugo raised his eyebrows slightly, causing his scar to stretch.

Did I say something wrong?

"You are remarkably well informed—for a half-blood," he commented, his eyes narrowed thoughtfully. Diamond gritted her teeth and tried not to let his remark hurt. "Ragor wants to gather souls, and to do that he needs to be nearby when the slaughter begins." He shrugged his big shoulders before continuing, "But no one is sure if that's all he wants. Devouring a soul's energy immediately after death is an insatiable need for him. It makes him stronger—but only for a time. And Ragor is a wraith who has been starved of souls for thousands of years. Now he gluts. When he arrives at the wall with his army, none of us will have time to starve."

Diamond shuddered at the implications of Hugo's words. Even if the wall kept Ragor out and, by some miracle, he gave up on Valentia, the rest of Avalonia would be destroyed. "Why, though? What does a powerful lord of darkness desire once he has devoured all the souls in Avalonia? What is left for him?"

Hugo frowned as though he didn't really want this conversation. "The other kingdoms across the Rough Sea, I suppose."

"So why aren't people from Valentia fleeing? Why isn't the Queen allying with the other kingdoms and planning for an attack? Valentia's an island city; surely there are boats or ships or something that can get people out?!" Diamond exclaimed. It was ludicrous to keep so many people under the constant threat of eternal torture at the Wraith Lord's hands.

"The Queen has discouraged her subjects from leaving. Did you know that Ragor was once Lord Commander of the armies of Erebos, the God of Chaos?"

Diamond shook her head.

"Well, he was. And my Queen is as ancient as Ragor. She has fought him and defeated him before. She knows how his mind works. Valentians have confidence she will defeat Ragor. They believe in her, and have every faith the shield and their Queen's eternal power will protect them from harm—as do I."

Diamond couldn't quite believe what she was hearing; not only did those last words sound somewhat forced, but surely people weren't so blindly trusting as to believe their ruler was going to save them—that one fae queen was powerful enough to keep them safe against an invading army of dead things.

"But the shield is thousands of years old. Every book I've ever read, every story I've learned as a child, says it is there to protect the Rift Valley and Valentia from the fire of the guardian's, not to stop an invading immortal or his army."

"True, but most people in Valentia have chosen to forget the shield's reason for existence. Remember, dragons have been gone from Avalonia for at least a thousand years. Even if tales and rumour suggest they have been seen in the Fire Mountains." His throat bobbed as he swallowed. "If you try and bring a long-dead body back into Valentia, the shield will turn it to dust. Therefore, the theory of our Master Commander is it will stop soulless creatures, like Dust Devils, from entering the city. To get his army into the Rift Valley, Ragor will have to destroy the wall and the shield. The mortal prince's city, Stormguaard, fell because there was no shield."

"Did many die?" Diamond whispered, almost afraid to ask.

"Yes." His voice was hard. "Thousands of innocent people perished and many more had their souls ripped from them in those final moments when the city fell...the prince and I saw too many suffer before we escaped."

Diamond shuddered at the thought of seeing a soul ripped from a person. "Will the shield stop all his soldiers?" she asked, thinking about the Seekers.

"No. Ragor has many monstrous creatures in his army besides Seekers and Dust Devils. There are Wolfmen, who people say were the first shape shifters but who displeased Erebos so he kept them in between forms as a punishment. They cannot scale the smooth Rift Valley wall. And Battle Imps, which are ugly as a warthog's backside. Big, muscly, bald and blue. They're too clumsy and heavy to even try. Neither is Ragor a battle leader given to patience—despite his eternal life. He wishes to conquer, and to do it quickly he will use giants to try and destroy the wall. It is heavily manned by Prince Oden's forces; and in addition to the Queen's forces, the gates that provide access for those without wings are warded by the Queen's magic. Have you been to many cities?" he asked.

The change in subject threw Diamond. Startled she met his questioning glare. "No, I haven't," she answered truthfully.

"Hmm. Well, remember what I said: every city has its dangers, especially for someone like you. The city guard will not help a half-blood in trouble, and neither will most of the people. You have no rights to safety—or anything else. If you wish to stay alive, or not end up pressed into service in a whore house, do not trust anyone or go anywhere alone." Warning laced his voice.

Diamond scowled to cover her inadequacy and fear.

Hugo kept his eyes focused in front of him and continued, although Diamond was at a loss to explain his patience and willingness to enlighten her.

"Diamond," her name rolled off his tongue and for a moment surprise flickered in his eyes. It disappeared so quickly she wondered if she had imagined it. "Valentia is swollen with refugees, people who are desperate and hungry and homeless. It is a dangerous and desperate place right now," his massive shoulders shrugged slightly. "But if Ragor is hunting you, it will be safer than wandering this forest."

Her belly clenched and her chest felt like it was being squeezed. That tightness was all she could concentrate on for a moment. She shut her eyes.

Breathe. In. Out. In. Out. Her father's voice. For a moment grief stole her senses. Deliberately, slowly, she inhaled a breath through her nostrils. After a time she opened her eyes, avoiding looking at Hugo's fearsome face. Valentia was going to be far from a safe haven.

Chapter Six

The aroma of cooked meat drifted up her nose. In control of her anxiety and breathing once again, Diamond forced some meat between her teeth. Juices ran across her tongue and down her throat, but still it was an effort to swallow. Eating seemed disgusting when her father would never taste another meal.

"Eating is necessary," Hugo told her matter-of-factly. "It will give you at least some strength, and food is scarce in this forest now. It may be your last meal for a while."

Diamond pulled a face but continued until her portion disappeared. It settled like a brick in her belly. Thankfully, Hugo seemed content to sit quietly until she had completed the onerous task. He quickly passed her his water skin.

"Here, drink," he ordered.

She hesitated. *Why would he share anything of his with a half-blood?* The scar twisted his left eyebrow out of shape as he raised his brows. Diamond didn't have the strength to argue or care. Coolness washed down her throat, unsticking the lodged food. Handing it back, she gave him a weak smile, quickly looking away from his scarred features. Ignoring her discomfort, he placed the water skin down on the floor beside his bent knees.

"So why is a Queen's guard so far north?" she asked, curiously.

"Prince Oden's scouts saw Cranach's pack heading north through the far reaches of the forest. They seemed to be avoiding any confrontation with our troops, and they only ever do that when they are hunting someone specific. Prince Oden wanted to track them and find out who they were after—and why Ragor was willing to risk his Seekers for it."

"I asked why you are here," Diamond clarified, frowning at his evasive answer. "You are a Queen's guard and not in servitude to the prince, unless your allegiance has changed."

His eyes turned to endless black. Diamond cringed away, trying to calm her sudden fear. She needed to learn to curb her tongue. The smart-mouthed comments she had always snapped back at her father would not be tolerated by this warrior.

"I go where my Queen sends me—and report back on matters of importance."

"Oh, well, I guess it must be disappointing to know they were only looking for a lowly, unimportant half-blood like me," Diamond responded caustically, ignoring her own advice about her mouth and staring across the cave into the dancing flames instead of into Hugo's obsidian eyes, not sapphire—obsidian—the colour of death and shadow.

The other fae warriors were silhouettes against the glowing fire light. Some were busy cleaning their weapons, others were talking quietly or laying down to rest. Diamond concentrated on them, watching Tom's skinny shadow as he turned to look at her, his attention resting on Hugo. Diamond could almost hear him asking if she was alright. She gave him a reassuring nod.

"Why would it be disappointing?" Hugo asked, contemplating Tom. "Ragor wants you dead for a reason. We just have to find out why. We will join Prince Jack, tomorrow then head back to Valentia. My Queen is ancient and has knowledge forgotten to mortals like us. She will perhaps be able to work out what he wants from you."

Diamond didn't want to meet the fae Queen at all, but his words told her she would have no choice in the matter. Escaping him before they hit the city walls was her only chance. Clenching and unclenching her fists, she did her best to control yet another panic attack. If only her father was here; he had always been able to anchor her, help her control her worst attacks. Cold and shaking, she resisted the urge to grasp her necklace. It had belonged to her mother. No one could have it, not the Wraith Lord, not this guard, and definitely not the powerful Queen. It was hers.

"We will find the prince not too far south of here. I know General Edo wishes to meet with his monarch. I expect he will want to re-join the prince's army as soon as you are safe," Hugo continued, oblivious to her turmoil.

"Oh." It was the only response Diamond could muster, her lips tingling as they always did when she felt panic grip her. Hugo didn't seem to have anything else to say either. Staring into the dying flames, she wondered what was to happen to her if General Edo did join with his prince. She had no idea what she was going to do in Valentia as she would be homeless with no money for food and absolutely no idea about how to survive in a city full of desperate people.

At least Tom was with her. Her friend's shoulders were slumped forward, misery and grief written in every line of his body. Diamond pressed her lips into a tight line, shame burning inside her. He had lost everything because of her. She should go and comfort him. *But what if he spurns me? Have the others told him I am to blame?* Tears burned her eyes. *What does the future hold for us both now? Will he ever forgive me?*

Tom's silhouette became distorted as her eyes blurred. Diamond would not cry again. Not in front of Hugo. Shame burned her cheeks as she remembered crying into his shoulder until she had no tears left to shed. Worrying about the future, hers or Tom's, was pointless; they had to make it to the city first.

Her thoughts must have shown on her face.

"Don't worry. If anything else hunts you, we will kill it. You will get to Valentia," Hugo promised, his deep voice rumbling over her and giving her goose bumps.

Diamond twisted to regard his terrifying visage, not doubting for a moment he spoke the truth. In those few seconds it struck her Hugo did not look as old as she had first thought;- in fact, if she chose to disregard the altering effect of his scar, he did not look that much older than her.

"How old are you?" she asked curiously, narrowing her eyes as she studied his face.

"Nineteen." Hugo answered shortly, studying her right back.

"Nineteen!" she exclaimed. "No. You're a lot older than that."

Her stomach tightened, twenty was considered fully mature in fae males. Her knowledge of fae customs was thorough, thanks to her father. Most fae males didn't choose a life mate upon maturing these days, certainly not if they had obligations to their Queen; but just the awareness that Hugo could want someone enough to make that binding pledge made Diamond fidget. He raised his eyebrows quizzically almost as if he could read her thoughts.

"Thanks," he drawled.

"S-sorry." Diamond stuttered, cringing at her insensitivity. "I didn't mean that the way it sounded. You don't look old at all. It's just with your beard and all that has happened, it's difficult to tell...." Heat flooded her face as she rambled, digging a bigger hole for herself. Amusement flicked the corners of his mouth upward, accentuating his scar. Its ugliness mesmerised her.

"It's just that—well—you seemed to kill those things so efficiently and quickly; it looked like you'd been doing it for a very long time."

All levity in his face disappeared. "I have," he responded, not volunteering any more information.

Nerves made her mouth work before her brain could stop her. "So how old were you when you became a warrior?" she asked.

His eyes glinted sapphire again, his face expressionless as he looked at her. "I am not just a warrior. I am a Queen's guard and I have always been one. I was given to the Queen as a baby, like all the Queen's guards are. It is considered an honour by many parents to gift their son to the Queen. I was raised and trained by my brother guardsmen. My Queen ordered me to take my first life when I turned twelve years old. So you could say I am an efficient killer; it's what I do—kill on the orders of my Queen." His face was blank, but she didn't miss the slight note of bitterness in his voice.

Diamond swallowed, not really knowing how to respond. She rubbed her arms as a strange prickly feeling washed over her skin. Hugo looked her up and down and changed the subject. Just like that, the feeling disappeared.

"It will be cold in the forest for you dressed like that," he said frowning meaningfully at her bare legs.

Diamond bristled, immediately flushing bright red as his gaze rested on her exposed thighs. She resisted the urge to pull what was left of her skirt down further. Never had her skin been this exposed to the scrutiny of a boy. But Hugo was not a boy, he was a mature fae male. Suddenly Diamond found it difficult to speak.

Embarrassed she hastily knelt on the hard floor, ignoring her stinging grazes, and curled her feet underneath her. She tugged her short skirt down as best she could. Silently the big warrior got up, his movements controlled and powerful, and walked over to his pack. He might only be nineteen but Diamond already knew he could kill with as much efficiency and grace as he moved. Hugo sank to his haunches and quickly pulled out a spare pair of leggings, some clean linen bandages and a pot of salve. Turning back, he chucked them to her one at a time, then put the water skin down on the ground within arm's reach.

"If you roll those up and tie something around your waist, they will at least cover your skin. And if you don't want to get an infection, you need to clean and dress your wounds, especially those nasty scratches on your neck. The goddess only knows what filth that creature had on his claws," he advised, then lay down near her and propped his head on his pack.

Diamond frowned, resolved to not think about where Cranach's claws had been. She swept the water skin up in one jerky movement. Wincing and steadily ignoring Hugo, Diamond cleaned her wounds before carefully dabbing the disgusting smelling salve on her neck. Thankfully, it dulled the pain almost immediately. With the dagger Hugo had given her, she cut a strip of linen bandage to tie around her waist, then pulled on the ridiculously large leggings. After she had rolled the legs up and knotted the makeshift belt round her waist, they weren't too bad a fit. She immediately felt warmer. Glancing at Hugo, she muttered an awkward, "Thank you for the leggings, commander."

"Hugo," he replied. "My name is Hugo. Use it until we reach Valentia." It was almost an order.

Diamond considered refusing, but saw no point. Instead she nodded.

After applying the salve to her remaining grazes, she felt an odd, almost comforting warmth wash over her skin and a mildly uncomfortable tugging in her chest. An inexplicable urge to lay down next to Hugo overtook her. Besides, it would look rude to find somewhere else to rest, and she was too weary to seek out Tom or General Edo.

In a fluid movement, Hugo leaned up and passed her his pack. "Here, rest your head on this," he instructed.

Flustered and surprised, she took it. It was a strange gesture given the reputation of the Queen's guards for being callous and cold-hearted. Through narrowed eyes he continued to watch her as she settled herself on the hard floor.

"Go to sleep, Diamond. I'll keep you safe," he told her.

Exhausted, she closed her eyes. Hugo watched her unwaveringly, a frown creasing his scarred brow when she opened her eyes a few minutes later to check if he was still there.

The Queen's guard did not relax or sleep until the girl's breathing had settled and her strange mix of human and fae features relaxed in true sleep.

Chapter Seven

Hugo shook Diamond awake at dawn. Around the cave the warriors were sitting around talking quietly. The boar had been picked clean of meat and its carcass had been deposited at one side of the cave. Hugo placed a large leaf with some scraps of meat on it beside her. She eyed it with distaste. It looked mostly like congealed fat and sinew.

"Eat," commanded Hugo gruffly, then wandered over to sit near General Edo.

Not hungry in the least, Diamond picked up her food and made her way to the yawning cave mouth where her friend sat staring out at the endless forest. Beautiful golden pink hues stained the sky. Tom shuffled to one side as she sat down.

"Hey," he greeted her.

"Hi," Diamond responded, leaning her head on his bony shoulder. "Did you sleep?" she asked quietly, not really sure what to say to her best friend.

"No. Not really." He paused and took a breath before continuing, "I kept thinking about what might have happened if I hadn't run away like a coward. M-my mum...she might still be alive if I had been braver. I should have gone in and at least tried to help her, but I didn't. She's dead because of me—" his voice broke.

Diamond balked. It was so unfair to let him think that. "No, Tom, that's not true. If you had gone in, likely you would be dead too." Tentatively she grasped his hand, then lowered her voice. "Tom, those things, they were after me. Your mother, my father—all those other people—they died because of me, no one else. None of it was your fault. Please. Please stop thinking that."

Tom frowned in disbelief and pulled away from her. "You? But why would they want you?"

Diamond clutched her necklace and shrugged, "I don't know. That creature wouldn't tell me why, only that he had been sent to kill me. So you see, you should not feel guilty. It is only me who carries the burden of all those deaths."

Tom made a non-committal noise and put his arm around her shoulders. "Yeah, well, even if those things *were* after you, you can't blame yourself for what happened to the town. You didn't ask them to come, and you couldn't have stopped them, so...." he assured her with a shrug.

Diamond hugged her friend.

"What are we going to do now?" she whispered, although the question was rhetorical.

His bony chest rose and fell in a deep sigh. "I don't know, but we'll find our way. We are not children anymore. Out there is a world far bigger than anything we are used to, and we are going to have to learn to survive in it."

He fell silent, his gaze distant. Diamond knew this mood in her friend. He did not want to talk about it anymore. Neither did she. Silently, side by side, the two childhood friends watched the sun rise. The stars faded from view but Tu Lanah continued to glitter like a huge watchful eye. Diamond knew the ice moon would get larger and lower over the coming months, until at winter solstice it would kiss the earth while the winter storms raged.

Neither of them noticed the warrior approaching with a slight smile on his full lips. "Hey," said Zane, kicking at Tom's leg with the toe of his boot.

Tom glanced up, frowning at the hazel-eyed fae. "What?" he replied.

"You told me last night you wanted to learn to fight. So come on then, get off your skinny arse and learn." Tom scowled at the fae warrior. "Unless you're too much of a cowardly little bastard to try," Zane taunted. Tom was on his feet in an instant. Zane chuckled. "That's the spirit," he laughed. "Don't let your grief grind you down, boy, or it'll kill you out here in this forest."

"I'm not a boy," snapped Tom, a flush to his cheeks.

Diamond suppressed a smile at Tom's instant reaction.

Zane's wiggled his eyebrows and looked Tom over, then winked, which inflamed Tom further. "Oh, I can see that. But you need a bit more muscle on that skinny frame to be of much use."

Tom huffed and grabbed the sword Zane held out. "See you in a bit," he mumbled to Diamond and followed a smiling Zane.

Hugo tracked the progress of the new tutor and pupil alliance to the far depths of the cave, then he leaned back against the cave wall and continued his conversation with General Edo. His voice resonated through the cave as he recounted the war that had resulted in the young prince losing his city and his kingdom to the Wraith Lord.

Diamond listened intently, hoping to learn something new.

A roaring in her ears wiped away Hugo's voice. Her vision fogged and Diamond suddenly found herself in a black and silent void. She stared in confusion at the emaciated woman who stood before her. Her face would have been remarkably beautiful if she wasn't so painfully thin. Long, greasy tresses of silver hair hung to the woman's waist, covering her long white robe that was yellowed with age and filth. Blue, despairing eyes met Diamond's. But it was the screams piercing the air that filled Diamond's head, and a sense of unending hopelessness that truly terrified her. Wraiths, figures of mist and darkness, writhed around the woman. They reached out their shadowy limbs, trying to fight their way through the quivering haze of light that trembled around her. Diamond gasped, trying not to clutch her hands over her ears.

Instinctively she knew the light was the woman's energy, her magic and her life force, and it was flickering like a candle about to be extinguished.

"It is time," whispered the woman, reaching out a bony hand and touching Diamond's necklace, then her heart. Warmth bloomed in Diamond's chest.

"The prince needs you, and soon every living soul in this world will need you," the woman rasped urgently. "Go now. South. A guardian is free. "

Diamond screamed as the woman faded, replaced by burning red eyes and a huge maw lined with black teeth. Dragon fire engulfed her, heat searing her skin, melting it from her bones. It sucked the oxygen from her lungs. She couldn't breathe! She was burning! A piercing wail of terror escaped her lips.

Abruptly she was knocked sideways and big hands rolled her swiftly on the stone floor as the vision left her.

"Wake up!" bellowed a harsh voice, a stinging blow landing on her cheek before hard fingers clutched her shoulders and shook her. Gasping for air, she hit out at the flames still licking her skin.

"Diamond! Stop, wake up!" Another slap rattled her brain and her eyes flew open, immediately latching onto Hugo's. Sapphire sparking with silver flame held her completely in thrall. Then he blinked and that tether broke. Smoke curled through the air above Hugo's head. Amazingly there was no pain—she was not burnt, and neither was he. But it had felt so real. She collapsed into his grip like a rag doll.

"What the hell happened?!" he barked, pulling her off him. "The air around you just burst into flame."

The muscles in Hugo's jaw tightened as he looked her over. General Edo stood just on the periphery of her vision, watching them intently. A pale-looking Tom stood immobile next to him. A puzzled expression flitted over the general's brow as he regarded Hugo before his narrowed eyes rested on her again.

"We need to go south," she blurted out urgently, ignoring Hugo's question, not because she didn't want to answer, but because she couldn't explain what had just happened. "The prince is in danger," she said with a trembling voice. Hugo eyed her as though she were mad. "Please. We have to go. Now!" she implored, trying to control the shaking and utter panic that threatened to turn her into a useless mess.

"Why? What just happened? Are you a witch or some sort of magic wielder?" he barked suspiciously. "Is that why the Wraith Lord wants you?" he growled. "My oath requires me to take all magic wielders to the palace or kill them."

"I don't know what just happened!" she cried in truth, trying to ignore his last words. A violent shudder racked her body. Diamond closed her eyes briefly against her fear and confusion. A dragon. A guardian—oh gods!

"Please. We have to go!" she cried her voice high pitched as she grabbed at Hugo's calloused, leathery hands. She had to get him to understand! They had to go south. "Please...." she whispered imploringly, unaware of the strange brightness in her violet eyes. "I am not a witch or magic wielder," she sobbed. "I'm not. I'm not!" she almost wailed.

"Fine," he growled, his face cold as he stood and began barking orders out to the already waiting warriors.

Trembling, Diamond felt around her face and hair.

"It's okay. I don't know what just happened, but somehow you are not burned," General Edo told her, inclining his head toward Hugo. "He saw the flames and moved faster than anything I've ever seen before to get to you. Damned weird thing happened when he reached into them to grab you, they went out immediately, as if he sucked them inside himself."

In her confusion Diamond missed the narrow-eyed, assessing look General Edo cast at Hugo as the guard strode back to Diamond.

"Come on, let's go," Hugo said pulling her to her feet and holding out his arms.

General Edo bristled. "She will come with me," he said squaring up to the younger man.

Diamond honestly didn't care who she went with but Tom snorted, "No offence, but I'm not being carried by any of them again today," he said, huffing at Zane.

Zane grinned like a wolf and drawled, "Aw, do I make you nervous?" A couple of the other warriors smirked at Tom's reddening face. "Don't worry. I like my men with more muscle."

Hugo growled, "Quiet, Zane. Now is not the time."

Zane bowed his head slightly, but Diamond did not miss the way his eyes flicked to Tom. Fae males were not singular in their sexuality.

Does he like Tom? she wondered.

Tom, however, deliberately ignored the warrior he had been sparring with only moments before. "If I have to hitch a ride, I'll go with you, general," he grumbled. "At least I know you."

General Edo snarled at the boy and eyed Hugo coldly. But Hugo held his gaze, dominance pouring off him. They did not have time for this. Diamond swallowed hard and stepped into Hugo's body. An invitation.

The general eyed her glacially, as if she had committed an offense. "Look after her," he warned Hugo, resting his hand meaningfully on his sword. "She is no threat to your Queen."

Hugo raised his eyebrows a fraction. "I will make that decision," he replied, sending Diamond's blood cold. "But for now, I give you my word I will keep her safe."

Diamond let Hugo lift her, one arm under her legs and another around her shoulders. Carrying her effortlessly to the lip of the cave entrance, he extended his wings and stepped into thin air. She squeezed her eyes shut, convinced they were about to fall to the forest below. Her stomach dropped and cold wind ruffled her hair. Steeling her nerve, she peered down, wishing she hadn't when all the blood rushed from her head. The ground was a sickeningly long way down.

"Trust me. I won't let you fall," he said.

Trust him? Is he mad? Of course she didn't trust him, not after that last comment. But she didn't know what other choice there was. Twisting slightly, she gripped tightly onto his shoulders, not caring if he thought her gutless. At least if he decided to drop her she would not immediately fall.

His eyes flicked over her body. "Did you get burned anywhere?" he asked stiffly.

"No." she answered, although she had no idea why not if the flames were real enough to create smoke. Her stomach tightened at the prospect of finding a dragon in this forest. Goddess above. A dragon! One of the legendary guardians to Eternity, the land of the gods. Red eyes flashed in her mind.

The vision, if that's what it was, had drained her. Her head felt too heavy for her shoulders. Diamond rested her cheek against Hugo's chest, turning her face into his tough jacket and away from the cold wind. It must have made him uncomfortable because a few seconds later he hitched her up and re-adjusted his embrace, tightening his grasp on her.

Onwards they flew, an impressive band of airborne warriors, their golden wings glinting in the sunlight. Hugo led them over the endless forest canopy, his own wings dark against the ashen sky, letting himself be guided by Diamond's instincts.

The weather shifted, becoming grey and stormy, whipping the trees into a frenzy. It became harder for the warriors to fly; much to Tom's chagrin, General Edo had to pass him on to another fae. She did not know whether to worry for her friend or not, as Zane shouldered a surprised Karl out of the way and hovered in front of the general with a comical mix of tight-lipped contrition and quiet pleading. Tom looked desperately at Karl, but the other warrior just shrugged helplessly at Zane's behaviour.

"It seems he likes you, so it's either him or you walk," Karl grinned. "I'm not going to fight that grumpy bastard for you."

Tom swore viciously but allowed Zane to take his weight. Diamond found it hard not to smile at the incongruous sight of her friend being carried like a child by an overbearing, heavily muscled fae warrior. Tom might be terribly skinny but he was still six feet tall and would weigh a considerable amount. Something told Diamond Zane would not struggle. Even if he did, he would not pass Tom to another.

Hugo showed no trace of fatigue or wanting to pass her to one of the others. Tilting her head back enabled her to study his face properly. It was then she noticed his eyelashes weren't white. They glinted as he blinked. They were silver, like the sparks in his eyes. This close the ridged, scar stood out stark and proud against his dark golden skin. Wanting to trace a finger along it, she wondered if it hurt him. As if he felt the weight of her scrutiny, he slowly and deliberately met her gaze and held it. Heat warmed her cheeks and she looked down.

They left the dense northern forest, flying south east. Hugo refused to rest, taking heed of Diamond's increasing anxiety for a prince she had never met. None of the warriors complained, all of them beating their wings hard to keep up with him. The forest below looked like a winter storm had ripped it to pieces. After a time the sulphuric smell of rotten eggs began to infuse the air, overpowering her senses. Covering her nose with her hand didn't stop the gags rippling up her throat.

A circle of flattened and scorched trees appeared in the devastation. Ash floated in the air and covered the flattened ground in a smoking grey blanket. Diamond had never seen anything like it. Hugo and the general hovered, surveying the unnatural sight before them. Zane held back, glancing down at Tom, who folded his arms over his chest as he steadfastly ignored the big warrior. The others, their faces betraying their uncertainty, remained in formation behind General Edo. At the centre of the wreckage a vortex of black mist twisted and raged from the ground into the black clouds above. A strange feeling bloomed inside her, as if something inside that mist called to her.

Movement fluttered at the edge of Diamond's vision, distracting her. "There!" she shouted, pointing down to the ground on their right. Tapping Hugo's shoulder quickly to get his attention, she leaned in towards his ear. "I saw something move. I know I did."

"I need to put you down." Tension rippled through Hugo's body as he spoke. There was a fallen, charred tree trunk almost hidden by ash below their feet. She pointed to it trying to keep her hand steady. Her heart thumped against her ribs at the thought of him leaving her alone, but even though he had not said it, Diamond got the feeling Prince Jack Oden was also his friend.

"There," she said, keeping her voice strong. He nodded. When her feet hit the ground it took her a moment to recover her balance.

"Stay hidden and don't move from here," he instructed brusquely then shot up into the turbulent sky.

Diamond crouched down, hiding behind the fallen tree, one hand clutched tightly over her mouth and nose. The smell of sulphur was overwhelming. Saliva rushed her mouth. Heaving, she spat it out.

A low, pulsing rumble spread through the earth, shaking the ground and making her insides quake until a sudden ear-splitting roar deafened her. She instinctively dropped to the ground and screwed herself up into a ball, clutching her hands protectively over her ears. Mercifully, the roar was short lived. Coarse, warm ash slipped between Diamond's fingers as she pushed herself up and peered over the top of the tree trunk. Swirling mist, blacker than any shadow she had ever seen, was sucked up inside the lungs of a huge creature. Standing taller than any tree, its massive, scaly tail swished dangerously close to Diamond's hiding place.

Terror trapped the scream in her throat. Her vision had been true! And if this beast existed, so too did the goddess and every other legendary nightmarish creature she had hidden from under her bedclothes as a child. The enormity of that thought paralysed her.

Lunaria and her war with the god of Chaos. It was all true.

This roaring, malevolent creature was a guardian. Ice crept along her veins. It clearly did not answer to the goddess Lunaria. *Who does it answer to—the god of Chaos?*

Red eyes rolled and raged like pits of fire. Black bony ridges protruded all the way up his spine, from the end of his barbed tail to the base of his big skull. There three twisted red horns curved outwards from the dragon's ridged forehead, surrounded by smaller spikes that thrust from the side of his massive head and jaws like a macabre halo.

The beast swung his tail in a huge arch, crashing close by into the ground that the fallen tree bounced and a branch hit her stomach and knocked her off her feet. Gasping for air, she scrambled up and ran as fast as her shaking legs would take her. Away, away from this creature of fire. Gas burned her lungs, her eyes watering until everything blurred. Trying not to breathe in the poisonous cloud, she made herself sprint. This creature was far more terrifying than any Seeker. In the vision this red-eyed dragon had incinerated her.

Sweating and breathless, she reached the edge of the ash circle and dived down behind a bush, staring in horror at the harsh beauty of the beast. It was close enough for her to see each individual mirrored, black scale. Acid drool dripped from the dragon's huge maw, smouldering on the ground where the slimy globules landed. Stretching back its reptile-like mouth, it bared row upon row of hideously sharp, black teeth. Fear rippled through her at the sight of them. Cloying heat sucked oxygen from the air, making it unbearably difficult to breathe. Crawling forward on her hands and knees, she cried out as spikes of scorched twigs dug through her leggings. Gasping, she collapsed down on the ground, salty sweat trickling into her eyes and mouth.

Where is Hugo? Panic threatened her vision, her lips beginning to tingle. All she could see were shadows and smoke. Her eyes desperately searched through the sparse forest, her brain not registering how odd it was for her to wish for him rather than her childhood friend or the general who had always been part of her life. That weird tugging sensation pulled at her insides, and she knew beyond any doubt Hugo was coming.

A movement in the trees caught her attention. Strangely, it was opposite to where she had seen the flash of movement before. A young man near Diamond's age, tall and lean with curly brown hair, ran forward. A sword hung down his back, its ruby hilt glinting as angrily as the dragon's eyes.

He has to be the prince. What is he doing? she thought incredulously. *He's right in the path of the dragon's gaze. Is he mad?*

The prince reached for something, and she realised there was a huge black and white animal lying on a bed of branches and leaves. A water leopard! Then she remembered what Hugo had said. Their lands were the lakes and mountains that bordered the Barren Waste Lands. Prince Oden's allies.

Diamond instinctively knew the animal was hurt. Its black barbed tail swished, hitting the prince's leg as if trying to get him to leave him. Clearly the stubborn prince wasn't paying attention. Neither of them would escape the dragon's attention.

It rolled its massive head, triumph making its whole body quiver. Anger and desperation laced the water leopard's bellowing roar. Animal eyes sought her out an instant before a growling voice echoed in her head, making her jump.

'Save him!'

Without any thought for her own safety or the fact she had heard the big cat's voice in her head, Diamond launched herself into a run, ash plumes bursting from beneath her feet.

Chapter Eight

Hot prickly sensations ran over Diamond's sweat-drenched skin as she charged toward the prince, Hugo and everyone else forgotten in her haste.

'Your energy—your magic. Use it to shield, to protect.' The emaciated dream woman's voice echoed weakly in Diamond's head. The spark of heat the woman had ignited within Diamond's chest burst into uncontrolled flame, shifting rapidly through every cell in her body; muscle, sinew, bone, they all burned with something Diamond could not comprehend.

'Magic.'

The word whispered through her soul, leaving her fearful of what that might mean if she lived through the next few minutes. Diamond pushed thoughts of Hugo's threats aside. Right now, instinct told her to let this power flow. The woman's aura stayed with Diamond, a misty presence quivering on the periphery of her consciousness commanding the magical energy within her in a way Diamond could not do herself. Encouragement and support flooded Diamond's mind.

'Free it,' urged the woman's voice. A peculiar milky film covered her violet eyes. Far from obscuring her vision, the magical sight sent the world swirling with colour, a kaleidoscope of energy exploding from the living magic of the world. Diamond did not have time to admire the beauty around her.

Level with the dragon's front claws, she skidded to a halt, panting hard. Waves of blistering heat coursed through her body, becoming more difficult to contain with every passing second. Alive and impatient, it wanted out—out of her body. Her eyes flew to the vulnerable prince. The air crackled and energy flared around Diamond's body. Unbound from its prison, magic engulfed her, turning her skin and hair into a river of silver and white light. The woman's control on Diamond's magic slipped and it fought for release. The dragon gave a bellowing roar and Diamond exploded into movement, running faster than she ever had before.

Orange scales glowed underneath the dragon's neck, turning molten and flowing like a turbulent river of lava. Moments later, dragon fire surged forth towards the prince and the water leopard.

Fuelled by anger and despair, magic swirled like a lightning storm around her arms, crackling through the air. Throwing her arms forwards, an orb of white energy exploded from her hands. It engulfed her, the forest and the dragon's prey in a huge protective bubble, abruptly cutting off the flame from around them. Diamond ground her teeth. The power flowing from her felt dangerous and far stronger than her ability to control. But there was no choice; if she could not dominate it, they would all burn. The huge dome of magic held a strong protective force against the torrent of dragon fire.

Horrible, terrifying minutes passed. Sharp, agonising pain saturated her arms. She could not, would not fail.... Her shield stayed strong even when the flames ceased and the dragon began battering the dome with his spiky tail, boiling with unchecked rage when his fire could not burn through.

"Keep going!" ordered a familiar deep voice. An almost painful wrench at her chest had Diamond raising her head. The movement caused the world to spin and rivulets of sweat to trickle down the groove of her spine. Hugo stood near the two figures on the ground, surrounded by a halo of blue and silver light, his sapphire eyes glowing with flickering silver flames. Caught by that glow, new strength and purpose surged through Diamond, bolstering her trembling and weak limbs. It boosted her but not for long.

"Do not stop!" Hugo commanded harshly as if he sensed she neared the end of her strength.

Her throat was burning and dry, her lungs heaved as darkness fogged the periphery of her vision. Despite her determination, all of it drifted away like mist on the wind: the shield, the forest, Hugo. She was floating, looking down on her physical body from a long way off. It was lovely and peaceful out here. This was the edge of Eternity. No sound penetrated, no roaring disturbed her mind. A serenity that was truly beautiful beckoned her. It would be wonderful to float away and be swept up in that never-ending tranquillity where the sun shone and the stars played.

Painful and insistent tugging dragged her back, crashing her awareness back into her body.

"*Diamond!!*" Hugo bellowed, close enough now to touch her.

His voice hit her like a slap to the head. Shocked, she gazed at the beautiful silver serpents of energy that reached from him, nipping her as they wound around her arms. That invisible tie jerked her closer to him even as his fiery eyes tethered her to her physical body and to him.

The dragon's wrath was terrifying. He attacked her shield, trying to smash his way through. Molten red eyes fixated on her with murderous intent, but Diamond was too exhausted to notice. The prince crouched next to the water leopard, wide-eyed and white-faced as he watched her.

"Hold that shield, Diamond!" Hugo demanded, concentrating only on her.

To Diamond, nothing else existed but the touch of his energy and the midnight blue and silver fire of his eyes. The dragon continued to pummel the shield, his barbed tail causing a cacophony of crackling and flying sparks. Fire rained down but still she held firm, small and pale against the might of the beast.

Her throat felt raw, and darkness fuzzed the edge of her vision. Hugo's eyes narrowed. Tingling shot through her body. Involuntarily her muscles tensed as if his strength had just poured into her, forcing her to stay upright.

"He's leaving!" shouted Tom from nearby.

Diamond vaguely registered General Edo landing next to her but did not break her hold on Hugo's eyes. It didn't matter what the general thought. If she moved or lost concentration, the shield would fail and they would all die. Right now the lives of these warriors were her responsibility. Panting and gritting her teeth until they hurt, she fought wave upon wave of dizziness. Not until Hugo told her it was safe, that they were all safe, would she stop.

Long terrible minutes passed. Sparks coloured her vision and still Hugo stood in front of her, commanding her gaze, the muscles of his jaw clenched tightly.

"Can—I—stop—yet?" she forced the question out between gasping breaths. Sweat ran into her eyes, her body shaking so hard she was on the verge of collapse.

The warriors and newcomers stared at Diamond in awe as she hardened her resolve and kept the shield going. Her magic burned strong but her body was failing, even with Hugo's borrowed strength.

The black dragon snorted and flapped his wings. Snarling, he eyed the young prince who—in turn—was staring at Diamond. Dishevelled and shocked, he sat on the ground next to the injured water leopard. The dragon's smouldering gaze rested on Diamond and then Hugo, committing their image to memory. Intelligence and cunning shone in those red orbs. A moment later his great head tilted upwards as if listening. Giving a loud frustrated screech, he snapped out huge bat-like wings and launched himself into the grey clouds.

"You can stop," replied the general after another minute or so. Grey, incredulous eyes looked from her to Hugo, who was still holding Diamond in his thrall.

Hugo gave the slightest nod. Agreement. Blinking rapidly, Diamond broke their bond. Her legs collapsed instantly. The soft covering of ash broke her fall, but as her cheek hit the ground a fit of retching and vomiting took hold. The general put a steadying hand on her shoulder, but even as he did so the harsh features of his face blurred and the world closed in until darkness took her. The last thing she saw was Hugo's sapphire eyes as they lost their fire and turned to ice.

Chapter Nine

Hugo reeled. What she had just done....

He swallowed hard, it had been incredible, impossible even. Never had he felt magic so powerful and unending. Not even the Queen's felt so vast. It scared him—even more so now. He had sensed it beginning to devour her soul, her mind. It would end her if she did not learn to dominate it.

The sight of a shield emanating from her hands had left him frozen, too shocked to do anything but stare until he had seen her weaken. A strange kind of rage had thundered through his blood then; even now he couldn't comprehend his overwhelming urge to protect her. *Using magic is banned by the Queen. I shouldn't have helped this girl....*

His hand found one of the daggers secured to his thigh as his eyes drifted to her too-pale face. She had looked so small pitted against such a mighty beast. Avoiding his blades, Hugo curled his fingers into fists, fingernails digging into his skin. He cursed his desperate need to storm over and scoop her up of the floor. Inexplicably, his magic jerked him a step toward her. She was so vulnerable right now. A growl rumbled up his throat, nearly choking him as he swallowed it.

Capturing Diamond's gaze and commanding her had been ridiculously easy. Their magic had instantly merged; hers—wild, joyous and determined to find freedom; and his—experienced and hidden, striving to dominate and tame hers.

Underneath that magical struggle Diamond's fear and exhaustion had tugged on his chest. She had needed him to keep her going, to hold her mind and body steady, and—without a second thought—he had done it.

Except he felt anything but steady right now. It was indescribable, their merging power and the rush of belonging. Hugo shook his head, trying to clear the buzzing in his ears.

Realisation dawned. No. It couldn't be true.

With resentful eyes he stared at her, not wanting to believe it.

Nexus bonds didn't exist anymore. They were a myth, the substance of old wives tales. But so were guardians, and one had almost burnt them all to a crisp.

Hugo ground his teeth together, scowling darkly when he seemed unable to tear his eyes off Diamond.

He was being absurd. Showing any interest in this girl, magic driven or not, would be far too dangerous—for them both. Despite himself, his stomach flipped at the sight of her unmoving and pale on the ground. Staring hard, he made sure she was still breathing, hating the emotions that made him check. Muscles quivering, he controlled his body.

It was now clear why Ragor sought Diamond. Her magic was not red, green or gold...it was the level of magic from dreams and stories. It was the sort exhorted in religious texts as being inherent of the goddess herself: it was white magic. Such a powerful gift, and one that could wreak destruction across vast lands—or kingdoms, if she learned to control it.

Hugo wrenched his magic back inside himself as it tried to reach her, forcing himself to think like the guard he was supposed to be. The Queen would want this girl under her control, not Jack's. Hugo was powerful enough to absorb enough of Diamond's magic to weaken her, but it was too vast and protective of its own existence for him to destroy it. Even if he took her within the dampening effect of Valentia's shield, her magic would only be suppressed.

Darker thoughts troubled him. The Queen would consume this girl's wild magic—and then he would be ordered to kill her, as he had countless other magic wielders. Hugo stifled his familiar rage and disgust. Killing was as easy as breathing; age, creed, origins—it didn't matter, he always followed his Queen's orders; there was no reason not to.

The general glanced suspiciously at Hugo. Quickly and with practiced efficiency, Hugo schooled his features into an icy mask, then turned to the mortal prince who was still staring at Diamond with a look of wonderment.

"Jack, are you hurt?" Hugo asked in a steady voice. He looked his friend over.

"No. But only because of her," Jack answered, sounding as overawed as he looked. Then he seemed to shake himself. Back in control, his attention moved to the older warrior. Hugo helped him up. "So who are our new friends, Hugo?" asked Jack, dusting himself down.

General Edo shifted his steely eyes from Diamond to Jack and immediately pushed himself up to his considerable height. With some amusement Hugo realised this could get messy. He had known immediately who the older warrior was, even before asking. General Edo was a legend amongst Jack's army, renowned for his fighting skills, clever mind and friendship to King Oden.

"Prince, this is General Amsal Edo. He was in the town Cranach led us to." Hugo hid a wince, this was getting worse for the prince. "General Arades Gillon was there too. He died in the fighting. It is his daughter, Diamond, who lies on the ground. The Seekers were hunting her."

Jack sucked in a breath between bared teeth as he heard the names of those mighty generals, warriors who had once been loyal to the Oden Dynasty. The prince's expression turned colder than Hugo had ever seen it. Unfazed, the older man's regard remained steady and assessing, weighing up the dishevelled young man in front of him. Jack slowly reached over his back and grabbed his sword pommel.

The prince had been a small child when the legendary warrior had left Stormguaard. It occurred to Hugo that rather than seeing General Edo as an ally, Jack might see this powerful fae as a threat. After all, he was one of the two generals King Oden had named guardians of Rhodainia until his son reached the age of eighteen and could be crowned king. Arades Gillon, Diamond's father had been the other. Hugo supposed the mortal king had expected to live long enough for one or other of his generals to return home. Jack was only two months away from his eighteenth birthday and not likely to turn over ruling his broken kingdom or his campaign against Ragor to a complete stranger even for so short a time, no matter what their name was.

Hugo smiled inwardly and forced himself to remain out of this meeting. Jack would only tell him to piss off if he tried to protect his friend. Since they had survived Stormguaard and Hugo had returned to his Queen, it was hard to accept that the politics of Jack's court were none of his business. His Queen had charged him with discovering why the Seekers travelled north and, if possible, bringing the reason back to Valentia. *Those* were his orders, nothing else.

"So, you are my king's son," purred General Edo.

It was a statement, not a question. Tilting his head slightly to one side only served to make the hulking general more predatory. Jack tipped his head back to keep eye contact as the tall fae warrior took a slow deliberate step forward.

The prince wisely held his ground. Jack knew the score. He would have to prove himself strong enough to lead or, according to Rhodainia's laws, this fae could take control of his army and his people.

Hugo hoped Jack had the sense to note the general's tough square jaw and the iron arm muscles that bunched as he curled his fists around the pitted, scarred pommel of his heavy blade. It was clear to Hugo's trained eye General Edo favoured his left side. Wings, covered in golden armour, extended fully in challenge, ready to be used as a weapon themselves should the need arise.

Jack unsheathed Dragonsblood, the sword his father had commissioned for him upon his birth. Not once did his eyes leave the general's. Slowly, one by one, his leather clad fingers loosened then wrapped back around the fierce ruby-eyed, silver and gold dragon pommel. It was hard not to admire such a beautiful work of art, even for Hugo, who had no interest in elaborate weapons. Blades, whether elaborate or not, were tools of death and agony.

"I like that you are not scared of me," the general chuckled, although his voice held no humour. "The last time I faced you with a sword, you nearly shit your princely breeches. Let's see how much of a man you've grown into, shall we?"

Jack held Dragonsblood up in the air, studying the shining blade. The ruby-eyed dragon glinted angrily as if sensing the tension in the air. Jack cocked his head, rage burning in his eyes. "Oh, I've grown up plenty, general. Whereas you have only got older and slower since you deserted my father."

"Slower!" laughed General Edo contemptuously. "We'll see. And I am no deserter, prince. But that is not important now. What is important is that you prove to me that you can wield that sword with the skill of a warrior—as your father expected—and that you are worthy of carrying it." He gave a small laugh, his eyes glinting with mockery. "When your father gave me my last orders, you couldn't even lift this sword off the ground. You always were a small, feeble child easily driven to anger. So—*little prince*—has anything changed? Are you man enough to lift that blade and fight me? Or are you a weak little boy?" he challenged, narrowing his eyes and pacing in front of Jack, sword drawn, looking every inch the warrior he was.

"No. I have not been a weak boy for a long time. I am heir to the throne of Rhodainia, and you should be on one knee begging my forgiveness for deserting your duties. The duties my father gave you—general," Jack uttered the last word with a contemptuous snarl. "You should have been there to guide me, to help me when I was too young to understand what I was doing. I lost my family's heritage because you left my father to his fate. You have been a deserter for nearly fourteen years. *Fourteen years!* You, general, have no right to order me to do anything! *Anything!!*" he roared, his face red, his eyes angry.

But Hugo knew Jack well. They had spent too much time together for him to miss the flicker of loss and hurt in his friend's eyes. There was no answering flicker of regret or softness in the general.

"Your father was my king and my friend. I have the last orders he gave me in my pocket. But now is not the time to explain myself to you, prince. If you want my allegiance and my help, you need to earn it. The first step is to prove to me that you can use that," he gestured to Dragonsblood with the tip of his own sword. "Then I will consider whether I am going to bend my knee to you or take over leading your broken kingdom...*little prince.*"

Even Hugo cringed at the arrogance and scorn in General Edo's voice. They had spoken at length in the cave about Jack and what had happened in the grasslands of Rhodainia. General Edo was a clever and calculating man. Hugo knew this attitude was an act, but it was a good one. Jack was about ready to explode with white hot rage. Jack's warriors shuffled closer, their feet sending tiny plumes of ash into the air.

"Highness?" Roin, Jack's captain questioned his voice tight. Zane and Karl stepped up beside him, swords drawn.

"Stand down," Hugo growled at the burly, broad shouldered warrior's.

Jack scowled at Hugo's interference but nodded to his captain. Immediately his men shuffled back, still looking nervous and on edge. Zane prowled towards Diamond, and Hugo tensed; then he noticed the other warriors now stood in the spot between the general and Tom. Zane nodded to them.

The general swished his sword through the air with utter delight, then without warning lurched and swung his blade down towards Jack. Metal clashed against metal as his blade was barred by Dragonsblood.

Jack had been waiting.

Chapter Ten

Diamond stirred at the sound of clashing swords. Unobtrusively, Hugo eyed her with concern. Her skin looked ashen. Hugo tried to ignore the way his gut clenched as Tom pulled her onto his lap and rocked her against his skinny body. But it was Zane who eyed Hugo warily, who tracked his movements.

Hugo snarled. Completely out of character, he couldn't stop himself striding over to the two friends. Her magic called to him. Gods help him, he was behaving like a fool.

"Let go of her," he snarled at the boy.

The cowardly runt paled, but did not let go.

"Tom, don't pick now to start being brave," advised Zane, his voice careful and even.

Tom looked up at Zane, clearly unsure.

"Go ahead. Hugo will not hurt her," Zane reassured Tom.

Hugo met Zane's knowing look, hating that the other fae could see right through his possessive actions. Deciding to ignore it, he bent down and swept Diamond away from Tom's embrace. With her cradled in his arms, he strode back to where he had been standing. Hoping everyone else's attention was on the fight, Hugo guiltily pulled her closer to his chest. Soothing warmth seeped from her into him. Hugo inhaled deeply. She smelled like ash and magic and something undeniably feminine; flowers and sunshine. It stirred something deep and predatory in him, something utterly impossible.

She slowly stirred, and he warily watched her as consciousness returned. Horror flashed across her pale features as she twisted to see the source of the metallic clashing.

"What's going on? Why are they fighting?" Diamond asked.

"General Edo has just met Prince Oden," Hugo responded flatly. Heat bloomed across his chest as she moved in his arms. "They're getting to know one another," he explained, surprising himself by the wry humour in his voice.

She paled even further. "But they'll get hurt! You have to stop them."

"No, they won't. Not seriously. The general will stop when he has an answer to his question."

She stilled and stared at him. "What question?" she demanded.

"If Jack, who lost his kingdom to war and death, is more capable of donning the mantle of leadership and ruling now than he was when he lost his kingdom," Hugo said, deliberately lacing his voice indifference.

Diamond's eyes widened. "Leadership? But he's already a leader—a prince. What in Chaos is Uncle Amsal thinking? That's it. Put me down," she ordered harshly.

Hugo ignored her demand, unwilling to let her go.

The force of her punch vibrated into his shoulder. "Put me down now, Hugo, or I'll poke your eyes out like I did that damn Seeker!" Her violet eyes burned with indignation and fury.

Caught off guard by her fierce spirit, a rare smile tugged at Hugo lips. He quashed it immediately. *What in the goddess is this girl doing to me?* Smiling was not something he had done since he had returned to Valentia; there usually wasn't anything worth smiling about. Besides, the scar on his face pulled his mouth up in an ugly grimace and exposed his teeth like a beast's when he did. It was repellent. Women generally found it gruesome. He had suffered ridicule for years at the hands of the malicious royal court sycophants. He managed to ignore their snide glances and whispered insults—most of the time. But occasionally, just to entertain himself, he allowed himself to put the fear of death in them. All it took was a snarl and they would nearly piss themselves in fear.

Diamond glanced at his scar as it twitched. She did not recoil as he expected.

"As you wish, but stay near me and don't interfere. This is something Jack has to do. He needs to prove himself to General Edo in front of his men or he will not maintain authority over either," he warned her.

She nodded once, but he didn't for one second trust her to stand on the side-lines. Slowly, and with more reluctance than he wanted to admit, he lowered Diamond's feet to the ground. She pushed away from his chest, then walked towards the two fighting men.

Hugo sauntered up beside her, not fooled for a moment. She frowned at him, but he just lifted an eyebrow and glared at her. "Close to me, half-blood," he repeated in a voice laced with threat.

Her nostrils flared. "Don't order me around, faery prick," she hissed insultingly between gritted teeth.

Hugo almost grinned at her feistiness—almost.

Jack staggered and fell, knocked on his back by the hilt of the general's sword. He spat a globule of blood to the ground, then wiped the back of his hand over his split lip with a loud curse. His brown eyes met Diamond's and widened as they exchanged a look. Gritting his teeth, the prince sprung back to his feet and lunged at the general's legs, knocking him off balance with a shoulder charge.

Hugo ignored his sudden surge of resentment toward Jack and made himself watch impassively. Jack was a good swordsman, but he was not as strong, or apparently as vicious, as the older warrior. Hugo tried to trust the general not to keep this fight going too long. He understood General Edo wanted to push Jack, to see what the younger man could do before agreeing to take orders from him. Hugo didn't want to interfere—but he readied himself to take the general on if it looked like he was going too far. Jack was still the future king of Rhodainia, after all—and Hugo's friend.

Jack's soldiers gripped their swords and surrounded their prince. Some faced in, some out. Not daring to get too close to a bunch of distrustful, aggressive fae males, stood a bunch of rag tag human survivors, strangers Jack had picked up on their travels. One woman and four men. Hugo did not want to know anything about them. Jack always did this, found strays that slowed the progress of the group down. The fae warriors either ended up carrying them or the entire group had to walk. He snarled as one of the humans caught his eye, an arrogant smile stretching thin lips over rotten teeth. Hugo's fae instincts flared.

Zane sauntered up beside Hugo.

"His name is Freddy. The woman said he is a nasty little bastard. Has tried to get under her skirts several time already." The warrior's astute eyes drifted to Diamond. "I'm telling you so you can protect her. Just like I feel I want to look out for him," Zane huffed wryly and inclined his head at Tom. "It seems we've both been blindsided by our inconvenient fae instincts."

So Hugo *had* been careless with his emotions. But Hugo trusted Zane. He was arrogant but not vindictive. Hugo grunted his thanks and stepped closer to Diamond.

Freddy chose that moment to give a gleeful smile at the sight of Jack's blood running from his split lip. Hugo hoped this fight ended soon, before any of the soldiers, particularly Roin, decided to try and put a stop to it. Now that would delight Freddy to no end. Jack's loyal captain had once been a smithy and he was one of the strongest human males Hugo had ever met. He had to be to command respect from a mixed force of men and dominant fae. A fight between Roin and the general would get messy, judging by the general's prowess with a blade. If Jack's men so much as tried to slow General Edo down, he would cause carnage.

Diamond hissed as Jack landed a heavy blow on the general's jaw but was then floored himself by a sweeping kick to his legs. Angry at them both, she took a step forwards with flashing eyes. Amazed by her expressive face, Hugo quickly wrapped his arms around her and held her fast. Zane chuckled and stalked back towards Tom, whose fury-filled eyes were fixed on them. The warrior stood in front of Tom, big broad shoulders obscuring his view. It seemed Zane had Hugo's back where Diamond was concerned.

He pulled her firmly against him and almost forgot about the others as his heart vibrated through her slim body. The top of her head reached his collar bone, so he leaned forwards until his cheek rested against hers. This close, her scent made his senses swim. His magic involuntarily surged around them, winding through her energy and increasing his heart rate. Swallowing hard, he tightened his arms.

"I said to stay near me," he growled as convincingly as he could in her ear, whilst biting down on an urge to smile at her defiance.

She twisted her head and glared furiously at him. "Let. Me. Go," she hissed, her body writhing against his grip, against him.

Confused by the heat that flushed up his neck, Hugo pulled away slightly. "Keep still," he warned, his voice ominously quiet, "or I will make you."

Immediately her movements stilled, the fire dying in her eyes only to be replaced by doubt. Hugo kept his face blank, hiding his unease. Consciously he made his voice gentler and more reassuring. "Just watch. I told you I won't let either of them get badly wounded."

He quickly glanced around, relaxing when he saw there was no one else close enough to hear his uncharacteristic tone of voice. Slowly, he unwound his arms but stayed mere inches behind her in case she decided to take matters into her own hands. Or Freddy, who kept eyeing Diamond like she was his next meal, decided to make his move.

Surprisingly, she didn't step away from him.

Jack swung his blade down, but this time misjudged his timing. Weeks of very little food had weakened him, and it was starting to show. The general parried, then struck with such speed and force even Hugo's eyes could not see his blade. A powerful blow drove Jack to his knees as he twisted to block. Jack's gloved fist closed around some ash, throwing a handful in the general's face. The general roared as it burned his eyes. Jack seized his opportunity and exploded with an uppercut. At six feet two inches tall and made of sinew and muscle, his fist crashed into the general's jaw, sending him staggering. Jack did not allow himself to be arrogant and grin, but he couldn't help glancing at Diamond. It was a typical Jack move, and it cost him.

Diamond did not look impressed, only horrified, when General Edo recovered quickly enough to slam his own fist into Jack's jaw. Jack's knees buckled and he fell unconscious in a heartbeat.

Chapter Eleven

Diamond rushed to Jack, ignoring Hugo's warning growl. She rolled the unconscious prince onto his side before any of his men could get there, then launched herself at General Edo, her face furious.

"What in the name of Chaos did you do that for?" she raged at him. "The prince's men could cut you down in a second. Are you insane? Do you want to die too?" she yelled, tears shining in her eyes. Losing her childhood uncle would be more than she could bear right now.

But the general was panting. Panting and grinning like he had just had the best time. Diamond couldn't believe what she was seeing. Before she could release the tirade of anxiety burning a hole in her chest, Hugo grabbed her arm and yanked her away. The general watched Hugo seize her and did nothing, only turned away from them, his wings still armoured and outstretched.

"Let go of me, you—"

"Leave him. He needs to talk to the men now," Hugo interrupted her, his voice infuriatingly calm. "Do not interfere, Diamond. Whatever you think, this was necessary, and the general has the prince's best interests at heart."

"Best interests!" she spluttered disbelievingly. *They are all mad.*

But Hugo held her gaze steadily. "Yes. If it is any of your concern at all, General Edo will explain when he is ready; until then, go and sit with Jack and let the general do what he does best—lead these men," he finished.

Diamond pushed her hands onto her hips and glared at him. *No one gives me orders. Who does he think he is?* But winning a staring contest with a Queen's guard was not something she could manage. He cocked a dark brow expectantly and she dropped her eyes.

"Fine! I'll sit with him. No one else seems bothered anyway," she muttered, plonking herself on the ground next to Jack. That wasn't strictly true. Jack's soldiers had not been given time to check on him. All the men and women, she noticed now, had been gathered together by General Edo.

Hugo threw her a warning look over one broad shoulder as he strode over to join them.

It was hard not to listen to General Edo's explanation to the soldiers. He gave a rousing speech, easily gaining their trust and support. Darkness settled around the group as he confidently organised the warriors. Diamond shivered, cold seeping into her clothes. It was a relief when Tom came and passed over a water skin. Together they cleaned up Jack's face.

"Are you alright?" asked Tom, studying her face.

"Not really," she sighed, plopping down onto her rump. "The whole of my childhood has been built on lies and illusion." She stared at her trembling hands, hands that could wield magic. "Do you think my father knew about my magic?"

"I don't know." Tom raked his hand through his hair. "If he did, and kept it to himself, it would only be to keep you safe...you know that."

Pain lanced her chest. Both her father and General Edo had hidden who they really were from her. *Why would my dad do that? Was the man who comforted me when I was sad, who picked me up when I fell, who told me I was his beautiful jewel, just a stranger? Did I ever really known him at all?* Tears pricked her eyes.

It was easier to ignore the storm of thoughts than confront her hurt and grief. For a while she bent her knees and rested her head on her arms, closing her eyes. Soft voices murmured through the trees, but it seemed everyone was trying to be as quiet as possible.

Diamond felt physically sick when she thought about that wild magic coursing through her bones and blood. *Did I really let it consume me so much my soul drifted into Eternity?* She squeezed her arms tightly around her knees.

Hugo. She wondered how he had managed to give her enough energy to keep her grounded, why he had done it. Now she knew he also had magic while living in a kingdom that abhorred it. *Does that make him a hypocrite or a born survivor?* she wondered.

When she opened her eyes again it was nearly dark. Tom had disappeared. Typical. Diamond shuffled uncomfortably. She needed to answer the call of nature. The prince lay on his side, an arm flung over his face, sleeping peacefully. Pushing herself to her feet, she carefully picked her way through the scorched trees to a bit of forest, thick enough to obscure her from view. Uncomfortable performing such personal necessities in the open, Diamond rushed herself, almost peeing over her boot when her oversized leggings got caught around her knees. After cursing under her breath, Diamond fixed her clothes then stood still and listened. Silence enveloped her.

Alone, she allowed her shoulders to sag, letting her weariness and grief weigh her down. The fierce need to see her dad nearly choked her. Just once, she wanted to see him so she could tell him she loved him. She hadn't told him for such a long time, and now it was too late. Giving into the sobs that had been brewing all day was almost a relief. So much of her life had been a lie, but it had been hers—and now it was gone. Diamond sank to the ground and wept until only a hollow emptiness remained.

Diamond swiped at her wet cheeks. No amount of crying was going to change what had happened and bring him back. If she was going to survive she had to find a way to deal with his loss...and get away from Hugo and the fae Queen. Diamond didn't understand how or why she had magic, but she knew the fae Queen would not tolerate it. Unleashing her magic like that, no matter who it had saved, had set her on a dangerous path.

Around her, sinister shadows seemed to pulse. Diamond tensed. Completely still, the only sound she could hear was her own heartbeat. Pushing hastily to her feet, she hurried back towards the circle of guards. Suddenly, a shape materialised from behind a fallen tree trunk. She stifled a squeal, not wanting to bring Jack's warriors or Hugo down on her head for leaving the prince.

"There you are," purred a tall, skinny man. He blocked her way forwards. "I've been looking for you. The name's Freddy," he gave a sly grin, sidling closer.

Diamond conceded a step. His eyes glittered with a dark menacing amusement that had her hackles rising immediately. Alone in the dark with him was not a good place to be. Pointedly she ignored the hand he held out. It was only just possible to see the scowl on his face.

"Now there's no need to be scared. I just wanted to say thank ya t' the pretty girlie that saved us from the dragon."

Just as Tu Lanah emerged from the clouds, Freddy gave an unpleasant smile that revealed rotten teeth. Another step closer and his hand snapped out. Diamond recoiled before he could grab her wrist, a chill skittering down her spine. This disgusting worm of a man was not a soldier. He was one of the refugees the prince had found hiding in the forest. Freddy cocked his head to one side, his tongue flicking around his lips in a lewd kind of way. Excitement gleamed in his furtive eyes. The thrill of the chase—a human predator. Her body gave an involuntary shudder, her instincts screaming at her to run.

"Aw, come on, me lovely. It's a long time since I've 'ad the chance of saying thanks to a lady for 'er help. Why don't yer let me escort you back to the others? 'Ere, take me arm. Yer look so cold." His voice was intimate and quiet as he slowly raked his eyes up and down her body. "I can warm yer up if yer let me."

Diamond swiftly shook her head. "No thanks, I'm warm enough already," she said, her eyes darting about for an escape route.

"Diamond!" barked a deep voice from nearby.

"Yes! Over here!" yelled Diamond, relief making her knees weak. She had met men like Freddy before. She knew what he wanted and it wasn't to thank her or escort her back to the others.

"What the hell are you doing out here on your own!" Hugo berated her as she ran towards the mass of shadow that seemed to solidify into his body as she got closer. "Why did you leave the prince?"

"I was on my way back," she said defensively.

Hugo stared coldly over her shoulder at Freddy. Instantly a feral snarled curled Hugo's lip.

Freddy plastered an arrogant grin over his face, but got the message. Whistling tunelessly he sauntered back to the others.

"Stay away from him. He's dangerous," Hugo warned, frowning down at her like she was stupid enough to seek the creep out.

"I already figured that out," she snapped before she could stop herself. "I'm not stupid!"

"Come on. I'm taking you back," he said, ignoring her tone. Instead he regarded Freddy's receding back, a murderous glint in his dark eyes.

Taken aback, Diamond registered his hostility. He must really hate Freddy to allow her to see anything other than his cold facade. Hugo's sapphire eyes drifted back to her. For a second he looked perplexed and silence fell between them. Leather creaked as he squared his shoulders. When she dared look at his face again, only ice remained. Prepared to walk the short distance back, she raised her eyebrows in surprise when he held out his arms.

"I will take you back," he said.

Footsteps nearby, followed by a grunt and the unmistakable sound of someone relieving their bladder made Diamond jump. Without another thought she stepped into Hugo's warmth, let him slip one arm under her legs and his other around her back. Lifting her in his arms, he held her securely against him.

It was far too dark for either of them to see the fury and frustration on Freddy's face as he turned and watched them go.

Diamond guiltily enjoyed the sensation of heat seeping from Hugo's body into hers. He smelled of musky sweat, earth, leather and something she couldn't place. It was a heady mix that invaded her senses, and in the minute or so it took to reach the clearing she could do nothing to prevent the hot flush that surged on her cheeks. It was thankfully dark enough to hide her blush as he landed and released her.

Diamond moved toward Jack. At a look from Hugo, Jack's two guards backed up and after a cursory. "Don't go into the forest on your own again," Hugo ordered as left her with them.

Diamond stuck her tongue out at his receding shadow.

Endless and vast, the night sky twinkled with thousands of stars. Unobstructed, Tu Lanah was so bright it cast oddly shaped shadows on to the ash from the skeletal burnt trees. She wrinkled her nose before plonking herself down next to the sleeping prince. Every time the grey ash was disturbed an acrid smell drifted up. It was disgusting.

Diamond found it impossible to relax. Her nerves jangled every time someone strode nearby. Meeting Freddy again filled her with dread. Perhaps if she stayed near Hugo or the prince, he would leave her alone.

General Edo decided it would be safer to stay near the clearing than travel the dark forest at night. Barking orders, the man who had been seen as eccentric and odd by the town's people of Berriesford was unrecognisable to her. This stranger was tough, uncompromising and utterly sure of himself. In the dim light it was hard to see Tom, but she could hear him. He seemed happy to mix with the soldiers.

Left to her own devices, her heart became heavy. It hit her how very alone she was now.

Jack groaned and awoke long enough for his two guards to help him, an arm over their shoulders, to limp to a nearby burnt tree. He collapsed to the ground and, after a quick swig of water and a weak smile in her direction, he promptly fell asleep. She hoped that was normal and that he hadn't been concussed by the general's blow to his head. Dithering, she wondered what she should do now.

"Diamond!" barked General Edo from across the clearing. "Please sit with the prince until he awakens. I need his guards for watch duty. Be ready with that...magic of yours if we get whiff that dragon is coming back for us," he ordered.

The two guards nodded to her and walked briskly to their new general. Diamond sat down next to the prince again. Every now and then she heard Hugo's deep tones and the general's rumbling voice. It made her feel safer to know they were both nearby. Tired but too unsettled to sleep, Diamond endeavoured to use her magical sight, wanting to know if she could use it at any time. It took her many attempts to figure out how to do it, but she eventually found herself holding her new perspective for longer and longer. Something about tapping into her new skill, or magic, or whatever it was helped her relax but she wasn't sure she could summon such vast amounts to form a shield again without the woman's help. Taking her time, she studied the energy that flowed around her. Between the beautiful iridescent energy of the ancient trees, little animals scurried, their aura bright and varied as they snuffled through the ash looking for food. Diamond kept quiet about them. The general had said no fires, so capturing the poor things for food would be pointless.

Jack dozed beside her, snoring every now and then. Groaning inwardly she watched a figure with energy unlike anyone else's prowl closer and stop nearby. Hugo's aura was a beautiful, shimmering sapphire blue, interwoven with tendrils of silver that writhed around him like protective serpents. He came and sat silently next to her, tilting his head back against the tree trunk, his broad shoulder almost touching hers. Her breath hitched in her throat at the sheer power and warmth, she felt as a silver serpent nipped gently at the back of her hand then coiled around her arm, binding her to him as he closed his eyes. She stiffened, not sure how she felt about that touch.

"Relax. Try and sleep for a while. I'll stay until my next watch," he said.

Too tired to wonder why he was showing any interest in her at all, Diamond did her best to relax and soon found herself drifting off to sleep.

The night passed in snatches of wakefulness interspersed with nightmares. Each time she woke, panicking, breathing hard and scared as hell, she felt Hugo's body shift toward her, his energy touching her skin, soothing her until she slept again. Hours later, without a word, he left for his watch.

Chapter Twelve

Weary and missing the security of Hugo's presence, Diamond remained next to Jack as she tried to ignore the damp, creeping cold that seeped into her bones. She shivered, hugging her knees for warmth.

"What's up, little girlie? Lost ya body guard, 'ave ya?" Freddy's voice grated in her ear.

Hot stinking breath smothered her, his closeness making her skin crawl. Lurching quickly away, she tried to grasp for her dagger but was too slow. Freddy grabbed her hair, jabbing the point of a knife to her neck. Diamond froze instantly.

"Good girl. Now, me an' you are goin' for a walk and I'm gonna say thanks properly fer savin' me life."

A disgusting, lustful chuckle rippled down her neck as he shoved his nose in her hair and inhaled deeply. "Hmm. Lovely," he purred.

A sick feeling started in the pit of her stomach, the beginnings of a scream churning in her throat.

Jack stirred but stayed asleep. She wondered if she should wake him. Diamond went rigid as warm fingers, Jack's fingers, grasped the material of her oversized leggings and gently tapped her leg. A silent request. In the dark, trying not to give herself away, Diamond shifted her hips toward Jack, hoping desperately he could see the dagger tucked in her waist band. Jack's hand slowly moved up her leggings.

Trying to distract Freddy, she slowly turned her head to gaze up at him and whispered, "I wondered when you'd come for me. I've been waiting for you. It's boring as hell babysitting this useless excuse for a prince."

Freddy yanked at her hair, and it was all Diamond could do not to squeal as his blade nicked the soft skin of her neck.

"Really?" he snarled.

The dagger slipped out of her waist band.

"Yes," she whispered with as much conviction and longing as she could summon. "Someone like you is so much more exciting than—"

Jack's prone shadow burst into movement. Freddy screamed as Jack cut the tendons and muscle of his forearm at the same time as he pushed Diamond sideways. Suddenly the pair was fighting and slashing, grunts of effort and pain exploding from them.

Diamond yelled at the top of her lungs, "*Hugo!!* Help!!" It was the only name in her head.

Jack barrelled into Freddy, sending him sprawling. Diamond blinked, searching desperately for Hugo's sapphire energy. It was nowhere to be seen. Jack grabbed Freddy's injured arm and twisted it. Screaming, Freddy toppled, clutching Jack's shirt front on the way down. Diamond cried out and scrabbled away through the ash, but not quick enough. The two men fell right on her, driving the breath from her lungs. Freddy grunted as Jack fell atop of him. Their weight crushed her face-first into the ash. She couldn't breathe!

Suddenly Freddy's weight disappeared, his body flying into the shadows. Hugo roared with rage, his eyes glittering like bright blazing stars.

"Look after the prince," he growled down at her and shot after Freddy. At first all she heard was Jack's rasping breaths, each one laboured and rattling ominously. With as much strength as she could muster, Diamond pushed Jack off her legs. A dark patch stained her leggings.

"Prince? You're bleeding. Help! Prince Jack's hurt!" she shouted frantically.

Guards were already running her way. Even as she pressed her cold shaking hands to the wound on Jack's ribs, her spine stiffened. There was something else, a low pulsing rumble getting closer and closer. The unmistakable sound of big wings beating the air.

The guards bellowed a warning, but it was too late. A deafening roar shattered the forest followed by a column of yellow flame that burst across the night sky. The dragon spewed his fire in a great arch, his red eyes blazing as he searched the shadows below. Diamond screamed as he looked right at her.

All hell broke loose. Voices yelled and bodies dived for cover that would be useless against such a creature. Above the din of the dragon it was hard to hear Hugo as he roared orders from somewhere in the trees.

"Prince Jack! Please. Wake up! We have to get out of here," she sobbed as she violently shook his lax body.

The burnt forest canopy crashed in around them, splintering burnt trees. Debris and sulphuric air swamped the two figures on the ground. Diamond screamed but could do nothing as talons as long and sharp as swords scooped them up, taking branches and earth with them into the dark night.

The wind bit at Diamond's face, reaching icy fingers in through the thin material of her clothes. Disregarding it, she concentrated on wiggling her numb fingers and toes to get the blood flowing again. The dragon had been flying over the forest canopy for what seemed like hours but, she reasoned, was probably a lot less. It wasn't even full daylight yet.

There was no hope of figuring out where they were being taken as the terrain below was just more forest. Strangely, Diamond saw the flash of a wolf's pelt among the trees, as if it were somehow keeping pace with them. Diamond's arm snaked around the unconscious prince's back, pressing hard on his wound. The bleeding had almost stopped but he was terribly pale. The dragon's grip was relaxed enough to breathe but that was it, there was no hope of wriggling free. She looked at the long drop to the forest floor. Even if they could escape, they would be killed or fatally injured in such a fall.

In the distance a long winding river glinted like a ghostly snake in the dawn light. An idea bloomed. *Could it work?* The dagger that had been scooped up with the dirt was balanced precariously on Jack's hip. It glinted invitingly. Hoping it wouldn't fall, she shuffled her hips and painstakingly wiggled her other arm free from where it was trapped next to one of the dragon's claws. Relief flooded her when the cold metal hilt of Hugo's dagger was gripped tightly in her hand.

"Prince Jack! Highness!" Her head nudged his insistently and she shouted loudly in his ear. He stirred and his eyes opened, looking cloudy and confused. It took only a few seconds for him to register the pain from his wounds and remember. There was no time for more explanations or to worry about issuing orders to this royal.

"There's a river coming up. When I tell you, hack and stab at the root of that talon. Cause this monster as much pain as possible."

"Why? What are you going to do?" he asked, sounding dazed but he moved his fingers so he could grasp the dagger.

Please don't argue, she thought. "I'm going to hurt it—at the same time as you," she told him with steel in her voice. This had to work.

The river loomed closer. She blinked and focused on the shimmering water. It seemed to disappear off the edge of the earth, misty air hanging above it. Her stomach lurched and she rolled her eyes.

Great. A waterfall. Still, it doesn't matter. It has to be better than where this dragon is taking us.

Colour, dazzling in its intensity, swathed the forest—but Diamond had no time to admire it. Instead she tried to block out the possibility they might both die from the fall or because she had no idea what she was doing with her energy.

Breathe—concentrate. Embers of magic flared to life inside her. Desperately she pulled at them, focusing on nothing else until they surged free. Release, freedom—magic. Even in this dire situation, it was hard not to feel a smug satisfaction for finding her magic. Sizzling heat travelled up through her body and down her arms, escaping out through her hand. Letting instinct guide her, Diamond concentrated on the dragon's scaly skin just where one black talon bulged through. Bone and flesh exploded into the air, followed by a roar of agony. Jack stabbed up and down with all his strength on another talon bed, swearing loudly and forcefully as scaly skin and blood covered him.

Diamond felt her stomach lurch. Fresh air and weightlessness. It had worked. Seconds later Diamond slammed into the fast flowing water. Cold engulfed her, stealing her breath as the water swept her away in a torrent of noise and confusion. She fought the urge to inhale and scream. Then she was falling again. Down and down, out of control.

Wham!

Another hard sheet of water. Diamond barely registered the stinging force of the collision; once again she was at the mercy of the powerful flow. Lungs burning, she resisted her need to breathe and was tossed and thrown, the world whirling by. Another weightless fall and the cascading water trapped her in a never ending tumble.

Down. Go down, she thought. Using the last remnants of her strength she forced her arms and legs to move, swimming down to the floor of the pool. It was calmer here. Digging her fingers into the gravel and bedrock, she dragged herself away from the heavy curtain of tumbling water. Once free, she propelled herself upwards and broke through the surface, coughing and spluttering loudly. The water grabbed her again, taking her with it.

The fast, vicious flow slammed her into rocks and floating debris, but Diamond was a good swimmer and used the current to help her; she swam with and across the churning flow, keeping her head up as best she could. After an eternity of exhausting toil, the river bank was within reach. Ignoring her numb, bleeding fingers, Diamond triumphantly grabbed a protruding root. Diamond doggedly kept hold when the fingers of her other hand slipped on slimy mud and grass. More tree roots curled like smooth snakes under the clear swirling water; Diamond quickly braced her feet on them, fighting the flow of water.

The dragon bellowed its wrath, swooping down the waterfall before banking straight back up to the skies, still searching. She couldn't stay here. This guardian was an intelligent and clever being. It would follow the course of the river, and she needed to be long gone by the time it did. Using the roots as leverage, she grabbed handfuls of the long, spiky grass and hoisted herself onto the river's edge, landing on her belly.

Trembling from bone deep cold, Diamond scrambled to her feet, slipping and sliding on the damp ground and mud as she bolted for cover under the nearest tree. The bark was rough under her hands, her heart slamming against her ribs as she leaned against it, lungs heaving.

Here the banks were wide apart, allowing for a more gentle flow. Heading downriver was the most sensible option. Jack certainly would have been too weak to fight the wild current. Fearing he might have drowned, Diamond launched herself in to a run. She had to find him, alive or dead. A few minutes later she spotted his inert body on a lower section of bank. He must have used all his remaining strength to drag himself out. Diamond raced towards him.

"Prince Jack! Highness!" she yelled.

Pale and sickly-looking, his breath came in shallow gasps. Diamond had once seen a man slashed in a knife fight in the town marketplace. Her father had knocked the assailant out cold before pressing hard on the wound in the victim's chest, but it had done no good, the poor man had still bled to death. She swallowed, trying to remain calm even as panic bloomed. At least the big gash in Jack's side had stopped bleeding. Sinking to her knees at his side, she gently shifted the material to get a better look—and hissed.

Deep layers of skin and muscle had been laid open. Clumsy with her numb fingers, she managed to lift his shirt and quickly assess the other two ragged cuts on Jack's back. Jagged, they looked far worse but were not as deep. Diamond hastily pulled the prince's shirt straight and anxiously looked up. The black dragon swooped over the river and waterfall. He would find them if they stayed here in the open. She cursed as it roared with frustration. But she needn't have panicked; with wings outstretched to catch the wind, it turned and headed away.

"Prince! We need to get out of here. Wake up!" she shouted in his ear, shaking his shoulders hard until he moaned. "Come on!" she pleaded, trying again. "We should head into the forest, away from the river."

Doubt flooded her as she looked into the darkness that surrounded them. *What if there are Seekers or Battle Imps—or worse—in there? What can I or the injured prince do against such creatures?*

"My name...is Jack," rasped the prince resolutely. His eyelids opened and gave her an unobstructed view of his dark brown eyes awash with pain.

Diamond bit her bottom lip in consternation but knew there was nothing she could do for him until they got away from the river. "Can you stand?" she asked anxiously.

"With a little help," he panted, grunting and gritting his teeth as she helped him up.

Diamond looked around his back; the wounds had started bleeding again.

"Leave it. We'll get into the forest and then deal with my wounds," he uttered with colourless lips on a deathly pale face.

They staggered as quickly as possible into the gloom of the trees and left the rush of the river behind them.

Chapter Thirteen

Hugo soared through the biting wind, leaving the devastated clearing far below. He landed solidly on the lip of small cliff.

Inside he was burning, burning with such wrath his facade was ready to shatter. Unable to contain himself any longer he opened his soul and let his raging magic erupt. The shimmering wave of shadow hurtled harmlessly into the empty sky. Panting hard, he expanded his back muscles and threw his metallic wings outward. Release was fleeting.

A raw animal power clawed at his bones, at his soul, boiling his blood as it too clamoured for release. He would not give in to the beast inside him. He would not. For months they had battled. It wanted to dominate him, control him, and the longer Diamond was missing the more wrathful and vicious it became. Another wave of burning heat and roaring rocked his mind.

No. Not yet, Hugo commanded, pitting his iron will against its insistence.

A shapeshifter had once told him how it felt to have another being living as a symbiont with one's soul, how it had sometimes made him feel not only insane but lost. But that shapeshifter had been young when he had yielded to his baser side, it had taken him years to become its master.

Hugo slowed his breathing as the beast settled, but he could fit seething at being cowed yet again. Hugo knew this battle for dominance was far from over.

In the clearing far below, Jack's soldiers and warriors tended the wounded and went about breaking camp. A vicious snarl curled Hugo's lips. Freddy needed to be hunted down. Hugo longed to feel that repulsive little bastard's neck snap under his fingers. Attacking Diamond had sealed his death warrant. But that would have to wait—for now. Hugo's stomach boiled with self-reproach. Diamond and Jack had been snatched from right under his nose. His magic had tried to alert him, to warn him his Nexus bond was in danger, but he had resolutely ignored such absurd feelings. Being tied to anyone, in any way, did not sit well with Hugo. But Diamond's scream had sent his blood cold.

Him. She had called for him, not General Edo or Tom.

His fingers shook as he rubbed his face. Gods, the fear in her scream had shattered his steely control last night. Reaching her had consumed him and, for a few frightening seconds as he scented her blood, all his training and common sense had fled. It was the sort of foolish mistake for which he would flog any other guard. Not only had he lost his focus, he had left her alone with an injured man without knowing how badly she was hurt. Instead he had gone running after Freddy, wanting to rip the little prick to pieces.

Well, there was no changing what had happened. General Edo had made plans and given orders, and Hugo had been happy to let him—but now it was time to leave. His desperate need to track Diamond down drove him to distraction. She could be dead by now or hurt and in pain. Magic thrummed through his veins in response to his thoughts. He absentmindedly rubbed at his chest, a derisory snort exploding from his throat when he realised what he was doing.

Below him the charred and devastated forest canopy stretched into the distance. Bright greens and golds should be apparent in late summer this far north, but an unhealthy tinge covered the Avalonian forest and became worse the further south they travelled. Finding game to hunt and food to forage had become increasingly hard as Ragor's malediction spread. It didn't matter, he was still leaving—to find her, to bring her to safety. Or this thrashing beast inside him would burst free of the restraints of Hugo's flesh and bone and hunt her anyway.

Hugo closed his eyes and breathed deeply. Merging his magic with hers, Hugo had sensed a deep confusion and fear of the power she wielded. It was clearly a new and overwhelming discovery, and one she stood no hope of controlling without assistance. He laughed bitterly. *Help? I cannot help her.* His oath required him to take her to his Queen, and he was under no illusion that action would eventually result in her death. He swallowed that sickening thought, extended his wings and stepped into the air. Right now, retrieving her from the resurrected guardian was the most important thing; he would deal with the rest later.

General Edo watched the Queen's guard return with hard grey eyes. The older man's mood had been dark and unforgiving since the attack. He had whipped the men into order, viciously putting down any that had questioned his authority.

Hugo squared his shoulders. The general was an intimidating, powerful male but so was Hugo. He had suffered beatings and whippings on a daily basis as a trainee of Queen's guard and those days had hardened him to fear of physical violence. Hugo simply was not scared of this fae.

The growl he emitted grotesquely twisted the scar on his face. Not many things scared him now. In Hugo's world, Lord Commander Ream and the ancient fae Queen were the only ones to fear. Being what he was and the way he looked, Hugo was usually the one instilling fear in others.

"General," Hugo nodded curtly, noting the general was clasping Dragonsblood in one big hand.

"Commander," the general returned, watching the younger man's approach.

Hugo waited. The general was clenching and unclenching his jaw. Hugo couldn't force the man to speak, so he crossed his arms over his broad chest and waited patiently.

"I know you are going to leave," General Edo said, his voice gravelly and deep. "You hide it well, but I can see your anger. You blame yourself."

Hugo steadily held General Edo's gaze. Deliberately he did not affirm the general's suspicions.

General Edo grunted then continued. "I have spent my life watching and sizing up men, especially males who are at the right age to become distracted from their duties. You're instincts are telling you to find a mate, and I can see you have a connection with Diamond."

Hugo kept his face carefully still but his stomach tightened. Yes, he had a connection with her, but not in the way the general meant. He wondered if this old warhorse really had picked up on his confusion about Diamond and their magic. It was hard to believe as Hugo had only just acknowledged their bond. Clearly he needed to be more careful with his behaviour. Hugo waited, continuing his cold dead stare, a stare he had perfected years ago.

"Oh, don't worry, Hugo; I won't share my thoughts with anyone, especially not the Queen—at least not unless you force me to. But her father was my best friend, and I had a hand in raising that girl. She is as close to a child of my own as I will ever get."

The general rubbed his large scarred hands over his face. "I know

I can't give you orders, commander, but we both know that no matter how interested you might be, you cannot pursue Diamond as a mate. However, I would very much appreciate it if you would find her and my crown prince—and bring them back."

For a long moment Hugo made a show of considering General Edo's words. It gave him time to suppress his smile of relief. He nodded his head as if making a decision.

"I will meet you at Sentinel's Cave in four weeks with any news I have," he said unemotionally before bending his knees and launching himself into the clear dawn sky, a flash of sapphire blue wings.

Chapter Fourteen

Diamond and Jack staggered through the forest until the prince's legs became too weak to take his weight. They collapsed next to a bubbling stream, Jack landing on his belly and panting hard. Diamond kneeled on the damp bank and carefully lifted his shirt; she hissed at the blood oozing steadily from the deep cuts. Jack's clothes were sodden with the red fluid.

"That good, eh?" Jack mumbled, sweat trickling down his brow.

"That good," agreed Diamond wryly.

They were resting under the canopy of a large tree. Empty nutshells littered the ground; taking one of their hard, reddish brown cups about the size of her fist, she swiftly shuffled across the ground and leaned out into the flow of the stream to scoop up some clean water. She returned to Jack's side to gently move his shirt up and dribble the water across his exposed flesh, sluicing out the three wounds.

"Do they need stitching?" he panted, squeezing his eyes shut against the pain. Beads of sweat formed on his brow.

"This one does," she said, indicating the long slash wound that followed his rib line. "But we don't have anything to sew with so I'll try and make you a dressing; that will have to do."

She had difficulty keeping her voice light. Jack looked up at her and gave her a watery smile. Diamond smiled back, ignoring the knowledge that infection would set in quickly out here in the forest. It could be possible to stop it, or at least slow it down with the right herbs. She sat back on her haunches and used Hugo's dagger to cut a strip off what remained of her dress. She rinsed off as much dirt as she could in the stream and then set about cutting more strips.

"Now that we've stopped running, I guess we should introduce ourselves properly. Hugo told me your name is Diamond, and my name is Jack. Not prince or Your Highness," he chided weakly.

"Hello, Jack," she replied with a small smile.

"So how did you end up with Hugo? And how is it you and your father were living in the same village as General Edo?" he wheezed, trying to distract himself from his pain as she refilled the nut shells with more water.

She dipped a cleanish bit of cloth in the water, then gently but thoroughly cleaned his wounds before answering. Diamond's nimble fingers worked surely as she told him all that had happened to her over the past few days. Concentrating on her task helped her cope with the raw grief in her heart. In between clenched teeth and growls of pain, Jack asked her many questions. Then they got to the subject of her magic.

"Diamond? How did you control your magic if you didn't even know you had such a gift?" he asked curiously as he tried to sit up.

"Hey! Don't sit up! Now you're bleeding again," she said with an exasperated sigh, glad of a reason not to answer his question. She had not known what to do, and admitting she had voices in her head giving her instructions made her sound mad.

"Look, I'll gladly answer all of your questions later, but right now we need to bind your wound. If we clean the others regularly, I think they will heal. They aren't as deep," she informed him, successfully changing the subject.

Jack's brown eyes watched her, his lips twitching as she cut yet more off her skirts.

"If you keep cutting, there'll be nothing left of that dress," he observed, a hint of amusement in his pain-filled eyes.

Diamond huffed a laugh and smiled back. "S'all right, I'll start on your shirt next, Your Highness."

He raised his eyebrows and, even though he still looked grey and in pain, he managed a cheeky smile. "Really? Well, I've known women who want to get the shirt off my back before, but this is a bit desperate, if you ask me."

She couldn't help but chuckle. Teasing her and trying to lighten her anxiety was a nice gesture.

"Indeed. Well, prince, you can keep your shirt on for now. Come on, sit up slowly. Can you help me knot this material together? I'm just going to change this water and get us some to drink, then I'll bind your wound."

When she returned, Jack had his eyes closed, pain etched on his face. Tomorrow she would search for some wild roots to help heal him. Diamond was no herbalist but her father had shown her some basic herb lore as she grew up. Gently she shook Jack awake then bound his wound tightly.

Temperatures plummeted during the night. Diamond shivered next to Jack, her thoughts straying back to the others. *Had they survived the dragon fire? Had Hugo?* She swallowed that uncomfortable thought. When Freddy had attacked, she had screamed for Hugo, not her childhood uncle or her friend, but for the guard who had enthralled her. She didn't know if he was still alive in a kingdom that abhorred and killed those with magic. It didn't matter. She clutched his dagger to her chest, remembering the warmth of his body as he held her. Those memories did nothing to keep her warm now though, and soon her shaking body woke Jack.

Placing an arm around her shoulders, he pulled her in close. At first she was embarrassed and couldn't relax, but he just dozed off, his arm slipping a little. With Jack asleep Diamond tried to calm her mind, but the sounds of the forest kept her on edge. Shifting her vision was not reassuring, the aura of the forest was dull here and nothing, no life, moved among the undergrowth.

Fear skittered down her spine. *Food. Tomorrow. I will deal with that problem tomorrow.* Her stomach grumbled painfully as if in response to her thoughts. To distract herself she studied Jack's aura. It was tinged with a sickly grey. Diamond shuffled even closer to the prince. He couldn't become sick out here; he would die. Then she would be truly alone. Tears pricked her eyes as she let her head rest on his chest, listening to the sounds of the forest with one ear and his heart beating with the other.

The past two days had been awful. Jack was shirtless, his body pale and dirty. The soiled garment was being used to carry more nut shells containing the rough poultice Diamond had made. Jack had been in far too much pain to travel on that first day, so Diamond had used the time to search out useful herbs and grind them into a paste. It would work better if they could boil it down to make a salve, but a fire was not an option. Flames and smoke would just invite danger.

Jack walked in front of her. A frown furrowed her brow. Purulent yellow fluid soaked his makeshift bandage. She eased herself closer to the prince, wrinkling her nose.

"Jack, we need to clean your wound again," she said, tentatively touching his shoulder to get his attention.

Over the past day Jack had been prone to snapping at her. He squinted, his brown eyes bright and unfocused. Not for the first time

Diamond wondered if Jack really knew where he was or if the infection raging through his body was clouding his mind.

"No. We can't stop—it's too dangerous," he bit out, wincing as he stumbled.

Diamond clamped her mouth shut, not brave enough to question him more. *Common girls don't question the judgment of princes—do they?*

Jack weaved between the tall, dying trees, narrowly avoiding bare branches that stuck out like the macabre fingers of a skeleton. Diamond shuddered in the gloom and eeriness of the forest. Her hand curled tightly around the cool metal of Hugo's dagger. The object gave her a sense of safety, a connection to him—even if it wasn't real. Her magic stirred unhappily as she called to mind the silver serpents of his energy wrapped soothingly around her arms.

It wasn't until the light dropped that Diamond realised how late it had become. She had been totally absorbed on putting one foot in front of the other. Now it was hard to ignore her aching muscles. Late summer this far south should still be warm—but it wasn't, the air was frigid. Weak and exhausted, shivers racked her body.

Glancing at Tu Lanah, a frown furrowed her brow. It would be another six months until the moon was at its lowest point on winter solstice, but storms would rage during the months before that. She shivered again and hoped the storms wouldn't come early. The Festival of the Moon on winter solstice had always been Diamond's favourite celebration, full of laughter, music, dancing, food—and love. It was a celebration of the goddess of creation. A night full of magic, where devout fae believed the females of their race were the most fertile.

Cramps twisted her stomach. Her life in Berriesford might not have been full of riches but going without food for such a long time was not something Diamond had experienced before. Exhaustion tugged her mood even lower. She didn't know how she was going to stop Jack's infection or keep them fed. It was impossible for Jack to hunt in his current state. She blinked back tears and scanned the forest.

And where in chaos are we? Jack had led them in a weaving roundabout route for hours. *How can I get us anywhere near Valentia if I don't know which way to go?*

Diamond shifted her vision. Jack's energy hung like a stagnant grey shroud around him. Fear of him dying made her throat hurt.

"Jack? How do you know which direction Valentia is in?" she

asked tentatively.

Silence. He seemed to be concentrating hard, his skin pale and covered in a sheen of sweat.

Risking getting her head bitten off was worth it. "Jack! You need to tell me where to go, which direction to head in or we aren't going to make it. You're sick and you're becoming confused. Jack!" she barked impatiently.

Unfocused eyes stared at her. The prince swayed unsteadily on his feet and just for a moment his eyes cleared.

"I'm sorry, Diamond," he panted and swallowed. "If you follow...the moon. The glow. It stays in the east...until after winter solstice," he rasped. Diamond could only watch in horror as his eyes rolled back in his head and he collapsed to the ground.

"Jack!" she cried.

With trembling fingers she felt for his pulse. Sobbing with relief when she felt the rapid flutter beneath her finger tips, Diamond looked about helplessly. A rocky outcrop jutted from a nearby slope. Diamond dragged Jack's unconscious body towards it a few feet at a time. It took most of her remaining strength but, at last, panting and sweaty and determined, she had him underneath its lee. At least it would provide some shelter. Dreading what she would find, Diamond unbound Jack's wound. A fetid aroma hit her. She gagged, wrinkling her nose in disgust. Quickly she cut a strip off her dress, wrapped it around her fingers and scooped out the pus. With no water to clean the festering laceration, she packed it with the herb poultice and left the dressings off, letting it drain.

Diamond stayed awake through the long and lonely night, scooping out the poultice when it became pus-stained, and replacing it until every last bit was gone. There was nothing else she could do.

"Except pray to the goddess," she mumbled to herself. And that's just what Diamond did, fervently. All night her mood bounced between worry for Jack and fear for herself if he died. She didn't stand a chance of surviving on her own.

Halfway through the next day Diamond allowed herself to leave Jack long enough to search out the nearest stream. After thirty minutes of walking, she came across a clear bubbling flow. Relieved, she single-mindedly used the empty nut shells to spend the day fetching water to fill up a small dip in the rocks near Jack. When satisfied the pool was full enough she carefully and patiently dripped water in between Jack's parched, cracked lips, beseeching him to drink. Dribbling water across his wounds, she washed the pus away as best she could.

Over the next two days Diamond searched the forest nearby for more herbs, ignoring her hunger and ever-increasing weakness. Foraging for yellow berries and any edible roots yielded only minimal success. But at least it gave her something other than loneliness and fear to think about.

Three days later the prince's fever broke, and his eyes flickered open.

Diamond's shoulders sagged, a small sob escaping her. "Nice of you to come back, prince," she whispered, wiping sweat off his forehead with a damp piece of cloth.

He looked at her silently, then fell back into a more settled sleep. That night when she checked his energy it had a flicker of blue among the grey. Thanking the goddess for her favour, Diamond lay next to Jack's prone body and held his cool hand as she tried to sleep.

The following day Diamond helped Jack shuffle slowly and painfully towards the stream. There they stayed for the next three days. She worked tirelessly as Jack rested, searching the forest for more herbs and food. Fallen nuts littered the ground and she discovered grinding them down released a foul smelling oil. After testing it on herself with no reaction, she mixed it with the herbs to make a salve. By the fourth day Jack was just about strong enough to walk.

"Diamond? I really am strong enough to travel now. We need to leave. If we stay much longer, we will starve. Even the trees are dying. Ragor's cursed troops must be overpowering its energy," he said, chewing on a tough reed root.

Diamond knew he was right. It was hard to keep track but at least two weeks had passed and they were both gaunt and bony.

Together they set a slow pace towards the bright orb of Tu Lanah. Each night Diamond cleaned Jack's wounds and then lay next to him on the ground, periodically checking his energy. It was becoming bluer and brighter every day; even his mood was lighter. A smile curled her lips. He had even taken to teasing her again.

The next morning sunshine burst through the trees, casting glittering beams to the ground. Since waking three hours ago they had been walking into even thicker forest. The going had been tough and rocky. Diamond leaned back against the rough bark of a tree and sucked in big breaths of cool air until her tired breathing settled. Jack mirrored her, his chocolate brown eyes resting intently on her face. A flush bloomed over her cheeks at his unwavering regard. After a few moments she risked meeting his eyes.

"Thank you," he said, looking at her intently.

She nodded, aware he was thanking her for saving his life.

"You're welcome, Prince Oden, but I owe you thanks as well."

"Do you?" He sounded genuinely surprised. "What for?"

"Saving me from Freddy," she replied while meeting his eyes, hoping he could see she was sincere. "If it hadn't been for you, Freddy would have—" she coughed disgusted by thoughts of what Freddy would have done to her. "Anyway, I'm really sorry you got hurt because of me," she finished awkwardly.

"Hey, I can't think of anyone else I would rather get attacked for than you," he teased, then brushed his fingers down her hot cheek and grinned. "Besides, it meant I got your undivided attention for a few days. It's been more than worth it to get to know you better."

He gently grasped her chin, and she felt herself drowning in his deep brown eyes. She gulped, not quite knowing how to handle this handsome, charming and self-assured prince. He was so out of her league. Forcing herself not to panic, Diamond withdrew from his touch. It wasn't that his touch felt creepy or wrong, not like the traders who had tried to corner her over the years; it was quite the opposite, in fact.

"And I mean that. I hope I still get your attention when we get to Valentia and you are once again surrounded by warriors with wings who could whisk you away at a moment's notice. Particularly a certain large one with blue wings," he chuckled but she didn't miss the serious undertone in his voice. He took her hand, his face altogether more serious. "Perhaps you should stay in the Rift Valley in my camp. It will be much safer for you than Valentia." A gorgeous smile stunned her, and his tone lightened. "Then we can spend time together in more...luxurious surroundings. My camps even have beds...." he wiggled his eyebrows suggestively.

Blowing air from her lips, Diamond gently but firmly pulled away. The prince studied her, looking amused at her discomfiture. Despite Jack's stunning good looks, Diamond couldn't help but compare him to a certain scarred and fearsome Queen's guard. Jack's warmth and friendliness was nothing like the cold strength Hugo exuded; yet Diamond longed to be lost in this forest with Hugo, not Jack. Which, she reflected, was ridiculous considering he was as likely to kill her as save her.

Jack's eyes narrowed thoughtfully as she focused on him again. "Diamond, I'm only teasing—about the bed thing, I mean. But not about the city. You will be safer if you stay away from it."

Diamond didn't doubt it. With a weak smile at Jack she turned and began walking again.

Chapter Fifteen

Diamond lost count of the days. One day of marching through this ancient part of the forest was much like another. Death caressed the old trees; their twisted trunks and heavy moss covered boughs bare of leaves. Even the tall firs that clung to the rocky slopes were mostly naked. Millions of fallen pine needles formed a deep carpet that made walking hellish and running impossible.

Jack grabbed Diamond's hand.

"Move quicker," Jack whispered, pulling her along urgently. "Wolfmen track nearly as well as Seekers."

This part of the ancient forest was riddled with Dust Devils and Wolfmen. The atmosphere was utterly still, so devoid of any breeze it was impossible to tell how close the monstrous creatures were from the stink of rotting carrion. Diamond gagged and swallowed her nausea.

It had been terrifying to find so many enemy soldiers here. Jack had thought the Wolfmen would avoid this part of the ancient forest, just as the fae did. Apparently they believed the 'heart' of Avalonia was haunted by tree spirits who dragged their victims into the trunks of their chosen tree and slowly devoured their prey over months, sometimes years.

Diamond shuddered. It was true the forest had a mysterious feel, as though eyes constantly watched her. But it seemed Ragor's monsters did not respect folklore and legends.

Diamond clutched Hugo's dagger in her cold hand. She was painfully aware it was the only weapon they had and was nowhere near enough to defend themselves effectively. With no breeze to blow away their scent, the miles of undulating hills and twisted ancient trees were a death trap. They were easy prey.

Diamond found she couldn't lift her feet properly and began stumbling. With immense effort she righted herself and pushed on. The ancient forest seemed to despise them, sharp branches clutching at the remains of her clothes. Jack yanked her into a thicket of spiked undergrowth to evade a shuffling party of Dust Devils. His hand was firm over her mouth, stopping the whimper that escaped her as the thorns pierced her skin. They waited for what seemed like hours to ensure the Dust Devil patrol had long gone. Her nerves were fraught, the utter stillness of the forest and the constant smell of death terrifying. Jack squeezed her trembling hand and guided her onward.

"Stay alert," he hissed, his dark brown eyes surveying the shadows between the army of trees in their path. "Hugo told me once that Leaf Fairies inhabit this part of the old forest. Nasty creatures they are. They have three rows of teeth and can devour a human body in seconds, right down to the bone," he told her, turning his chin slightly over his shoulder whilst keeping his eyes forward.

Diamond shuddered with revulsion. "How big are they?" she whispered, nervously imagining fae as big as Hugo but with massive rows of fangs and sharp claws.

"About as big as your hand, but those rows of teeth are as sharp as needles; they devour their prey in swarms and have a temperament more brutal than an injured Battle Imp."

"They sound charming. How do we fight them if we meet any?" she asked as she stepped closer to Jack's side despite her attempt at a light tone of voice.

"You don't," said a deep male voice from behind them.

Diamond spun on her heels, dagger out. Her mouth dropped open and her heart jumped wildly against her ribs.

Jack followed suit, pushing her behind him protectively. "Hugo!" Jack exclaimed incredulously, a wide smile spreading over his face.

Diamond felt blood rush up her neck and into her cheeks. The sight of Hugo's towering figure stunned her into silence. She blinked to make sure he wasn't an apparition.

"How the hell did you find us?" asked Jack, disbelief colouring his voice.

"I followed your scent," Hugo responded, his voice devoid of emotion. He stared intently at Diamond.

Diamond could not take her eyes off his face, nor could she help the rush of relief she felt at seeing him. He was alive and unharmed....

Jack laughed, not bothered in the least by Hugo's cold demeanour. Obviously pleased to see his friend, Jack strode up to the Queen's guard and gave Hugo's shoulder a solid thwack. Diamond winced. Clearly Jack was confident Hugo would not read any disrespect into the gesture and retaliate.

"I know I smell a bit ripe, but I didn't think it was that bad," Jack laughed jovially.

"Not your scent, prince. Hers," Hugo stated. The weight of his amazing eyes bored into Diamond.

Jack's smile slipped but he recovered quickly. Both of them missed the thoughtful frown he gave his friend.

Diamond felt new heat sear her cheeks, not ready to consider how he knew her scent well enough to track it. Lifting her chin and steeling her nerves, she held his dark look until he turned his attention to Jack.

"You look better than I expected, prince," commented Hugo, scrutinising Jack's movements through slightly narrowed eyes.

"Yeah. I should be dead from infection by now. But," he smiled indulgently at Diamond, "I had a lot of help, some top class healing and a very patient healer."

Jack stepped back to her side and clasped her hand in his. Hugo briefly glanced at the gesture and met Jack's challenging gaze. Unable to meet Hugo's eyes, hers dropped to the ground as he continued talking. A burst of anger and embarrassment clenched her belly tight. It shouldn't matter what Hugo thought. What she did was none of his business. Even so, she was annoyed with Jack for his proprietary gesture. Silently but firmly, Diamond disengaged herself from his fingers.

"How did you get away from the dragon?" Hugo asked tersely.

Diamond's legs wobbled when she stepped sideways away from Jack, pretending not to notice when Hugo clearly registered her movements. She hoped Jack would take the hint and let her go. She would not be marked as any one's property, prince or no prince.

"Diamond used her energy and I used your dagger," said Jack, his voice steady, though his brief glance at her was questioning and somewhat amused.

Inwardly Diamond cringed. She and Jack had become close but that did not give him rights over her.

"Oh?" Hugo asked, turning his attention to her again. Curiosity burned in his eyes but was replaced seconds later by a blank stare.

Diamond bristled.

"We should go, prince. You can tell me while we walk. I meant what I said about the Leaf Fairies. If we stay here too long they will detect our presence and I don't fancy being their next meal," he said, dismissing Diamond with a turn of his big shoulders.

A scowl creased her features. Not that there was really much point as Hugo didn't look at her again.

Days passed and still they trudged on through rolling glens and across gentle slopes. Food was scarce, and only Hugo had the ability and the weapons to cover enough ground to hunt. Sometimes he was gone for hours. Diamond hated his absence almost as much as she hated his cold attitude towards her when he returned, only to become even more confused by him when night fell and he chose to rest close by her, letting his energy wrap her in warmth and comfort.

On the rare occasions Hugo did catch a squirrel or scrawny bird, they would stop. Both he and Jack were adept at making fires, but once their meagre meal was cooked, they extinguished the flames quickly and left the area, eating as they walked. The terrain changed, the hills becoming gentler as they headed down towards the coast. Deliverance from this hideous nightmare was near. Diamond was both relieved and terrified about what would happen to her when they got to Valentia. She wondered if Hugo would allow her to stay hidden with Jack.

Nights fell quickly, always cold and crisp. Through the canopy, millions of bright stars twinkled. Diamond blinked and used her gift to guide her in the dark. Hugo's energy swirled in a sapphire and silver cloud, like a beacon in the gloom. When her footsteps stumbled, his energy shot back and steadied her, drawing her closer to him. Swallowing the butterflies in her belly she walked more quickly, trying to keep up with him. Even though she didn't like to admit it, she felt far safer with Hugo by her side. Jack was an experienced soldier, but Hugo had a quiet viciousness and power about him that Jack didn't possess.

As she studied Hugo's wide back, he seemed to disappear into the inky shadows. Diamond blinked furiously and he came back into focus. Her tired mind was playing tricks on her. Wearily she dragged her feet through the pine needles. If they didn't stop soon, she would collapse. But under the moon-lit sky, Hugo pushed them unrelentingly onwards. Diamond silently cursed his lack of consideration for anyone else.

"Hugo? Please, can't we stop?" she eventually dared to ask.

"No. We are to meet General Edo in less than a week, in a cave that is flying distance from the Rift Valley wall."

"Sentinel's Cave?" questioned Jack, his voice contemplative.

"Yes. If we don't push on, he will leave without us."

"Can't we get to Valentia without him?" Diamond wearily asked.

"Unlikely. Ragor's forces will be thick around that section of forest. We will stand a better chance if we band together with Jack's soldiers. Besides, there are too many humans now to fly everyone to the wall, and anyone who tried would get shot down by arrows."

"Oh," said Diamond, a shudder rippling through her at the thought of having to fight her way through the monsters they had been evading for weeks.

Jack stepped passed her. He and Hugo talked in low voices as they walked. Diamond found she was too tired to care what they were talking about.

Chapter Sixteen

Hugo eventually capitulated. "You two rest here. I will take first watch." He met Diamond's eyes before prowling away.

Once again his bulk morphed into the shadows, and Diamond lost sight of him within seconds. Sighing, she turned to Jack.

"Shall we?" he shrugged, his eyebrows wiggling comically.

Diamond had to smile, then looked with distaste at the rough ground he indicated.

"Come on, I'll keep you warm until my watch. It seems to annoy my good friend, which is as good an excuse as any other to get close to you," he grinned, mischief glinting in his eyes.

Diamond punched his shoulder playfully.

"What? It's true," he defended himself. "Besides, I enjoy winding him up. His heart has been dead for far too long." He shrugged. "It's good to see some sort of emotion in him."

Diamond wondered what he meant as she lay down next to the prince who had become her friend. They lay on their sides, spooned close enough for body heat but not touching. For a while Diamond gazed at the stars twinkling though the skeletal trees. She liked Jack; his humour and friendship had kept her going, but she didn't want his warmth, she wanted Hugo's. She wanted to feel the touch of his magic brushing her skin when he was nearby. Watching the shadows for his return did not help that need, and it felt like hours of tossing and turning before she slept.

Surprisingly Hugo did not disturb either of them until dawn. Diamond awoke the instant his warm fingers shook her shoulder, then cringed at the stony look on his face. Jack was clasping her hand to his chest. Guilty and embarrassed, she flushed and glared back defiantly. Holding Jack's hand was not a crime. But under the accusing glower Hugo aimed her way, she lost her nerve and dropped her eyes.

Jack sat up, unaware of the tension and with his curly hair in disarray. It was an effort not to shrink from him when he treated her to a languid smile and brushed a lock of hair back from her face.

Hugo growled, and her head shot around to look at him, her eyes flashing. He had no right to disapprove of anything she did or who she did it with. It was none of his business.

Jack looked up at his friend and frowned a little. "Just give us a minute, Hugo. Diamond needs to sort out my wound," he ordered in a careful and even voice, but she knew he had sensed the undercurrent between her and Hugo when he rested his hand on her arm and gave it a squeeze.

Hugo prowled to a large fallen tree, his movements laced with restrained power. After lowering his bulk down, he took out one of his daggers and began tossing it in a precise, lethal rhythm. His sapphire eyes watched unwaveringly as Diamond dipped her fingers in the remains of the salve. The weight of his regard made her fingers tremble. Jack shrugged off the surcoat Hugo had given him and leaned over his knees, his scars expanding along with his muscles. The long gash was almost healed now, but the new tissue was swollen and raised and would tighten up if left alone.

"You don't have to watch," Diamond snapped at Hugo.

Jack raised his eyes and stared steadily, challengingly, at the guard. Diamond's anger flared. Jack was deliberately goading his friend.

"I know, but I'm comfortable now," Hugo drawled, clearly not intending to move. His eyes glittered at her obvious discomfort. Jack smiled tightly over his shoulder at her but remained silent. With cold fingers she gripped the makeshift jar filled with nasty smelling salve as if she wanted to crush it, resisting the violent urge to throw it at one of them.

"Well, I'm not rubbing this into you again whilst we have an audience," she uttered at Jack, furious with them both.

Jack clearly wanted Hugo to see her do this and, although massaging his wounds had not bothered her before, it felt far too intimate now. What was it Jack had said, that it was *'good to see some sort of emotion'* in Hugo. Hugo watched her intently, making her even more self-conscious. Her annoyance grew along with the redness on her neck and face. *What sort of game are they playing?*

With rough hands, Diamond massaged the salve into Jack's skin, not bothering to apologise when he winced. It served him right. She refused to look at either of them throughout the whole process.

"There. I'm not doing that again," she said heatedly and threw the salve in Jack's lap. Wiping her hands down her bodice, she caught a flash of amused satisfaction in Hugo's eyes as she stalked haughtily past him.

The days were dry; although dark clouds gathered on the distant horizons, the rain never reached them. Hugo's water skin hung empty from his waist. The damn thing taunted Diamond. She scowled, watching it swing with the movement of his hips. Her tongue stuck to the roof of her mouth, her thirst raging. The only moisture they had found was when night fell and a thick blanket of mist crept in. They had resorted to resting near any bushes that still had remnants of leaves, licking the moisture off to sooth their throats before the daylight and warmth stole it away.

The forest eventually transformed into a bleak and barren land devoid of any life. The silence grated on Diamond's nerves. Old gnarled trees twisted their way towards the sky, their naked boughs covered only in yellow and green lichen, their fallen leaves rotting under foot. It was disturbing to be engulfed by so much decay day in, day out.

The sun dropped slowly behind the trees, disappearing in an orange and red shimmer of fire.

Diamond shivered. Her ragged, torn leggings hung from her bony legs, no protection at all against the plummeting temperatures of the night. A constant ache pounded against her skull and her limbs dragged, heavy with exhaustion. She kept her own counsel, not wanting to seem weak, especially to Hugo. Hugo seemed unaffected by the lack of food and water, except that the skin around his eyes seemed to have sunk. His beard had grown longer, obscuring his face. He had lost weight too. Diamond stubbornly refused to admit her exhaustion to either of the two men. Jack had become more withdrawn the closer to Valentia they got. Diamond felt sorry for her friend. His gaze often rested on the skyline as if dreading what lay beyond. Clearly he did not relish returning to his responsibilities.

An old quarry loomed up out of the gloom. Clumps of soft green moss glowed in the silvery moon light, covering the uneven ground like a velvet carpet laid over great chunks of granite. Hewn hundreds, possibly thousands, of years ago from the nearby rock face, they lay scattered, half buried by earth and time. Like a small ethereal haven, the quarry's damp atmosphere gave life to leafy bushes and vines that grew in long twisted ropes, clinging tenaciously onto the sheer rock face.

"I'm going up there to keep watch," Jack stated.

Hugo grunted his acknowledgment then stalked around inspecting the plants. Diamond watched him for a while, wondering what he was up to. All of a sudden he merged with the shadows, then disappeared entirely. With the gloom and her head aching so fiercely Diamond gave up searching for him. It was either magic, or she was just so tired her eyes were playing tricks. Either way, his disappearing into the shadows like that was—disturbing.

Exhausted, she wandered over to a flat rock and lay down, letting her aching limbs rest. Dry sticks cracked underfoot as Hugo returned clutching a handful of what looked like sponge. A large knife dangled from his other fist. He sheathed it with practised ease and precision. Nervous as ever when he was near, Diamond chose to look at his boots, not his face.

"Here," he said sitting down next to her.

Forcing herself upright she blinked and changed her vision. The silver strands of his energy only wavered around him now, looking depleted. She swallowed her sharp intake of breath. It frightened her to know he was getting weaker.

"Chew this. It has moisture in it. It will help sooth your throat, just don't swallow the sponge," he rumbled quietly.

Diamond took the piece of yellowish, spongy-looking plant, eyeing it suspiciously before deciding to trust him to put it in her mouth and chew. The juice was sweet and gloriously cool as it ran down her throat. She swallowed and groaned with pleasure, sensing his energy stir as he smiled a little.

"Thank you so much," she whispered gratefully. Warmth caressed her skin for a moment before withdrawing. It was the same feeling of belonging and security that bloomed through her chest every time he was near. Suddenly shy, she twisted a loose strand of hair around her fingers.

Hugo turned and cocked his head to one side, a small frown creasing his brow as he watched that outward sign of her agitation.

"Are you okay?" she blurted, not really knowing what else to say. They had not really spoken since he had found them, only the occasional word.

His eyes widened in surprise. Belatedly she realised he probably didn't get asked about his well-being much—if ever. The corners of his mouth tilted into a smile. "Yes—thank you, Diamond." Her name rumbled across his tongue, soft and gentle.

Her throat dried out, and she squirmed a little under his gaze. Every single word she knew disappeared from her head. After a moment he reached out, slowly and carefully, and caught her overworked fingers.

"You will have to cut that bit of hair off if you keep twisting it into knots," he chastised gently, pushing her hand into her lap. "And that would be a real shame." His hand lingered against hers.

Her magic stirred at his touch. A spark of heat deep inside her flared to life. She tried shuffling her position a bit to distract herself, but his energy pulsed against her exposed skin, magnifying her feelings, inciting her magic further. Diamond pulled away. If she never released her magic again it would be fine by her.

"You, on the other hand, look completely exhausted. Why don't you lie down? Try and sleep," Hugo suggested, turning and gently pushing her down.

Diamond sank onto the hard cold rock, her eyes not leaving his. Exhaustion washed over her in waves. As she drifted off to sleep Diamond was dimly aware Hugo stayed by her side. A guardian, silently watching the stars.

Chapter Seventeen

A frown etched Hugo's brow. His shoulders slumped as he rested his head on his knees. Time alone with Diamond was ridiculously precious to him.

Jack had been goading him daily since Hugo had found them. Every time the prince had touched Diamond or slept near her, Hugo had wanted nothing more than to rip her away. His friend knew him well enough to see how Diamond was impacting his emotions, and the little prick had taken to fawning over her every chance he could just to get a rise out of Hugo. He huffed a chuckle. *Damn if it was working!* The trouble was he had a feeling Jack was enjoying winding him up far too much.

Hugo didn't mind that his friend could see how he felt. Hugo had learnt to trust Jack. Agonising guilt squeezed his heart; another ruler, another place.... He pushed those memories violently away.

Hugo rubbed his face and glanced down at Diamond. He was utterly unprepared for the way she made him feel. Whether it was because of their magic or something far deeper, he didn't know, but Diamond had effectively knocked down the wall of ice encasing his heart. For years he had watched other warriors fall in love, had seen them meet a life-mate and make a blood bond, an ultimate commitment that bound two souls until death severed it. Now his own world had shifted in a way he had never expected. It terrified him.

Tipping back his head to stare over at Tu Lanah, grinding his teeth until they hurt. It did not matter what he felt or what his heart and soul craved. He had to hide his feelings. Recently matured males were possessive and confrontational, particularly around anyone they wanted; male or female, human or fae, it did not matter in the least. And he was no different. Despite all his training, Zane and Jack had seen the change in him. But both he and Diamond were in for a whole heap of heartache and misery if he couldn't build that emotional wall back up before the Queen noticed.

Hugo had only let himself care for a girl once, and he had been a young teenager then. Naive and lacking experience, his first, tentative love had grown into a full blown crush.

Fear slithered down his spine. There were so many reasons he needed to distance himself from Diamond....

Pale and gaunt, even in sleep she looked unwell. Mist swirled around his feet as he pushed himself off the rock and stepped stealthily around her outstretched legs to squat in front of her. Goose bumps covered her bare, mottled skin. He let his eyes examine her body in a way he had been unable to do whilst she was awake. Her hip bones stuck out through the remnants of her dress, making her waist look painfully thin. One arm rested across her chest, and her other hand was pushed under her hollow cheek. She was too thin and fragile to last another four days in this forest without food and water.

Unfastening the straps of his armoured shoulder plates and arm guards, he let them fall to the ground, then he shrugged off his tunic and laid it over her. The garment was big enough to drown her, but relinquishing it gave him a sense of satisfaction he hadn't felt in years. Its meagre warmth was the only protection he could provide from the damp and cold. His leather surcoat now adorned Jack's shoulders.

He pulled some tendrils of silver hair off her face and ran his big calloused fingers lightly across her cheek, careful not to wake her.

Hugo pushed himself up with a sigh. He doubted she would understand him leaving, but he had to get help or she would not make it to Sentinel's Cave. Hugo knew General Edo would wait for a few days, but not indefinitely. With a heavy heart, he brushing his lips against her forehead and whispered a soft, "Goodbye." The salty tang of her sweat mixed with her sweet summery scent, which filled his senses as he licked his lips. With a soft growl, he stopped himself from kissing her again.

He tapped into their Nexus bond and stretched out his magic, pushing through her mortal flesh, finding that tightly bound flame in her soul. He longed to free it, to let it soar and merge it with his own, to find out how powerful could they become together. But it was not a burning flame that he found, only a weak, dying ember. No. It could not give up on its host. He teased that flame, taunting it with his serpents and shadow, challenging it to break free, to be stronger.

Her back arched, a small whimper escaping her cracked lips as she shifted her frame toward him. He pulled back guiltily. Such intimacy, even for the right reasons, was wrong without permission. Forcing himself to leave her, he went to find Jack.

Hugo did not armour his wings when he extended them, instead he saved his energy for what he knew would be a long and exhausting flight. The exquisite hues of blue and silver seemed to absorb the silvery moonlight as he beat his wings against the cold night air. Seconds later he landed twenty feet from the prince, nodding a curt greeting.

His relationship with Jack was sometimes strained. Jack was irritated by his coldness and reserve since Hugo had returned to serve his Queen. It was deliberate on Hugo's part. It had to be this way for them. Hugo's track record with friends—and his Queen—had proved dangerous and destructive. The ghosts of his past reminded him to keep his distance.

Hugo squared his shoulders and fixed his eyes on the dishevelled prince. Hugo pressed his mouth into a tight line. He didn't want to leave Diamond with Jack. They were already close, and relying on each other would only force them closer. Hugo scowled. Jack's relationship with Diamond was not and never could be his business—Hugo belonged to the Queen. Even so, his gut tightened painfully as he thought of Diamond being seduced by the handsome prince.

"I have to go." Hugo winced at the deep growl in his voice and crossed his arms over his chest in a defensive gesture. His leather armour creaked as he moved. "If I don't get help from Sentinel's Cave, Diamond will die from starvation. Her body is giving up."

Jack cast his eyes over the horizon and down at the dead trees, still alert, still watching carefully. Hugo ground his jaw as Jack made him wait for a reply.

"It's alright, Hugo. I'm not blind," Jack said quietly. "I can see she's getting too weak to make it. Could you carry her to the cave?" he asked with a frown. "Leave me here."

Hugo shook his head. The thought had crossed his mind more than once, although he would not admit that to Jack.

"No. I am too weak. I wouldn't make it. It will take me at least a day to get there on my own. If you can keep her alive for another three days, I will bring back help. Don't deviate from this course, prince. If you keep pushing on, I will find you again." Hugo twisted to unstrap a long silver blade from his back and offered it to the prince. He would not leave them defenceless.

Jack nodded his thanks as he fastened it around his body, pulling the leather straps tight.

"Take this as well," said Hugo, passing him another dagger. "Something is draining this forest of life; probably a large force of Dust Devils. I can't be sure. Do you think you can avoid it until I can get back to you?" Hugo surveyed the horizon, narrowing his eyes at the glowing moon. "And watch the skies for that dragon. I don't know how it exists or what sort of guardian it is, but I doubt the goddess is controlling it. It's searching for you—and for her, now."

A dark cloud floated ominously in front of the moon, casting them into shadow. Unable to help himself he added, "Take care of her, Jack." His voice was as heavy with meaning.

The moon resurfaced, reflecting the feral lights in Hugo's eyes. Jack looked down toward the shadowy quarry where Diamond slept, his face suddenly tight, his eyes hard and his voice cold when he twisted back.

"It is nice to see you can feel something for someone, Hugo. But the closer we get to Valentia, the more I worry about the girl who saved my life. Will you protect her, Hugo, like you so desperately want to? Or will you lead her into the serpent's lair?"

Hugo did not answer, he could not.

Jack sighed. "Do what you need to do to get help, Hugo. Rest assured that I am capable of keeping her safe. And after we are back in Valentia and you have returned to your Queen's side, I will still make time for her; you, however, cannot. You know as well as I do that no matter what you feel for her, you can never have her. Whereas, if I want to, I can," he finished, his voice heavy with meaning.

Hugo grunted a response, not trusting himself to speak lest he punch Jack's teeth down his throat. The prince was right. No matter what he wanted, Hugo had no business taking an interest in any woman other than his Queen. He curled his fingers into fists and stepped off the cliff before he did something he might regret. Shifting his wings against the invisible eddies of air, he armoured them as he hovered for a moment, looking down towards the sleeping girl. Without another thought for the Prince of Rhodainia, the big warrior disappeared into the midnight sky.

Chapter Eighteen

Diamond careened into Jack's back as his feet ground to a sudden stop. They'd left their pitiful excuse for a camp well before dawn. Trembling with fatigue, she was utterly depleted, unable to summon the energy to change her vision anymore. Laying down and curling up into a ball was such an appealing thought. Sleep. She wanted to sleep. But Jack was so stubborn he would just pick her up and carry her to the cave that Diamond now believed was imaginary.

Hugo had covered her with his tunic the night he had left. It had kept her warm for the past four days, his scent enveloping her completely. When she wanted to give up—like now—she imagined those powerful arms cradling her against his chest. If she wanted to feel that again, to see him again, even if it was to scowl or to yell or to do nothing but look at him, she had to keep going.

Inhaling deeply, the irrational anger she had fought for days simmered in her belly. *Why did he leave me?* Her braided hair swung as she shook her head. No, not just her—them.

It took longer than it should have to right herself after a stumble. There had been so little food, just a handful of mouldy berries and some stagnant water from a dried-out stream bed. Its rotten taste still lingered in her mouth, making her want to throw up.

Her eyes burned, but she had no tears, almost as if her body had dried out completely. It had been stupid to think Hugo cared about her. Diamond's throat hurt as she swallowed. *What does it matter?* She was being ridiculous. Hugo owed her nothing. Damn him to Chaos and back. *Why do I want him?* She shook her head. *Why not Jack?* At least the prince was free to be with who he wanted. But instead her heart had picked a Queen's guard, who was completely off limits and saw her as a burden he had picked up along the way.

"Can you smell that?" Jack whispered over his shoulder, his brown locks lank and greasy, his gaunt face covered with a thick beard.

Her footsteps immediately stilled as Jack cocked his head and listened intently. They had left the borders of the ancient forest three days ago. The trees weren't quite so barren but the wind pushed their boughs against each other, causing them to groan and screech as if speaking.

Diamond stared at Jack's back, not daring to move. For a few minutes he did nothing other than tightly grasp the hilt of Hugo's sword. Giving a nod, he indicated they should move on.

Diamond stepped through the rotting vegetation, avoiding the twisted ropes of ground-dwelling ivy and any sticks that might crack loudly under foot. Jack's tension grated on her nerves. The sweet, rotting stench of decaying flesh clogged her nose, stronger and more pungent than ever—that foul miasma that accompanied Dust Devils. Fear prickled her skin, tickling down her neck, stoking her magic. Diamond winced as the crystal, clutched protectively in the dragon's claws of her necklace, absorbed that fear. It absorbed her emotions, heating until it scorched the tender skin between her breasts. She yanked it away from her body just as Jack stopped dead in his tracks.

"Stay here. I'm just going to check ahead. Something's not right," he whispered without even looking at her.

Diamond sank to her haunches, keeping utterly silent. It was difficult to hear anything above the banging of her racing heart. Wishing for Hugo right now was pointless; he was probably back in Valentia at his Queen's side, giving Diamond no more thought than he would an insect. Lost in her turbulent thoughts she missed the sound of dead sticks cracking nearby. An explosion of movement and sound erupted around her, crashing and guttural roars coming from every direction. Diamond jerked herself up, but not quickly enough. A heavy blow landed on her jaw, knocking her off her feet. Hitting the ground with a jolt, air burst from her lungs.

The stink of carrion overpowered her as the Dust Devil crashed down onto her chest with its full body weight. Her scream was cut off when the rotting corpse lifted its leather covered fist and, with a grunt, slammed it into her face. Colours exploded across her vision a split second before agony cascaded across her face. Her lip exploded, the metallic taste of blood filling her mouth in a nauseating rush.

All she could hear was shouting and grunting and swords clashing. Another heavy blow sent agony detonating through her skull. Diamond felt herself slipping into unconsciousness, her body light, floating as if her arms and legs no longer belonged to her. The Dust Devil roared with triumph, his rotten breath hitting her straight in the face. She blinked to clear her vision, but it was no good. Panic gripped her chest, stealing any sensible thought. *I am going to die!*

The gloved hand grabbed at her throat, squeezing and cutting off her air supply; simultaneously his other arm moved. Diamond saw his sword glint in a shaft of glittering sunlight. No. She would not let him kill her. Not without a fight. Writhing underneath his weight, Diamond bucked, pushing her hips up to unbalance him. Fear and desperation lent her strength. She wriggled her hands free, clawing at the monster's half-rotted face and dead, soulless eyes. Skin tore under her desperate fingers, but it was no use—his dirty hand remained fast to her throat. Diamond willed herself to stay conscious even as her lungs burned and her vision faltered. Blood pooled in the back of her throat and she gagged, unable to swallow or spit, as the monster squeezed the life from her.

"Diamond!" she heard Jack's voice bellow somewhere in the distance. Still fighting for her life, she couldn't turn, couldn't look for him. There was the high pitched whine of a sword being swung, a thump as the Dust Devil's head hit the ground, then a split second later black dust exploded in her face. She immediately sucked in gulps of air, sobbing and choking with relief.

"Diamond? Diamond!"

Jack swore as he beheld her face but could do nothing to help as a blue, heavily muscled creature ran up behind them, growling and swinging a large axe.

"Get up!" Jack bellowed at her, blocking the hard blow from the creature's weapon with Hugo's sword.

She scrambled unsteadily onto her feet. Dazed and in pain, she half stumbled, half fell to the nearest tree trunk. Keeping her back to it she sank down, her knees unable to take her weight. It was impossible to think of anything other than the agony throbbing through her face and head. Blood filled her mouth. Gagging, she spit. Blood clots splattered the ground even as more ran down her face. Jack appeared at her side, panting heavily. He was covered in black dust and blue blood.

"Get up! *Now!*" Jack roared and, with a grip like iron, yanked her to her feet. "Run!" he bellowed and began sprinting over the ground.

Diamond had never run so fast in her life. Trying to match Jack's stride, she jumped roots, sprinting as swiftly as her wobbling legs would take her. When she faltered and nearly fell, Jack grabbed her arm and dragged her along. Despite the adrenaline pumping in her veins, she knew he could have gone faster without her.

"Diamond, where's the dagger Hugo gave you?" Jack barked

sharply. "Get it out now! You are going to have to fight if you want to survive. To kill a Dust Devil you need to take its head off. Go for the neck."

She nodded, although her chances of hacking a head off with a dagger made her want to laugh hysterically. Her emotions stormed. Heat and magic seared through her insides, crackling around in her belly like exploding fireworks until the pain of keeping it contained nearly drove her to her knees. The dragon crystal was hot enough to blister and burn her skin. Clutching Hugo's dagger like a lifeline in her right hand, she closed her eyes. Inhaling Hugo's scent deeply, Diamond used it as her anchor and panted through the panic threatening to render her completely useless. A loud sob escaped her ravaged lips.

"It's alright, Diamond—just fight as hard as you can, for as long as you can," Jack grunted, stepping back now so he was right next to her.

But it wasn't alright, not at all. This wasn't like before. With Hugo nearby she had been able to control her magic. This time her power felt different, wild and savage. Blood ran down her chin. With every sob and shuddering breath she took, more dripped onto Hugo's tunic. Hot tears blurred her vision as power thrummed through her veins, coursing through her exhausted body and burning into her very bones. She fought the urge to scream.

Clutching Hugo's dagger in a hand that didn't seem her own, she forced herself to breath. *In. Out. In....* Just like her father had taught her. The world seemed to narrow to that one need—to breathe.

Jack fought on alone, taking on a heavily muscled Battle Imp, a blue monstrous creature that stood nearly seven feet tall. Its body was hairless, with pointed long ears and dark fathomless eyes. Wide jaws opened in a grotesque smile as it struck at Jack with a vicious-looking barbed and curved blade. Jack side-stepped with ease, then ducked. In one swift move he gutted the creature, splattering Diamond in foul smelling blue blood.

Jack cursed, moving to shield Diamond's body with his own. He stood over her, panting and facing the shadows as she fell forward onto her knees and hands, tears streaming down her face. Her brain wouldn't work properly. This couldn't be their end—overcome by magic or sliced apart by monsters. Panic crushed her chest, her face and hands numb. Jack dropped down in front of her and pulled her into his arms.

"Diamond? It's alright. They've gone for now," he told her.

"Something else has taken their attention."

She trembled against him, the heat inside her belly guttering into a flame rather than a raging fire. Her head dropped to his chest as she sobbed.

"It's alright, I've got you," Jack murmured into her hair, "but we have to go." Gently he pulled her to her feet. "Come on. We need to run," he said, keeping hold of her hand.

Chapter Nineteen

With every step Diamond took, her skull and face pulsed with pain. She wondered if her cheek bone was broken. Blood caked her chin, forming a dry crust on her teeth, and she had no saliva left to wet her raw and painful throat. Without warning the world tilted and her legs gave way. Collapsing on the ground, waves of nausea hit her, and it was impossible to fight the blackness fogging her vision.

"Oh shit! Diamond? Come on. Don't give up on me. You have to get up," Jack urged, running a hand through his sweaty, blood soaked hair. Taking a ragged breath, the prince squatted in front of her. Anxiety swamped his gaunt, handsome face.

"Diamond, listen to me. Stand up—then I'm going to carry you," he said, gently cupping her throbbing chin in one hand as he pushed the silver threads of blood-caked hair from her eyes with the other.

She couldn't understand him. His voice seemed such a long way off, just muffled words and confused sounds. *I wish I could just close my eyes and drift away,* Diamond thought, exhausted.

Jack swore quietly then stood and raised his sword, staring intently into the trees ahead. Diamond whimpered. Her whole body ached as she looked up at him through the slits of her half closed eyelids.

"I'm sorry, I need to...." Jack's voice was suddenly choked off as a huge arm snaked around his throat. Diamond couldn't even scream as he was pulled backwards.

"Get up! Run!" he choked out, his eyes wide.

But she couldn't, her body just wouldn't work. Three shadowy figures appeared in front of them, arrows nocked in their bows, ready to fire in an instant. Something was amiss; they faced the forest not Jack.

"Hello, Jack," growled a deep voice. "Don't move and don't shout. You are walking straight into the path of your enemy."

Diamond tried to focus on Jack's attacker. His voice was

wonderfully familiar. Hoping she was right, she squinted up through sticky eyes at the large shadow.

"Hugo!" breathed Jack. His tired face lit up and his shoulders sagged in relief. He looked closely at the men, poised, watching the shadows, ready to strike in an instant. "Diamond, it's okay. These are my men," Jack said looking down at her.

"By the goddess, Jack, you look rough!" exclaimed Hugo with a quizzical twitch of his eyebrows whilst shoving Jack back up on his feet. "I thought you looked bad when I left, but hell's teeth, prince!" he grimaced taking in Jack's blood-stained clothes and sword.

"I'm fine, but Diamond isn't. This blood is mainly hers," Jack answered.

Diamond was vaguely aware of Hugo squatting down in front of her, his back to the others. He swore quietly but she could only stare at him in a daze, unable to speak. Tears of relief pricked her eyes as she looked at the concern in his. Pulling a disgusted face, he gently touched her lip and swollen cheek with his thumb. She dropped her eyes in shame. Her face must be a mess. Hugo clicked his fingers and someone passed him a water skin. Lifting her head with one hand, he held the water skin with the utmost care and gentleness against her torn lips.

"Drink," he ordered gruffly and tipped a few drops of the blessed liquid onto her tongue.

Throbbing pain stung her lips. Diamond swallowed with difficulty, coughing as the dried blood became sticky in her mouth. Hugo tipped more water between her lips, waiting patiently for her to rinse and spit out clots. Putting the water skin down, he ripped material off his shirt, using it to gently clean up her face whilst Jack had a drink. She winced as he dabbed her lip.

"Sorry," he mumbled.

"Thank you," she rasped, her throat still raw.

Before she or Jack knew what was happening, Hugo had hoisted her into his arms and stood up. "The general is waiting in Sentinel's Cave. It's not far away now." His deep voice rumbled through her chest into her bones, and to her shame she could not stop herself grabbing on desperately to his shoulders. Hugo tightened his grip as he felt her push against him.

"There are more of Ragor's soldiers ahead. Another large squadron. Bigger than the one you just fought," he told Jack.

Jack swore, jamming his sword into the ground at his feet. It swayed side to side.

"How big?" he asked, his nostrils flaring.

"At least one hundred fifty strong—probably more, it's difficult to tell as they're hidden in the forest," Hugo answered gravely, holding Diamond tightly against his chest.

Belonging rushed through her at the feel of hard muscle and heat against her cold body. Startled, she wriggled a little. He glanced down, holding her eyes. Arms of steel tightened, and he raised an eyebrow, snarling a little. Immediately her movements stilled. But she wasn't trying to escape him, completely the opposite in fact.

"This squadron of Dust Devils travels with Battle Imps and Wolfmen, just like Ragor's main host; not to mention they have a giant swelling their ranks," Hugo said, keeping eye contact with Jack.

Jack ground his teeth together, his jaw muscles clenching and unclenching rhythmically. "Where are the rest of my soldiers?" the prince asked quietly, staring at Diamond, who had nestled into Hugo's warmth. For a moment Jack's eyes softened and a worried frown creased his brow.

"General Edo is commanding your men. He has ordered a rotational guard to watch the enemy nearest the cave, the remainder are sheltering and resting inside the cave," Hugo informed Jack in clipped, precise tones.

Jack grunted in acknowledgment. "You said you'd take three days to get back to us, Hugo. It's day four, what happened?" he asked coldly.

Hugo bristled. Diamond could feel his muscles tense all around her. His chin lifted proudly, and there was a slight pause before he answered. "We needed to deal with the Wolfmen that were tracking you and end the rest of the squad you just fought before we could get to you safely," he explained stiffly.

Jack grunted and Diamond felt her stomach lurch. They had been tracked by Wolfmen? She felt limp. Suddenly she was happy not to be standing up.

"Fair enough," said Jack almost dismissively. "If it isn't far to the cave, I'll take Diamond whilst you show us the way," he said, gesturing at her with his chin.

Hugo glanced down, holding her eyes. His grip tightened and he snarled a little. Not at her, but because of Jack's words. With an almost imperceptible movement of his head he seemed to ask: *"Do you want to go with, Jack?"*

Her emotional turmoil at seeing him again was overshadowed by such a deep, deep relief that he was here to take care of her. A tear ran down her cheek. No. With all her heart she wanted to stay in his arms. She pushed her body against his, gripping him like a life line.

"No, prince. You are exhausted and need to recover. I will take her," Hugo replied.

Jack opened his mouth to argue until he caught the way Diamond was clinging to Hugo. Clamping his jaw shut, he stared hard at her.

Guilty for wanting Hugo so badly, she made herself push back and rasped, "I can walk by myself." Her lip started bleeding again.

"No!" both men declared at the same time.

"Fine. You take her, Hugo," Jack acquiesced but held Hugo's challenging gaze for a moment longer. "But think about what I said before."

Diamond looked from one to the other, wondering what Jack meant as Hugo gave a cursory nod. Tight-lipped, he allowed Jack to give the order to move out.

"Let's go. No flying. I don't want anyone taken down by an enemy arrow. There are already more of them than there are of us," ordered Jack.

The group moved stealthily through the gloomy trees. Surround by warriors, Diamond felt safer than she had for weeks. Hugo's arms were wonderfully warm and she couldn't help but tighten her grip on him and snuggle closer into his chest. His warmth and musky scent over ran her senses. Strength seeming to flow from him into her. Her head wanted him to put her down—he was a guard, a *queen's* guard—but her heart wanted him to hold her tighter. Frustrated, she shook her head at her chaotic thoughts.

Hugo flashed her a quick look. "Something wrong?" he asked innocently, his eyes glinting with amusement as if he knew exactly what she was thinking.

"You can put me down, Hugo. I can walk," she told him, her words muffled by her swollen lip.

"No."

Diamond scowled at his refusal but that just seemed to amuse him more.

"We both know you don't really want me to," he stated. "And don't scowl, it's making your lip bleed all over me and you've already ruined one of my tunics," he reminded her.

Secretly pleased, she crossed her arms and huffed loudly, then found herself utterly transfixed as his lips twitched in a broad smile. His scarred features twisted in a grotesque way but Diamond didn't notice. Her eyes did not stray from his mouth. Her heart clenched.

She had just made this ruthless warrior smile.

Soon, with nothing else to do but stare at his face or rest, Diamond let her exhausted, starving body relax. The rhythmic sway of Hugo's powerful body was so soothing and she felt so safe and warm. By the goddess, she was tired. Lulled by the heat radiating from Hugo's body, her eyelids became heavier and her head drooped onto his chest. His scent and magic cocooned Diamond, comforting her.

Hitching her up, Hugo tightened his grip and resettled her weight. Briefly he glanced down, doing his best to hide his satisfaction when she murmured with contentment and nestled her face into his chest.

Chapter Twenty

Diamond sat with her back against the cave wall watching Jack. Catching her eye, he smiled but it was strained and tired. Her returning smile was a little forced. Since being back with his men, Jack had left her to her own devices. Not that he had a choice really. Diamond leaned her head back and watched him, feeling the gap between them widen. It had begun to sink in, what and who he was. It left Diamond with no illusion as to her unimportance compared to him. His responsibilities would distance them, not to mention her blood. Although she didn't think Jack as shallow as the Avalonian ruler. Rubbing her temples she squeezed her eyes shut for a moment. It would be nice to be free to pick her friends for once, or to have a friend who accepted her for who she was, rather than shunned her for her mixed blood.

Focus on the positive things, she told herself. *Valentia is a busy trading city with huge ports. It must have goods and people arriving from the other kingdoms all the time. Surely heritage won't count for so much there?*

A headache pounded behind her eyes. But maybe it did. Hugo had already warned her that as a half-blood she had no rights, no protection under Avalonian law. She would just have to be really careful where she went and with whom. Tom had been her only friend back in Berriesford; nothing need change, she didn't need other friends.

Diamond sighed. She was being foolish. Of course things would change, her whole life already had. Trying not to think of her father, she rubbed the bridge of her nose and studied the big warriors and tough-looking soldiers that filled the gloomy space.

Sentinel's Cave was large, its entrance hidden amongst a cluster of ancient, moss covered boulders. Small holes allowed rain and moisture to drip in from the earth above, and the rock wall she leaned against was obscured by a covering of green, velvety moss. Further inside the cave where it was more protected, the walls and floor were dry. Clearly it had been used as a hideout or guard station for years. There were cooking pots piled beside a stone fire pit and several mounds of old dried moss on top of sticks and pines needles that seemed to serve as makeshift beds.

Diamond's tired eyes stung, so she leaned her head back and closed them for a moment. The first time she had suffered a nightmare she had awoken with sweat coating her body and running between her breasts. Terrified and trembling, she had found Hugo kneeling next to her asking if she was alright. It had been too dark to see his face, but she was sure she had heard concern in his voice. Without asking, he had settled his bulk next to her, his sapphire and silver energy had wrapped itself around her protectively; Diamond had not even thought of protesting. Twice more nightmares had jolted her awake. Each time Hugo had reached out a big hand and rested it on her shoulder, gently rubbing his thumb against her neck, calming her. Even now Diamond was left with a sense of gratitude for him watching over her.

The protection and warmth of the cave was wonderful after being so long out in the open. Bags of supplies lined the far wall next to a row of full water skins. It seemed an age since food had last passed her lips. A painful ache rumbled through her belly at the thought. She rubbed at it, sorely tempted to sneak over and rummage through the sacks. A tall female warrior lounged against the wall near the bags, clearly supervising them. With long, light brown hair and sharp features, she was perhaps the most intimidating female Diamond had ever seen. Her eyes wandered over Diamond, completely disinterested, before moving on to rest on Roin.

Perhaps not, thought Diamond, discounting the food. It was not worth a confrontation with such a female.

Damp-loving plants crawled up the ancient rocks near the cave entrance, their spiral bright green stems intertwining and hanging down to conceal the cave from the outside. Soldiers guarded the hidden cave mouth, coming and going for the past few minutes as they swapped the watch, their faces drawn and bodies tense.

The water leopard, Trajan, crouched near Jack, flicking his barbed tail. Clearly they were communicating through telepathy. Jack shook his head vehemently. Snarling, Trajan stood.

Diamond gaped in amazement, never having been this close to a water leopard before; she was stunned. He was huge, his head easily as high as Jack's chest. Peculiar gill-like structures stood out at the base of his jaw and black markings covered his white fur. But it was the exposed bony ridge of spine that travelled from the base of his huge skull to the tip of his barbed tail that drew Diamond's attention. He was beautiful in a savage, dangerous way. Clearly he had recovered well, only the scab on his chest wall any indication of a recent injury.

Diamond's eyes widened as Tom pushed himself off the ground and bowed slightly to something Jack said before following Trajan out of the cave. Tom had never been that respectful to anyone before.

Tom had also lost weight, but when she had spoken with him this morning, he had been far more positive about the city than she felt. Zane, who stood guard next to his prince, watched Tom disappear before his eyes drifted to Diamond's. The hard planes of his face split into a sheepish grin and he shrugged. Even with a split lip, Diamond found it hard not to smile back. So Zane *was* interested in Tom. She wondered if Tom realised the broad-shouldered warrior ribbed him every moment he could because he wanted Tom's attention. Probably not.

Diamond knew Tom wasn't interested in girls. When they had just reached their teens they had decided it was time to experiment with their first kiss. It had been a weird experience for both of them, more sloppy and uncomfortable than passionate. They had both shrugged it off and decided not to repeat the process with each other. Tom had experimented once or twice with other partners but he had never wanted anything serious.

Diamond hoped a tough warrior fae like Zane would not be too overbearing or possessive of her friend. Tom would hate that. Still, her eyes watched Zane's attention shift back to the cave entrance. Maybe Zane was more than just a bit interested. At least Tom would be cared for and safe if he found a partner in a fae warrior.

More weary-looking warriors returned from watch and went to rest quietly on the moss beds near Jack, who was now talking quietly to an archer with sinewy strong arms covered in intricate swirling tattoos. Her eyes must be tired, she decided, because those tattoos seemed to be swirling like the markings on a fae's wings.

Thinking of fae—Hugo stood tall and rigid in the shadows, his eyes constantly scanning the cave and the men, running over her every now and then, making her skin prickle with awareness. The hilts of his swords were visible over his shoulders, glinting in the dimness of the cave. His beard was matted, but he had cleaned his face and hands. Diamond, on the other hand, had blood leaking down her face again from her torn lip. With a jerky motion, she used

Hugo's dagger to cut a piece of the blanket someone had given her and held the scrap firmly against her lip. She winced. The split must be deeper than she thought. Maybe she should see if someone could stitch it for her.

"Hi," General Edo said gruffly, sitting down next to her. He propped his large forearms on his bent knees but did not look at her.

"Hello," she answered, feeling a little awkward but not sure why.

"So, do you want to tell me what happened to you?" he asked quietly, studying her swollen black eye, bruised cheek and the scrap of blanket pressed to her lip.

"Aren't you going to order me to?" she asked wryly.

"No. I'm going to order him to tell me," he said with a nod towards Jack.

"Why did you fight Jack the day the dragon took us?" Diamond asked, picking at a loose thread on her ragged dress. She still hadn't forgiven him for that.

The smile he gave her held no amusement. "I needed to assess very quickly what sort of man Jack is." He paused glancing at Jack. Diamond waited, trying to be patient. He seemed to be weighing whether to tell her more, then he took a deep breath, "Before I found you and your father in the north, I was King Oden's primary. That meant not only was I a general in his army and responsible for planning and executing his campaigns in the west against Ragor, I was also his advisor—and friend. Along with your father, I took responsibility for and commanded the Combined Army of Rhodainia. It was the greatest army in the world...." he said shaking his head in what looked like disbelief.

Diamond kept quiet. *It must be hard to see that army in tatters*, she mused, feeling sorry for him. Her father had told her of the army. It had never occurred to her to ask how he knew so much about it. Only now did her perception of him as a lowly woodcutter strike her as foolish. He shouldn't have known how to fight so well or talk with such authority and diplomacy to the town sheriff and his men.

General Edo didn't notice the tightening of her mouth.

"For hundreds of years men have been conscripted to fight alongside Rhodainia's own soldiers, though most would apply to their monarchs or leaders to be allowed to serve. The Combined Army has been in existence since Ragor was banished to the Barren Waste Lands by Lunaria thousands of years ago. His monsters were contained by us. Your father was a good friend and an even better general—until he left with your mother."

Diamond tried not to react to the bitterness in his tone at those words. He coughed, and when he spoke again his voice was neutral. "Your father and I advised King Oden on battle strategy as well as coordination and execution of any attacks. In fact, we advised on most things: patrols, supplies, even who should be on his council or promoted to captain of his personal guard." He took a deep breath and sighed sadly. "After Jack was born and the Queen died, King Oden wrote a decree and placed it in the king's vault deep under Stormguaard. The king's council witnessed it and I was given a copy, as was your father."

Diamond sat up straight. "What did it say?" she asked quietly, gasping when he pulled a yellowed wrinkled piece of parchment from his pocket and handed it to her. Diamond carefully straightened out the wrinkles. Not even half way down the page she stopped. "Is this real?" she whispered, incredulous.

"Yes. I've carried this with me for the last fourteen years. The king is dead and his son is not twenty. That means either your father or I should take the responsibility of regent. King Oden ordered us to give guidance to Prince Jack and involve him completely in the running of Rhodainia. Now your father is gone. It falls to me to decide if Jack is competent to continue ruling until his twentieth birthday." He turned to look right at Diamond, and she almost shrunk from the ice in his eyes.

"About eighteen months after the king released your father from his service, he found out something about your mother. He wouldn't tell me what it was but ordered me to find Arades and Tanelle and bring them home. He told me if Arades refused, I was to stay and protect them both and that I should not return to Stormguaard until they agreed to return with me. Now my king is dead and so are your mother and father. When you are safely in Valentia, my responsibilities will lay with His Highness over there." His voice faded.

"I see," she said. It was clear she was not going to be his responsibility anymore. Diamond kept her face down so he could not see how much that hurt her.

"Do you?" he asked quietly.

Time to grow up and fend for myself, she thought and lifted her chin. "Yes, I do. I understand you have a decision to make about Jack and your position in his court. To do that you cannot stay with me." She frowned. "I don't understand why King Oden would want my mother and father back in Stormguaard, though." She winced again as her lip started bleeding.

"I wish I could tell you. All I really know is your father left the city to be with your mother. He had not known her long before they were married. He once told me it took the blink of an eye for him to fall in love with Tanelle—that they had some sort of deep bond and were meant to be together. I laughed back then. I never was one for sentiment of that sort."

His voice faded and Diamond did not miss the thoughtful look he gave Hugo. Diamond saw Hugo glance at them both and dropped her eyes. General Edo smiled slightly as he awkwardly patted her hand. "Now I utterly believe him. Anyway, I had to assess if Jack is a capable leader. Challenging him was the only way I had to weigh him. Now I know he is not a coward. I also know how easily he can lose his temper and make a mistake. I've also had time to talk to his men and build up a picture of what sort of leader he is. Besides, he got you back safely—with a little help from Hugo."

Diamond didn't feel like pointing out she had saved the prince's royal behind, not the other way around.

The general's boots scraped against the stone as he shifted his position. "We are soon going to have to fight hard to get past that legion of rotting corpses and monsters camped between us and the Rift Valley. I have to decide whether to let Jack lead or whether to take leadership away from him."

Diamond stayed silent, not really sure if Jack would let the general take anything away from him or that Jack's men would follow the general. They sat in silence for a few minutes, then he gently took the parchment back, rubbed his eyes with both hands and gave a big sigh.

"I'm grateful to those two young men for keeping you alive. Arades will look on them both with favour from Eternity. Your face will heal if you get a couple of stitches in that lip, but we have a lot to overcome before we can get to the safety of Valentia and any healers. Stick close to Hugo. I will be with the prince, so neither of you need worry about him. Anyway, I have a feeling Hugo won't refuse to protect you. Do exactly what he says and you'll stand a chance of staying alive. Understood?"

Diamond nodded wearily, wondering how happy Hugo would be about his babysitting duties.

"Good. Then I have something to do," he said quietly but resolutely.

Diamond glanced over at Hugo as the general left her. Her breath caught in her throat and her stomach jumped painfully as his sapphire eyes met hers. Resting her forearms on her knees, she broke that contact, shocked but pleased to see General Edo sink to one knee in front of Jack.

He's made a decision then, she thought with a mixture of relief for Jack, and regret for herself. She really would be alone if the general resumed his duties—it seemed Tom was comfortable being with Jack, and Zane was not likely to give up on her friend, looking at the way he kept glancing longingly towards the entrance. Determined not to think about what was to become of her in the city, she concentrated on the group across the cave instead.

Jack's reactions went from shock to disbelief as the general presented him with the yellowed parchment and an explanation. Her heart went out to Jack as he sank to his knees and read his own father's hand writing. Again and again he read it. His pale face and tight expression said it all. No one spoke to her or paid her any attention at all, they were all too busy watching Jack and General Edo. Standing, she headed for the entrance but changed her mind about getting some fresh air when she felt a sharp tug in her chest. Turning, she found Hugo staring at her. His eyebrows twitched up as he shook his head slightly.

She sat back down on the ground, irritated with herself for giving in to his silent command.

"Arse," she muttered, flashing a dark scowl in his direction. An amused smile curled Hugo's lips, and he lifted one dark brow. It was then Diamond realised she had forgotten how good fae hearing was.

Chapter Twenty-One

Diamond felt bored. Tom did not return, and Jack stayed occupied with his warriors. They came and went, wanting orders or giving their prince information. Pushing herself up she wandered around to stretch her stiff muscles. Roin, the captain of Jack's guard, was handing out strips of dried meat and some dried yellow berries from the line of food sacks. Standing behind Roin, the female warrior smiled as Diamond approached. It made her seem slightly less threatening.

Thanking Roin, she sat cross legged on the damp ground trying to eat. Blood rolled down her chin as her lip opened up again, the stinging pain made her eyes water. She winced and swore under her breath. Roin watched her struggle for a moment, then took pity on her.

"That needs stitching," he stated as he squatted in front of her and took hold of her chin, inspecting her mouth gently.

"Yeah? Know any good seamstresses?" she mumbled.

He grinned widely, his tough face suddenly transformed and his grey eyes sparkling. "Yes. Me," he stated proudly. "Ask Unis." He nodded at the female warrior. "I've sewed her together enough times," he chuckled.

"True," Unis smiled back. "He's obviously in the wrong job. Needs to be a seamstress and sew pretty dresses all day long," she drawled. "He'd look better in a dress than that armour…wouldn't you say?"

Roin flipped his middle finger and grinned before reaching for a pouch in his tunic pocket. After cleaning his small needle he sat on a boulder and instructed her to kneel in front of him. Roin then gently prodded the bruised tissue around the split.

"Trust me," he smiled reassuringly, as she winced.

On the other side of the cave Hugo abruptly turned his head in their direction, almost as if he felt her discomfort. Breaking off his conversation with the tattooed archer, he strode over, his hands resting on the daggers at his hips.

Diamond immediately shrank back from the hard angry look on his face. Roin glanced up calmly. Unis and Gunnald sauntered closer.

"Something wrong, Commander Casimir?" asked Roin curiously whilst still inspecting Diamond's lip.

"Do not touch her," Hugo growled at Roin.

Roin raised his brows, "Why not?" His voice was still deceptively calm, but Diamond did not miss the stiffening in his shoulders.

A moment's hesitation from Hugo. "Because there is nothing to numb the pain for her," Hugo hissed, his fists curled around his blades.

Roin raised his eyebrows in surprise at the reaction from the normally unemotional Queen's guard. "Maybe not, but her lip will continue bleeding and will get infected if it is left," he replied reasonably.

"Roin, Diamond is my...responsibility. I will get her lip stitched when it is safe to do so. Not here in this dirty cave with nothing to numb the pain," Hugo insisted. He looked directly at Roin, threat pouring off him.

What is he doing? Diamond thought anxiously. Jack's captain only wished to help her.

"Move away from her, Roin," Hugo growled.

She suddenly remembered who and what Hugo was: a cold-hearted killer.

Staring mutely at him, Diamond shuffled away from them all.

"Commander," warned Roin in a low voice. "You're frightening her. None of us will hurt her," he said in a calm voice.

Hugo shot Roin a baleful stare but Roin did not seem at all perturbed; he just reached out and patted Diamond's shoulder.

"Don't worry. It seems the commander sees your well-being as his responsibility." He winked at her and lowered his voice. "Fae and their instincts, ehh?"

Diamond flushed, suddenly realising what he meant. Her eyes shot to Hugo, who looked like he was about to throttle the grinning captain. Hugo opened his mouth to speak but the whoosh of an arrow stopped him.

Thunk! It struck flesh. A loud agonizing scream had Hugo spinning on his heel towards the entrance. He stepped directly in front of Diamond, shielding her as the others burst into action, heading for their prince.

"Stay behind me!" he commanded, his eyes already scanning the cave and the men, analysing the situation.

The men resting on the moss beds jumped up, immediately drawing their weapons. General Edo bellowed orders, and Gunnald, the tattooed fae, raced to the entrance and returned fire with his elaborately carved bow. Diamond's mouth dropped open. The bow glowed, along with Gunnald's tattoos. He loosed arrow after arrow in such quick succession she couldn't follow his movements. He had magic! And it seemed he had no hesitation using it in front of Hugo.

Diamond's throat tightened as the roar of hundreds of Ragor's men resounded outside the cave. Arrows rained down from the small holes above. Hugo spun and grabbed her around the waist, moving so fast he was just a blur. Her feet left the floor, breath exploding from her lungs as her back slammed against the moss-covered wall. Another hail storm of arrows thudded into the packed dirt at their feet. Wide-eyed, Diamond gripped onto Hugo's body as she scanned the cave for Jack and Tom. Jack was pushed right up against the back of the cave shouting something at Hugo, who glared at the prince. The general was bellowing and gesturing wildly with his sword.

Blood roared in Diamond's ears but she heard Jack's voice holler at Hugo, "Get her out of here. *Now!!*" His brown eyes met Diamond's startled gaze. "No," she whispered, shaking her head. She didn't want to leave her friends.

Without hesitation, Hugo grabbed her hard around the waist, pulling a sword from across his back at the same time. "Hold tight and do not let go," he ordered her. "We're going."

"But we can't leave!" she cried. "What about the others? *No!*" she shouted, hitting ineffectually at his massive shoulders.

It made no difference. He pulled her against him, lifted her with one powerful arm and ran to the exit. Dark blue wings unfurled and armoured, then they were airborne. Even in such a dire situation Diamond was startled by the speed of that transition. Wind rushed by her ears, and it was all she could do to hold on around his neck. The whine of arrows dogged them. Hugo dipped and rolled with incredible skill despite her legs, which dangled and swung around uselessly, threatening to pull her weight from his arm.

"Get your legs around my waist," he roared.

Petrified, she flung her feet up, but she was weak and unable to clench the muscles of her thighs. It was no use. Her legs slipped time and again. Diamond clenched her fingers into Hugo's leather armour until her nails threatened to rip off, terrified that if his grip faltered, she would plummet to the ground. As they flew unsteadily over the forest canopy it became clear she was upsetting his balance, but there was nothing she could do. His knuckles turned white where he gripped her waist.

Diamond flinched back as the fletch of an arrow kissed her face a split second before it slammed into Hugo's shoulder with a sickening thud. It tore through his shirt and into his flesh just under his shoulder guard. Reeling backwards, his wings lost their rhythm, pounding unevenly against the air as he tried to stop spiralling down towards the dead trees.

The grey, wiry hide of a Wolfman flashed in the corner of Diamond's vision. With amazing skill Hugo flipped himself around as it leaped for them. Muscled, hairy arms reached for her, long claws gleaming before Hugo skewered it on the sword in his hand. The creature roared before going limp, its dead weight dropping them like a stone. Hugo released his sword and, in one swift movement, enclosed Diamond roughly in his arms, wrapping his wings around her. Barely seconds passed, before they crashed through the tree's and hit the ground. Over and over they rolled. Hugo slammed into something and jerked; suddenly the cage of strength and armoured wings was gone. Her body was thrown from his protection. The forest floor ripped her skin to shreds as her momentum drove her tumble onwards. She collided with a tree trunk and her skull cracked against the solid wood. Through sheer will she stayed conscious, crying out as pain flooded her body.

The undergrowth crashed around her, teeming with monstrous creatures. Growling and snapping, their eyes glowed with blood lust. In shock, she could only stare stupidly as they came to destroy her.

Hugo rolled to his feet with fluid grace, the remains of the dark arrow sticking out from his shoulder. Blood streamed from the puncture wound, reducing his skin to a pale mask as it drained down his chest. Sapphire eyes searched the undergrowth, turning obsidian as he found her. Roaring with rage, the Queen's guard became a powerhouse of wrath, as dark and unforgiving as any of the creatures surrounding them.

Drawing a dagger from his waist, he sliced off the end of the arrow before throwing himself into a shoulder roll to reach his sword on the ground. In less time than it took Diamond to take a shuddering breath, he had sheathed his dagger and pulled his second sword off his back. He began cleaving his enemy with stunning speed and viciousness. A mist of shadow swirled around those silver blades, doing his bidding, aiding its master by forming spears that pierced where he willed.

Diamond forced herself to get up and managed one step towards Hugo before a hard, muscled arm encircled her throat and began squeezing. Panic had her clawing at the arm as her throat was crushed.

Battle Imps could not speak, but this one bellowed a roar loud enough to get Hugo's attention. Hugo slashed open the gut of a Dust Devil with one sword. He fluidly changed his stance and took its hideous head off with a graceful slash of the other before turning to face the Battle Imp. He said nothing but his eyes flashed a warning just as he dropped one sword and loosed a dagger from his hip. A whip of shadow appeared from Hugo's body, grasped the moving blade and propelled it forwards with unimaginable speed. With a thud it embedded in the forehead of her attacker. Diamond fell to her knees, gasping for breath as the blue monster toppled backwards away from her.

"Get up!" bellowed Hugo, scooping his fallen sword from the ground and sprinting over. Grabbing the back of her clothes, he hoisted her to her feet. She swayed unsteadily, staring in horror at the wound in his shoulder. He lithely leaned past her and yanked the blade from the Battle Imp's forehead.

"Pull yourself together," he barked, throwing her up against a tree and shaking her shoulders hard. His eyes were black orbs of magic and swirling shadow, no trace of sapphire blue. This, she realised, was his warrior's face. He quickly assessed her, his face becoming tight. Diamond stared at him in awe and wondered if he saw energy like she did.

"What can I do?" she whispered, her voice shaking.

"Fight or die, Diamond," he uttered harshly.

Fear made her bowels watery as her hand closed around the smooth metal hilt of her dagger. She jerkily pulled it from the sheath Zane had given her. Finding courage, she nodded and set her lips in a tight line. His eyes cleared and she peering into sapphire and silver pools, then the colour was gone, becoming darkness once more.

"Fight until your last breath. Do not give up or they will take your soul," he warned grimly. Spinning away from her, he cleaved through his enemy. Vicious snarling and the stench of rotting flesh and blood filled the air. Running feet thudded toward them. Hugo spun on his heel, hacking down Wolfmen and Dust Devils until they fell like leaves at his feet. They were appearing from all directions, too many for him to handle alone, no matter how fast he moved.

Minutes passed as Diamond cowered against the tree, her heart banging with fear. Hugo was going to die and it was her fault; she'd weighed him down—and now she was useless.

A Dust Devil ran at her, his sword raised, rotting bits of skin hanging in mangled ribbons from his face. Diamond thrust the dagger into his chest but it did not stop him. He barrelled into her, sending her staggering against Hugo's back.

Without faltering, the Queen's guard threw out his front leg to take their weight, then turned, throwing her off him. Blade angled up, he swung and cut off the Dust Devil's head in one brutal movement. It exploded into a cloud of black dust that covered them both. Hugo roared with pain. A Wolfman jumped out of Hugo's reach, clutching a rusty iron blade dripping with blood. The attack drove Hugo to one knee but it did not stop him. A second later he was back up, his face icy calm. Snakes of shadow thrust out from Hugo's bare wrists, lashing the Wolfman to the spot, and Hugo quickly pivoted, gutting his assailant in one swift move.

An oncoming volley of arrows whined through the air. Hugo shoved his body up against Diamond, protecting her. A couple pinged harmlessly off his armoured wings, while the rest of the volley shot past. She gaped wide-eyed up at him. He had just protected her with his body—with his life. He stared down at her, looking just as shocked. Her nostrils flared as she scented his blood. Instantly she dropped to one knee. Blood pumped down his thigh. His breathing was ragged and fast, but he did not stop scanning the shadows for more attacks.

"Hugo!" Diamond cried, stuffing her dagger back in its sheath. Icy fear wrapped around her heart as she desperately tried to staunch the bleeding.

"No! No! No!" she sobbed, her eyes wide as she looked up into his sweating face.

His eyes looked like pieces of black glass against his ashen skin. He blinked, lightly brushing his blood-caked fingers over her cheek and, for a moment, sorrow flashed in his face. No, she would not let him die here. *This is my fault!* This would not be happening if he hadn't been forced to protect her useless hide. Blood oozed from his wound, dripping between her fingers and running down her wrists and arms in ruby rivulets.

Without questioning her instincts, she closed her eyes and spiralled down inside herself. Fear and an urgent desperation to save

Hugo morphed into a wild furnace of heat. She opened her soul and spurred that ember of magic to burn, to grow, until it pulsed through her veins. Feeling the warmth of Hugo's blood against her fingers fuelled that power. It raged so fiercely she struggled to contain it. Letting the pressure drop from his wound, her hands and clothes plastered with his blood, she stepped out from behind the tree. Hugo looked at her askance, his face bone white from blood loss. He tried to grab her, swaying as he missed.

"Diamond! Get back here! *Now!!*" he yelled, reaching for her with serpents of shadow and silver. She smiled, trying to reassure him this was the right thing to do. Irritation, anger and something akin to fear flashed in his eyes as she easily brushed away his magic.

"Cover yourself with your wings," she commanded, her voice gravelly with suppressed power. Hugo took one look at her opaque eyes and wrapped his beautifully etched and armoured wings around his body, kneeling down within their protection. Burning waves of magic racked her flesh and bones, but the pain was tempered with a deep sense of release, a freedom she had never experienced before. As before, her mind soared free of her body, searching through the shadowy sentinels of the trees.

Hugo roared as if he felt her release. Shadow and silvery tethers of light reached for her. But such freedom made her giddy. She wanted to fly free of restraint, away from those tethers, until she saw the cave. Jack and the warriors fought valiantly. Gunnald's bow was still glowing, his quiver replenished with a never-ending supply of arrows. Tom fought bravely, Zane by his side shouting insults and encouragement. This time the lure of Eternity did not triumph. Her friends needed her.

Forcing her unconstrained soul earthwards, she slammed back into the familiar feel of flesh and bone. And screamed. Gritting her teeth she fought to control the omnipotent, white hot power pulsing through her body. The burning hot energy clawing at her insides was agony; it wanted freedom. Light and heat consumed her in painful waves. Hugo could not help her this time; she could feel his magic trying to reach her but her own roared in defiance. It did not want to be protected, it wanted to protect.

Another huge Wolfman lumbered towards Hugo, claws out and arms raised. Enraged, her power unleashed itself in a blast from her hands and body. That wave of magic tore through Ragor's soldiers, instantly turning their flesh and bones to ash. Trees were ripped up by their roots and the sheltering Queen's guard was flung facedown on the ground, his wings glowing as his body sucked her power into his own.

Diamond sensed the death of the Wolfmen and Battle Imps. She felt their energy transform into something insubstantial that blew away like mist on the wind. Her mind registered that the immediate danger to Hugo was gone, but she could not stop. Her heart raced painfully fast. A familiar feeling of panic and helplessness consumed her. Revelling in her fright, her magic seized control of everything but her consciousness and her soul. Rooted to the spot, Diamond's body became as rigid as a plank of wood.

Her magic greedily fed from her emotions, devouring what remained of her anger until only terror remained. Terror for herself and for Hugo, who was sprawled on the ground nearby, somehow still alive. Power coursed like poison through her veins, seeping onto her skin and into the air around her. Bright and hot, it did not understand it was devouring her and, in so doing so, was killing itself. Pain gripped her racing heart, beating so fast she feared it might explode and cleave her chest apart. A scream of agony and desperation splintered the air as the enormity of what she had done registered. She had allowed her magic to take control. Without Hugo's influence it had triumphed over her will. Now it would rage untamed and kill all those she had sought to save.

Chapter Twenty-Two

Hugo crawled on his belly, raking his fingers into the dirt, his finger nails breaking painfully as he dragged his bulk towards Diamond. Her magic pulsed against his, savagely trying to stop him from reaching her. An entity in its own right, it wanted power—it wanted to control its host. It was too new, too young to recognise its Nexus and welcome a joining.

Determined not to let the magic triumph, Hugo forced his body to absorb it, just like before when Diamond had fought the dragon. Its power would overwhelm her; kill her if she did not learn to dominate it. Absorbing magic was part of his gift. It only made him stronger. Quelling his terror of losing her, he relentlessly pulled himself across the ground. He would not let her die. Almost overpowered, he reached his goal. Bellowing, Hugo flung both arms around Diamond's legs and yanked her feet from under her. With a thump she hit the ground. Her magic flickered. Hugo seized his chance and heaved his bulk on top of her, curling his fingers into her shoulders.

"Diamond. Stop! You'll kill everyone!" he shouted in her ear and shook her viciously. "Control it! Force it to obey you!"

Horror filled her violet eyes as the skin on his face began to burn. Pain hit him only when his wrists and hands began blistering. Even with their Nexus, his body had reached its limit. Unable to absorb any more magic, his blood began to blaze.

"*Stop!!*" he snarled at her, his face a mask of agony. Holding her arms he pinned her to the ground, but it was a useless move; magic poured out of her body, thrashing against what it believed was a threat to its existence. Diamond blinked and his stomach clenched as tears ran from her deep violet eyes. Desperation shone in their depths. Balking, he knew immediately what she was asking.

"Kill me!" she whispered hoarsely. "Don't. Let. Everyone. Die."

Hugo could not do it. He could not kill her. If it was anyone else, anyone at all, he would have slit their throat in a second. But it wasn't. Leaving her was unthinkable, and he could not slam his fist into her already mutilated face to render her unconscious; not just because of the remorse he would feel, but if he let go of her arms, she would turn him to ash. Hugo roared with rage and frustration. With no idea how far her destruction reigned across the forest, he made his decision.

Forcing his jaw open, he drove his second set of teeth through his gums. Needle sharp and pointed they snapped into place. Even on the precipice of burning to death, Hugo knew he would have to mark her where no one else, particularly the Queen, would ever see the wound he left.

Hugo looked into Diamond's frightened eyes, prayed to Lunaria for forgiveness, and ripped her dress open with his teeth to reveal the silky pale skin of her breast underneath. Lowering his head he gave a feral growl and sunk his teeth into her soft flesh, sucking hard.

He released the venom from his poison glands, which wrenched a scream from her. Her spine arched against his grip, and her energy weakened. Good. She fought for another five beats of her heart, each one pulsed through him, loud and consuming, then mercifully she was unconscious.

The roar of energy settled. With his teeth still embedded in her flesh, Hugo pulled Diamond into his arms. The warmth of her blood filled his mouth. It ran sweet and pure down his throat. Hugo's world shrank to the feel of his tongue brushing against her skin and to the taste and feel of her clutched against him. He became utterly lost as her essence filled his senses. His jaw muscles convulsed as he drew more and more from her, savouring every drop of her sweetness. His heart raced, his conscious mind changing from desperation to a fog of desire. A raw, animalistic need almost overcame his instinct to protect her.

But her ashen face told Hugo how near to death he was pushing her weakened body. Giving a feral roar of dissatisfaction, he forced his needle-sharp teeth back under the cover of his gums.

Breathing raggedly he closed his eyes and lifted his face to the sky, the veins on his neck engorged as her blood pumped through him. The animal inside him thrashed in ecstasy as his magic and blood mixed with hers. Taking control of himself was the hardest thing Hugo had ever done. He had never felt such primal need as he did right now for the woman in his arms. And he fought—he fought with every fibre of his being to stop that beast inside him from exploding through his flesh and bones—until, growling with discontent, it capitulated. Panting, his eyelids flickered open to focus on the deep bite wound that bled profusely. It distracted him immediately.

Shaking badly, Hugo lifted Diamond until he could push his lips against her soft skin and force saliva against the wound. The coagulant in his saliva would staunch the bleeding and trigger the healing process. Growling in self-disgust, he had to use every ounce of self-control not to drink more of her.

"I'm sorry," he whispered into her ear, lowering her and crushing her against his body. With burned and bloodied hands, he gripped the back of her ragged dress, her blood-stained a silken spider's web around his bunched fists. Fleetingly he wondered what would happen to him if his Queen were to taste his blood now. She was the only other fae he knew of who had the ability to use the bite. The Queen used her venom to control the minds and bodies of her guards. Hugo grimaced. Thankfully, and for reasons Hugo did not care to think on too deeply, she had not bitten him—yet.

Diamond would not remember what he had done to her; although the reaction of the guards he had seen bitten by the Queen every winter solstice was the only experience he had to go on. With all his heart he hoped he was right. If she had no memory of it, she would never find out what his bite meant. Utter control of her body, and even her mind, was now his if he wanted it.

That thought terrified him. Despite his fearsome reputation, Hugo did not want that sort of control or power over another person, especially not Diamond. Such a determined spirit deserved to be free of control.

Covering the livid puncture wounds with the remains of his tunic that Diamond still wore, he looked up to the perfect blue sky. Ash curled into the air as the forest settled. It was then he noticed the strange stillness that surrounded them, almost as if Diamond's magic had sucked all the sound from the air. Hugo used the silence to breathe deeply and pull himself together.

Legions of golden-winged warrior fae flew overhead, their metallic armour glinting in the midday sun. It was an impressive site. Soon enough his senses settled and sound returned.

Swords clashed in the distance. The cave.... A deep bellow rocked the silence. The roar of a giant.

But all Hugo could think of right now was the girl in his arms. She was as still and deathly quiet as the forest around them. Cradling her tightly against his chest, he prayed to the goddess and willed her to overcome his venom.

Revealing what he had done to anyone, even a healer, was not an option. The Queen's court was like a nest of viper's waiting to strike. No one could be trusted. If the Queen found out....

Hugo took a deep breath to quell the terror in his heart, and he unconsciously touched the scar on his face. No, she would not find out.

Hugo could not bear the guilt and horror as Diamond's breathing became shallow and slow. His venom was killing her. Even with the small amount he had released, her body was too weak and frail to beat it.

He quickly scanned her. Unbidden and unexpected, a wave of wild desire rushed his body. Her blood, her taste was still so strong in his mouth. It clouded his senses and made rational, sensible thought almost impossible. He groaned, driving his face into her hair, hating himself for such feelings when she was so vulnerable. Snarling, he fought to control himself, battering down his aching need to make her his mate.

Yes, they shared a Nexus bond, but he could not blame that for how much he wanted her. He did not care that she was a half-blood; this stunning, spirited female was his perfect match. He shook his head in disbelief. *How can this be happening to me?* It was ludicrous to covet her; it was beyond dangerous for them both. He squeezed her tightly. That bite—not the venom, but the blood he had swallowed— was the first step in becoming mated. Twice. They had to swallow each other's blood twice before they were mated. But for Diamond to survive the Queen's attentions, Hugo had to crush any feelings he had for her.

Chapter Twenty-Three

Hugo gently pushed the blanket down to reveal her soft skin, which was forever marked by him. His eyes followed the gentle curve of her breast, clenching his teeth so hard he nearly broke them. His fae instincts raged so strong right now he couldn't think straight. Taking a deep breath, he concentrated on the wound. Bile burned his throat at the sight of the bloodied yellow fluid leaking from the inflamed skin. If Diamond didn't get to a healer soon, she would die.

Lowering her to the ground next to him, he gently brushed the hair from her face and looked to his own injuries. Blood oozed steadily from both wounds and the burns on his hands and face were agonising. Setting his jaw, he ripped his leggings open. The deep slash wound on his thigh was still bleeding. Good. He pushed the fingers of one hand into the wound, grunting and swallowing down the agony and vomit that rushed his mouth. Beads of sweat trickled down his face as he scooped out the congealing blood. A small, gelatinous mound now sat in his cupped fingers. Hugo quickly smeared the thick clots on Diamond's breast. The dark red blood looked obscene against her pale skin. There was a slight hiss as his blood and the leaking venom mixed to form a thick brown scab. He eyed it with grim satisfaction. The anti-venom in his blood would help her fight the drugging effects of his poison.

He carefully pulled her shredded clothes back up. By now a pool of bright blood had formed under his thigh. Dealing with his own wounds was his next priority. He gritted his teeth, stubbornly ignoring his dizziness. Now was not the time to be weak. Hugo sucked at his saliva, spitting globules into his palm until he judged he had enough of the coagulant mucus to cover the gash in his leg. Smearing it on, he hissed loudly as it began to work. Stinging and burning, it sealed the exposed blood vessels. When he was done, he checked the bite one more time, sighing with relief when it looked less inflamed.

"Good girl. Fight it," he whispered in her ear, gently brushing his lips against the soft skin of her cheek. It was time to declare their existence to the warriors above. The best healers in Valentia were at the palace, which meant bringing Diamond there was imperative.

Dragging his injured leg, he stepped out from the shadows and devastation and into sunlight. He waved his arms at the warriors above.

On high alert, their fae eyes noticed him instantly. Twenty warrior fae landed nearby, some hurrying over to help him, the others forming a defensive cordon. Their troop leader seemed momentarily stunned to see Hugo, then the leader's clenched right fist, the first two fingers extended, hit his left shoulder thumb inwards in a smart salute, his golden brown eyes taking in Hugo's uniform and ravaged appearance.

"Commander Casimir? Captain Elexon Riddeon. What can we do to assist you, sir?" the warrior fae asked, his tone clipped and efficient.

"Some water and clean bandages for me. The lady needs a healer. Once I have bound my wounds I will take her back to Valentia." Hugo's response was curt, as these warriors would expect.

"Of course, sir. Fedron." Elexon indicated to the soldier who stood behind his left shoulder.

Hugo's hackles raised immediately. The warrior had to drag his gaze from Diamond. He did nothing to disguise the hunger in his eyes before he handed over a water skin. Hugo accepted it but stepped between the warrior and Diamond, squaring his shoulders and blocking Fedron's view. The slight growl Hugo omitted was nothing short of lethal. The warrior's face became impassive but Hugo did not miss the amused spark in his eyes. Hugo's fingers twitched, instantly wanting to smash a fist into the warrior's face.

"Fedron, step away from the commander," ordered Elexon, his observant eyes narrowing, though strangely not at Hugo.

Fedron smirked and moved sideways, a move that put him in sight of Diamond once again. This time Elexon stepped to block him. A casual move but Hugo still noted it.

"What happened here, sir?" the captain asked quickly, trying—but failing—to distract Hugo from Fedron. Elexon's alert golden gaze raked across the clearing, taking in the devastation and Diamond, who lay unconscious near the fallen tree.

Hugo considered his words carefully before answering. "An enemy attack at Sentinel's Cave. Prince Oden, his general and his men are trapped there. I can still hear a giant. Prince Oden will need assistance to kill it." There was a breathless quality to his voice that he hated as he wrapped a bandage tightly around his thigh. It made him sound weak. Explaining himself to these men was not necessary; besides, keeping how the devastation had happened to himself was imperative if Diamond were to live.

"Inform Havron and go to the prince's aid," Elexon ordered Fedron. Fedron stared long and hard at Diamond, his delay in complying on the verge of insolence before he saluted his superior.

Hugo did not have chance to straighten and slam his fist into the warriors gut before Elexon barked, "Now, Fedron!"

As Fedron disappeared into the sky, Elexon released his sword pommel. Hugo met Elexon's steady gaze and nodded slightly. A move that the captain returned. From the corner of his eye Hugo saw a warrior move towards Diamond, bending down to slip his arms around her. Hugo took two swift steps to his side and snarled savagely, realising too late his behaviour was way out of character for a Queen's guard. He found he didn't care in the least.

"Don't touch her! I'll take her," he growled, curling his fingers into fists and using all his self-control not to kick the fae backwards and away from Diamond's prone figure.

The warrior immediately stepped back, looking warily at Hugo's menacing expression but Hugo did not notice, he only concentrated on Diamond's face. As soon as he was by her side his magic found the cowed, trembling ember of hers, amplifying his already possessive instincts. Wincing and steeling himself to ignore the nauseating waves of pain that shot through his ravaged body, Hugo crouched down. Gritting his teeth, he hoisted Diamond into his arms, aware the other fae were watching him closely.

"Sir, are you sure you don't want one of my men to take her?" Elexon asked with concern.

Hugo didn't bother answering. She was so delicate and so precious to him now, he didn't care how much pain he was in; he would get her back to Valentia and the healers himself. Growling with determination he straightened up, scowling at Elexon's men, who now stood back, their faces impassive. Good. At least if they were wary of him they would stay away from Diamond. He unfurled his wings but knew he had no extra strength to armour them.

Elexon's eyes narrowed a fraction. He understood how weak Hugo was by that omission. The warriors followed Hugo into the air. Elexon ordered six men with him to escort Hugo to the distant island city; the rest he ordered to re-join Fedron.

Hugo ignored the warriors, not caring if they were there or not. Distant clouds shrouded Valentia, obscuring the Queen's tower completely. Hugo set his jaw. It was just less than thirty miles across the Rift Valley back to the city. That distance carrying a person, even uninjured, would be hard. Hugo prayed the blast of energy he had absorbed from Diamond would give him enough strength to get there. He inhaled deeply, her scent sending his heart tumbling. He could do this. Hugo resolutely set a punishing pace and headed toward the city, squashing the voice of reason in his head that told him she was not his and never could be. His life belonged to the Queen.

Part Two

The City

Chapter Twenty-Four

The silver-haired girl lay on the bed, her skin pale as death. The healer bathed her face, then straightened. She urgently spoke with the Queen's guard, who stood grim-faced and dirty by the door. He nodded once, waited until she had left the room and dropped to his knees beside Diamond, anguish apparent in every line of his body.

Diamond's insides were aflame. Broken buildings and shadowed walkways stretched ahead of her. A city of shadow and lost souls. She staggered toward the rift in the darkness where a pulsing light beckoned. A way out! Forcing her limbs to move, she ran—only to find her way blocked by a familiar foe. The lost souls screamed his name in terror.

"Sulphurious."

The mirror-black dragon slammed down in front of Diamond, his vicious talons crushing the ground. Scorching red eyes bored into her soul, simmering with malevolence. Molten fire rippled up his long neck, his hideous mouth gaping wide. Screeching with effort, Diamond pitted her pathetic shield of magic against his fire, tears of exhaustion and utter despair running down her dirty face. She had fought through this endless night hoping her saviour would come, but hope had turned to despair. Outstretched, her arms shook violently. It would not be long before she was at the end of her strength. Sparks of dragon-fire pierced her shield. Crying now, her eyes darted every direction, looking for an escape.

She felt him before he appeared—her tormentor. Ice coated her stomach. It was too late, she realised, for anyone to help her now. A faceless figure emerged from the flames, wreathed in darkness. Only endless, eternal shadow writhed under the cowl where his face should be. Panicked, she strengthened her shield with every last drop of energy she possessed.

The figure raised a skeletal hand and flicked her magic aside like it was an insignificant irritation. Slowly, deliberately, he stalked up to her. Emptiness filled her mind, despair eating at her heart. Then the screams started, a screeching, wailing cacophony that threatened to rip her skull apart.

The dragon cowed down before the power of its lord and master, watching the death of the half-blood with intent red eyes. Studying his withered fingers, the figure huffed an icy chuckle, shaped them like a claw and drove them into Diamond's chest. Pain surged, ripping a scream from her throat.

This, she understood now, was the power wielded by the Lord of Chaos; endless pain and suffering were his to command. Indescribable cold gripped Diamond's heart, consuming her until her very blood and bones froze. A scream for the person who had already saved her so many times jammed inside her ice-filled lungs. Petrified, Diamond realised this would not be a peaceful death, there would be no Eternity for her, only darkness and Chaos.

Wraiths prowled nearby—waiting—waiting for her to die. They shrieked her name, their skeletal hands grabbing her as their lord relinquished his hold on her dying heart. Their fingers of mist and shadow turned to icy spikes that dug painfully into her flesh, dragging her toward a yawning black abyss.

A voice echoed in the distance; a male voice, rich and deep. It became louder and more insistent until he was yelling frantically for her to fight, to live, to come back to him. Diamond felt a rush of hope as a familiar power tugged frantically at the magical embers in her soul.

The wraiths faltered. Responding to its mate, that ember flared to life. Crackling heat surged through her veins, warming her flesh and bones, melting the ice encasing her heart.

Instinctively Diamond released a forceful blast; it leaked from her hair, her skin, her eyes. Even in such a weakened state the light was enough to send the wraiths screeching into the abyss, into the safety of their dark world. Disorientated and weak, she stumbled. Vast unshakable strength invaded her body.

"Diamond! Come back to me. Run!" her saviour yelled over and over.

Sobbing, Diamond ran with every ounce of her remaining strength towards the voice that ordered her back from the abyss.

Warm hands gripped Diamond's shoulder's, shaking her firmly. The voice still called her name, commanding her to return. But unlike moments before, it now sounded very real. Slowly, through the fog of her mind, she became aware of the softness of the bed underneath her, the warmth of the velvety blankets and the glorious downy pillows that supported her hot, sticky head. Her eyelids flickered and the shaking stopped. Breathless and spent, Diamond was unable to move or speak. Tears of relief leaked from her eyes, burning a trail down her skin into her hair.

"Thank the goddess," Hugo's voice murmured into her ear, so familiar but so soft and full of worry she almost didn't recognise it.

Cracking open her heavy eyelids, everything looked foggy. Focusing was impossible, even breathing was an immense effort. She tried to speak, to ask where she was but only a whimper escaped her dry lips.

"Shh. It's okay. You're safe for now. I will take care of you. Go back to sleep," he urged softly. Dry, cool lips lightly grazed her forehead and she murmured, unable to form words of thanks to the warrior who had brought her back from the demon and the darkness.

Chapter Twenty-Five

The young healer clicked her tongue. She disapproved of the fusty air in the room and threw the purple drapes wide open. Sunlight hit the Prince of Rhodainia in the face, causing him to moan in protest. The healer's brown hair was swept back from the soft features of her face and secured in a tight bun. Her grey dress and white apron were neutral and professional, as was her expression. Quickly the healer dipped a curtsey to the handsome young man who had not left her patient's side since yesterday evening.

"Sorry, Your Highness, but the air in here needs freshening up, and Isla Norr has given me instructions to do what I need to do to get this young lady up and about today."

"Of course, Rose," said Jack rubbing his eyes before pushing himself out of the large armchair that he had placed next to Diamond's bed.

For five days Hugo's self-control had been balancing on a knife edge, and he was still trying to keep his head and heart together. For two of those days he had fought with Diamond, pouring his magic into her whilst everyone else thought him a silent guard by her door. No one, not even Rose, noticed when he leaned against the wall for support or had to blink sweat from his eyes with the effort of giving Diamond the strength she needed to survive whatever hell she was in. Hugo knew his actions were dangerous to them both, but he could not leave her any more than he could stop breathing.

Serene and peaceful, she had been in a deep sleep since the shadows had left her soul. He had felt their coldness and greed as they tried to take her from this life into theirs. His magic had raged at the thought. Anxiety tightened his chest, though the current calmness of her magic reassured him.

"And we can't upset Isla Norr, now can we?" Jack commented while giving Rose a well-practised smile.

Rose dipped her head demurely but not before Hugo caught the edges of her mouth curling up in response. He tried not to roll his eyes at Rose's all too predictable reaction to the prince's charms.

Isla Norr was the Queen's personal healer and was a formidable force of nature for one who was supposed to be kind and caring. The stern female fae had accepted the mantle of Principle Healer to the Queen fifteen years ago. Since then Principle Norr had run Valentia's academy of healers with iron discipline. Even the Prevost of the Acolytes deferred to her judgment.

Hugo had reluctantly handed Diamond over to the healers and patiently let them do what they could to cure her. They had stitched her lip, but none had dared try and throw him out of the room whilst they bathed her cut and bruised skin with the herb- and spell-infused water until she was almost unmarked. Knowing Diamond would be mortified by being naked and helpless in front of him, he had politely turned away but kept his magic near her until they had completed their task. Rose had then dressed Diamond in a stark white night gown that covered her from her neck downwards. Hugo hated it. In his opinion it looked far too much like a death shroud.

A mass of silver hair fanned out from Diamond's head, covering the pillow. Not for the first time he struggled to hide his dismay at the stains and clumps of dried blood that made it dull and lifeless.

Never mind. Rose will sort that out today, he reassured himself.

Jack lifted his arms above his head and stretched, giving a moan of pleasure at the release on his inactive muscles. He strode over to the window with a sigh, leaning on the sill and peering out at the clear blue sky. After a few minutes the prince twisted back to face Hugo.

"I'm going to have to leave her today. The war council and the Queen are expecting me at this morning's meeting. I have delayed them as long as I dare," Jack said, studying Hugo steadily. Hugo studied him right back, keeping his face blank and nodded once. Jack's gaze did not falter but his eyes narrowed.

When the prince and General Edo had arrived yesterday, three women had been tending Diamond's battered legs. Hugo had been kneeling by her bed holding her hand. Jack had been instantly annoyed to see Hugo so close to Diamond. In fact the prince had been unable to mask his anger as Hugo had stood with difficulty and move back to allow him and General Edo to get to her side.

For the first two hours Jack, General Edo and Hugo had kept a silent vigil by her side. They had all refused to leave the room until Isla Norr had personally threatened to cast a sleeping spell on them all, saying there were private things that needed doing for the young lady that should not be witnessed by any of them. Even Hugo had been ushered out, although he remained on the other side of the closed door, feeling for the essence of her weak magic. The next day Jack had sought permission from the Queen to move Diamond to a room of her own with bathing facilities. Since then Hugo had left her side only to allow the healers to clean and stitch his wound and apply salve to his burns before re-establishing his position as Diamond's personal guard.

"You know, the lovely Rose here is going to wake Diamond today. Maybe this will be a good time for you to rest and eat—and, err, take a bath. You stink," said Jack bluntly, as a breeze from the open window sent the foul stink of old sweat and blood eddying around the room.

Rose gave a snort of laughter as she walked into the bathing room to check the water.

"I agree—when she is awake," answered Hugo stubbornly, staring at Jack with his dark glittering eyes. "But until then I will stay here."

Jack held Hugo's gaze, his face tight. "Hugo, you're being a stubborn ass. The Queen will know you have refused to leave. Damn it! You are putting her at risk by staying here," he declared, squeezing his hands into tight fists.

Hugo remained silent, although behind his back he clasped hands together so tightly they hurt. Jack was right.

"What happened between you two in the forest, Hugo?" Jack asked. The prince waited expectantly for an answer.

Hugo just looked steadily at his friend and said nothing, outwardly portraying only icy calm whilst his insides roiled. He *had* been stupid. Jack was so utterly right that Hugo wanted to hit him—or something. The nearest wall would do. The fact that the Queen hadn't sent for him to report, or thrown Diamond straight in the dungeons, filled him with dread. His Queen was like an adder waiting to strike. Hugo felt sick.

"Whatever it was flattened half the forest, nearly burnt your skin off and left her unconscious. You know there will be questions, especially from your Queen," Jack stated.

More silence.

"Hugo, you forget I am *your friend*. Don't keep shutting me out. Ever since you came back here to your Queen, you've been nothing but a cold-hearted shadow of who you were in Stormguaard." The prince strode up to him and cocked his head. "I haven't seen you laugh or smile in months. Is that what she does—steal any joy from your soul?"

Hugo slumped a little, the breath whooshing from his chest. "Yes," he whispered.

"Then don't let her steal Diamond. Anyone who knows you can see how much you want her."

Hugo's eyes shot to Jack. "What do you mean?" he asked hoarsely.

"Oh come on, Hugo. You lived around me and my soldiers for nearly three years. We can all see how you act around her. Besides, you're fae," he said as if that explained everything.

Hugo ignored that. "What do you mean you can see how I act?" he persisted.

Jack gave him a quizzical look. "Hugo, I have never been able to wind you up about anything, let alone a woman. But with her it's as easy as breathing. You look like you want to rip apart anyone who talks to her, let alone anyone who might hurt her."

Hugo opened his mouth to protest but, smiling mischievously, Jack quickly continued and smacked Hugo's shoulder good-naturedly. "Yes, you do. Like in the cave when Roin touched her. We all thought you might lose your cool completely. It gave us all quite a fright." Jack cocked his head and grinned. "You're behaving like a fae who has found a mate. Have you, Hugo?"

Hugo scowled and snarled, but that just made Jack bark a laugh. Behind them Diamond stirred, drawing their attention. Jack's face lost any levity.

"She saved my life, Hugo. I owe her. If you don't want her to be in danger, if you want to *protect* her, let me take her from here. Help me get her away. You know the Queen will kill her for the magic she can wield." Jack's voice turned almost pleading.

Let her go.

Those words of reason echoed in his head, but still Hugo remained silent. Selfishly, he didn't want Jack to take her away. His throat constricted in panic at the thought of her leaving. But she deserved to be safe. *Can I do it? Can I defy my Queen, get Diamond out of the trap I have woven for her and get away with it?* He opened his mouth to ask Jack how, then clamped it shut as Rose came back out of the bathing room, clicking her tongue disapprovingly.

"His Highness is right, sir. You need to care for your own injuries or you'll get infected," said Rose, oblivious to the last part of the conversation. "Besides, when the young miss is awake, she will need to bathe—and you cannot stay for that. It's not seemly," she said flushing at Hugo's dark look, but she raised her eyebrows expectantly. "Not this time, sir."

"Understood," Hugo answered, his eyes flicking to Diamond then back to Jack. "When she is awake I will leave."

Jack sighed, running his hand through his hair as he watched Rose. "Alright, Hugo. I'll drop it…for now. But we will speak of this again—and soon," the prince promised darkly, looking back out of the window at the Queen's tower.

Hugo hated the building that emerged from the centre of the grey granite palace. It loomed up to the sky like a ridiculous, huge phallus, its bulk dwarfing every other building in the considerable grounds. Constructed from pink marble, veins of glittering crystal wound through the stone. On a sunny day the whole thing seemed to soak up the light and glow, its massive structure making it visible for miles up and down the coast. There were more than two hundred rooms in the tower alone, housing the Queen's opulent throne room, her council chambers, private kitchens, her own personal apartments and training rooms for all the Queen's guard's; there was a school and an armoury—not to mention her own dungeons under the foundations. Hugo shuddered at his memories of those awful, stinking cells.

"I need to go and prepare myself for my meeting," said Jack puffing his cheeks out. "I also need to introduce General Edo to my council and commanders today," he told Hugo.

The rug muffled his footsteps as he walked over to Diamond. The prince leaned in and lightly kissed her forehead before he straightened and squared his shoulders. He stroked a hand gently down her soft cheek. When he turned, Hugo's eyes were obsidian, his face carved from granite. Unfazed, the prince only nodded grimly to the Queen's guard as he walked out of the room without looking back.

Chapter Twenty-Six

Rose opened the windows, and a gentle sweet breeze caressed Hugo's sticky skin. His body stank worse than a sewer, and he must look a gruesome sight, covered in filth and blood, his clothes torn and his weapons encrusted with dried blood and guts. His chin was covered by a thick beard, half of which was burned off, and his mouth tasted like something had died in it.

"When will you wake her?" he asked Rose, schooling his features into neutrality.

Rose's eyes were big and wary as she glanced at him. "Well, now is as good a time as any." She smiled timidly, "Would you like to help me?"

He said stiffly, "Err.... If you tell me what to do, I am willing to help." He concealed his surprise. It would be a miracle if Rose hadn't been ordered to pass on information about Diamond and him to Isla Norr or the Queen. He just hoped that no healer knew enough of ancient fae customs to understand what the mark on her breast was.

"Please come closer." Gulping, Rose beckoned him over.

It was then he noticed the phial in her hand. Instantly suspicious he glowered at it and snarled slightly.

"It's alright, sir," Rose soothed, following his gaze and trying to sound brave. The girl was human but had watched him stand over Diamond day after day without sleep or food. Clearly Rose was well aware of how protective he was of Diamond—that in itself made Rose a danger to them both. Hugo ignored his training, which told him to threaten Rose to ensure her silence.

"This is just to reverse the sleeping spell. It will not harm her, commander; I promise. Just talk to her. She will be disorientated and scared when she wakes, and your voice seems the only thing to calm her."

Hugo nodded curtly after giving the phial another suspicious glare. Noticing Rose's flushed face and the way her hands shook made him scowl harder. The shaking worsened and, for the first time in years, he felt a pang of remorse at using who and what he was to intimidate someone so kind. Rose had been here nearly as much as him. Despite that, he couldn't bring himself to smile. Being this close to Diamond even so many days after the bite had his heart pounding so hard he was sure Rose could hear it.

Only Rose had seen him kneel by Diamond's bed and hold her hand to his lips. But it wasn't until they were alone that he would lean in until his face was buried in Diamond's hair or his lips brushed her ear. In those precious stolen moments he would whisper nonsense to her. Rose was right; Diamond always stilled, almost as though she were listening to him. It was easy to tell her of his deepest thoughts: of wanting to take her somewhere far away, of escaping the servitude of the Queen. Vocalising his dreams made them seem more real. Their Nexus, his brutal existence as a young guard, he told her things he had never shared with anyone else. Hugo held back a derisive chuckle; it had been easy because there was no judgment—or pity—in the eyes of an unconscious woman.

Each time the evil that lurked between this world and Eternity tried to steal her breath and take her soul, Hugo had controlled his panic and called to her, plunging his magic deep into her flesh and bones, winding it around the struggling ember of her own. His Nexus. Rare, beautiful, spirited. He would not let her die. Weak himself, the dampening effects of the city shield had been hard to overcome; but with sheer determination he had managed it, pulling and yanking at that tiny spark of hers until it flared brightly. His heart had raced with unaccustomed fear until she answered his commands to run from death, until her chest began to rise and fall as she breathed once again. That was, until the next time.

He watched Rose tip three tiny drops of a red liquid onto Diamond's lips. It ran along the full length of her mouth before her tongue flicked out and she licked it away. Rose was far too preoccupied with Diamond to notice the sudden flush that crept up Hugo's neck.

"Talk to her. Bring her back," was all Rose said as she held Diamond's hand.

Hugo knelt down on the floor, his infected thigh wound bleating with pain. Leaning forward until his lips brushed the shell of her ear he whispered her name, sending his magic flowing through her, calling her back to wakefulness.

Chapter Twenty-Seven

Diamond smiled as that beloved voice gently coaxed her from her dreams back to reality. She followed it as she always did, knowing he would lead her to safety. Quickly, she realised he wanted her to wake. She dimly registered his warm fingers lightly brushing her cheek. Instinctively, she turned her face into that powerful hand, murmuring her contentment. All too soon it pulled away.

A whimper escaped her parched throat, but the warmth did not return. Laying quietly, Diamond allowed her mind to begin functioning. The world around her slowly took shape; the wonderfully comfortable bed, her head resting on a soft feather pillow, the cool sweet breeze that blew gently over her skin. Something else tickled her nose as well—salt, she mused, she must be near the sea.

Her eyelids flicked open, wanting to see Hugo to thank him, to throw her arms around him.... But it was not Hugo smiling down at Diamond, it was a girl about her own age with relief in her chestnut brown eyes.

"Hello," the girl beamed. "I'm Rose. I am your healer."

Diamond stared at her uncomprehendingly. Outside, voices rumbled and gravel crunched as someone walked on a path under the open window.

"Healer?" she rasped. Her memory had become distinctly hazy in the last few minutes. Coughing to clear her throat she tried again. "Where am I?"

"You are in Valentia. In the Queen's palace," Rose explained, giving Diamond time to absorb that piece of information.

Diamond stifled a sob of relief. They had made it! Or at least she had.... Her tongue stuck to the roof of her mouth as she spoke. "Hugo? And the...the others? Where are they?" she croaked, dreading the answer.

Rose gave her a conspiratorial smile and perched on the bed next to Diamond, holding her patient's shaking hand. "They're all alive," Rose said reassuringly. "In fact, I think they have all been in here at some point," she giggled. "Even the water leopard; Trajan, is it? Anyway he healed well and the skinny boy, Tom. I've been looking after him as well. He came in here to keep the prince company for a while until I made him go back to bed."

"Why?" interrupted Diamond quickly. "Did he get hurt?" Tom had never been any good with blood or pain.

"Yes. A cut on his arm, but don't worry—he's fine now. And then your guard, Commander Casimir, Hugo as you call him," she searched Diamond's face and frowned. "Well, he has refused to leave until just now. And the prince.... Whew!" She fanned herself and faked a swoon, giggling as Diamond blushed bright red. Rose's light-hearted manner did the job of distracting her patient from the worry in her heart.

"Would you like a drink?" Rose asked, picking up a glass of water from the bedside table.

Struggling to sit up Diamond took the cold glass. Ice chinked and, with a shaking hand that Rose had to steady, she took a big gulp of water, swallowing and moaning with pleasure as the ice-cold liquid washed across her tongue and down her dry throat. Rose, still prattling on about Jack, got up and walked into the next room.

"Now you just relax there for a minute and get your bearings; I'll check the bath for you. Isla Norr wants you up and about today—and no one goes against the Queen's healer...." her voice faded to muffled sounds as she walked into the bathing room.

Diamond let her head flop back against the soft pillow and studied her room. It was huge. Far larger than any bedroom she had ever seen. A big bay window, lined with a seat, let in large amounts of light. Little diamonds of glass cast hundreds of tiny rainbows across the floor and walls, and big purple velvet drapes were twisted back then secured with gold cord. The room was spotlessly clean and stunningly beautiful. Ornate rugs covered the wooden floor, and large tapestries of the forest and the sea covered the granite walls. There was a small writing bureau against the wall opposite, and a large armchair covered in blue silk sat by her bed. It faced her as if someone had been sitting in it. In the other corner stood an elegant dressing table with an oval mirror.

Diamond wondered what she would wear if she got up today. She had absolutely nothing to call her own now. She peered under the covers and grimaced. A white nightgown covered her. It was truly awful. She wrinkled her nose just as Rose stepped back in and said her bath was ready. Rejecting worries about what she didn't have, Diamond pushed back the warm covers and allowed the other girl to help her sit up. She clutched the edge of the bed for a moment as a wave of dizziness hit her.

"It's okay. It will pass. It's probably the after effects of the healing potions and spells. And you have been very ill," Rose informed her gravely, her brown eyes full of concern. "I thought you had died at one point. I ran to fetch Isla Norr but by the time I returned, Commander Casimir told me you had rallied and were breathing properly again."

Tears shone in Rose's eyes. Diamond's stomach flipped as she held the healer's hand, unable to express her gratitude to this kind stranger. Her own throat bobbed as she thought of Hugo and her dreams. It had been death she was running from and him she was running to. Suddenly she wanted nothing more than to see him.

"Thank you for taking care of me, Rose," she said with a shaky smile, hoping to make Rose feel better whilst pushing away her own wants. Thoughts of Hugo were beyond foolish. He was back with his Queen; now that Diamond was alive she was no longer his problem. He would not have time for her.

A delightfully cool breeze tickled her bare feet and ankles. For a moment Diamond allowed herself to gaze out of the window at the blue sky. Fluffy white clouds zipped happily by. The sight of something so naturally beautiful lifted her heart. Even with Rose's help, getting to the bathing room was a slow and painful process.

"I—err—I can manage now," Diamond stuttered breathlessly as she stood looking down into the enormous sunken marble bath. Tendrils of steam danced lazily up to the ceiling, inviting her in.

"Okay. There are oils in the bath that will help you heal and dull your pain," Rose informed her cheerfully.

Diamond turned and looked pointedly at the door. Being unconscious and bathed by others was one thing. Even though she felt weak as a baby she did not want anyone else in the room whilst she had a bath.

Rose got the message and pointed out the robe that hung in one corner. "I'll be back in an hour to help you dress," she said, closing the door with a click.

Diamond let her nightgown slide off her shoulders and stepped out of the puddle of cotton at her feet, wondering what exactly Rose had for her to wear.

A fresh lemony scent filled the air, mixed with the aromatic scent of herbs. It tickled her nose as she inhaled, then she shivered with anticipation. She couldn't remember the last time she had bathed in warm water. It had been weeks, weeks of trekking through an endless cold dead forest. It had been before her dad had died and her world had been turned upside down. Ignoring her burning eyes, Diamond thrust away her grief, not wanting to deal with it yet.

At one end of the bathing room there was a long, ornately decorated mirror. Walking up to it she studied her reflection, pulling a critical face at what she saw. Diamond had never been vain. Ridicule and insults did not allow for that behaviour, but the girl staring back at her from the mirror was a stranger. Her hair was matted in dirty, dull clumps. Her face was thin and angular. Her cheeks were sunken and her breasts smaller than they had been for years. The outline of her ribs was far too obvious and her hip bones jutted out painfully against bruised thin skin. Diamond swallowed her distaste. Huge, sunken violet eyes stared back at her, dominating her face.

"Oh!" she gasped, noticing a jagged wound covered with an almost translucent brown scab on her left breast. It felt rough under her fingertips. Not painful as such, just very sensitive. Diamond frowned and peered down. With two fingers she gently moved the soft swell of her breast. It looked like a row of puncture marks. Even with all her other wounds, this was a peculiar injury to have sustained in such a place. Mystified, her frown deepened. The goddess knew the rest of her was covered in old wounds and yellowing bruises too. Something about that thought didn't fit, but having no better explanation Diamond turned away from the mirror and dipped a toe in the scented water. It was beyond wonderful, an utter luxury. Wobbling down the three steps, Diamond bent her knees and sank down, groaning with pleasure as the warm, silky water embraced her battered body.

She lay weightless in the bath for what seemed like an age, letting the sting of her wounds ebb away whilst enjoying the peace and absolute luxury of the bathing room. No one disturbed her. She moved and her necklace bumped against her chest. Sensing her relaxed mood the crystal pulsed gently, warm against her skin. Instinctively, her fingers touched the jewel. No one had taken it. A relieved smile curled her lips. Through the water the facets of the jewel radiated a kaleidoscope of pretty rainbows around the room.

After relaxing for a long while, Diamond drummed up some

energy and laboriously scrubbed the ingrained dirt from her skin with a yellow soap that smelled of flowers and honey, then started on her hair. It took three washes to get the grease and blood out. When she had dealt with that she patiently picked the dirt from under her broken nails. Exhausted but not wanting to endure the humiliation of being helped out of the bath by Rose, she forced herself up.

The filthy water was cold and the steam had disappeared by the time she emerged from the bathing room clad in the cotton robe. Winding the towel around her head Diamond padded over to the dressing table to study the silver hairbrush on it. Smiling she ran her fingers over the beautiful engraving. She could use this, she realised with a smile. Girls like her just didn't own beautiful things like this.

Shaking the towel off her head, she let her hair fall in messy tangles to her waist just as there was a brief knock and her bedroom door opened. With a jolt of surprise she stiffened and twirled to face the huge warrior striding in. Hugo stopped abruptly, his hand on the door knob as he saw her standing in a thin bathrobe with her wet hair cascading in a silver curtain down to her waist.

Chapter Twenty-Eight

Diamond was struck dumb. Her voice dried up and her heart tumbled around in her chest as though it were suddenly loose. Hugo looked so different; younger and ruggedly handsome, despite the scar that stood out on his face without his thick beard. Achingly familiar eyes regarded her cautiously. Except—her stomach dropped—there were healing burns on his skin.

Did I do that? Diamond didn't know what to say.

His eyes slowly dropped, his gaze travelling over her body, taking in *everything* about her. A flush burned her cheeks as he inhaled. Tension simmered in the silence, his regard making her extremely aware that she was naked underneath the robe. Hunger flickered in his eyes as they lingered on the outline of her breasts but was gone so quickly Diamond wondered if she had imagined it. A shy smile curled her lips when it occurred to her he looked almost as uncomfortable as she felt.

"Hello, Hugo." The tremble in her voice made her cringe and her voice dried up.

Swallowing, Hugo squared his shoulders. Newly washed and still wet, the blue streaks shimmered in his raven hair. It had been braided back from his face, accentuating the harsh lines of his jaw and neck. The black tunic he wore was embroidered with intricate whorls of blood-red silk that swirled across his massive shoulders and down the contoured muscles of his arms.

Both his tunic and leggings were covered by a sleeveless, thigh-length leather jerkin that was imprinted with a fierce sea serpent. It was fastened tightly with thick leather straps and buckles that strained over his broad chest, cut to reveal the weapons belt circling his trim waist. Daggers hung from it, vicious and gleaming. Diamond grazed her attention across his face, then up over his shoulder to the Silverbore swords that were in place on his back. Menacing, they glinting in the sunlight that streamed through the open window.

Breath rushed from her chest as if his overpowering presence sucked it right from her. He looked dangerous, scary and utterly stunning.

"Diamond. I—err—didn't realise you were not dressed. Please forgive me," he rumbled in his rich, deep voice.

Her knees trembled at the memory of that voice challenging her, ordering her to live. They stared warily at each other, seconds passing, marked only by the small carriage clock ticking on the dressing table. Diamond's memories of the last time they had been together were hazy, but she knew Hugo had saved her life. She couldn't remember how exactly, but there was utter certainty in her heart that he had. Her breath hitched. The last thing she remembered was losing control, and the terrible, consuming heat and pain that tried to rip her chest apart.

Rose had said Hugo had not left her side for days, that he had neglected himself in order to stay with her. That voice—she swallowed a sob—she remembered her dreams so clearly. The demon lord, the dragon and that bone chilling cold. Tears glistened in her eyes. Hugo had called her back from the darkness and shadows, he had ripped her from the clutches of death more than once.

Diamond impulsively walked forward, her bare feet silent on the rug, until she was staring up into his sapphire and silver eyes. Balancing on her tiptoes she reached up, placing one hand on his shoulder and the other behind his head. Her cool hands pulled him down. Surprise flickered in his eyes but he did not resist her gentle demand. The kiss she brushed on his scarred face was gentle, and she carefully avoided his burns.

As her lips contacted his skin, she felt him flinch back. Realisation dawned. Her own looks had incurred enough ridicule over the years. His scar loomed close to her lips. It had never bothered her, but.... She had noticed even Tom had blanched and looked quickly away when Hugo's face twisted as he spoke. Perhaps this tough, cold guard was not as immune to the judgment of others as he would have everyone believe.

Pulling back very slightly, she allowed her eyes to meet his, then slowly and deliberately she leaned back in, her fingers curling into the blood-red embroidery of his tunic. She kissed him just above his mouth where his skin had knitted back together in uneven lumps. The scar was surprisingly soft under the caress of her lips, and she lingered to inhale the clean spicy smell of him.

"Thank you, Hugo," she whispered, her voice trembling. "I

remember you in my dreams. Y-you made me live. I-I won't forget it. And Rose—she told me you wouldn't leave me, that you guarded me while I slept. I don't know how to thank you," she finished, a tear running down her cheek.

Hugo didn't seem able to say anything. He squeezed his eyes together as if in pain, then nodded his head. When she pulled away she was shocked to see his cheeks flushed pink. Another revelation. Still, she supposed, a Queen's guard was unlikely to receive any spontaneous affection or thanks—ever. A quick swipe with the back of her hand dried her cheeks.

She gently took hold of one of his freshly bandaged wrists and lightly touched a burn on his face. "Did I do that?" she asked feeling sick with guilt. "I'm so sorry.... I-I don't remember...."

Nodding, Hugo jerked away from her touch. "It was not your fault," he stated roughly, then hesitated a moment before taking a deep breath as if forcing himself to speak. "But understand, you will not be able to use your magic from now on. The shield—and my Queen's enchantments—will stop you. You lost control in the forest and flattened more than a half mile of it. It is against my Queen's laws to use magic in these lands, and such a capacity for destruction puts everyone in this palace at risk, and that is not acceptable."

"I understand," Diamond replied hanging her head. "I'm so sorry, Hugo," she added. "I never meant to hurt you. I truly don't remember anything of the forest other than such painful heat and-and losing control of my body."

She gulped down a mouthful of air, with a small sob. The calloused finger he placed under her chin scraped her soft skin as he tilted her face up again. His eyes commanded her attention—not that she wanted to look away.

"Diamond, I don't blame you for my injuries. Really I don't. You have an astounding and powerful gift. It's just that it's wild, untamed...." For a moment his voice was soft and gentle. Then he seemed to remember who and what he was. His step back felt like a huge rift to Diamond, especially when he hardened his features again. Swallowing and taking a steadying breath, he forced his next words out.

"I am no longer your friend, Diamond. I am a Queen's elite guard and I follow only my Queen's orders. You broke the Queen's laws by using magic and, as of this morning, my orders are to stop you if you try and access your magic or become a danger to anyone in this palace. Do you understand what that means?" he asked harshly, his eyes like glittering coals.

Diamond paled. "Yes, I understand," she whispered, her eyes going to his blades. Hugo had made himself crystal clear. His orders were to kill her if she touched her magic again. Dropping her eyes was the only way to hide the sting of his betrayal. Trembling, the soles of her feet brushed on the rug as she shuffled backwards—away from him. Feeling small and vulnerable, her fingers twisted against her robe, pulling it tightly around her body until, dissatisfied, she folded her arms protectively over her chest.

Her breathing hitched and sped up. She had been so stupid believing there had been any connection between them; Hugo belonged only to the Queen. He may have planned this all along. He may have saved her, only to trap her in the court of an immortal who killed people possessing magic.

The walls of the room pressed in on her—there had to be a way out of here.... Her mind raced. She would *find* a way, somehow she would get away. Panting, small panicked breaths, she fixed her eyes on a pulled thread in the soft rug under her feet. Lightheaded now, her lips began to tingle madly. Failure to control her fright always rendered her useless, and now there was no one to help her.

Breathe. In...out...in... out, she told herself, remembering her father's calm voice as he taught her how to control her panic attacks.

Hugo clenched his jaw and squeezed his fists tight until his knuckles turned white. The Queen's guard was fighting a private war with his oath of duty and the overwhelming need to explain himself to the girl cowering from him. Never before had she seemed frightened of him.

Diamond felt him suddenly reach out with his magic. Warmth caressed her skin, his boots silent on the rug as he took a step closer. Lifting her chin defiantly, she beat back her tears and took a slow deep breath, trying to regain her equilibrium.

"Diamond, I would never...."

Before Hugo could finish his hesitant words, the solid oak door to her room was thrown wide, smashing into the wall. A shower of dust exploded into the air. Two heavily armed Queen's guards marched in, their hard faces intent and predatory. In unison they focused on Diamond.

Chapter Twenty-Nine

Squealing, she spun on her heel and darted for the bathing room. At least she could lock herself in there. Light glinted off a blade as the first guard pulled a dagger and lunged, grabbing for her.

The second guard immediately spun between her and Hugo, his sword angled and defensive as he faced the larger warrior. Still shaky and weak as a baby, Diamond didn't stand a chance of escape. Rough fingers clenched a handful of material on the back of her robe and yanked her to a halt. The cotton ripped until she was cruelly exposed from her neck right down to her buttocks. An instant later an iron hard arm wrapped around her throat.

Terrified, she fought and twisted and screamed but the guard kicked the back of her legs so hard numbness shot down to her feet. Collapsing in a heap on her knees, all it took was a swift slam of his boot in her back and she fell face first into the rug. The impact knocked her senseless. Before she could comprehend the speed of her capture, that same boot kicked her hard in the ribs. She bleated in agony as at least one rib fractured. In a heartbeat her captor was crushing the back of her neck with his foot, pushing her face into the floor. She couldn't breathe couldn't breathe couldn't breathe....

Panting in shallow gasping breaths her world focused only on getting air into her lungs.

"What are you doing?"

Diamond had never been more relieved to hear Hugo's deep bass voice. It resonated through her panicked brain, as cold and icy calm as she had ever heard it. She tried to cry out to him, but her voice was just a pathetic whimper. He wouldn't let them hurt her—she didn't think.

"The Queen ordered us to take this filthy magic wielder to the dungeons," said the other guard's voice, equally ruthless.

"Then I will take her. She is my prisoner, under my control." Hugo's tone was superior and laced with the promise of violence.

Metal chinked. A heavy footfall...then another.

"Really, commander? And can you control her...or yourself? I very much doubt that," the voice sneered, full of loathing. "That's why she sent us, isn't it? The Queen's magic-wielding dog was let off his leash long enough to find a mongrel bitch of his own to play with. When will you learn, *commander*, that the only female you are allowed to covet is your Queen? Bed as many whores as you want. Force them to stare at that ugly face whilst you rut upon them, but don't you remember? Even the Queen's pet cannot get away with actually caring for one. Maybe this time when our mistress unleashes the Lord Commander on you both, I will get to hear her—and you scream—get to watch as he—"

Diamond flinched at the sound of breaking bone. Summoning up the energy and courage to struggle against the weight on her neck, she wrenched her head around just as a limp body crashed to the floor beside her. Through her foggy vision she could see the guard's off kilter jaw and bloody, broken nose. It was impossible to feel sorry for him; she felt only a fierce satisfaction that Hugo had got rid of one of her attackers.

"Let her up, Attion—now," Hugo ordered the remaining guard.

There was a pause whilst her captor considered his options. Clearly he didn't fancy his odds, and Diamond couldn't prevent a sob as the weight of the guard's foot lifted off her neck. Before her brain could process her ability to move again, rough hands shoved under her arm pits and hoisted her to her feet. Dishevelled and in pain, Diamond was spun around to face Hugo. Wincing she stooped forward to hold an arm across her cracked ribs, the torn material of her robe flapping open, exposing her back down to the curve of her buttocks. Hugo did not even glance her way, although Diamond could feel his magic pushing against her, wild and raging. The weight of his gaze remained fixed on the guard, wholly black and as cold as death. His eyelids did not so much as flicker.

"You disgrace that uniform," Attion spat, ignoring the groans of his fallen comrade. "This creature is nothing but dirt under your boot. Her blood is sullied—*mixed*," he jeered, "and you attack your own brother for her? Your actions are treasonous. She deserves less than a clean death at our gracious Queen's hands."

"Do not speak anymore," Hugo warned, his voice icy. "You do not have leave to attack any prisoner without express orders from Lord Commander Ream or the Queen. Did you receive orders to beat—or kill—the girl?"

The other guard pursed his lips, his nostrils flaring in defiance.

"I didn't think so. Give her to me. I will take her to the dungeons myself."

"No. My orders are to—"

"And I am your superior," Hugo growled, his dark eyes flashing dangerously. "Release her now and I will let you chase my shadow down to the dungeons like the rat you are."

Hugo's hand shot out faster than Diamond's eyes could follow. The guard seemed stunned, his mouth dropping open and his eyes popping wide as huge fingers curled around his throat, crushing his wind pipe. "She maybe a filthy magic wielder," Hugo snarled, "but if you lay a finger on her again, I will rip out your throat and watch as you choke on your own blood."

He shoved his face right into the other fae's, his voice low and menacing. "You were there all those years ago.... You watched him torture Tawne. Do not make the mistake of thinking I have forgotten, Attion," he drawled the fae's name with such venom Diamond cringed away.

The guard's lip curled in contempt, though he paled significantly. "You are a fool, Hugo. Our Lord Commander will delight in punishing you—and her—for this. Just give her to me," he wheezed, unable to talk properly with Hugo's fingers wrapped around his neck. "I will see she gets to the dungeons alive."

Fear encased Diamond's heart. *Alive? Is there a chance one of these guards will kill me? Oh, gods, I am in such deep trouble. And what did he mean Hugo would be punished for helping me?* Even in her dazed state, she knew Hugo had attacked these fae out of fear for her; if she knew why he had attacked his brothers, so would his Queen. She didn't understand why he would put himself at such risk.

Anguished and confused, she stared at the ice in Hugo's eyes. Cold air brushed over the bare skin of her back. She shivered violently. Attion and Hugo had both seen she was naked beneath her robe. Black eyes flickered her way. Humiliated at her helplessness and vulnerability, she dropped her gaze.

"I expect that to be so," Hugo replied, unfazed by Attion's words. "Our Lord Commander can torment me at his leisure, just like he does the rest of you, but the difference between us, Attion, is that the cruel bastard cannot kill me, no matter how much he wants to. I am after all, the Queen's dog. So.... Let. Her. Go," he enunciated each of those last words very carefully.

"No. Do not," countermanded a chilling female voice from the doorway.

The despair of a million painful deaths raced through Diamond, stopping her heart for the merest moment. It was as if all those poor lost souls screamed out for help with one gigantic voice. Diamond closed her ears and walled off her mind, grabbing on to the only thing that seemed to hold her steady. Hugo. But his magic was suddenly hidden by a vast and oppressive darkness that rippled around Diamond, stealing her breath.

"This disgusting creature should be grovelling on her belly in my presence, defiled as she is by the goddess' magic. Her ghastly pale looks ridicule the darkness of our true lord. I do not wish to look on her repulsive face any longer. Guard Sarou." Attion's name was a command.

Diamond knew it and went lax as Attion grabbed her wrist. In a second she was flipped face down on the floor with his knee on her naked back.

Chapter Thirty

The swish of silken material eddied around the room as the Queen of Avalonia stepped closer to her commander.

"I sent these men to arrest this magic wielder, Commander Casimir. Tell me, why are you here—again? You gave me your report and it was duly noted you excelled in your duties by keeping her alive for my use. But do not think that my gratitude extends enough to protect you from punishment if you return to this vile creature again without my permission."

A soft bump vibrated the floor. Hugo knelt before his Queen his head lowered in subservience.

"Of course, Your Majesty," he answered, his voice impassive, holding no hint of the aggression or anger he had shown Attion.

Diamond held her breath, as frightened for Hugo as she was for herself. He should not have helped her; it had been foolish to return to her room at all, even if he had only intended to warn her not to try and run.

"So tell me, commander, why did you return?" The Queen's voice held ice and steel.

"My Queen. I came to inform the *magic wielder* she is now your prisoner, and if she wishes to live, she must prepare herself for a life of repentance in whatever way Your Majesty sees fit."

Hugo sounded so sincere, his voice holding enough disgust Diamond wondered if she had imagined him ever calling her magic a gift. The pause following his words seemed to go on forever. Diamond tried not to whimper as her spine and ribs screeched in pain. The metal shin guards Attion wore dug deep into her skin as he shifted his weight.

Finally the ancient Queen spoke. "Indeed. Well, you have illustrated your...unwavering adherence to my rules once again, commander. As I heard you point out, I did not expressly order these guards to harm my prisoner, merely apprehend her. I wish time to consider what to do with a half-blood who contains enough vulgar magic in her veins to flatten a forest. And it seems you do, as always, have my best interests at heart."

The Queen's attention shifted to Diamond's naked back. The weight of that ancient gaze had Diamond trembling under Attion's bulk.

"You will attend me in my chambers and more fully explain your actions against your brothers, Commander Casimir." Her voice became contemplative. "But even I am beginning to think this half-blood may be very, very useful to me after all," she mused.

There was another pause as the Queen turned to consider Hugo. Diamond's shoulder screamed in pain along with her ribs as Attion shifted his considerable weight against the arm he had wedged up against her spine. Shame and horror filled her in equal measure when his fingers brushed lightly down the curve of her ribs and waist. She realised no one else was paying her any attention. It was impossible to cry out or fight pinned to the floor as she was. Relief flooded her limbs when he snatched his hand back.

The Queen spoke again, her voice thoughtful, though still icy. "For now the girl may stay in these quarters and enjoy the hospitality of my palace—which she *will not* leave. You will ensure she has two experienced guards at all times. They will report back to you, Commander Casimir. You are now her gaoler. Ensure she is healed well enough to attend dinner this evening. I want my court to see the benevolence of their Queen toward such a creature. It will please some and confuse, if not anger, others," the Queen stated with a satisfied smirk. Silk rustled and the oppressive atmosphere lifted as the immortal glided from the room.

Attion lifted his weight from her back but Diamond could not get up. Agony grated along her ribs as she slowly rolled onto her side, hugging her knees and warily watched Attion heave the other guard to his feet and drag him from the room.

Chapter Thirty-One

Silence settled.

Hugo stared at the doorway, eyes narrowed and head cocked to one side. Diamond could not, dared not, move. Her body began to shake uncontrollably. All her father's stories suddenly made sense. The small brass carriage clock ticked away the minutes.

Eventually Hugo deemed it safe to close the door. A metallic lock clicked into place. Quickly he returned to her side, dropping to his haunches. "Diamond? Oh gods. I am so sorry. I didn't want this.... I never should have brought you here, but you—"

"No. You shouldn't!" she spat. "But you did. You are one of her men. You knew what she would do to me."

He looked at her hopelessly, his mouth opening and closing like he wanted to say something, but the words would not come out.

"Why?" she whispered again, tears running down her cheeks. "Why didn't you leave me in the forest? At least there I stood a chance of surviving."

Magic tingled along her skin, seeking to soothe. "I—"

A banging on the door stopped him from answering and he withdrew instantly.

"Miss? Let me in. Are you alright?" Rose anxiously cried.

"Let her in, Hugo," ground out Diamond. She didn't want anyone else to see her like this, but Rose was the only one who could help her now. Agony burst across her ribs with each shuddering breath she took.

Hugo nodded curtly, his face shutting down completely. Diamond found she did not care. Striding to the door he unlocked it and yanked it open.

"The Queen wants her healed enough to attend dinner this evening. This is your responsibility, Rose. Do not let me down," he snarled, leaning into Rose before she got more than two steps through the door.

Diamond wanted to defend her new friend, who paled and stared up at Hugo with wide, frightened eyes. Diamond curled her fists, wanting to punch that snarl off his face. "Leave her alone!" Diamond barked.

The poor healer blanched even further as she took in Diamond's ripped robe and curled up posture on the floor.

"Your guards will station themselves outside this door," Hugo informed Diamond curtly, his eyes narrowed as he looked at her window. "Do not try and run. There will be guards outside too. Rose, make sure she is dressed suitably for dinner. I will return to escort you to the dining hall."

"I am not going to eat with you and that-that—"

"Careful, Diamond. She is still my Queen. For reasons that are beyond me she has allowed you, a magic wielder and a half-blood, to live and enjoy the hospitality of the palace. Do not force my hand. Contrary to your belief, I don't want to have to throw you in the dungeons—or kill you," he said, staring down at her.

"Surely as a filthy, magic wielding, mongrel bitch, I should just eat in my room and not taint the pure blooded in this palace," she hissed, humiliated and hurt by the names he and the other guards had used.

Hugo's face was impassive, his tone unyielding. "No. Dinner is served in the great hall at seven every evening. The Queen will attend with Jack, and clearly she wants you there too. Do not make the mistake of thinking it was anything other than an order," he warned.

Diamond tried to sit up but couldn't. Her eyes burned with unshed tears and only gritting her teeth stopped her from crying out. Rose immediately ran to help her but Hugo reached her first.

"Don't touch me."

He just scowled and hoisted her up into his arms. Ignoring her protest he carried her to the bed and, with complete and utter gentleness, placed her down. That care nearly tipped her over the edge, but she held her tongue, more confused than ever by his contradictory behaviour.

"Rose will find a way to heal you, and I will return at six forty-five to escort you to the dining hall," he informed her.

Diamond's shoulders slumped. There was no way out of it. Fear shuddered down her spine. This could either be a dinner or just an opportunity to heap public humiliation on her in front of people who clearly abhorred magic. *But Jack will be there,* she reasoned, hope flaring in her heart. Maybe he or General Edo would help her escape this nightmare.

Hugo's eyebrows drew together into a frown. "You will be sitting with me. Not with Jack," he said coldly.

Diamond tried to hide her dismay and shock. *Can he tell what I'm thinking?*

"And don't try to access your magic. If you so much as touch it, I will know. I have discretion with my orders, so please don't force me to violence. Neither you nor Rose will tell anyone else why you have these guards—or what happened here today." Menacingly he took a step closer, then slowly and deliberately looked around. "This is a nice room. If I feel I can't trust you," he turned his attention to Rose, "...or *your* loyalty is put in to question, the palace dungeons will become your quarters—for both of you. It's not a nice place to be—dark, reeking cells full of murderers and traitors. Think about it." With that, Hugo turned and strode out of the room, slamming the door without a backward glance.

Rose watched him leave then stared at Diamond. After a few moments she pressed her lips into a tight line, becoming the efficient healer once again.

"Right. Stay there, and don't move until I get back. The only thing that will heal your rib in such a short space of time is an Acolyte potion."

"A what?" rasped Diamond, confused, sick to her very core and ready to pass out.

"The Acolytes are healers...magical healers. They are the only ones in this city allowed to openly use magic. They are religious zealots who worship the Lord of Chaos."

Diamond shuddered. "I thought the Queen killed all magic wielders."

"Oh, she does...unless she wants something from them." The words lay heavy between them, but Diamond wasn't thinking of herself, she was thinking of Hugo. Rose wrinkled her nose and continued. "They are chosen and brought here as children—like the Queen's guards. Kids mostly don't know how to hide their magic, or even that they should. Sometimes they are dumped at the palace gates, or their own parents report them to the city guard. Fancy your own parents willingly handing you over to such a life—disgusting!" she uttered. "I normally avoid the Acolytes; they have their own section of the healers' wing, and for years have been using the main temple in the city. Their Prevost answers only to the Queen and Isla Norr. Most of the acolytes are power hungry and cruel and abuse their positions. But I know one that will help us. He will have a potion that will work. I'll be back as soon as I can."

Before Diamond could tell her not to go, Rose practically ran from the room. Silence settled around Diamond like a heavy blanket. She released a shuddering breath as she wondered what the immortal monarch wanted with her. Whatever it was would be horrible and likely painful. Rubbing her side did not erase the feeling of Attion's unwelcome touch nor prevent fear skittering down her spine at the thought of ending up in some dark, damp, stinking dungeon.

As familiar as her heartbeat, the tingle of a panic attack crept from the tips of her fingers up her arms and across every part of her body. Gasping, the walls began closing in, crushing her. *Breathe, breathe,* she told herself over and over, trying to expand her lungs against the pain of her cracked rib. *In...out....* Remembering her father's calm voice was bittersweet but it helped.

Rose returned about half an hour later but did not comment on Diamond's pale face or shaking hands. For a while Diamond did not even notice she was back. Her concentration was utterly focused on keeping her hands still and her breathing steady. Her father had often reassured her she would grow out of her attacks, and she had not had one in the months leading up to his death. Now, since her life had gone to the rats, they were out of control—just like her life.

Diamond had lost any sense of power over her destiny. With cold hands she gripped the folds of her robe. She had to start mastering her emotions again. She had to. Otherwise she would not endure whatever the Queen had in mind for her.

Rose clasped a small bottle between her finger and thumb and held it out. Inside swirled a thick green slime that seemed to pop and bubble like it was alive. A small tendril of grey vapour curled from the bottle neck. Diamond wrinkled her nose as the smell of stagnant water and something vile wafted by.

"What in the name of Erebos is that?" she asked in disgust.

"The foul tincture of a petrified fire toad, but—" Rose added quickly at the look on Diamond's face, "it will heal your bones in an hour—so come on, just take it."

"Is it safe? It looks like it might grow legs and wriggle around my insides," Diamond muttered warily.

Rose snorted. "No, it won't grow legs, but if the toad hadn't been petrified by the Acolyte, a pin prick of its slime would poison you. Your eyes, your nose and your mouth would leak blood until you choked. So chop, chop, bottoms up and all that." The healer grinned and put her hands on her hips in a threatening manner.

Diamond grimaced and tipped the slime into her mouth. It fizzled and popped as she swallowed.

"Urgh! That's worse than the mouldy yellow berries I had to eat in the forest," she grumbled.

Rose thrust a glass of water at her and made Diamond drink that as well. That done, Rose found Diamond another robe then lay next to her on the bed and held her hand.

"This is going to hurt," she warned.

The healer wasn't wrong. Diamond panted and sobbed through the next few hours. Rose stalwartly held her, comforting her with murmurs and gentle touches. In turn Diamond gripped onto her new friend like an anchor, lost within a whirlwind of anxiety and pain. Eventually, with Rose's calming touch and soothing words, Diamond settled. As the hours passed, the pain in her ribs dulled to an ache. Exhausted she fell into an unsettled sleep until Rose gently shook her to say she had to leave for her other duties.

"The guards were already outside when I came back earlier," Rose informed Diamond quietly. "I don't know what the Queen wants from you, but I'll do what I can to help you."

Diamond tried and failed to swallow the lump in her throat at the sincerity of Rose's words. A single tear rolled down her cheek. "Thank you, Rose. But you have already helped me enough," she said wiping it away. "I don't want you to get in to trouble because of me," she said softly.

But Rose just gave a small smile. "Try and rest some more. I'll be back later and we'll get you sorted for this dinner."

Diamond got up and listlessly sat by the open window watching people meander around the immaculate gardens. Around lunchtime, one of her guards opened her door. She shrank back against the wall as he stepped in to watch a maid bring in a tray of food. The older woman didn't even try and hide the disgust on her face as she banged the tray down on the nearest surface before walking out without a word.

Diamond wondered if everyone she met from now on would hate and fear her. Diamond's fingers found her throat as her breathing hitched. Anxiously she grasped her necklace. Tonight was going be truly awful. Not hungry in the least bit but determined to build her strength back up, Diamond hobbled to the tray. The food was surprisingly high quality—for a prisoner. Fresh bread, cheese and chicken. It was delicious but Diamond couldn't force much down. Her stomach was no longer used to large amounts of food, and coupled with the fear gnawing at her belly, she began to feel queasy after a few mouthfuls. Pushing the tray aside she went back to her vigil on the window seat.

In the middle of the gardens a large fountain spouted from the stone figure of a woman in a long flowing dress. The water's tinkling tune soothed her frayed nerves. Diamond closed her eyes and inhaled the subtle scent of roses. Soon her exhaustion tugged her into a deep sleep.

Chapter Thirty-Two

Diamond nearly fell off the window seat when Rose came bustling back in. Following closely on her heels was a maid with dark blonde hair and gentle blue eyes.

Outside, long shadows crawled over the fountain goddess, swathing her in a cloak of darkness. Diamond shivered at the sight despite the warmth in the air. Above the palace the late summer sky burned with fire. It was hard not to feel humbled by such an amazing sight, a true reflection of the power of the goddess. In the background the little carriage clock chimed telling her it was five-thirty.

"This is Kitty," Rose informed Diamond, sitting down next to her, poised and with her back straight. Her eyes were sharp as she met Diamond's. "She will be your maid from now on. Her duties include ensuring your room is clean and tidy and helping you with your personal care if you need it. We have...err...mutual friends outside the palace. You can trust Kitty. If you need me she will find me...day or night, do you understand?" Her voice was heavy with meaning. The healer got up and nodded to Kitty who was carrying something in her arms.

Kitty smiled a friendly, "Hello." Then she pulled off the cotton cover to reveal a beautifully embroidered pale blue dress. The fabric was soft and so light it floated through the air as if disturbed by an invisible breeze. The white flower embroidery and tiny crystals were so delicate they did not weigh the material down, only twinkled like raindrops in sunlight as it moved. For Diamond it was hard to tear her eyes off such a beautiful thing. There were other items of clothing too, including a blue shawl, silk undergarments, a boned corset and pretty shoes that matched the dress.

Diamond gasped and immediately blushed at the sight of the undergarments, which were far more expensive and sensual than any she had ever seen, let alone owned. "Goodness! Where are all these from?" she asked incredulously.

Rose smiled broadly, a proper smile that lit her face and warmed her brown eyes to melted chocolate. "It seems you have a benefactor. This was delivered from Malloy and Son." She rolled her eyes. "That has to be *the* most exclusive boutique in the city. There were instructions for all of this to be delivered to you so that you can wear the dress for dinner tonight. Whoever it is also sent these."

She gestured to the other items a breathless-looking older man carried into the room and unceremoniously dumped on the bed. He left without a word. There were clothes boxes and parcels, boots and a new thick black cloak. Smaller paper wrapped packages sat among the pile. One had a red satin bow. Rose picked it up and peered at the label.

"This one says 'for this evening' on it," she told Diamond, holding it out expectantly.

Diamond took it. With shaking fingers she undid the bow and pulled off the packaging. Inside a small grey box sat a hair comb. It was a stunning piece of intricately formed silver. Vines and flowers inlaid with glittering amethysts. Diamond had never seen anything like it.

"Wow!" muttered Kitty and Rose in unison.

"By the goddess' good graces! Who would do such a thing?" blurted Diamond, completely baffled as she tried to think who it could be. With shaking fingers she peeped inside another paper package to find hair pins and cosmetics.

Rose shrugged, then grinned. "I have no idea, but after what happened earlier we aren't going to worry about that. What we *are* going to do is make you the prettiest girl in that dining hall tonight, if only to stick one very large middle finger up at the Queen...oh, and every other small-minded imbecile in her court."

Despite all her fears, Diamond couldn't help but give a wry smile. Oh, how she would love to arrive poised and beautiful like a true court lady and not cowering like a dirty half-blood peasant to be stared at and cursed. Carefully Diamond reached out and touched the soft material of the dress.

"I've never owned such beautiful things before...." she whispered reverently.

Rose gave a snort of disbelief. "Sorry, but I can't believe someone who looks like you has never worn a pretty dress before, even if you haven't had such expensive jewellery."

Diamond flushed, embarrassed. "Well, I haven't," she countered, a little defensively. "My father never had the money to spend on things like pretty dresses. Our clothes were for wearing and working in, not partying...." her voice petered out as she thought of her home and her father.

Rose beamed. "Well, at least getting ready and wearing this gorgeous dress will be fun, then maybe one day we can go shopping together. This is the finest city in Avalonia, after all."

"That would be lovely, Rose. Maybe one day we will."

Their eyes met and both girls forced a smile knowing that day was unlikely to come, but it was a nice thought nevertheless. Rose continued in a firm voice, "There are shops here that sell the most exquisite clothes. Traders come from as far away as Gar Anon to sell their wares. There are even rare silks brought thousands of miles along the silk road from the Sky Desert."

A shadow crossed her face. "Or at least there are sometimes. Things are a little scarcer now."

"Because of the war?" Diamond asked quietly.

"Yes, partly, and because the seas are becoming rougher with the beginning of the winter storms. Only sea captains with magic can navigate them. And as you can imagine, only those who are extremely brave or very stupid come here with magic. Besides the ice moon is unusually low, lower than it has been for years. Some of the Acolyte's have been proclaiming it is the curse of the goddess; that she will bring the wrath of the ice moon down upon us all for forsaking her. I think that's just scare mongering and nonsense. The goddess would never harm her people. And there are others in this city who feel the same." Rose dropped her voice and glanced at the door. "We believe it is the Lord of Chaos who will unleash his wrath, not the goddess." She moved in so that she could whisper in Diamond's ear. "Do you know of the story of Erebos and Lunaria?"

Diamond shrugged and shook her head. "Only what I've read in history books."

"Well, it is a long tale, too long to recount, right now. But I will speak as we brush your hair." Rose led Diamond to the dressing table and indicated for her to sit on a stool. She picked up the silver hairbrush, running it gently through the length of Diamond's locks.

"This world was not the only thing created with magic. Lunaria was a child of the gods and was herself created with magic, like their other children. As the children learned to wield their own magic they created many wondrous things: the stars, the moon, the sun, and the darkness of time and space in which to put them. As their powers grew they created vast new worlds; but Erebos did not care for these worlds of sunlight and souls that Lunaria and his sisters made, he wanted darkness and anarchy. As they created, so he destroyed. Lunaria and her three sisters: Alethia, the Goddess of Truth; Amnousia, the Goddess of Vengeance and Nuava, the Goddess of Love, fought for our world, one they had created together from magic. Eventually the other goddesses became tired of war and left Lunaria to fight Erebos and his armies alone. It did not end well for either of them. To protect those she loved, Lunaria sacrificed herself to her brother, and Erebos has not been seen in the flesh since he smote her down." Rose hesitated and glanced at Kitty. "I understand there is much more to this story but I have never been allowed to hear it."

"Why not?" asked Diamond, enthralled.

"Because it is a sacred story that is protected by my friends. All I can tell you is that there is a scroll. The Veritas scroll. It is an enchanted parchment written in the blood of Alethia. When Lunaria was killed by Erebos, Alethia returned from Eternity. In an attempt to preserve information that might help save our world if Erebos should somehow return, she transcribed the vision of Krato, the high ruler of the guardians of the gods. The Scroll of Truth cannot be destroyed by anyone other than a child of the gods or a god himself, but the Queen has it, and has banned any but her guards from seeing it for over a thousand years."

"Then how do you know about it?" Diamond quipped, raising her eyebrows cynically.

"Very funny," smiled Rose. "My friends have a copy—of sorts."

"No offense, Rose, but what has that got to do with me?" Diamond was getting agitated now. Time was ticking away, and Hugo would return for her soon.

"Because it says when Erebos finds a magic wielder, a vassal, strong enough to contain his magic, he will return...to the ruin of us all, and that only the blood of the goddess can stop him."

The reverence in Rose's voice sent shivers down Diamond's spine. For a moment all three girls were quiet.

"But no one thinks that's me, right? She doesn't think I'm a vassal for a dark god—does she? I come from the north. I'm half fae and half human—I'm nothing special...." Diamond swallowed, "I'm not strong enough to be a threat to anyone," she whispered.

"Oh, she doesn't want to destroy the vassal. You have to remember that she worships Erebos and has spent the last thousand years brainwashing the weak, sycophantic minds of many of her people into worshiping him too. No, the problem is once the vassal has been found, the Queen is powerful enough to bring Erebos back to this world."

Diamond froze as voices echoed through her bedroom door. Rose pulled away, her head cocked. After a moment all became quiet. A guard change.

"But as you say you don't exactly seem the type for the Lord of Shadow to covet. Still, don't let on you know about that scroll—to anyone. The knowledge might get you killed. Right. Let us forget that story for now and get you ready for dinner. If you are to stick one in the eye of our illustrious Queen tonight, you must look your best."

"Must I? She might throw me in the dungeons or execute me for daring to look nice," Diamond muttered, taking Rose's cue to change the subject.

"I doubt she'll throw you in the dungeons," said Rose, grimacing. "She could have done that earlier. No, she wants something else and to get it, I think she needs you whole and healthy—for now at least. Come on, I want to make sure you rival her perfect beauty, then we can show that idiot of a commander what he's missing!"

Diamond felt her cheeks heat at that comment but held her tongue.

"Kitty's an absolute genius at this. Let's get started," Rose said, taking charge and ordering Diamond to stand and take off her robe.

Diamond kept her face blank as they dressed her, embarrassed beyond measure at being helped into her underwear and the tightly fitting, blue boned corset. She briefly felt a jolt of unease that her benefactor knew her size so well. But then Kitty slipped the dress over her head, and she forgot to worry about that.

Diamond gasped. It was beautiful. The delicate material caressed her bare skin like a warm summer breeze, floating in gossamer folds around her legs and ankles. Thankfully the bodice and three-quarter length sleeves covered most of her bruises. Kitty pulled the laces tight down the back, accentuating Diamond's small breasts and the tiny curve of her waist. Diamond balked, trying not to pay attention to her lack of curves. *So much for rivalling the voluptuous Queen*, she thought bitterly.

"Ouch," she muttered as Kitty yanked and pulled, before fastening the laces in a bow. Her newly-healed rib protested but Diamond completely forgot about her discomfort when she looked in the dressing table mirror. Her hands shook as she ran them reverently down the dress. She had never dreamed of owning, or ever wearing, a dress like this.

Nerves roiled in her stomach. Diamond's experience of large gatherings was limited to town hall festivities in Berriesford, not a banquet hall in a palace surrounded by lords and ladies; these people who would be staring at her, hating her for what she was and the magic in her blood. She lifted her chin. She would walk in that room at Hugo's side, with her head held high; she would not cower from the mighty Queen or anyone else—no matter what they did to her.

Kitty plaited and wound her hair into a pattern of beautiful swirls at the back of her head, leaving some to hang in waves down her back. The quiet maid adroitly fixed the stunning hair comb among a nest of silver curls. It glittered prettily as Diamond moved her head.

"Well, I suppose you deserve to preen a bit. You look incredible." Rose laughed as she laid out an array of kohl, powders and lip rouge.

At a blank look from Diamond, Kitty smiled. "Would you like some help with this too?" she asked gently, her soft blue eyes twinkling.

Diamond nodded gratefully. "Yes, please. I've never worn cosmetics before."

"Of course. Here, let me show you." Kitty artfully covered Diamond's bruises with cream and powder until they were virtually invisible, then went to work on her eyes.

When she had finished, Diamond slipped on the low-heeled satin shoes and surveyed herself in the full length mirror. Her jaw dropped. This wasn't the same person she had seen earlier that day. Despite being far too thin, she actually looked pretty. She beamed at Rose and Kitty, who smiled back.

"Well," said Rose with a satisfied smile. "You will certainly rival Her Majesty. You look stunning."

Diamond blushed as a loud knock resounded on the bedroom door.

Chapter Thirty-Three

Hugo went still and gaped wide-eyed. A strange kind of elation filled Diamond at his unguarded expression, but her confidence and pleasure were short lived. Snapping his jaw shut, his face became unreadable. At his withdrawal, her elation crashed in splinters around her.

All Hugo said was, "Good, you're ready. Let's go."

Clearly cross, Rose thrust her hands on her hips and frowned. He stubbornly ignored her stare. Deflated and confused by the ache in her chest, Diamond couldn't meet the sympathetic eyes of her new friends. Quickly bidding Rose and Kitty a good night, she followed Hugo out of the heavy wooden door into the dimly lit stone-flagged corridor. Feeling suddenly silly in her pretty dress, Diamond scowled at his back. She shouldn't have expected any reaction other than indifference from him.

Expected? No. Hoped? Yes.

Tears stung her eyes. Oblivious, Hugo marched in front.

Two Queen's guards flanked them. It was an alarming experience having ruthless killers at her back and Hugo ahead. Walking swiftly, he led her up staircases and down corridors until she was dizzy. Utterly lost, she tried to match his long stride. He did not look at her again, just strode on ahead expecting her to keep up. After days of inactivity and weeks of starvation, Diamond's heart began to race uncomfortably; by the time they reached the more illuminated part of the palace and music reached her ears, she was breathing heavily and shaking with fatigue.

"Hugo. Please. Slow down," she panted, a sheen of sweat covering her brow. "I need to rest."

Hugo turned and nodded to the guards at her back. They stepped back, watching her like hawks. Diamond leaned against the wall, trying not to throw up. Hugo's shadow loomed in her peripheral vision, but asking him for help was out of the question. Clearly he had dropped any pretence of caring about her. Pursing her lips she deliberately avoided his continual regard.

"Here," he said eventually, holding out his arm to her. "Let me help you."

"No," she ground out between clenched teeth. Glaring defiantly at him she pushed herself off the wall. "It's clear where your loyalties lie, *commander*. I don't need your help."

"Diamond—please, just take my arm." His voice sounded softer now, his eyes concerned.

"No. You've made it very clear you don't give a shit about me, Hugo," she spat bitterly. "I am nothing to you, even after everything we've been through," she replied, swallowing her tears, and lifting her chin.

His hand reached out. "Diamond...."

"Well, who do we have here?" interrupted a voice from behind her.

Diamond's stomach flipped. "Jack!" she breathed in a rush of air.

So happy to see him—to see anyone other than Hugo—she ran to him, ignoring the glares of her gaolers. Jack's guards stiffened but he just waved a hand at them and they stood back.

"Hey!" he laughed, opening his arms as she almost bowled him over.

Diamond wanted to cry with relief. He looked so handsome, so strong and actually happy to see her. He was an anchor in a world spinning with unknowns and fear.

Disentangling himself from her desperate grip, he held her at arm's length. His twinkling brown eyes inspected her thoroughly, his gaze roaming down to her satin-clad feet, back up over the length of her twinkling gossamer dress. Heat radiated from her cheeks by the time he'd finished his inspection.

"You look—wow." Jack shrugged as if at a loss for words. "Stunning." He held her hands gently. "And so much better than you did this morning. You really worried us there for a while."

"Sorry," she smiled sheepishly. It was ridiculous in the circumstances but Jack's compliments made her glow inside.

Hugo's face was thunderous. *'Do not tell him of the Queen,'* his gaze snapped in no uncertain terms.

"And as much as I would happily stand here all night and hold you, we have to go in that room for dinner. So? Shall we?" Jack said, placing her hand in the crook of his elbow.

"Err...." Diamond looked nervously at Hugo. Dark eyes glittered in a face that resembled carved granite.

"Oh, Hugo won't mind if I steal you away for a while—will you Hugo?" Jack drawled, winking at the Queen's guard, but Diamond did not miss the challenge lacing his words. Something passed between the prince and the Queen's guard in that moment, but Diamond did not care.

Not daring to look in Hugo's direction, she clung to Jack's arm as they approached the giant double doors of the dining hall. Two smartly dressed servants pushed the heavily carved doors open.

Diamond stared in awe. On each gilt door a green and red sea serpent coiled through a breaking silver wave, staring fiercely at whoever dared approach. The servants bowed low to Jack and stayed low until Hugo passed them.

Jack turned his head and smiled down at her, his eyes reflecting the glimmering light from the chandeliers that hung from the vaulted ceiling. Her fingers gripped his silk-covered arm nervously.

"Don't worry. You'll be fine," he reassured her, completely unaware of her predicament as he patted her hand. "Come. There are some people here who are desperate to see you," he said, watching with amusement as General Edo spotted them and strode down the hall.

Diamond gaped. The general wore ornate metal and leather armour emblazoned with a dragon. Jack's sigil. His jaw was clean shaven and his wings glinted impressively. He was like a force of nature approaching, and she couldn't help but smile. The general's grey eyes widened as he took in her appearance, but he greeted his prince first, bowing smartly to Jack.

"Good evening, Highness. Our seats on the dais are ready when you are."

When the general turned his attention back to Diamond, she was a little surprised by his reserve. He did not kiss her or hold her; she was not a child anymore, she reasoned.

"Well, young lady, I see you are recovered. That is good—we all thought you might die," he said with an edge to his voice that caused Jack to frown.

"Err, thank you—unc—I mean, general," she replied and smiled at him. "The healers have been amazing. And it's good to see you looking so well too. Your new armour is very impressive. You look nothing like the man I knew who lived in the woods."

"Indeed. Well, that is how it should be now that I have re-joined Prince Oden," he answered with a tight smile.

Maybe he is just tired or worried, she reasoned, confused and hurt by his aloofness. She tried again. "And I'm so glad to see you unharmed. I wondered if you had made it...." her voice petered out, distress stealing her voice.

Jack smiled understandingly and patted her hand but the general turned his head away. "We did—all of us, because of you." Jack was obviously trying to reassure her, but his eyes narrowed slightly at his new general.

Diamond wasn't entirely convinced they had survived because of her, more likely in spite of her. She knew her magic had killed Ragor's soldiers but she had no idea what had happened after that. All she could remember was Hugo's eyes as she had burned him. *Did I really ask him to kill me?* Her head throbbed. It was all so hazy.

Jack gave her a bright smile, so she fought her anxiety. He was studying her intently, like he often had in the forest.

"Do you know what happened to Tom?" she coughed, clearing her throat uncomfortably.

"Who me?" chimed a familiar voice from behind.

She whipped her head around and exclaimed with relief. Tom looked pale but otherwise healthy. As she chatted and caught up with her friend, she did her best to ignore the threat hanging over her head and the staring, hateful faces that followed her progress around the room. Needing the support of someone, Diamond clutched tightly to the arm of the mortal prince.

Chapter Thirty-Four

Hugo was having difficulty keeping his face blank. Diamond was holding onto Jack's arm like it was a lifeline. *What is Jack doing?*

Any pretty, well-bred girl in this room would fall at his feet; there was no need to heap such attention on Diamond. Hugo's chest tightened as Diamond glanced at him fearfully. Being who and what he was often shamed Hugo, but he always hid it, always pushed it away. This time he couldn't. The remorse and guilt he felt at biting her—at bringing her here—was breaking him in two.

Stifling a sigh he stood back against the wall, watching as her guards scanned the room. They were standing a respectful distance away but close enough to stop her if she somehow became a threat. Hugo's teeth clenched and unclenched, his scar twisting enough to garner glances from those nearby. For a moment he distracted himself by staring at them until the overdressed fools nearly pissed their breeches and scurried away.

He quickly found the two Queen's guards again. They hadn't moved. His shoulders relaxed minutely. The fae he had grown up with hated him for the favour their Queen showed him. He should be dead. They all knew he had magic but none of them, not even Lord Commander Ream, knew what it was. He only ever used his darker talents when his Queen forced him, but even she had no idea how dark those magical depths went. Bile burned his throat and he thrust those thoughts away.

It would not take much for these guards to find an excuse to hurt Diamond. Word would already have circulated through the tower after what he did to Attion and that other prick. Not for a second did he think his Queen or his 'brothers' believed he didn't care about the girl from the north.

Accusing faces, pale phantoms of the dead, echoed in his mind, as they often did. The Queen wanted powerful magic eradicated from her kingdom, or so she said. Hugo tried not to growl. He had seen what she really did to those with magic. She was insane, driven so by her belief in her dark god and his eventual return.

Erebos was as much a tale of darkness and evil as Lunaria was a tale of light and goodness. The dark and the light as it always was in fairy stories and legends. Good magic verses evil magic.

Ridiculous children's tales. It was true his Queen allowed her Acolytes to live but, like him, that was only to serve whatever darker purpose she had in mind for her kingdom.

For years it had been Hugo she had sent with her other guards to hunt down babies born with any other colour wing except gold. Gold meant a small amount of magic, enough to manipulate the metal in their blood and learn how to armour if the child were taught how, but not enough to be a threat. Hugo's gut twisted painfully and the hunger he felt as he smelled the delicious royal fare suddenly turned to nausea. It wasn't just the children he had brought before her that sickened him. No. It was every single person who had done nothing wrong except be born with magic of one kind or another and stupidly let it show.

Hugo released a heavy sigh. Atonement for his crimes would come eventually, of that he had no doubt. Until then he would find a way to protect the one person that meant more to him than his own life ever could. Squeezing his tired eyes shut he smoothed his features back into neutrality. It wasn't hard, he had learned at a young age to hide his feelings, to give nothing away—not even as he saw Jack brush a lock of hair from Diamond's face and wrathful anger flared in his gut.

Jack glanced at Hugo but he did not wink or smile as he had done in the forest, instead he brushed the beautiful comb that twinkled in Diamond's hair and whispered something in her ear. Hugo swallowed his jealousy as she blushed prettily.

It was nearly three years since the Queen had ordered Hugo to assist the prince with defending Stormguaard. He had not intended to become friends with Jack. But Hugo had spent two years fighting the Wraith Lord alongside the mortal prince. Spending time with Jack and the Rhodainian army had been illuminating. In fact, learning some of Jack's men, like Gunnald, had magical gifts they openly used for war had taken him months to accept. Rhodainian fae had gifts far beyond anything Hugo had ever seen; not just golden wings but the glorious hues of green and red that were never allowed to live in Avalonia.

Gunnald's swiftness and accuracy with a bow had astounded Hugo almost as much as seeing people, human and fae, use magic in their everyday lives. Being so far from the shield and the Queen, he had allowed his own magic to stir. It had revelled in its freedom. Hugo had been able to hone that growing power and train it in a way he never could have in Valentia. Without fear of reprisal he had used his ability to assist Jack's campaign against Ragor on many occasions, earning him a level of respect and friendship from Jack's men that he had never known before.

Despite magic, Stormguaard had still fallen to the overwhelming numbers of Ragor's army. Jack had pulled back the remains of the Combined Army to the borders between Rhodainia and Avalonia. Together, Jack and Hugo had sought out the enigmatic Master Commander Riddeon, and joined the remains of the prince's army with the Queen's warrior legions.

Commander Riddeon had welcomed the reinforcements. As one large force they fought many hard and bloody battles and had even reached the point of pushing the Wraith Lord's forces back when the Queen had ordered her troops to withdraw. Even the stoic and professional Master Commander Riddeon had been unable to hide his shock and disagreement with that order.

Hugo clamped his lips tight and exhaled. The more time he spent away from the cloying influence of the immortal Queen, the more unsettled he became—unsettled to the point he found himself questioning why he hadn't deserted long ago.

His tongue found the rough skin inside his cheek, pushing at his scar. No. He knew why. Any thoughts of escaping his miserable existence had been crushed long ago. That was until he had found himself looking into the most beautiful violet eyes he had ever seen. Diamond had entwined herself into his soul so deeply he would do anything to keep her safe. Her blood was eternally imprinted on his, just the beginning of a blood bond that he had no right to pursue. A shiver rippled through his body and he swallowed. He had marked her with his venom; even if their Nexus didn't exist, they were connected, bound by that act alone.

It had been so easy to sense her anger and disappointment at his inability to protect her from his Queen. He didn't know if he should feel relief or regret that Diamond had no idea about their bonds. He allowed himself a small smile; perhaps he should feel a measure of both. He could imagine her blazing anger if she ever found out. Venom, magic and blood; an intoxicating mix, one that could destroy them both if the Queen were to find out.

Clinging tightly to Jack's arm, Diamond flicked yet another wary glance his way. Hurt and fear flared through their invisible link. Unknowingly, he rubbed at his chest. A group of young lords who were slightly drunk and a little loud stepped in front of him and he lost sight of her for a moment. Hugo stayed where he was, though, and let his thoughts drift back to early this morning.

Weary and in pain, he had left Diamond's room to take care of himself. Lord Commander Ream had been waiting. Instantly, Hugo's senses had screamed in alarm. The Lord Commander was the coldest and cruellest fae male Hugo had ever met. He was loyal and protective of the Queen to the point of obsession. If Commander Ream deemed Diamond to be a threat in any way, he would kill her in an instant, with no regrets.

Hugo had silently followed him and entered the Queen's private chambers. Completely unconcerned for his wellbeing or the gash on his leg, oozing pus through stinking bandages, his Queen had bid Hugo kneel. With hard green eyes, her voice calculating, she had questioned him again and again about Diamond and her abilities. Such an interrogation had coated his stomach with ice, and hiding the overwhelming protectiveness he felt for Diamond had been nearly impossible.

A peal of sweet laughter reached his ears, jolting him out of his reverie. Diamond's eyes sparkled as she let go of Jack's arm and graciously took General Edo's. Hugo eyes narrowed. The general did not look particularly pleased. In fact, he looked almost reluctant to escort Diamond. It was an odd reaction given General Edo's determination to help his friend's daughter reach safety.

A distant trumpet heralded the Queen's imminent arrival. Squaring his shoulders, Hugo braced himself to see her. Today's events had left him anxious to the point of wanting to grab Diamond and run. But that would be downright foolish. He was too recognisable and there were too many spies in this city for him to get far.

Fixing his blank gaze on Diamond, he took several deep breaths. The only way to keep her safe now was to do what the Queen wanted and bide his time. Not only did he need to convince his Queen that he did not care about Diamond, he needed the goddess' favour to outwit her immortal mind.

Chapter Thirty-Five

Hugo watched Diamond's face fill with fear at the sound of the trumpets before she mastered herself. Her terror seeped through to him, and he watched her already pale face drain of colour entirely. Desperately thin, she looked like she might collapse any moment; despite that, he thought she looked utterly stunning. Her ethereal looks were completely at odds with the average Valentian, as were his, but he thought her captivating. Her eyes glittered almost as much as the delicate folds of her dress, which floated around her like a twinkling mist. Her silver locks looked beautiful piled on her head in a mass of curls, braids and waves, and he stifled an overwhelming urge to walk up and pull away the beautiful comb that nestled among it. He wanted to see those silver tresses tumble down so he could run his fingers through them, over and over. The urge became almost unbearable, and he leaned up against the wall, crossing his arms to stop himself.

Hugo realised he wasn't the only one who had heard her laugh or was drawn to her either. His throat constricted as he scanned the room. Guards and lords and even some of the more brazen servants glanced over at her. Curious gazes followed her, but it hurt his heart to see interest turn to hate and disgust as those same people recognised her as a half-blood. Keeping his face neutral, he hoped none of them would seek to hurt her tonight.

A trumpet blared again, sounding the arrival of the Queen and her entourage. Hugo pushed off the wall and strode forward, glad to have an excuse to position himself near Diamond again. Her only response was a disparaging glance, accompanied by a blast of magical anger. Hugo absorbed it and glowered down at her, forgetting she had no idea what she was doing.

Keeping hold of the general's arm, she took no further notice of Hugo as they all waited for the Queen to be seated on the elaborately decorated dais at the far end of the hall.

Jack winked at Diamond, glancing at Hugo as he kissed her hand before elegantly turning on the ball of his foot and marching purposefully down the hall towards his seat. Respectfully, the other guests began to take their places. Hugo addressed General Edo, who seemed more interested in his prince than the girl on his arm.

"Sir? I will escort Diamond to her seat if you wish to accompany His Highness." Choosing to ignore Diamond's furious frown, he gave a slight nod to the older man.

The general nodded, passing Diamond's hand over without any hesitation. He did not even look at Diamond, let alone bid her farewell as he strode after Jack. Hugo kept his face impassive when hurt flickered in Diamond's large eyes.

Hugo did not hold his arm out to her, he did not fancy the humiliation of her rejection in front of this crowd of people. Instead, grabbing her elbow, he gently but firmly propelled her to a table not far from the dais.

Fuming at his touch, Diamond rubbed her arm when he let go. With flushed cheeks, her bejewelled eyes only served to enhance her beauty. Hatefully, she cursed him under her breath. Jerking her, he shoved her down onto her chair, a bitter taste coating his tongue. He shouldn't have expected anything else. He had practically delivered her to the Queen, then stood by whilst his subordinates beat her and then he, not them, had threatened to throw her in the dungeons.

"It's not polite to call names," he snapped under his breath, raising his eyebrows in warning.

"It is if you deserve it," she shot back through gritted teeth, her back straight and her chin angled defiantly.

"Why? Because I brought you here? Diamond, I saved your life. Do you think there was another choice?" he asked bitterly. Instantly his magic flared to life, reacting to her stormy emotions. He growled. This was an unbearable situation. It was always exhausting hiding his magic when he was with others, and right now, trying to curb the angry waves of energy pouring from him was nearly impossible. "Do it again and I'll spank you like the ungrateful child you are," he fumed.

"Really? What, right now? I doubt that," she sneered. "It would degrade you too much, especially in front of these small-minded morons—and those guards who, correct me if I'm wrong, are your inferiors. And what about your Queen? You wouldn't dare demean yourself in front of her. Would you?" Challenge laced her voice. "No, you'll wait until we are alone again and then attack me. Or perhaps, commander, you'll let your friend Attion do it for you. Maybe you'll let him do more than just grope me with his filthy hands while you grovel on your knees for your Queen," she jeered, disgust and shame pulsing from her.

Hugo's heart briefly stopped as he digested those words and her emotions slammed into him.

Attion had done what?! Rage fuelled a sudden surge of heat that seared his blood and pounded through his head. Hugo stared at her, his nostrils flaring as he fought for control, but he did not give in to his magic's demand for release; instead, he mastered it, rolled it into a tight ball and thrust it inside a cage, not forgotten or extinguished but saved—for later.

Hugo took some deep breaths, fighting to keep his face neutral in the onslaught of his feelings and hers—confusion, hurt, fear—but even they were overshadowed by her rage at him. Suddenly, he wanted take her up on that scornful challenge. He wanted to show her that he did not care what any of these people thought. She did not understand that bringing her here had been the only way to save her.

In a flurry of twinkling gossamer material, Diamond twisted to face him and he released a large relieved breath, making it sound like an angry huff. Her defiance in the face of all that was happening to her lifted his heart. Her fear of him, and this court, wasn't so great it had curbed her spirit; if anything, she was more defiant. Using his best dominant stare, he fixed a glare on her; then suddenly, out of nowhere, despite her taunts and the anger pulsing against him, he had an urge to laugh.

Even the shadow of his Queen and the sadistic Lord Commander Ream could not prevent the corners of his mouth twitching up at the thought of throwing her over his knee and spanking her perfect rear until she squealed. He cracked a wider smile when she snorted her irritation and crossed her arms over her chest, giving him the cold shoulder.

"Go to hell!" she hissed, clearly furious. "None of this is funny!"

He coughed, bringing his amusement under control. His voice softened and he gently touched her arm. "No, it isn't," he agreed. "But I'm not laughing at you, Diamond. I'm just happy you can still find it in you to tell me to *go to hell* after everything that has happened today."

Those amazing violet eyes flicked to his and he saw her hesitant smile, then felt her desperate need to believe him. "Are you?" she asked softly.

"I'm sorry if I hurt your arm," he said sincerely, sitting down on the chair next to her and leaning in close enough only she could hear him now. "And I am sorry for bringing you to this palace. It truly was to save your life. I am also sorrier than you will ever know that I am sworn to serve the Queen," he said quietly, and although he had no idea why he uttered those words out loud to her, he found he meant them with all his heart. Apologising for his Queen could get him executed on the spot. Yet it was true. Hurting Diamond was the last thing he wanted, and it was suddenly important she knew that.

Diamond's dress sparkled like it was peppered with bejewelled raindrops when she turned toward him and held his gaze. Captivated, he could not look away. For a few seconds they stared at each other, lost to the people around them. Her head tilted to one side as she scrutinised him. Without thinking he pushed his magic against her, caressing her and willing her to feel the truth of his words. Her cheeks flushed and her throat bobbed.

"I believe you are, Hugo. In which case I forgive you," she declared with quiet dignity, then smirked coyly at him. "But only if you promise not to throw me over your knee and spank me in front of all these lords and ladies."

"Alright," he breathed, swallowing his relief. "But only for tonight and only if you behave." Eyes glittering, he cocked his head and released a throaty chuckle. "Otherwise I *will* whisk you away where we are alone, throw you across my knee and spank you until you beg me to stop," he drawled, delighting in her flustered reaction.

Seconds ticked by as he pinned her with a meaningful stare. His heart pounded as her emotions raced from doubt, to embarrassment, to anticipation before her face lit with a dazzling smile. His heart stopped. What a strange sensation to make someone happy, to make them smile.... Hugo caught his breath and tucked that beautiful image away in his heart.

"Fine," she agreed breathily. "I'll behave—for now."

Still flushed, she dropped her eyes and gave him one last shy look through her lashes before turning away to talk to Tom, who sat next to her.

No longer distracted by Diamond's flushed cheeks, Hugo blew out a breath and, still smiling, glanced up. Then froze. Jack glared at him and the Queen's green eyes regarded him with cold speculation.

Stupid! Stupid!

Hugo had not smiled or relaxed like that in front of anyone since he had been a child, and never in front of his Queen. Jack's glare said it all. *How could I have been so heedless of where I was?* Kicking himself he forced his blank gaze to briefly meet his monarch's. With his heart thumping fearfully in his chest, he bowed his head in respect. *Did I just condemn Diamond?* Shapely, full lips twitched in the merest smile but it was that icy immortal gaze, fixed upon Diamond, that sickened Hugo. Predatory and utterly focused, it was the look a cat gave a mouse before stalking it, pinning it and devouring it until nothing but a pile of bloodied bones remained.

Chapter Thirty-Six

The dinner seemed interminably long. Jack caught Diamond's eye and gave her a supportive smile, then levelled his attention back to General Edo. Despite Jack's presence, Diamond's insides were churning. Being stuck in this hall was awful. The hateful glances from strangers, the Queen sitting elegantly poised on her dais, the guards; it was all becoming too much. Her eyes darted around nervously, not trusting anyone, not even Hugo.

He served his Queen.

The food arrived, beautifully presented and cooked to perfection. It was certainly more extravagant than anything Diamond was used to. Soups and terrines, followed by succulent roast chicken and vegetables. It smelled wonderful, but Diamond just nibbled.

Hugo frowned sideways at her. "Aren't you hungry?" he asked shortly, as she pushed a lemon tart around her plate.

She sighed, wondering that he asked such a stupid question, given her situation. "Not really. To be honest, the thought of eating makes me feel sick," she responded tightly.

The look he gave her was steady and assessing before he grunted and turned his concentration back on his own food. Diamond had noticed how little he ate as well. He kept on glancing under hooded brows at the Queen. It was hard to keep up her cheerful responses to Tom's good humour and ignore Jack's frequent glances without begging them both to help her.

A bone deep weariness invaded her body and mind. She stifled a yawn behind her hand, her eyes blurring as she stared at her cream covered dessert.

"Have you finished?" asked Hugo, so close his warm breath fanned her cheek.

She gave a start. "Err—yes—thank you," she said guiltily, blowing air out of her cheeks. Had she really been slouching forwards, almost asleep?

"Stay awake," he warned her. "The Queen will consider it insulting if you fall asleep in her presence, and you absolutely cannot leave until she gives you permission."

Diamond took a sip of water, leaving her wine glass alone. She nodded, trying to shake off the exhaustion that made it so difficult to concentrate. Her eyelids began to close. Under the table a large hand squeezed her leg hard enough to send a ripple of pain up her thigh and startle her awake.

"Stay. Awake," Hugo ground out between gritted teeth. "She will punish you, and me, if you fall asleep."

Diamond blinked hard and nodded. "Sorry," she whispered, not daring to look up at the fae Queen. Despite Hugo's mood changing like the wind, the last thing she wanted was to get him in trouble. He kept his hand resting on her leg. She should push him away. But the warmth of his touch seeped through the delicate material of her dress into her skin. It was a strangely proprietary move for a Queen's guard. Intimate and hot, his large hand curled around her thigh. Her senses honed in on that touch. Struggling, Diamond made herself listen to Tom, forcing out answers to his questions.

Keeping her body upright took such an enormous amount of effort, and it wasn't long before the muscles in her back began to shake. She swallowed her nausea, a light sheen of sweat breaking out on her brow. Suddenly the weight of Hugo's hand disappeared.

The Queen had summoned him. Power evident in every step, Hugo approached the dais. Bowing gracefully on one knee, he lowered his head before his mistress. Minutes ticked by. Shame burned on Diamond's cheeks for Hugo. The Queen continued to ignore him. Other people in the hall began to glance his way, many sniggering cruelly. Diamond fixed their faces in her mind. Jack was staring at Hugo, his face tight, clearly uncomfortable for his friend. General Edo, looked away, his face as hard as his grey eyes. The Queen, however, did not seem in the least bit bothered about causing Hugo such humiliation and carried on her conversation with the scarred, tough-looking warrior fae who sat to her right.

At that moment Diamond hated the Queen and this simpering court, so much she wished for control of her magic so she could turn them to dust. Seeing such a proud and fierce warrior be so submissive and treated with such contempt sickened her to her very core. Confused, her attention flicked from Hugo to the Queen—and found the glittering green eyes of a reptile fixed upon her. Diamond's heart jumped at the satisfied smile that curled the Queen's rosy lips. Remembering what had happened in her room, Diamond immediately dropped her gaze, her panicked breath catching in her throat.

The Queen was doing this to Hugo on purpose—for Diamond's benefit. Diamond stared down at her tightly clasped hands, not daring to look up again. Breathing rapidly, a familiar light-headedness swamped her. It didn't matter why. The weight of that ancient gaze crushed Diamond's exhausted body. Not sure how to help Hugo and paralysed by fear, Diamond tried to control her emerging panic. Diamond's thoughts became muddled, her brain foggy. Voices drifted around her, just snatches of conversation. Tingling numbed her fingers and lips, spreading until even her teeth felt numb. The clatter of cutlery and the chink of glasses made her head spin. It was an effort to remember her father's calming techniques, his gentle deep voice....

Breathe....

Gods, she was going to faint or vomit. Or something. An instant later her chair was pulled out from behind, nearly toppling her off. Hugo's hand slipped under her arm catching her.

"Say your farewells. You have Her Majesty's permission to leave now," he said stonily.

Diamond didn't want to look at his face, even her tired, panicked mind could pick up the tightness in his voice. The ire pulsing from him made her skin tingle. She mumbled a goodnight to Tom, who happily carried on chatting to the young soldier at his side. Diamond did not have time to bid farewell to anyone else, including Jack, before Hugo was marching her out of a door at the side of the room. Her guards fell in step behind them.

Fuzzy headed and clumsy, Diamond tripped over her own feet several times as Hugo paced along the corridors. His jaw was clenched, distorting the jagged lines of his scar. To others he might look emotionless but Diamond knew him now. The fury coming from him was almost too much to bare. Hot tears pricked her eyes. She wanted to turn back time and return to the forest. At least there he had let himself care for her.

Exhausted, Diamond ignored her better judgment and craved being held by him again, not pushed away. Blinking away her hurt, she focused on keeping up with his long strides. They passed from the well-lit, glass-roofed corridors of the main palace into the ancient stone ones. Hugo kept up the fast pace, marching down a long set of worn stone steps, not waiting to see if she was close behind him. Half way down Diamond got her satin-covered foot caught and tripped over the hem of her beautiful dress.

The world tilted. Crying out, she missed how quickly Hugo uncoiled his body and snatched her arm.

"Ouch!" she shrieked. Tiredness and pain overwhelmed her. Hot salty tears tipped from her stinging eyes and dribbled down her cheeks. It had to be her fault he had found himself in such a humiliating situation in the dining hall. It was the only reason he would be so angry with her. She tried to turn away from his dark glare but he was too swift.

He grabbed her shoulders spinning her back towards him, swearing so quietly that only she could hear.

"I'm sorry," she said quietly, her lip trembling. "I didn't mean to get you in trouble. Are you going to put me in the dungeons now?" she hiccoughed.

He sighed heavily, running a hand over his burnt face, looking nearly as tired as she felt. "No," he said shortly, glancing at the guards with an unspoken order. They didn't move. He snarled, taking one threatening step toward them. Reluctantly, they dropped back far enough not to hear him speak. Then his voice softened as he guided her down to the bottom of the steps. "I know what my orders are, Diamond, and I have never defied one. It would be foolish of me to begin now...for many reasons; but I will do my best to keep you from those dungeons and keep you safe as long as I can."

Unable to contain her relief, her tears turned into shuddering sobs. Hugo stepped sideways so the Queen's guards could not see their faces.

"You really are exhausted—and frightened, aren't you?" he asked, his voice and sapphire eyes gentle now. "Not even when you fought a mighty dragon, or were starving and at death's door in that dead forest, did you cry like this."

"That's because you were with me," she whispered before she could censor her response. His eyes widened slightly, but Diamond was too tired and too emotionally worn by the day's events to regret her words.

"This dinner was a really bad idea. I still can't work out why she ordered you to go," he said with a hint of concern in his voice. "You should be resting."

His free hand moved as if to caress her face but dropped almost immediately, his fingers curling into a fist. Her guards, his men, were still watching, even if they couldn't hear.

"Yes, it was a bad idea—but it wasn't as if either of us had a choice." She shrugged and attempted a watery smile. "At least I got to see everyone else. Besides, I wouldn't have gotten to wear such a pretty dress if you hadn't made me go."

His scar twisted, showing his teeth; but rather than being repulsed, Diamond relished it. It meant he was giving her one of his rare smiles. Tipping her head back to look up at him, she smiled in response.

"Come, let's get you back to your room. You need to get some sleep and recover. Maybe tomorrow we will discover what the Queen wants from you."

Diamond swallowed and nodded, but she didn't really want to know.

They turned a corner and the long shadowed corridor tilted alarmingly. Exhausted, she swayed unsteadily into Hugo. In an instant she was cradled in his arms, resting her head gratefully on his broad chest and absorbing his warmth.

The further he walked through the corridors, the less frequently the sconces glowed. Dim stone corridors passed by until Hugo's footsteps slowed and she realised they were back. His muscles tensed as he readjusted her weight and leaned forward to open the door. A curt order for the guards to stay outside, and the lock clicked shut behind them.

Silence fell; Diamond faked being asleep. Waking would mean leaving the security of his arms.

"Diamond?" he murmured, his voice deep and resonating through his chest. "You're back."

She snuggled closer and, for a moment, curled her fingers into the leather covering his upper arms.

She could hear the amusement in his voice as he said, "I know you're awake."

Sighing she lifted her head as he strode further into her bedroom, his footsteps muffled by the rug.

"You need to get undressed and into bed," he informed her as he let her legs drop to the floor.

Diamond couldn't support herself. Her knees wobbled from exhaustion and the sheer headiness of his magic's gentle caress. Of their own volition her feet closed the gap between them and her body swayed up against his, revelling in that solid wall of strength.

"You can help me undress," she murmured, resting her forehead against his chest. Unfastening all those laces and small buttons by herself would be impossible, said the voice of reason. "Or I could just stay here," she breathed, her heart clenching as it hit her how much she wanted the warmth of his powerful body against hers. There was nothing she could do to stop her body melting against his, so close she could feel his heart beating its fast rhythm. Her mouth dried out as she dared to peer up into his face, and placed her hands on his hips.

Hugo made a deep choking sound that rumbled through his chest, vibrating into her bones.

"Diamond. No. Don't. I—gods.... I need to go before I do something we both regret," he murmured with a husky and raw voice. She felt it, the moment his magic withdrew. Her stomach lurched with resentment.

"I understand, Hugo. What was it Attion said? Hmm? Oh, that's right. You can bed a whore but you can only belong to your Queen. How nice for you. But I am not a whore. No matter what your men think." She pulled away, her eyes burning. "I just need some help to undo this dress. I'm not asking you to bed me," she whispered, her face aflame. But she still held on to him, unwilling to let him go. "I'm not a whore, Hugo," she repeated in a whisper. But that did not stop her wanting him.

"Diamond, I know that. But—you don't understand—I-I can't undress you," Hugo whispered hoarsely, his throat bobbing as he swallowed and he curled his hands over her shoulders as if to push her away. But nothing happened. He just held her. Motionless, his eyes fixed on hers. She couldn't breathe. Then she felt his magic slide over her in a warm caress.

"Please, Hugo," she urged, not really knowing what she was asking for, help with her clothes or something far more dangerous.

His fingers tightened on her shoulders.

"Or I'll have to ruin this lovely dress and sleep in it," she added, before resting her cheek back against his chest, listening to the solid drum of his heartbeat. There was a long tense pause.

"Fine," he muttered eventually. Big hands found the fastenings and laces at the back of her dress and she leaned forward compliantly, absorbing the feel of his body against her. Guilt fought with want. He was a guard—her enemy. Quickly she shoved those thoughts away and slid her arms around his waist as he deftly worked at undoing her dress.

Warm fingers grazed her skin, tickling her. A delightful shiver rippled through her whole body and she smiled, squeezing her arms around him. Instinctively she pushed herself closer.

"Diamond...." he groaned. 'Stop...please."

But his actions belied his words as he slid his warm hands into the small of her back and held her to him. Their hips met and her bones turned to water. It didn't matter that he was her enemy or that he belonged to another woman, she wanted him. This was not the tentative attraction that she had felt for other boys, but the full blown desire of a female fae. Her body flared to life. He had just lit the furnace of her lust and she knew he would sense it. Heat pooled between her thighs, rippling through her core.

Heart pounding, she pulled back enough to see his face. Raw need burned through those stunning fae eyes, his nostrils flaring as he scented her reaction to his touch. Her eyes widened at the same time his did. She snarled, her finger nails digging deep into his clothes, trying to reach the skin beneath. But before she could yank him closer, he slid his thumbs over the curve of her waist and gripped her, pushing her firmly from him.

"No. I cannot take you, no matter how much I want to. I am not free to offer any more than my body."

Diamond opened her mouth to speak.

"No," he interrupted. "You deserve far more than I can give you. And things are complicated enough for us. Now go and get into bed," he instructed firmly, pulling his hands away.

At that small movement her dress slid from her shoulders, whispering softly as it landed at her feet. For a moment Hugo seemed too stunned to move, then he swore viciously and swung her up in his arms. The leather of his jerkin was cool and tough against her exposed skin. Refusing to feel guilt for wanting this, for wanting him, Diamond clutched at him, groaning with disappointment and frustration when he laid her gently on the soft bed and pulled away. Before he could straighten up she wrapped her arms around his neck and held him close, her cheek against his.

"I know we can't be together, Hugo. I know you are my enemy, but I don't care; I still want you." She kissed his cheek softly. "Thank you—for being so honourable, but right now I wish you weren't," she whispered in his ear.

Swallowing, Hugo swiftly pulled away and threw the soft blankets over her.

"Diamond?" His eyes glittered in the light of the dying fire.

"Yes?" she muttered, sleep dragging at her, despite the fading heat of desire.

"You are the most beautiful woman I have ever seen, tonight or any night, queen or no queen," he said quietly before he strode away, clicking the door shut behind him.

Chapter Thirty-Seven

"I don't know who your benefactor is, but they certainly are generous," declared Kitty wistfully, eyeing the high quality, burgundy satin gown Diamond wore.

It had arrived yesterday with the pair of low-heeled black leather boots sitting on the floor near her bed. A frown furrowed Diamond's brow. It wasn't right to accept so much charity from a stranger, but she couldn't return these gifts to a phantom. Uneasily she wondered what that unidentified person would want in return. Rose immediately waved off her concerns.

"I wouldn't worry. You can't give it back, and I'm sure whoever it is will make themselves known when they are ready. Until then," she shrugged, "enjoy it. There's precious little else to enjoy in this palace at the moment."

All three girls knew Rose was right. The Queen was an ever present shadow in Diamond's life, an unknown who could wipe them all out in a second if she chose to.

Kitty silently picked up the silver-plated hairbrush and brushed Diamond's hair until it shone, then fixed it neatly over one shoulder.

Before long Diamond was looking at herself in amazement. The face looking back at her was still thin but her violet eyes held a soft light, a strange inner glow that made them huge in her pale face. Turning away, Diamond swallowed her fear. Hiding her magic was only going to be possible if she kept her eyes down and avoided looking others in the face.

It had been three days since the dinner, and Rose had decided Diamond needed some fresh air and exercise. Arguing had done no good; Rose, it seemed, had a stubborn streak to match Diamond's. Diamond gratefully gave in and let Rose begin her plan of slowly building up Diamond's physical strength.

Diamond returned to her room an hour later to find Tom waiting for her. Squealing, she threw her arms around his neck, refusing to let go when he complained he couldn't breathe. Eventually she gave in.

"You look handsome," she teased, taking in the tunic that was embroidered with a dragon. It was far too big for him but he still looked good. More man than boy, she decided.

He grinned. "Do you think so? The general said I need to earn my keep...so, I've joined Jack's guard. I'm to start training tomorrow," he said quickly.

Diamond's face dropped. "But you can't! You might get hurt—or killed!" She grasped his arm, her anxious fingers digging in his sleeve.

Tom frowned, his voice turning sharp. "I'm not a child, Diamond. Jack is younger than me and has been fighting a war for years. Gods, he is to be crowned a *king* soon. And look at Hugo. He's only twenty, and already a commander. A *Queen's guard* commander! It's not all about age!" he barked and ran shaking hands through his hair. "Damn it, Diamond, I need to do something with my miserable life! Then maybe the next time my family—or—or friends are threatened, I will be able to fight back instead of being a useless piece of shit!" he yelled. He took a shaky breath, and she dropped her hand. Tom never raised his voice.

"I'm sorry," she stammered. "I just don't want you to get hurt," she said despondently and put her arms around his thin body to give him a tight hug.

He kissed her hair and held her. "Well, I'm not going anywhere yet. I'll be down in the barracks training before they'll let me join the guard. Jack said he will keep an eye on my progress himself. Diamond? Why haven't you left the palace yet? Is everything alright?" he asked, holding onto her shoulders and staring intently at her.

Diamond hated lying to him...but—dungeons. "Everything's fine, Tom. Don't worry about me."

"Well, just in case, why don't you ask if you can learn to fight too? You know, with that dagger Hugo gave you?" he suggested the twinkle back in his eye. "I'm sure Jack won't mind teaching you a few tricks if you ask him," he chuckled and winked at her.

She pulled a face and hit his arm.

"Hey! There's no need for that!" he protested, laughing. "I've seen the way he looks at you. Yeah, you know I'm right." He laughed as her face flushed.

"I don't know that at all," she denied haughtily.

He just prodded her in the ribs and grinned. "Well, if you don't, you should. And if you don't want Jack to teach you, how about Hugo?"

Diamond flashed him a filthy look but, rather than explain why that was a bad idea on so many different levels, she grinned. Time to get her own back. "Soo...tell me about Zane. Have you stopped playing hard to get and slept with him yet?" Then fell into peals of laughter at Tom's cherry red cheeks.

Two weeks later Diamond cringed as Tom took another blow on his ribs. Despite a grunt and a stumble, he did not give up. Being so gangly made him look clumsy and awkward every time he moved, but it seemed Tom was getting the hang of fighting with a staff now. He ignored her *whoop* of encouragement. He had made the mistake of looking over at her on his first day, but not since. His bruises were only just fading.

Diamond knew she should leave; getting Tom into trouble again was the last thing she wanted.

Glancing over her shoulder at her friend, she walked away from the patch of open training ground. It was strange not seeing Tom as often now, but they were not children anymore, and their lives were taking very different paths.

Her loneliness, constantly tinged with fear, had become a familiar feeling. Jack had gone out to the valley so she hadn't seen him since the dinner. Unsurprisingly, General Edo had gone with him. Diamond missed Jack far more than she should and, until today, had not dared venture out of her room alone. Kitty and Rose encouraged her to walk through the grounds with them every day, and they stayed to keep her company in her room when they could. But Diamond was still listless, waiting to see what her fate would entail. Without Rose and Kitty she would have gone completely mad.

Being watched every hour of every day and night by ruthless guards had worked Diamond into a regular state of panic. Daily anxiety attacks rendered her utterly useless. Controlling them with the help of her friends in the daytime was one thing, but once Rose and Kitty left, fear pushed against Diamond's mind, her muscles tightening until it felt like her spine might snap. With orders not to lock her door, she often sat with her back against it, petrified the elite guards might see fit to attack her again. Thankfully, Attion had never been one of her guards.

Uttering a prayer, she thanked the goddess, and Hugo, for their favour. But sitting on the floor with her back against the door all night, every night had left Diamond tired and aching. It was out of necessity she began to re-learn how to control her panic attacks alone.

Imagining Hugo's calming heat and magic wrapped around her body seemed the only way to retain her equanimity. The guards would not attack randomly she told herself time and again, until she began to believe it. It had taken five nights to persuade herself to move away from the door, and another two until she could lay on the bed and close her eyes.

Now, when Tu Lanah lit the dark night sky, her thoughts were much calmer. Every night Diamond delved deep inside her body, grasping the flickering ember of her magic whilst fixing Hugo's face firmly in her mind. Her magic never felt like it would break free and take control, but fear of what Hugo would do if he sensed her connecting with it stopped her from coaxing its diminished existence into more. It comforted her to know that it was not smothered completely by the shield or the Queen's spells, that it was still able to react to her touch and her thoughts.

Diamond had only seen Hugo four times since that night she had thrown herself at him; each time only at a distance, but she knew the guards reported to him about her comings and goings with Rose and Kitty. Occasionally his deep voice would resonate through her bedroom door; she would wait, hoping he would come in, only to curse him hatefully when he walked away.

Turning left, Diamond joined a gravel track. It meandered back towards the rear of the palace. Avoiding the front part of the palace grounds and the entrance to the Queen's tower had seemed the wisest course of action since she had been venturing outside.

Her dark green tunic—another gift from her benefactor—flapped open. Sliding it off revealed a sheer silk blouse. She glanced around but, other than her silent guards, no one paid her any attention so she did not worry. The chill from the early morning air had evaporated and glorious sunshine warmed her skin.

Her body felt stronger again. Along with increasing her exercise, she had forced herself to eat properly. There was no room in her plan for physical weakness. Diamond walked briskly, her feet crunching on the gravel as her stomach grumbled loudly. She would eat breakfast before going to the library to research.

Her guards always stayed near the doors of the massive library, convinced she might try and escape. It made her life a lot easier, not having to explain her reading choices, so she didn't care. Working towards her escape was the only thing keeping Diamond sane, and if the idiots wanted to believe she would actually try and run out of the front doors, then so be it.

A shadow fell across her path, blocking out the light from the sun. Instantly her steps faltered.

"Good morning, Hugo," she said tightly, sounding anything but welcoming as he landed in front of her.

Metal disappeared in a shimmer of blue and silver as he tucked his wings in behind his back. "Good morning, Diamond," he answered, equally guarded.

Diamond tried to stop her traitorous pulse racing as he ran his eyes over her, his gaze lingering on the soft contours of her breasts. She looked away and began walking again.

Hugo frowned. With one look—a silent command—the guards dropped back. He fell in step beside her before, without warning, spinning in front of her.

Unprepared for such an abrupt halt, Diamond banged into his massive body, momentarily stunned. Immediately irritated with him, she clicked her tongue against her front teeth. Her boots scuffed the gravel as she shuffled back—and gaped.

Garbed in his official dress uniform, Hugo stole her ability to speak. Blackened Silverbore armour gleamed against tough black leather. The outfit's whole upper body seemed moulded around his defined muscles, accentuating his broad shoulders, large arms and trim waist. Emblazoned across his chest was the fierce jade green sea serpent of the Queen's sigil.

Diamond wrinkled her nose in disgust at the sign of his servitude to the immortal Queen.

Hugo, in turn, cocked his head slightly to one side, studying her before taking one hesitant step forward. Diamond's feet did not obey her command to step away; instead she inhaled deeply, cursing the fae blood and instincts that made her do so. His musky scent rushed her senses, making her head swim. Angrily she stamped on her racing heart, trying her best to calm her unsteady breathing.

A curse slipped out under her breath as her legs actually wobbled. Ridiculous! She couldn't let herself be so affected by him. She still felt that familiar tug in her chest. How absurd to miss that magical touch so much. At his nearness, her magic flickered from an ember into a flame that licked along her bones. Diamond slowly raised her eyes to his face, her magic surging towards him.

He seemed taller than ever and twice as...well, everything: intimidating, handsome, imposing. She gritted her teeth. He was muddling her mind, that was all. She quickly pulled back her magic lest he feel it. Hugo's eyes widened, his fists clenching as his nostrils flared.

Too late. Damn! Diamond struggled to curb her thoughts and her magic. But no matter how hard she tried she could not command it to withdraw. Wild and heady, it danced with his, sending shivers through her whole body.

Avoiding that beautiful sapphire gaze, Diamond coughed and shuddered, squeezing her eyes tightly shut. Taking a deep breath she opened her eyes and resolutely distracted herself by studying his weapons, her own fists mirroring his.

They were both fighting whatever was going on between them. Forcing herself to step back Diamond took in the daggers sheathed on his waist and the knife hilts glinting in his vambraces. As always, his crossed swords sat snugly on his back. A few deep breaths and she again had control of her voice...if not her feelings.

"So? To what do I owe this unexpected pleasure?" she asked coolly, hurt that he had ignored her for over two weeks.

"The Queen has ordered your attendance at court this afternoon," he answered bluntly.

"What? Why?" she sputtered, her stomach lurching sickeningly. She folded her arms across her chest in an unconsciously protective gesture. *Breathe*, she told herself.

Hugo's eyes flickered at her stance, his body stiffening minutely. Diamond dropped her arms, her hands slapping loudly against her thighs. Sunlight glinted off his weapons as he stared intently. Hating herself for her weakness and hating him for her predicament, she wrapped a finger in her hair and began twisting it as her eyes darted about the gardens, looking anywhere but at the fae warrior who was both her friend and her enemy.

"I don't know. But my orders are to make sure you are there," he answered stiffly.

"Please, Hugo. I can't. Those guards—they'll hurt me again...you will...you'll...." She could not do this, she could not go with him—she gulped air. Her breathing was wrong—this was all wrong. They were going to kill her or hurt her. She wobbled sideways. Her mind wasn't prepared...she wasn't prepared...oh gods...she couldn't do it.

"Diamond," Hugo said softly, but his eyes flickered to her guards, who watched the couple through narrowed eyes. "Slow your breathing down."

Sparks flicked across her darkening vision. He stepped forwards. Diamond instantly stepped away from him. Fear stole her reason. The Queen....

Hugo grabbed her shoulders, so close now his scent made her head swim. Without thinking she blinked, gasping in surprise when her magic flared and her vision changed. Soothing and calming, his silver serpents wrapped around her arms, sliding over her skin, stroking her reassuringly. One floated and touched her face. Tears burned her eyes. She had missed his touch so much. Hugo angled his body so the two elite guards could not see the compassion on his face.

"Diamond, shh.... It's okay. Take some slow breaths. In through your nose...that's it, out through your mouth...keep going...slowly. That's it." Large calloused fingers reached for hers, disentangling them from her hair. "Leave your hair," he instructed gently, his touch lingering against her hands before he let go. "Do not let her do this to you. *Do not* let her break you. It is what she wants: to dominate and control you, to play mind games with you. Whatever she orders this afternoon, you do it. Do you understand? Then you will stay alive. You are strong enough to survive anything she throws at you, Diamond. You just have to believe you are."

Shocked by his words, she could only stare as he took a step back from her. It was hard to think straight with him so close and touching her like that with his magic. A laugh almost escaped her. How wrong he was about her. She couldn't even breathe through her anxiety. She was weak in mind and body, and the Queen knew it.

Unable to meet his eyes, she jumped when he lifted his gloved hand. He immediately dropped it when she flinched away. It was not that she feared him, quite the opposite. The memory of his hands against her bare skin, of his hips pushing against hers, made her cheeks flame. She studied his boots. Gods, how could she want someone so much it hurt to look at him?

Oblivious, Hugo stared at the strand of coiled silver resting against the side of her face. A frown etched his brow, his fingers twitching like he wanted to smooth the knot away. Then he pushed his wings out ready for flight.

"Come. I will take you back to your room," he said firmly.

"No! Thank you," she barked breathlessly.

"Why not?" Hugo asked, his face smoothing into its customary mask.

"Because you belong to *her!* Because you are my enemy. How many reasons do you want, Hugo?" she cried. "I just don't want to be held by you," she hissed, knowing that was completely untrue.

"Really? Because I seem to remember you begging to stay in my arms the last time we were together," he reminded her.

Diamond's cheeks heated as he took another step forwards and, a little hastily, she was forced to step back again.

Hugo raised his dark eyebrows. "Diamond?" he whispered, angling himself further from the two guards watching like hawks. They could not hear nor see his face now. "I am not your enemy. I know you feel your magic reacting to mine whenever we're close to each other—I know because I can feel it too," he said. His scar twisted ever so slightly and she saw a smile curl the edges of his mouth.

Mortified, Diamond covered her embarrassment with a scowl. "It isn't that...I mean—I can feel it but.... I-I'll walk back," she stuttered, her cheeks on fire now.

"Of course," he said, smiling widely as he studied her hot face. For a moment he didn't say anything before adding, "Enjoy your walk to the wall with Rose. I will fetch you from your room this afternoon at three thirty. And remember what I said: You are strong enough to survive anything she throws at you."

His words were like a bucket of cold water to her face. She paled. *What is his mistress likely to throw at me?* Not daring another look at him, frightened she may throw herself at his mercy and beg him to take her away from the palace, Diamond hastily turned on her heel and marched off along the track toward the rear towers of the palace.

Chapter Thirty-Eight

Rose donned a wool shawl and led Diamond by the hand. They walked through the manicured gardens and exited an ornately decorated metal gate that took them from the rear grounds into the large main courtyard.

Diamond's jaw dropped open. The palace was impressive from the rear gardens, but the scale and grandeur of the whole thing from the front blew her away. Elegant granite buildings of various sizes rose above her. Tall spires, topped with green flags, reached for the blue sky. Turning on the spot, Diamond could see how the palace was built on a large plateau. On one side ornate bridges spanned mighty fissures that seemed to drop away between the rocky cliffs to an ocean—or perhaps even the city below. A long gravel road led to the distant palace gates.

Diamond slowly raised her eyes. The Queen's tower loomed over her, pink and glittering and resplendent in the sunlight. Inside sat that wicked woman. Diamond turned away trying to calm her fear of what was to happen later.

Queen's elite guards stood at attention around the edge of the manicured lawn watching all new arrivals. Diamond wondered if she might see Hugo again. More guards, adorned in gleaming Silverbore and leather armour, lined the grand steps and stood to attention either side of the main door. Holy gods, Hugo was terrifying enough on his own, but all of these warriors together made a fearsome sight.

The courtyard was buzzing with carriages, horses and people; smartly dressed men, women and fae coming and going in a steady stream.

"Those gates you can see are about a mile away," explained Rose. "They're normally shut, but the Queen is holding court today. The rich and landed always attend her, especially since the Rift Valley is so full of refugees, not to mention Prince Jack's army. Most of this lot look like the lords who own estates in the Rift Valley. They are all fae, all territorial and are all well and truly disgruntled with the amount of refugees on their land. There is often trouble out in the valley because of it."

"How do you know so much?" asked Diamond curiously, never having been interested in the politics of her own home town.

"Oh. It pays to know people. You know? Maybe a gorgeous warrior...." She smiled and blushed, dropping her voice so the guards behind them couldn't hear.

Diamond's mouth dropped open.

Rose just grinned and hooked Diamond's arm, walking briskly along the side of the gravel road towards the distant gates.

"Rose! Really? You mean you have a...friend who works for the Queen? Holy gods, how d'you get away with that?"

"Shhh! We're careful, that's how," Rose said, eyeing the guards meaningfully.

Another thought struck Diamond, "Rose? Are you—you know—mated?" she asked, her cheeks warming. Not because she was embarrassed by the question but because she was thinking of someone else entirely.

Rose leaned in conspiratorially and grinned. "His name is Fedron, and he is twenty-four," she grinned. "And no, we aren't mated but," she winked and smiled wickedly, "if he asked me I would do it, be his mate, I mean. It would be a huge commitment but I...well, I guess I love him enough."

Not much of a declaration of undying love, reflected Diamond, but held her own counsel.

"He would need the Queen's permission, and the cold-hearted bitch issued an order months ago. None of her soldiers are to mate until the war is over." She shrugged as if it didn't matter, but couldn't hide her disappointment. "Fedron says he agrees. He says it wouldn't be fair to me to go through creating such a bond when he might be killed. It means sneaking around so his superiors don't find out, but that's okay—mostly. Kitty knows—and my friends outside the palace." She shrugged. "They don't really like him. They think he's taking advantage of me—but he's not." Her mouth turned to a stubborn line as if she were convincing herself, not Diamond, of those words.

It didn't sound okay to Diamond; if anything, sneaking around and trying not to get caught sounded dangerous. "Oh," she responded, not sure what else to say.

They walked in silence until Diamond turned back to get a view of the vast palace grounds from a distance. Towers, turreted walls and huge sprawling buildings with pointed spiked pinnacles stretched across the far breadth of the plateau. In front of the palace the impressive open grounds were dotted with groups of training soldiers and warriors. A large enclosure that looked like a barracks nestled up against the far outer walls.

"When we get to the palace walls, just behave like we're supposed to be there. The palace guards have better things to do than worry about two harmless women taking in a view of the city," advised Rose.

Diamond raised her eyebrows and glanced meaningfully at her guards.

"Oh them? They won't stop us. Their orders are to stop you leaving the palace or using magic; they won't give a rat's ass what else you do," she responded, grinning at Diamond's shocked expression. "What? I'm not always quiet and respectable, you know. Come on! It'll be a fantastic view of the valley today," Rose said. "It's so lovely and clear you can probably see the Rift Valley wall too."

In the distance warriors ran along the battlements, launching into the sky. "I wonder what they're so excited about, probably some training exercise," Rose said dismissively. "It's about six miles from the gates down to the sea on the east side of the island, and about three miles to the docks on the west," she explained, her steps speeding up whilst she told Diamond about the city.

By the time Rose had finished talking they were within forty feet of the largest gates Diamond had ever seen. It also became obvious something was happening outside the walls. Loud commanding voices bellowed for the gates to be shut. Diamond's ear drums rattled as a massive pulley system was activated to close the gates, which were clearly made for keeping invading armies out. She stared open-mouthed. In the shadows under the wall, eight huge beasts roared as whips snapped and men bellowed.

Ometons!

Heads down, their muscles bunching and straining under the thick covering of grey and white fur, the northern snow beasts dragged the massive gates shut. Diamond had only seen Ometon pelts when the Ice Witches came to trade at Berriesford market. Normally solitary animals, they were notoriously vicious if riled and had been known to hunt their unfortunate victims down over hundreds of miles, purely by blood scent when angered.

"You know, staying inside the palace walls might actually be a good thing. There have been terrible fights—and even riots—

breaking out in the lower levels of the city. Maybe that's what all the excitement is," mused Rose, frowning up at the ramparts.

From the barracks and around the city, airborne troops streamed into the sky, bows at the ready.

Diamond gaped. This was surely too great a response for a riot. The two girls grasped each other, unsure what was happening; even their guards looked back toward the palace as if debating whether to grab Diamond and return to their Queen.

Diamond felt a strange prickle along her arms the moment before a deafening roar rocked the sky. Petrified screams rang out in the distance. Diamond's body rocked with recognition, and she stared up at the huge shadow that glided high above their heads. A great horned head angled down. She could almost feel those red eyes searching for her.

Rose squealed and ducked as fire rained down from above. But the shield held. It crackled and glowed as bright and hot as the sun, but no flame pushed through its power. The dragon bellowed its fury and glided across the blue clear sky, turning on huge outstretched wings to make a second pass.

"What in the name of Chaos is that?!" Rose yelled, straightening up as more screams echoed from the city streets. Suddenly Rhodainian soldiers and Avalonian warriors alike burst into action. Some formed foot squadrons, others flew into formation, then headed out across the city.

"Quick! We need to get to the next section of wall. We'll be able to see better from there!" shouted Rose, dragging Diamond behind her.

"Why? Can't we just go up here?" countered Diamond, pointing at the nearest set of steps.

"No. Quickly. We must go this way," she urged, her eyes flitting to Diamond's two guards.

Another surge of dragon fire crackled against the shield. Rose began to run, holding tightly to Diamond's hand. They reached the base of some narrow steps and Rose hoisted her skirts.

"This way. As fast as you can, Diamond," she panted.

Diamond glanced over her shoulder. Her guards were only a couple of steps behind. The nearest looked as though he were about to grab her. Rose ran up the narrow steps first, then dragged Diamond up the top step past two burley soldiers who seemed to be guarding the stairwell. They eyed the two girls with a frown. Before Diamond knew what was happening, the two soldiers pushed in front of her guards and sliced a dagger across their throats. Diamond looked on horrified as blood spurted from the necks of her captors.

"Come on, this way," hissed Rose and without a backward glance at the dead warriors, grabbed Diamond's arm.

Then they ran through a throng of men who seemed to close together in the wake of the two fleeing girls, as if shrouding them. Soldiers and warriors alike, some with Jack's sigil, some with a serpent adorning their chests, surged around the turreted wall. Rose's hair came loose and fell down her back in a chestnut curtain. They were close enough to the edge of the wall for Diamond to see the twisted rooftops and chimneys of the sprawling city falling away to the ocean. Above them the ancient shield glowed faintly blue, forming a huge dome.

"It doesn't normally glow like that," panted Rose, glancing over her shoulder at Diamond. "It must be that monster's fire. Look, you *can* see it...the valley wall..." She pointed, still weaving between warriors who were too preoccupied by the sight of a mythical beast gliding over their heads to pay any attention to the two girls, or the two soldiers hurrying along behind them.

They seemed to be miles up in the air here and could see for eternity. The ridiculously steep sides of the island dropped away into buildings of all shapes and sizes. Apprehensively, Diamond craned her neck to get a glimpse of the labyrinth of streets leading down through the sprawl. Warriors darted through the air, heading towards the ocean where a ship exploded, sending smoke billowing into the air. The dragon flew low over the white-crested waves, a long column of fire igniting more vessels. Even from this distance it was possible to see the flecks of people diving into the water to escape the flames, only to find themselves plucked from the waves by large claws, thrown into the air and cooked alive before the dragon caught them in his jaws.

"Good goddess above!" exclaimed Rose, coming to a sudden halt to stare in horror at the destruction. "It's destroying ships and *eating* people...." her voice drifted away as she spun sideways to stare at the distant valley.

"Yeah, it's roasting them first though," confirmed a rough voice from behind Diamond.

"One of the others said he heard it was searching for her, or maybe the boy prince. What we need is a warrior like that bastard Casimir to fly this magic wielder thirty miles back to that damned forest and leave her there for it. In fact, sod that. The master's son could do it...couldn't he? You know, Rose, use those wings that makes you women lift your skirts so easy." Rose threw him a dirty look and he grinned.

"Seriously. If we dump her in the ocean outside the shield, that bloody creature might leave this city be."

Diamond stared at the soldier. Menace glinted in his eyes. She shuffled nearer Rose. Then it registered what he'd said. Hugo had flown her *thirty* miles, whilst he was injured himself.... *How had he managed such a thing?*

Rose glared, "Shut up, Ayk. Leave Diamond alone. Just do what you're supposed to do and get her to the master. Come on," she urged Diamond. "We need to get you out of here before those dead guards are noticed."

Once again Diamond found herself propelled onward, this time toward a tower door. Too shocked to fight or question, she stumbled through the entrance into the dark interior, her chest tight and panicky.

"Rose? Please. What's happening?" she panted, unsure whether to be pleased they were running away from the palace or scared she was fleeing with men who could kill so easily.

"Don't worry, they're taking you somewhere safe," said Rose, her face in shadow. Dust-filled sunbeams from four small arrow slits were the only source of light.

"Go on just do it. Hurry up! I need to get out of here," Rose urged, clearly not talking to Diamond.

Large arms encircled Diamond, holding her fast as the other man slammed his fist into Rose's jaw. Rose fell against the wall, her hands outstretched to save herself.

"Leave her alone!" Diamond yelled.

"Quiet," growled Ayk, putting one hand over Diamond's mouth. "Do you wanna bring the whole palace guard down on our heads?"

"Sorry, Rose," muttered the other soldier, "That will bruise nicely. But I hope it doesn't get my arse kicked by...."

"Dan! Shut up, you idiot!" hissed Ayk "Go, Rose. We've got her. She'll be fine," he tried his best to sound reassuring, but Diamond wasn't convinced.

Holding her face, Rose glanced back anxiously at Diamond.

"Trust them, Diamond. They will help you. Goodbye," she mumbled, then rather than going down the steps as Diamond expected, Rose ran back out through the door, disappearing into the clamouring soldiers.

Darkness fell again as the door slammed shut. A shadow stepped forward. Diamond wanted to fight. She was sick of being weak, of being pushed around and beaten like she was nothing, like her will didn't matter.

She bucked and wriggled. Dan stepped forward and pressed a cloth tightly to her face. A bitter herbal smell filled her mouth and nose. This was not a rescue! Desperately Diamond fought and kicked out trying not to breathe in the foul tincture.

"Oh, come on, girl. Don't fight it. We don't have time for this. 'Ere, back pocket, shove some more on," Ayk snapped at Dan.

The cloth left her face for a blessed few seconds, but her breathing was too panicked to scream before it was pushed back on, suffocating her. This time there was no choice, her body needed to breathe. She gasped a great lung-full of the foul stuff. Her mind became fuzzy and her arms and legs heavy. Unable to fight any longer, her body went lax.

"Saviour, my arse," muttered Ayk. He picked her up just as she blacked out.

Chapter Thirty-Nine

Hugo had deliberately avoided going anywhere near Diamond until this morning. Staying away was safer for them both, especially as his magic reacted wildly to hers, and he couldn't seem to stop himself wanting to touch her or comfort her in some way. Spies and informants worked every nook and cranny of this vast palace, and he wasn't stupid enough to think the Queen wouldn't hear about this morning.

Of course, Hugo also made it his business to know what Diamond was doing and who she was with, every minute of every day. Every six hours her guards changed. He often waited impatiently for their reports even though they had nothing much to tell him. Rose, Kitty and one visit from Tom had been Diamond's only company—so far. It seemed Jack had been too busy organising his own court and council to seek Diamond out; either that, or General Edo was keeping him too busy in the valley to return.

Hugo stretched out his wings and de-armoured them before relaxing his grip on his sword. The Silverbore blade sung as it cut through the air and slid home in the scabbard on his back.

Tallo Nosco nodded and grinned, "Thanks for the practice, commander. I'm glad to see you haven't become sloppy since you disappeared to the north."

The master-at-arms sheathed his own blade and bent to pick up his discarded tunic. The older male was all tough, lean muscle and scars; despite his advancing years, he was the only male Hugo had ever met who could challenge him with a sword. He was also the only fae in this palace Hugo ever let his guard down with.

"Anytime, old man," countered Hugo, grinning.

"Piss off—*old man,*" Tallo grumbled.

Hugo chuckled as Tallo flipped a rude gesture his way. The warrior who had once trained the young Queen's guard recruits grinned back.

Before their grins had faded, a deafening roar followed by a column of fire streaming high above the palace snapped them to alertness. Armour clattered across their wings. Together they gaped upward. Glowing sparks crackled across the ancient shield as it devoured the red hot dragon fire. A black-winged shadow glided past. Hugo instantly grabbed his armour off the dusty ground. Sweat ran down his face as he watched the dragon turn gracefully in the air.

"Holy shit! What is that?!" exclaimed Tallo.

"That is the guardian I told you about," responded Hugo, quickly fastening the armour around his broad torso.

Tallo dressed, becoming the calm and controlled warrior once again.

Hugo nodded and, as one, the two warriors bent their knees and launched upward, their metallic wings glinting impressively in the luminescent light of the shield. Hugo slowed to hover about forty feet off the ground, feeling suddenly torn. His responsibility lay with protecting his Queen. The tower glinted in the sunlight as if daring him to turn away from it. He closed his eyes and he heaved a frustrated growl, but his Queen was not the face burning brightly behind his eyelids right now.

"Commander, I must re-join my captains," Tallo barked, not bothering with a farewell as his momentum increased and he headed out.

Hugo beat his wings powerfully, his eyes flickering from the palace to the wall. A sudden surge of panic set his heart pounding. This wasn't his emotion, he realised quickly. It was muffled and shot through with disgust and fear.

Diamond! He whirled about. Remembering his reports from this morning, Hugo propelled himself toward the main gate. Rose was taking Diamond to view the city from the palace walls today. The main gate is where they would go.

A menacing black shadow glided close to the shield, then with a bellowing roar shot like a huge arrow down towards the ocean. A moment later Hugo heard far off screams. The air around him thrummed with energy, making his skin tingle. Spurring himself higher and nearer the shield, Hugo instinctively thrust out his magic, sending shadows crashing against the crackling blue dome. His muscles spasmed and it was an effort to keep flying forward as he forced his body to absorb the shield's might. When its energy began to burn in his blood, he yanked his magic back inside.

His silver wing markings flared brightly and his eyes blazed with molten silver fire. Shocked, he realised that the shield's extra power had enhanced his senses. He could hone in on the minutest detail and focus on each individual conversation if he wished. Hugo stopped, arched his back and roared up at the shield, his face inches from it. The beast inside him roared along with him.

Now. Let me out now, it urged. *Let me find her.*

No, he answered, forcing it back inside its cage.

Other warriors watched the Queen's guard warily from afar but none approached. To them, dark wings equalled dark magic. Hugo narrowed his focus on the wall. How right they were.

A crowd of guards gathered together on the second watch tower. Their faces were fraught with fear and indecision. They saw him coming and made a space, every one of them eyeing him with alarm. Then he realised why. Two bodies lay atop each other, thrown haphazardly into a dark corner of the tower wall. Their heads lay at a grotesque angle, exposing sinews and vessels, their eyes glassy in bone white faces.

"Who is in charge here?!" bellowed Hugo, trying to control the dread in his heart.

A tall thin warrior stepped forward. A fae captain. "I am, sir." The male saluted, outwardly calm.

"Where is the girl?" Hugo barked. Diamond had definitely been here; he could smell her, not to mention *feel* the remnants of her horror at those deaths.

"What girl, sir?" the man stuttered looking confused.

Hugo stared long and hard. His razor-sharp eyes zoning in on the male's large pupils, the sweat beading his brow, and his eyes that darted to his left farther along the wall when Hugo deliberately glanced back at the bodies. Faster than lightening, Hugo slammed his foot into the warrior's gut.

"Where is she?!" he bellowed. The fae landed on his back as Hugo pulled both his swords. "Tell me now or you die and so do your warriors," he threatened, thrusting one blade against the back of a young warrior's neck.

Barely into adulthood, the fae was younger than Hugo, maybe seventeen, and had clearly never seen any real fighting. A wet patch appeared on the boy's breeches. Hugo snarled in disgust and stepped sideways, but placed his second blade threateningly against the boy's stomach. They all knew he would kill every single one of them if they defied him.

"I-I don't know where they went. It was two soldiers; they took her and the other girl towards the next turret. That's all I know—I swear it, sir." This time the fae looked him in the eye as if willing him to believe. Hugo did not have time to wonder if he was lying or to punish him for holding back information.

"If you are lying to me, I will ensure you die an extremely painful death," he told the warrior. "See to it Lord Commander Ream hears of this," he ordered, inclining his head at the bodies. He pushed the young warrior away before launching into a run.

Hugo inhaled as he sprinted across the section of wall spanning the main gates. Diamond's scent was strong on the air, almost as if she were running next to him. Another group of soldiers gathered around a crumpled figure on the floor.

"Rose?" uttered Hugo, dropping to his knees by the healer. Her face was swollen as if she had taken a hard blow. He swore.

"Commander?" her face paled even as she tried to sit up.

"Where did they take her?" he asked.

She just stared at him.

"Rose!" he barked. "Where did they go? I need to get her back!"

Rose hesitated and shook her head as if clearing it, then turned to the nearby turret.

"In there," she breathed.

Not fae. Not flying, Hugo realised quickly, thanking the goddess.

The turret door slammed open as he barged through. It was dark inside save for the light from the arrow slits. He immediately stilled. Still buzzing with magic, his heightened senses picked up every sound from nearby. Listening intently, he didn't know whether to be relieved he hadn't run into a trap like a bumbling novice, or roar with frustration that she wasn't in here. His anger and worry grew.

"Where have they taken you, my love?" he whispered to the empty turret.

Ignoring the thrashing desperation of the beast inside him, he calmed his breathing and his mind, and *felt* for her. He didn't know how to work their venom bond properly yet, but magic was something he had known all his life. Absorbing more from the energised air was as easy as breathing. Hugo grinned and flexed his muscles. Rolling his neck, he melted into the shadows.

Following the sweet smell of summer flowers was easy, but curbing his rage was not. Mixed with Diamond's scent was the disgusting stink of human male sweat—and fear. Two captors then, he mused. Not that it mattered, they would be dead soon enough. Damp tickled his nostrils as he descended unseen into the darkness. His boots were silent on the stone steps as down he went past ground level and the tower guard room into the pitch black. He was nothing more than rippling darkness as he stepped onto the earthen floor of the lowest level. Only spare gate machinery was housed down in this musty, unused store. Hugo adjusted his vision until the piles of heavy chains and workbenches came into a foggy view. Clearly no one had been down here for a long while—except two reeking humans and Diamond.

Hugo followed his nose, prowling toward what looked like a solid wall. Anyone else would have missed the concealed outline of a stone door. He inhaled and smelled the astringent herb they had used to drug her. Monksweet. A plant the Acolytes used to stifle magic and render their victims unconscious. Effective but short-acting. A cold rage settled on his heart. He had no idea who would want to take Diamond, but he did know they were going to die, and painfully, if they had harmed so much as a hair on her head. Carefully, slowly, he placed one palm against the upper brick of the door that looked cleaner than the rest and pushed.

Stone grated upon stone. Hugo stopped to listen, his body coiled and ready. Nothing. Every move of his body was perfectly controlled as he drew his blades and stalked forward.

Chapter Forty

Murmured frantic whispering buzzed like the hum of an insect in Diamond's ears. It stopped as she groaned and cracked her eyelids. *What in Chaos?* Her thoughts were muddled, her mind thick and syrupy. *Where am I? This isn't my room....*

Outside, seagulls screeched and people shouted anxiously. A large group ran past the building, their feet stomping below the open window before fading away. Her arms were heavy, too heavy to move. Confused, Diamond opened her eyes fully and stared down. She was tied to a chair. Even as her mind registered that fact she felt the hard seat underneath her. Her head ached ferociously, and she couldn't make her body move.

"Here," came a muffled voice. "Drink some of this. It'll make you feel better."

Diamond swung her head away but large hands gripped her head from behind, keeping her still. Her captor held her nose, forcing her to drink. Lukewarm liquid hit the inside of her mouth. With no other choice, Diamond gulped and choked down the sweet solution until she wanted to vomit. Just before he pulled the cup away, she held a mouthful back, spraying it into his face. A petty defiance, but a defiance nonetheless. The man behind chuckled.

"There is no need for bad manners, girl. Our lord only wishes to speak with you."

Ayk! She would not deign to answer him.

That potion cleared her mind a little. Ayk had kidnapped her—and murdered two Queen's elite guards, just like that. No remorse, no hesitation.

Diamond squinted at the figure retreating to the window. His face was completely obscured by a black, featureless mask, which he was now wiping with his sleeve. He turned and looked outside, his head tilted down. They were upstairs then. Diamond cocked her head, listening to the madness of the city; the screams, the shouts, the distant roar of the guardian.

Blinking her scratchy eyes, she studied her captor. Broad shoulders, wide enough to block out the light, dipped to a trim waist. His cloak slipped sideways revealing golden wings folded almost flat into his back. A warrior then, Diamond realised, trying not to panic. *What in Chaos is a warrior doing kidnapping his Queen's prisoner?* Her eyes darted to the small door, and she took a deep breath, her heart beginning to race. She didn't know if she could get away from such a male without her magic. Probably not. The hair on her neck prickled as feet shuffled behind her and Ayk whispered with someone. Diamond wanted to laugh. She had been thrust from one prison right into another.

My life has turned to rat shit, she thought, dropping her head to stare at her dirt-stained leggings. A victim, that's all she was. It occurred to her that's all she had been for years. A bubble of self-deprecating laughter escaped. Without a doubt she had to be the most pathetic person she knew; even Tom stuck up for himself more than she did. The window warrior turned his head and stared long and hard at her. Feeling his gaze, she lifted her eyes. They sparkled vividly in her mirth.

"Is that mask supposed to scare me?" she scoffed before she could stop herself, a mad grin still plastered on her face.

The warrior turned back to his vigil by the window. "No," he muttered.

"Where's Rose?" Diamond asked, still foggy about what exactly had happened before she got here.

"Rose will be fine," he answered curtly. "I'll make sure of that."

And that was that, no more talking. Silent minutes ticked by. Diamond didn't know what she wanted to do more: laugh or scream. It seemed they were waiting for something—or someone. Tugging at the cord around her wrists only made her bonds tighten. With every vibration the strange silken rope dug into her wrists, becoming so tight her fingers turned white. It didn't take long to realise she needed to keep still.

The sun moved, its beams eventually bathing her in light and warmth. It must be afternoon by now, she decided as her stomach clenched. Hugo would find her missing soon; he would start searching for her. She jumped as a downstairs door banged and thumping footsteps climbed closer. Moments later the door swung open. Diamond stiffened defensively.

"Hello, Miss Gillon," said the newcomer. The fae by the window dipped his head in respect. "My lord," he said in greeting, then stood straight-backed as if to attention.

"Who are you?" Diamond rasped. It had been hours since her last drink. Her throat was so dry it was difficult to talk,

"I'm a friend, Diamond," he replied. Although he wore no mask, this man's voice was gravelly and distorted.

Diamond shook her head to clear her ears, trying not to shrink away as the newcomer approached her chair. He stopped in front of her and crouched on his haunches until his face was level with hers. She blinked, and blinked again. The man's face was twisted, his features contorted and rippling as though she were looking through a dirty puddle at him. It was distinctly nauseating.

"What do you want with me?" she asked, wishing her voice sounded stronger, less shaky.

Her captor's mouth twisted in a strange smile, reminding her of Hugo. She closed her eyes and wished with all her heart that he was here now, despite everything. He had fought for her before, and in her gut she knew he would rip these men apart for taking her, even if it was only because they had killed two of his men in the process. But no. It would be better if he didn't come, if she could escape on her own, get away from her new gaolers without him. If she could, it might be possible to run from the Queen.

The man continued, oblivious to her inner turmoil, "I want you to escape the Queen and live. I want you to save this world, and I want you to fight for Eternity," he said sincerely.

Diamond snorted with laughter, "You want me to live, to save the world—to escape? Oh, please. In case you hadn't noticed I'm trussed up like a pig for slaughter...by you, not the Queen." She yanked at her bonds and once again they tightened. She hissed in pain.

Her captor looked down and frowned at her bonds. "I am sorry about that, but please try and understand our nervousness with you. You annihilated over one hundred enemy troops *and* took out half a mile of forest with your magic. I couldn't risk you doing that to us before I have time to explain," he said, pulling a thin knife from his boot.

"Explain what?" countered Diamond, eyeing his knife warily. "And aren't I more likely to listen to you if you *haven't* got me bound to a chair?" she uttered through gritted teeth.

"Yes, but you would be wise to keep still. That is Haplotheria silk, the product of an ingenious little spider-like creature who kills its prey by crushing it with its web. This beautiful thread tightens against vibration and will not loosen by itself, so keep still, princess, and listen whilst I cut your bonds."

Diamond stopped struggling and gripped the arms of the chair to keep her hands quieted.

"You are no ordinary half-blood," he told her, leaning forward, the blade held loosely between tough, scarred fingers. Diamond leaned away but his breath became warm on her mouth.

The masked warrior stiffened as windows broke in a nearby building. It seemed the Valentian people were rioting and looting far too close for comfort.

"My lord, we need to leave. We can take the—" shadows hid the warriors eyes but Diamond felt him looking at her, "—the usual ways. You will have more time to persuade her of our cause in the safety of our normal haunts."

"Diamond—my lady. The drug we used has dampened your gifts in a similar way as the shield, but it will wear off soon. If I cut you free, will you give me your word you will allow me time to explain?" asked the lord. "I give you my word in return, you will be safe from the Queen."

"Safe?" Diamond snorted. "I doubt that you can promise to keep me safe from an immortal like her."

Warmth pulsed insistently in her belly, something familiar tugging at her chest.

"Fine. I'll make this quick, but you have a choice to make. This world needs you to live. Darkness will take us all if you die. There will be no more children, no more love or light, no more sun or moon—even the stars will fall from the heavens as Eternity itself is destroyed. Nothing but an endless void will remain. You can stop all of that. Diamond, your mother was someone very special...." He paused and took a breath, dipping his strange distorted head in what looked like reverence.

Behind Diamond something splintered and exploded. The tug on her chest ripped an answering wave of magic from her core. Rage, worry, fear. Hugo's raging emotions slammed into her, leaving no room for any other thoughts. Wood flew past her head in bits, some landing on her, some hitting the distorted man. Ayk and Dan only had time to grunt in shock before they fell, their hot blood hitting the back of Diamond's head in a gut-churning splatter. Diamond looked on in horror as Ayk's eyes glazed over and Dan's body landed in a twisted heap beside her.

The distorted lord was up and out of the door before Diamond could even blink.

Hugo ploughed through the debris, kicking bits from his path.

"No!" Diamond yelled at the disappearing figure, she needed to know about her mother! "Come back!" she screeched, twisting and fighting against her bonds until her wrists were dripping blood.

The window warrior spun swiftly in front of the door, facing Hugo with his sword drawn. Clearly he wanted to give his lord time to escape, even if that meant his own death. Before the door banged shut downstairs, Hugo stormed forward. The warrior flicked his wrist. Diamond gasped. Red magic. No Avalonian had red magic anymore. It ripple across the room like a wave of shimmering heat. Hugo roared, but not in pain.

Leaning into the onslaught of power he grinned with fiendish delight, darkness rippling around him. A shroud of silver-flamed shadow devoured the red wave, even as his powerful body charged forwards.

The warrior swore, desperately raising his sword in defence. Clearly he had expected a different reaction to his magical attack. Hugo's wrathful bellow filled the room as he drove his sword down. Metal jarred and sparked.

"You took her from me! I can smell her blood. Now you will die!" he promised, his voice nothing like his own. It was more animalistic than Diamond had ever heard.

The warrior blocked Hugo's blade with skill and precision. Red magic meant the ability to control heat and fire. Hugo's blade began to glow as the other fae heated it like it had come out of a furnace. Hugo grunted but did not let go. The white-hot metal did not burn him through the glove of darkness rippling around his hand.

"Stop this, commander! We are not your enemy," the warrior panted, blocking and spinning away from Hugo's blades with utter confidence and no small amount of skill.

Hugo did not answer, his only response was to blast the red magic away with a veil of darkness, parrying a strike and bringing his other blade down with such force the window warrior stumbled, almost driven to his knees. Hugo blocked the warrior's sweeping sword strike and stabbed him through the shoulder, before mercilessly slashing across the male's thigh. A move meant to incapacitate. The warrior dropped to one knee but somehow still managed to block Hugo's killing blow.

"Commander! Stop! She will be safer with us. If you take her back to the palace, the Queen will kill her! You know she will! We need Diamond to live! All of us do!" he panted, desperation in his voice now.

Diamond gasped as she saw the warrior's hand drop to his boot and grasp the handle of a small concealed knife.

"Hugo!" she yelled, fighting her bonds with all her might. Pain screeched through Diamond's wrists as the silk tightened. She screamed. It was going to cut off her hands!

Instead of killing the warrior, Hugo kicked his assailant in the chest sending him sprawling. There was a solid thud as the warrior's head smacked into the wall and he stilled. Hugo immediately twisted to Diamond, dropping to his knees in front of her. Blood ran from her wounds, dripping down the chair arms.

"Keep still," he ordered, pulling a dagger and slicing through the silken rope.

Sobbing with relief, she sagged against him before the pain started in earnest. Her fingers burned as blood rushed back in. Diamond whimpered, not sure what to do with herself.

Thoughts of the window warrior escaped them both. Hugo quickly slashed strips of material off his tunic. Dropping his blades he firmly bound her wrists, trying to staunch the heavy flow of blood. For a moment he leaned his forehead against hers and gripped each wrist as she fought to control her panicked sobs.

"Shh. It's alright. You'll be fine now. Breathe, Diamond. In...out...with me. That's it."

Slowly her mind returned to her. With her head leaning against Hugo's, they shared the same warm breath. She closed her eyes, her body responding to his. Her breathing slowed until it mirrored his own and she could swear she heard the distant beat of his heart.

The scuff of boots on the wooden floor had Hugo on his feet in front of her, blades ready. Diamond looked on as he faced the bleeding warrior, his face icy and calm.

"We are not your enemy," the warrior panted. Equally calm and with slow intent he sheathed his own blades.

"Kill me if you must. But you know if you take her back to the palace, the Queen will destroy her. Let her come with me, commander. Please. I give you my word I will keep her safe," the warrior appealed, holding his bloodied hands out to Diamond.

Hugo looked down at her, his brow bunched. Diamond shook her head frantically and grabbed at his tunic. He couldn't be considering it.

"No," he bit out at last.

"So be it. But you know what will happen now, and from what I've just seen pass between you, you are going to wish you had listened to me. You will both need our help one day soon; I just hope we can get to you soon enough. Until then...." he said and bowed low, his fist upon his chest.

Even Hugo looked stunned by that universal mark of respect. Bleeding and bruised the warrior turned and fled.

Chapter Forty-One

As if the goddess herself whispered in his ear, Hugo was certain that he must let the warrior go. Maybe they would meet again. Regardless, what sickened him most was that the male was right. Hugo *would* regret this selfish act, just as he regretted his decision to bring her to the palace.

Diamond stared up at him with wide, shocked eyes. He wanted to reassure her, to pull her into his body for protection and take her away from this mess.

"They know who my mother is—was," she whispered, her gaze flitting between her bleeding wrists and the fallen men on either side of her chair.

Hugo felt his heart go out to her. A life in the northern forest could never prepare anyone for all this pain and death. He dropped to his haunches and grasped her chin, pulling her face towards him so he could look at her.

"Diamond, look at me, not them. We need to get out of here," he said softly.

Her beautiful eyes focused on his face. "How? How did you find me?" she whispered, lifting her hand and laying it against his scar.

Hugo swallowed, he couldn't remember any women ever voluntarily touching his scar—or him—with such tenderness.

"I told you, I can feel your magic. I will always know where you are," he murmured, wishing he could share how true that was as he gently cupped a bloodied hand against her soft cheek. "And I wish I could promise to always keep you safe—but I can't." For a moment he couldn't move as she turned her face into his palm and kissed it.

He should have let the warrior take her; he didn't know what he was going to do now. His actions had been utterly selfish, his only thought to wrench her back to him. But now.... His mind raced with possibilities. Maybe they could catch that warrior. No. He sighed. It was hopeless. He had hesitated, and now it was too late. Hugo hung his head. He was too recognisable, but alone—just maybe she could make it to a trade ship and get out.

"You should run," he said quietly, knowing he would gladly return to his Queen empty-handed and suffer his punishment if it meant Diamond stood a chance.

Diamond straightened. "No. You need to take me back," she replied, her voice steady and determined.

"Diamond, I can't. That warrior was right. The Queen will destroy you. She will bleed your magic dry and then kill you." He swallowed his self-disgust and inadequacy. "You cannot go back—I will not be able to keep you safe."

"Yes, you will," Diamond whispered into his palm. A bitter taste washed through his mouth at the conviction in her words. "And if I don't go back she will punish you—I don't know much about torture, but I can guess she gave you this scar." She leaned in and, just like she had done once before, brushed her warm lips against it. "It's in your eyes and your magic every time I touch it."

"What is?" he asked, trying not to pull away from her ridiculous belief he was her saviour, or the feel of her lips against his scar. This was all wrong, she should be repulsed by it, by him, just like he was every time he saw his reflection.

"Fear," she whispered.

He balked and immediately scowled. "I am not scared of anything, not her—and certainly not you," he snarled, immediately defensive that she should think him weak in any way.

A small, understanding smile curled her lips, "Of course you're not, but I don't want her to give you anymore scars or pain because of me," she said.

His defensive walls crumbled immediately. It was strange to know another person was anxious for him. He huffed a wry laugh as he pulled her out of the chair, tensing his muscles when her legs wobbled.

"She will cause me far more pain by hurting you—so we are not going back. There is one place I can take you. One person who might help us."

The tunnel he had used would be their best means of escape. Now Diamond was safe and by his side, the beast inside him had settled along with his magic, and his sight was back to normal. Hugo could blend in with the shadows, become invisible and see well enough to negotiate the pitch black, but Diamond could not. And if her kidnappers had used these tunnels to get here, so might others. Besides, he would likely get lost in the old catacombs without

Diamond's scent to guide him. No, Hugo would explore them another time.

Diamond looked with disgust at the fallen soldiers, and he waited stiffly for her condemnation. He felt no regret. Diamond was his Nexus and they had tried to take her from him. Their deaths were their own fault...or their lord's. He needn't have worried; Diamond said nothing, keeping her eyes averted she stepped over them and peered inside the dark entrance.

"Where does that go?" she asked curiously.

"Honestly? I have no idea. I only know the tunnel I took to get here from the wall. There were entrances leading off everywhere and, without your scent to guide me, I think we would get hopelessly lost."

She blushed and refused to look at him.

"Summer flowers," he whispered in her ear, inhaling and stepping up close against her back. "That's what you smell like," he told her, letting his magic glide forward and caress the exposed skin of her neck. A shiver rippled through her body.

"We should go," he said huskily, coughing to clear the tightness in his throat. Now was not the time, no matter how much he wanted to pull her against him. Instead he took her hand, entwining his fingers with hers and guided her towards the door.

Chapter Forty-Two

They emerged from a rundown little cottage onto a dirty street. The tang of sea salt and fish laced the air, but it was the acrid smoke blowing inland that choked them. A heavy blanket smothered the city.

"Holy shit!" cursed Hugo, gripping her hand tightly, "I didn't realise those tunnels had brought me down this far. We're miles from where we need to be."

The small street acted like a funnel for the mass of people running for the docks. Decisively, Hugo dragged her along with the flow. Diamond gripped on tightly to Hugo's hand, hating the proximity of such a mob. They turned the corner on to the docks. Carnage greeted them. People lined the huge quays to watch. Pushing and shoving each other for a better view of the ships beyond the shield, the burning ships. The magnificent hulls were reduced to floating pyres that sent black smoke billowing skyward.

A large high-walled harbour and dock buildings loomed to the left, its entrance protected by a solid wall of warrior fae. They were a truly awesome sight. Gold wings held them steady, hovering from ground level to high in the sky. No ordinary fae would get past, and certainly no humans would dare try. Behind the wall of warriors, two huge war galleons were berthed safely in the harbour. Above each fluttered the Queen's sigil. The green serpents upon the rippling flags seemed almost alive as the breeze whipped them into a frenzy.

Despite the sight of those two magnificent vessels, Diamond smirked. It was impossible not to feel immense satisfaction at the sight of the Queen's armada being reduced to ash out on the ocean. Then she saw the bobbing heads of the sailors trying to swim for their lives and any satisfaction she felt dissipated into horror. Screams echoed clearly over the water, heads disappearing by the dozen under the wild, white-crested waves. The sea teemed with bodies, some thrashing and swimming, some floating face down. Fishing boats of all sizes had rallied to pull people from the sea, some already brimming as they returned to the docks. A few brave fishermen even risked the wrath of the dragon to venture beyond the shield to mount a rescue.

It didn't escape Diamond's notice that there were many half-bloods among the rescued and the dead. It was easy to spot them. Although many had fae traits, they still looked slightly different to full blooded fae. Deep yellow wings that were scarred as if they had been burned, hung wet and limp down the backs of some, and many had pointed ears, handsome faces or tall strong bodies. Hugo noticed where her attention lay and yanked her sideways.

"C'mon. You can't help them. And we have to get out of here," he urged.

Diamond frowned and pulled him to a stop. Rescued sailors from other kingdoms collapsed on the dockside. The dark olive skin and black hair of Houria; the forked, beaded beards of Gar Anon; even the ebony skin of the Southern Hotlands were in evidence. Her stomach tightened in anger at the obvious marks of cruelty on their thin, cold bodies. Lash marks striped their backs and the red welts of manacles discoloured their wrists and ankles. Slaves.

Fae were not good in the water; the weight of their wings became heavy enough for some of them to drown. It seemed the people of Avalonia were happy to sacrifice the unwanted, the unworthy or the downright unfortunate to the rough seas in their Queen's armada. How convenient for her to know that her bigoted people did not care enough about half-bloods or slaves to protest.

Well, they will now, snarled Diamond to herself. There were hardly any ships to protect their vast ocean doorway, and now these men and half-bloods could escape and cause havoc in this city. Diamond grinned and hoped some of them would.

A scuffle broke out nearby. A deep, heavily accented voice bellowed his rage as two city guards dragged a limp body from a fishing boat.

"No! She is my daughter!" A man with ebony skin shoved two guards away from the body on the ground and hoisted a young slim girl into arms rippling with hard muscle. He looked around frantically, for a moment his eyes met Diamond's and she felt the oddest sensation, a tug on her soul as if this man were important to her.... Tarnished blue metal gleamed against the dark skin of his forehead. A blue sun inlaid in his skin like a tattoo. It was impossible not to stare at the flames reaching down his temples to touch his jaw line.

But Hugo did not have time to study the docks. Ignoring her protests, he dragged her against the surging crowd, leaving the sun-marked man behind. Diamond blinked to clear the smoke from her stinging eyes.

Together they fought to escape the tightly-packed and aggressive crowd. Hugo growled, shoving people roughly aside. The atmosphere was laced with violence. With every stumble of her feet Hugo righted her, making encouraging sounds. Never once did he let go, and she gripped him back with equal fervour.

"Through here," he urged, just when Diamond wanted to give up and collapse to the ground. He pulled her past an upturned cart, weaving between its spilled load of empty baskets. A man lay on his belly next to the cart, his face beaten bloody. Diamond swallowed and did her best to ignore him. Blood and death were becoming far too familiar a sight.

Beyond the main street, Hugo tugged her into a small alley, then burst into a run. They sprinted from the noise of the docks, not stopping as they bolted across bigger streets or ran by groups of looters. The city passed by in a blur until Diamond's lungs burned and the metallic taste of blood lined her mouth.

Hugo pulled her to a sudden halt. Barely panting, he cocked his head to one side. The distant chime of a temple bell echoed. Four chimes. Hugo frowned and looked up at the strip of sky between the closely built buildings. A whooshing sound approached, becoming louder. Hugo pushed her against a building, flattening his recognisable wings against the wall. Warriors and city guard flew over in heavy formation, heading for the rioting city folk and the docks.

"She will know we are missing by now," Hugo said, looking down at her. Diamond didn't miss the anxiety in his eyes and felt her heart miss a beat. Hugo never looked anxious. "We need to get to the other side of the island," he told her, yanking her farther into a shadowed doorway as another group of city guard flew low over the roof tops, scanning the ground below.

"I know you're tired, but you have to run—as fast as you can, until it's safe to fly." Grabbing her hand, he launched into another sprint.

It was all Diamond could do to keep up with him. With heaving breaths she forced herself to move. Speech was impossible. Another street. Another. Once again Hugo spun smoothly, changed direction and grabbed her around her waist. Diamond found herself in the shadows covered by his body. A split second later inky darkness swirled, concealing them. It was hard to ignore the way her chest heaved against his even as city guards and warriors shot overhead.

"W-what was that?" she stuttered, as the darkness lifted. Tired. She was so tired.

"Later," was all Hugo said, as panicked screaming began in the distance. "They're clearing the docks. If we're going to make it, we have to fly now whilst their attention is elsewhere." Hugo's voice was urgent but steady. His sapphire eyes scanned her red and sweaty face. "Are you ready?" he asked, opening his arms. She quickly stepped into his warmth and wrapped her arms around his neck. "Legs up around my waist," he instructed.

She did as he asked, her heart racing. Metal chinked as he armoured. In the dimness of the alley the pattern of silver rivulets seemed far brighter and infinitely more beautiful than she had ever seen them before. A gasp escaped her as they turned to a pattern of silver flames.

"It's the power in the shield," he said by way of explanation, then hesitated before speaking again. "I can absorb it, feed on it. Somehow that guardian's attack is making my magic stronger," he told her, his eyes flicking warily to hers.

He had expected shock or distaste. Diamond stared right back. He must know that nothing about his magic, or him, disgusted her. She leaned in, wrapping her arms around him, her chin tucked into the curve of his neck. For a few wonderful seconds he just held her tightly, inhaling deeply as he let his magic wrap around them. Diamond tightened her arms and legs and squeezed him back, pushing her face harder into his neck. She wished for courage enough to tell him how she felt. He took a breath as if to speak but no words came out, only a huge shuddering breath as he shook his head. Magnificent and powerful, those wings began to beat against the air and his magic withdrew. Diamond hoped she would not regret letting that moment pass.

Chapter Forty-Three

They slowly crested the roof tops, Hugo vigilantly searching the sky. More airborne warriors and guards passed nearby, focused on the distant docks. They ignored the single Queen's guard and his charge. Hugo rapidly propelled them through the air, stealing Diamond's breath. Her tunic flapped madly, the cold air cutting straight through her sheer blouse to freeze her skin beneath.

Everything will be fine, she told herself, preferring to hide from reality by burying her face in Hugo's neck rather than watch where they were going. His arms tightened around her, his back and shoulder muscles contracting and shifting urgently under her grip.

The dragon was nowhere to be seen, only the smoking pyres of the dead ships were evidence of its wrath. Hugo headed over the jumbled rooftops, his eyes searching the city. Warily he watched the other fae in the skies, increasing his efforts and changing direction if any came too close.

Hugo was heading toward the ice moon. East. This side of the island was open to the raging weather blown in from the Rough Seas. Below them lay small battered quays and tiny inlets. Fishing boats and small trade vessels bobbed around on the turbulent waters, safe under the protection of the shield.

With her back to the direction they were heading and her face still buried in Hugo's neck, Diamond did not see the lone fae diving down across the slanted rooftops. Golden wings flashing he headed in at an angle that would obscure him from even the Queen's guard. Diamond snapped her head up as a familiar strong voice bellowed her name.

"Diamond! Commander! Wait!"

Hugo back winged and executed a swift defensive turn, holding her with one arm as he reached over and pulled a sword so quickly the blade was up before they faced the oncoming force of General Edo.

"What do you want?" growled Hugo with eyes black as night.

The general panted, a slight sheen of sweat on his brow. "Damn it, where have you been?" he blustered, looking at Diamond with concern. "Are you all right?" he asked quickly.

Diamond could only nod in confusion.

"Good. By the goddess, you had us worried. The Queen has all her guards out searching for you. The way she reacted when neither of you answered her summons to court was truly terrifying, even for me. Jack has sent out his own men to search for you." His big chest heaved as he caught his breath. "If you return to the palace, she'll kill you both," he warned, his keen grey eyes searching the skies. A group of fae launched over the distant palace walls and dived down over the sloping island city scape.

"Jack said I am to meet him at the goddess' temple in the middle district in one hour, regardless of whether we find you or not. Come with me and we will get you out of this mess," he told them earnestly.

"Jack sent you to look for me?" Diamond asked, her eyes wide.

"Of course he did. Diamond, he is beside himself with worry. You saved his life. He always intended to get you out of that palace, but if we don't go now the Queen's men will be upon you and there will be no hope of escape."

"Hugo?" Diamond whispered urgently.

Hugo stared at the general silently, suspicion pouring off him.

"Oh, by Erebos' balls, commander! We need to get her to safety. I know you care for her. Gods damn it! It's in your face every time you look at her—even when you try and hide it. Everyone can see, including your Queen. What the hell do you think is going to happen to Diamond when you take her back to that place? Do you think she will be allowed to live? She is as good as my daughter, I helped raise her! At least let her come with me, and she might stand a chance of getting away. Jack has already arranged passage for Diamond on a trade vessel. Hugo, if you want to go too, the captain is all about profit. I'm sure for a few more gold coins he will take you too."

Diamond felt Hugo's body tense with indecision as he looked over his shoulder at the eastern docks, then back at the general who tensely watched the distant group of warriors move closer.

"Fine," growled Hugo and sheathed his blade. His arm came back around her and adjusted her weight. "Lead the way, general," he said.

General Edo immediately dived down among the roof tops leading them away from the approaching fae. When they had skirted around enough of the city to hide them, he led Hugo back up towards the middle district. Ordinary fae with golden feathered or sheer wings zipped about, their movements urgent. Some eyed the warriors and gave them a wide berth, others did not even notice, intent on their own business. Below, the streets were littered with debris. Horses clattered over the cobbles, as those without wings either urgently returned home or tried to run for the valley. It seemed the dragon did not even need to directly attack the city to cause utter carnage.

A domed rooftop appeared ahead, its green and yellow lichen-covered curves a sorry sight. The temple of light sat in its own grounds, just as the one in Berriesford had, and looked equally as neglected. Large trees stood like sentinels, boughs sagging under their own immense weight. The burning pyre had long since fallen into disrepair and lay in a collapsed heap. General Edo circled over a nearby avenue lined with shops and pointed downward. It was large enough to land in and practically deserted.

Glass crunched under Hugo's boots as he smoothly landed, his eyes instantly scanning the buildings and shadows. His arms tightened around her shoulders as her feet slid to the ground. Cold kissed her skin as he gently pulled away.

Diamond was suddenly scared. "You won't leave me, will you?" she whispered urgently, worried that as soon as they met Jack, Hugo would return to the palace. They both knew the Queen's search would be unrelenting and her wrath like nothing on this earth if one of her elite guard deserted. Diamond's cold fingers clutched at his forearms as if her touch alone could stop him from going back to that life.

Hugo smiled reassuringly and cupped the back of her head in one big hand, then leaned down until his lips brushed her forehead. "No. I will never leave you," he whispered.

"Come on!" urged General Edo, running past them. "We need to get off this street."

They reached the end of the wide avenue within seconds. Both warriors leaned up against the wall of a large corner building.

Hugo peered out, checking the main thoroughfare. "Go!" he hissed, nodding at General Edo, who grabbed Diamond's hand.

"Run!" the general urged.

Together they surged across the street and darted in through a rusty iron gate. The temple garden was dim and cold. Eerie quiet sat upon it, even the city noise did not penetrate here. Their breathing and footsteps sounded far too loud. General Edo quickly pulled her off the path into the shadows under a Lyca tree. The large red leaves drooped down, almost touching the floor, its boughs creating a dim hiding place. Standing with his back to the red trunk, General Edo narrowed his eyes, searching the grounds and the temple's many arches. Finally his gaze assessed the main doors.

Hugo darted into the shadows of a yew tree opposite—and disappeared. Diamond blinked but said nothing. The general was too busy studying the temple to notice. Silently they waited. Nothing moved other than two seagulls that landed on an ancient archway and squawked loudly.

"Where's Hugo?" The general frowned after a few minutes. Nothing moved in the shadows. His whole body tensed, his eyes searching frantically.

"I'm here," Hugo rumbled, his voice barely more than a vibration directly behind them.

Diamond felt goose bumps rise on her skin, her magic flaring as he touched her reassuringly with his. How had he moved behind them without being seen or heard? Clearly her childhood guardian was wondering the same thing. Hugo ignored the question in General Edo's eyes and, with his swords drawn, stepped closer to Diamond.

"It seems quiet. The others should be here soon. What do you want to do—wait out here or go inside out of sight?" the older warrior asked.

Hugo looked from the temple to the general just as the iron gate gave a high pitched squeak. Both fae whipped their heads towards it. Immediately they all shrank back. Diamond held her breath, hoping it was only Jack. Her fingers clutched Hugo's tunic. A moment later she gave a nervous giggle. General Edo swore, then huffed a chuckle too.

"It's alright. I don't think he's come to get us," he muttered as a smallish black mongrel dog slunk nervously along the path. It hesitated at the sound of the general's voice, then bolted.

"Probably not," agreed Hugo, but he watched the animal leave through narrowed eyes. "But the Queen has all manner of spies working for her, and not all of them are human or fae," he muttered.

"We'd better get out of sight then," responded the general. "The goddess only knows who might have seen us land. These temples are always unlocked, so we need to make sure no one else has sought shelter here after what's gone on today."

He looked at Hugo and tipped his head towards the door. Hugo nodded, then focused all his attention on Diamond and ignored the general completely. She swallowed and tried to look calm, even though she felt anything but. Smiling a little he tucked a wisp of hair behind her ear.

"Stay close," he whispered, pulling something from his weapons belt to hold it out. "Here. I rescued this from the forest."

Diamond curled her fingers around the hilt of the dagger and looked at it in wonder. "I thought it was lost," she breathed, gripping it tightly.

Hugo cocked his head, a smile curving his lips at her expression. "No. Not completely lost—just astray. Now it's back where it should be—by your side." His voice was soft, the silver in his eyes glinting like stars in a midnight sky.

Her heart thumped. *Does he only mean the blade?* she wondered. When he gently brushed the back of his fingers down her cheek and kissed the tip of her nose, she had her answer.

"It's yours—don't you want it back?" she asked, stroking the cool metal with careful fingers. It belonged to him. Although it was much more than just a blade to her. It had kept her sane through her fear and loneliness in the forest. Every glance of that Silverbore blade had given her hope that Hugo would come for her, that she could be strong like him and survive.

"No, Diamond. It belongs to you—completely. By your side is where it should stay—always."

"Thank you," she whispered and blinked away her tears. It was only a stupid knife.

Chapter Forty-Four

They crouched down behind the once-alabaster wall. Green mould stained the ancient stone, and fusty damp tickled Diamond's nose. The dagger shook as she gripped it, ready to fight.

"You go first," whispered General Edo to Hugo.

Hugo adjusted himself to go and then hesitated. "No," he grated, frowning at the general. "You go. I'll watch our backs," he instructed curtly.

General Edo contemplated Hugo with hard grey eyes then nodded. Diamond released a breath. Now was not the time for a power struggle between these two dominant fae.

"Fine, commander. But be vigilant. Jack said he would be here, but—as you said—there are many spies in this city."

Fleetingly Diamond saw irritation in Hugo's eyes. Then his sapphire gaze rested on her, and softened in a way that made her legs weak.

"Stay close to me," he rumbled as General Edo bolted for the door. "I'm still not sure about this."

Sick with nerves, Diamond nodded. General Edo disappeared through the thick, white oak doors. Minutes passed. Diamond nervously flicked her gaze from the door to Hugo, her mouth so dry she could hardly swallow. Hugo vigilantly monitored the grounds around them, his attention flitting to the skies above too. The wind began to gust noisily around the outside of the temple grounds, bizarrely not touching the trees in the grounds. Diamond glanced up at the grey clouds forming overhead.

Minutes later the general cracked open the door again. He beckoned the two crouching figures urgently, his face tight. Hugo glanced around the temple grounds one last time then uttered, "Run!"

Diamond didn't need to be told twice. Head down, dagger clutched in her hand, she sprinted. Wings un-armoured and flat to his back, Hugo followed close on her heels.

Inside the temple was cold and held a curious atmosphere only an ancient place of worship can transmit. The door swung shut, which plunged them into darkness. Dirty stained glass windows, high in the domed roof, provided the only light.

Diamond's heart raced, her breathing loud in her ears. "Hugo?" she whispered fearfully,

"I'm here," he answered, his magic touching her, reassuring her.

General Edo swore and huffed, trying to turn the large door lock. The ancient metal grated, the big iron key protesting. He hissed, the iron burning his un-gloved fingers. Ancient and stiff, the lock did not want to turn.

"Here," said Hugo, "I'll do it."

He wrapped his hand in his tunic so the metal would not burn him. General Edo nodded and stood back, blowing on his burned fingers. His boots echoed as he took Hugo's place by Diamond's side. The moment Hugo had his back to them and leaned down to grasp the key, the shadows exploded into movement.

Queen's guards appeared out of shimmering air, so close Diamond could see their gleaming eyes. The general only had time to grunt before a sword hilt slammed into his temple. Cruel fingers instantly grabbed her wrist, wrenching it so hard her fingers loosened. Diamond shrieked in pain, her dagger clattering to the floor. Hugo did not stand a chance. Three figures materialised next to him, moving like lightening. One looped an iron cord around his neck and yanked it tight.

"Hugo!" Diamond squealed in terror. The roar in Hugo's throat was cut off, reduced to a strangled choking noise.

Two guards dragged Hugo backwards by his arms, kicking at his knees. He tried to fight—but with his magic suppressed by the iron, he could only partially armour his wings. The guards slammed several kicks into his belly. With bunched muscles, Hugo flung one guard away and managed to reach over his back for a sword.

"Tighten that collar! *Now!*" bellowed someone.

Hugo turned purple as he fought the iron cord squeezing around his neck. The nearest guard grunted as Hugo's blade sunk deep enough through his arm to grind against bone. The collar was yanked, and Hugo had no choice; he collapsed panting and choking to the floor. Diamond screamed in terror and confusion.

"Enough! Commander Casimir, keep still and you will live. Fight and injure any more of your brothers and I will tighten that iron noose around your neck until it burns clean through," Lord Commander Ream informed Hugo ruthlessly. "My Queen wants you returning to her side. But know this. I *will* kill you—slowly—if you so much as twitch in the wrong way." He stood over Hugo's kneeling figure, a merciless shadow. "My Queen's offer. If you return promptly to her side, deliver your prisoner *and* continue your devoted servitude to her, you will be forgiven for your incompetence—for losing," he snorted, "the magic wielder. Personally I'd wipe your traitorous hide from this earth, but I must defer to my Queen's wishes."

Diamond knew if they took her back, her life would be forfeit. The Queen would kill her—and maybe even Hugo. Her breathing hitched, her heart banging against her chest. *No. I will not go back!* She bucked and struggled to be free. The faceless guard clamped his arms around her like a vice, pulling her to his chest. A guttural warning rumbled from Hugo, but he did not fight.

"Quiet!" ordered the scarred Lord Commander Ream. His granite hewn features came into focus as he strode to within an arm's length, contemplated her with utter revulsion, then viciously backhanded Diamond's cheek. The blow sent her reeling, and blood exploded into her mouth. He bent down and retrieved her dagger from the floor, glancing over at Hugo in disgust as he recognised it.

"Cease your wailing, you mongrel bitch, or I will cut out your tongue," he barked cruelly. "I doubt the Queen will mind."

Terrified, Diamond immediately looked to Hugo. Nothing but scorching hate burned in those silver eyes. He shook his head. This was no empty threat. Diamond stilled, allowing herself to be captured like the meek little mouse she had become, the bitter taste of defeat and fear coating her tongue. Ream prowled closer, contemplating Hugo's dagger. Shaking uncontrollably, her bladder threatened to void. Ream raised his left hand and Diamond flinched. But all he did was run a finger gently down her cheek.

"Such a pretty face—for an abomination of our lord. I would like opportunity to get to know what makes you tick, what makes you scream the loudest, but—we don't have time," he purred, lust and excitement thick in his voice as he grabbed her throat with one large hand. A frightened squeal bubbled out of her trembling lips. Instantly he withdrew, his eyes cold as ice as he slammed a large fist into her jaw.

Diamond was half way to unconsciousness before pain blasted across her face.

"I told you to stay quiet," Ream snarled as darkness closed in and she sagged against her captor's embrace.

Chapter Forty-Five

Hugo forced the familiar black wall to descend on his emotions, holding back the rampaging fury inside him. He would kill these warriors. Moving his eyes slowly, he marked each face in turn. His magic was powerful enough to ensure they would not see him coming. He would play their games—for now. If he did not, they would kill Diamond before he could get this cord off his neck.

Not for the first time Hugo felt the weight of his inadequacy and guilt, which only served to fuel his rage further. Heat pounded through his blood, and the beast thrashed wildly against the cage of his body. Through his eyes it registered Diamond's limp form. Hugo gritted his teeth, his body shaking as he became consumed by its desperate need to protect her, to rip her to safety and release its wrath on these males who would harm her. It was an impossible need that had quickly become an obsession.

Hanging his head to hide his rage from Lord Commander Ream, he drove that need, along with his magic deep, inside himself until he choked on it. There was nothing he could do—yet.

He took a few moments to gain control before he raised his eyes. Diamond's face was already swollen and grossly discoloured. With detachment, he wondered briefly if her cheekbone was broken. The cord around Hugo's neck burned, but he did not try and remove it—he knew better.

Attion stared down at him, watching every twitch Hugo made. The point of his sword pushed uncomfortably against Hugo's leather-covered chest. Hugo met his gaze and snarled. Attion's mouth twitched, and he twisted his blade. Arrogant bastard.

"Let him up," instructed Ream, shoving Diamond's dagger into his weapons belt before turning to Hugo.

Attion dropped his blade and stepped back.

"You will not struggle, commander, but you *will* do everything I ask without hesitation. If you do not, when that magic-wielding filth wakes I will make her suffer. I will inflict such indignities upon her that when I am done she will not remember her own name, let alone yours—do you understand me?" he growled, shoving his face into Hugo's.

Hugo did not recoil but swallowed the nausea and guilt that threatened to burn a hole in his chest. His beast snarled. It recognised Lord Commander Ream as an enemy. Hugo heard its violent thoughts, felt its wrath burn in his blood. Sweating beneath his armour, Hugo kept all that malice off his face.

"I understand," he rasped in response, his throat painful and swollen.

"Good. We return to the palace. You can deliver your prisoner to your Queen and await her forgiveness. Attion!" Ream barked. "Take the mongrel. Commander Casimir need not bother himself with her any longer. Yohan. Nix. Take the general."

Hugo watched the two guards hoist up the general's lax body. He was no lightweight and even the two heavily muscled guards grunted with effort. Hugo wondered how in Chaos Ream had found them. He stifled his frustration and crushing disappointment. His chance to save Diamond, and maybe himself, had just been ripped from his grasp. It had been stupid to hope. He was the Queen's servant to command, a killer with a shrivelled soul—it was not the will of the mighty guardians or the goddess for him to be anything else.

Attion strode forward and pulled Diamond from the other guard. Her body was so light he lifted her easily. A groan escaped her and he hesitated, a rare frown furrowing his brow before he settled her against his chest. For one moment Hugo's protective wall cracked open, and he snarled viciously at the other guard. Attion did not seem to notice. He looked utterly transfixed by Diamond as her head tipped forward, leaving her cheek resting against his shoulder and her hair flowing over his arm and hand. A confused expression flickered across his face and, almost guiltily, he met Hugo's wrathful glower.

A second later all expression disappeared from his face. Hugo wondered what had just happened, but then he remembered what Attion had done to Diamond when she had been at her most vulnerable. He fixed an unwavering glare on the other guard, willing it to burn a hole in Attion's back as he turned away. At night when the darkness became his ally, Hugo would make Attion regret touching what did not belong to him.

Hugo wondered what was to become of them all as he followed

his commander out into the dull evening light. It had started to rain, grey ominous clouds hanging low overhead. The air was finally clear of smoke. It seemed the ships had burned themselves out or had sunk under the fierce waves.

Hugo tensed, tilting his head and straining his fae ears. The city was unnervingly quiet, almost as if it were waiting to see what was to happen next. The group of warriors armoured their wings and launched skyward, flying in silent formation up towards the palace and the waiting Queen.

Chapter Forty-Six

Diamond groaned. Serpents of invisible magic thrashed and nipped at her exposed skin like tiny insects. She tried—and failed—to brush them away. Cold wind whipped at her hair and clothes but she was so warm, held tightly against Hugo's chest. Waking up would only bring more pain. She turned her head into his chest, inhaling deeply, then gagged as a foreign male scent swamped her.

This was not Hugo. Her whole body went rigid. *Hugo, the general, where are they?* It took only a second for her to recognise the sharp pricks on her skin. Hugo wanted her to wake up. He insistently pushed his magic against her, those silver serpents nipping her as they often did when he was angry.

"Are you awake, half-blood?" grated a cold, familiar voice. Attion.

Diamond's heart flipped, feeling each place his hateful body touched hers. Common sense deserted her and escape became her only thought. She wriggled and fought, only to find herself clamped between arms of steely strength.

"Stop!" bit out Attion, his jaw clenched. He glanced at Lord Commander Ream, who flew in front. "If you struggle I will have to hurt you. Please—stop," he hissed. His eyes darted to her face.

Diamond was so surprised by his urgent plea that she instantly stilled and stared up at him, shock making her limp. Seconds later he relaxed his arms.

A familiar tug. Diamond whipped her head to where Hugo watched. Relief and alarm vied for supremacy in her heart. Hugo must have agreed to something terrible for Lord Commander Ream to release his bonds and allow him to fly free. Whatever it was, Hugo made no move to approach them. Attion glanced at Hugo, then down at Diamond, giving her a small nod of thanks. She scowled, not trusting this astounding change in Attion. His embrace remained gentle, and every now and then he glanced down.

They landed in neat formation on the manicured grass in front of the Queen's tower, and Attion dropped her feet to the ground, putting a large hand on her back to steady her. Recoiling from him and realising she was free, Diamond bolted to Hugo.

"Commander Casimir! Control your prisoner—*now!*" ordered Lord Commander Ream.

Before her mind could process that order, Hugo grabbed her wrist. She shrieked as he twisted and flipped her body over. In one swift seamless move, she was face-first into the ground, her back and arm pinned under his knee. Pain exploded up into her shoulder.

"Keep still," he warned heartlessly.

But Diamond didn't hear him. Panic bloomed through her chest, and she writhed and panted, fear and confusion stealing her sense; even the agony of her arm paled into nothing. Hugo was doing this to her, he had chosen his Queen over her.... Through her haze of anxiety and tears, she heard slow deliberate footsteps approach.

"Commander Casimir, move." It was a sharp, resolute order; with an unquestioning belief that Hugo would not disobey.

Hugo immediately complied. His weight disappeared. Diamond did not understand what was happening. *Why is Hugo doing this?* A groan of relief slipped by her lips as her shoulder joint moved back into place.

"Attion. Get her up. Your commander will not dirty his hands with this filth any longer."

"Hugo...?" she implored, looking up. Her voice was a pained whisper, a plea from her heart to the one who was tearing it in two. Those beautiful sapphire eyes looked away, and she felt her hope dissipate like mist on the wind. One small step and rough hands grabbed her hair, yanking backwards. Diamond was forced onto her knees, she gave up trying to control her breathing. Wide-eyed, she looked up at the fae warrior in front of her. Attion met her gaze steadily. She saw the words on his face, *'Don't struggle—please.'* It took all her self-control to not fight, but Attion's grip loosened and he pulled her to her feet.

Hugo kept his face completely empty, but behind that facade of granite he was raging. The girl who meant everything to him, who had become his reason for existing, was being led into a world of pain. And it was his fault. A wash of bile stung his throat when he saw Attion's gaze hold Diamond's. To these men she was nothing but an insect to be crushed under their boots. His arms hung lax at his sides, his fingers twitching with the need to destroy these guards and run.

Lord Commander Ream stepped in front of him and studied him coldly, then reached out and ran his finger with disgusting intimacy down Hugo's scar. Hugo had long ago learned not to flinch from this vile male's touch. Nauseous, he thrashed around behind his emotional wall, wanting to rip his commander's throat out with his bare hands.

"Do not presume to show her favour again or she will indeed feel agony for your weakness." Lord Commander Ream leaned in and added, "Your last plaything didn't beg enough. But I'm sure the Queen will give me longer to break you both this time—if you displease her." He shrugged and grinned and it was a truly terrifying sight.

On the outside Hugo remained emotionless, utterly still. He kept his eyes focused in front of him. Knowing it was for the best he caged his heart in shadow. Convincing everyone that he did not care for Diamond, that she was indeed just a dirty magic wielder owned by the Queen was the only way to keep her from the cruel torments of his commander.

Chapter Forty-Seven

Shaking and trying to find strength in something—anything—Diamond kept her head down, concentrating on the weight of the dragon crystal bumping against her chest. Several times she stumbled as their group headed up the wide steps into the gloom of the tower. At the head of the procession, side by side with Lord Commander Ream, Hugo had once again become a cold-hearted guard, a complete stranger. Diamond almost lost her mind, nearly giving in to her insane urge to run to him and beat her fists on his chest or scream in his face to get him to look at her—to at least *acknowledge* she still existed.

General Edo was being dragged, semi-conscious, between two hulking guards. How had this happened? No one had known where she and Hugo had been going.... Gods, even they hadn't known!

The dull corridors were empty except for the occasional sentry who watched their approach with blank faces. Attion kept his hand firmly under her arm and guided her after Hugo's hulking shadow. Lord Commander Ream kept his chin raised superiorly, his weapons glinting with every powerful step he took.

Diamond wanted to vomit. Her legs trembled so much she stumbled again, catching herself against the rough stone wall and scraping her hand. Attion tightened his fingers and dragged her back on her feet.

"Keep moving," he rumbled.

Dazed, Diamond allowed him to lead her like a lamb to slaughter. An ache bloomed in her chest as she looked at Hugo. Power and grace incarnate. But the beauty of his armoured wings seemed diminished, their silver markings flat, dull even. It made Diamond wonder if that moment of dazzling power in the alley had been her imagination. Her shoulders slumped; maybe everything about the way he had treated her earlier had been her imagination.

"Ensure the magic wielder has no weapons concealed under that tunic...or anywhere else," Lord Commander Ream ordered Attion.

Hugo turned his head and watched blankly as Attion grabbed her tunic and wrenched it from her shoulders, ripping her delicate shirt down the back in the process. Keeping his gaze cold and fixed on his task, Attion leaned around her torso, running his hands over her upper body, then sank to his haunches and slid his hands firmly and swiftly over her leggings.

"Take off your boots," he instructed. Diamond complied. "Nothing," he proclaimed.

Commander Ream dipped his chin in acknowledgment. "Commander Casimir, escort your prisoner—but I suggest you keep your hands off her when in sight of your Queen. Attion, keep pace behind. Do not let her run," he instructed.

Diamond expelled a breath as Attion straightened and took a step away. Her relief was short-lived; his fingers almost immediately curled around her upper arm and pushed her forward. Double doors decorated with sea serpents in gilt and green jade loomed before them, heavily guarded by warrior fae. Dressed in less ornate armour than any Queen's guard, their brown leather chest plates and green uniform marked them as palace guards. The guards quickly lowered their eyes and pushed open the heavy doors.

Hugo stepped in front of Diamond, his face blank. Pain tore her heart at the sight of his black fathomless eyes. Less than an hour ago those eyes had held concern in their sapphire and silver depths. Diamond stared ahead, unable to force herself to look at him.

Pink marble steps led down to a large room tiled in sea green marble. It looked like an expanse of glittering water. The opulence of the throne room stunned Diamond. Gold and jade sea serpents curled down each of the eight fluted columns, spreading their scaly tails up and across the vaulted ceiling above. They shimmered like living beasts, brought to life by the sunbeams glaring through the high windows.

Two dual headed serpents stood guard at the far end of the room. Their emerald eyes glittered in their golden heads and seemed to fixate on Diamond.

Diamond had only a moment to feel insignificant in the face of such grandeur before the weight of the Queen's hostile glare lit upon her. Heat licked along Diamond's bones, her magic rising to protect her. Suddenly unwilling to cower, Diamond straightened and looked around the room. Ignoring her magic was the only way to prevent it from breaking free. Taking a leaf from Hugo's book she deliberately kept her face blank and forced her magic back down inside.

At least twenty people sat behind a long table placed on one side of the throne. As one they studied the dishevelled young woman standing atop the entrance stairs wearing ripped clothes, with a swollen cheek and bloody bits of cloth binding her lacerated wrists.

Diamond tried to swallow, by now her mouth was so dry it was nearly impossible. Then her heart sank further. There would be no help or compassion from these people. All these staring faces had the fair complexion and brown hair associated with the Avalonian people; not one looked remotely like Hugo, with his honey bronze skin and blue black locks; and not one looked anything like Diamond with her large violet eyes and waves of silver hair.

Only three female fae graced the table, their gossamer pearlescent wings floating gently behind them like a beautiful butterfly's. Diamond had always thought pearl wings so very pretty and had spent most of her young childhood wishing and pretending that she could fly. The irony didn't pass her by. She was hated for being half-fae but had none of their useful traits: no wings, no sharp hearing, no acute eyesight. The only things she did have were her father's grace of movement and delicately pointed ears.

Disgust flitted over the face of one of the older females. Overweight as she was, the expression wrinkled her face so much her chin disappeared under the oversized collar of her yellow silk gown. She looked ridiculous. *Like an overdressed toad,* Diamond decided, matching the woman's disgust with her own.

Many of the faces at the table showed hate or revulsion. Diamond stared them down. A murmur rippled through the group and they mumbled under their breath at her audacity. The Queen balanced her chin lightly on the back of her fingers, her elbow on the arm of the throne and her green eyes glittering with malicious amusement as she watched Diamond's display of defiance. Clearly she was enjoying the scene being played out before her.

This beautiful Queen had a heart and soul of ice. She was nothing like the goddess of creation, who had gifted immortality to the rulers who had fought to save their world and people from Erebos.

Diamond curled her lip, taking in the loathing on the faces around her. It seemed the gift of immortality had become a curse of insanity, which had seeped into the mortals surrounding this viper. The Queen had taken hundreds of years to destroy the memory of her benefactor, waiting until all those who had known the goddess as their queen, and King Noan Arjuno as her devoted mate, had faded into legend. Slowly but surely she had warped the minds of her people until they worshipped only the dark god—until they believed he would be the one to give them eternal life after death. A belief that had driven her people to hate and intolerance.

Hard-faced council members and high ranking warriors scrutinised her. Diamond fought the urge to grip the front of her sheer blouse. Thanks to Attion the garment hung loosely from her shoulders, almost revealing her before these strangers. Hugo grasped her arm and gently but firmly urged her down the steps. Let these sycophants look upon her in judgment, but she would not be ashamed, not of her blood or her body. Lifting her chin, she snarled at her audience.

Then Hugo raised his voice enough that everyone would hear his words. "When you reach her grace, you will kneel. Three weeks ago you broke the Queen's laws by using magic. Today you insulted her benevolence by escaping. Because of you, two of my brothers were killed. Now you must await her judgment."

Diamond whipped her attention from the seated council. Lips pressed together, her contempt switched to Hugo. She had not run today, and he knew it. It seemed being kidnapped was not an excuse his Queen would care to hear. She lifted her wrists in front of his face, wishing she could slam both fists into his face. Everything he had said about helping her, about never leaving her, had been lies. He was a coward. A gods damned coward! Concerned only with protecting himself.

"You know that isn't true, you lying bastard!" she hissed.

Hugo just looked at her. Impassive. Unreachable. Before she could utter another word his large hand pushed her forward. They both knew it was pointless for her to fight or argue. The emptiness in his face, the utter change in him back to emotionless guard destroyed Diamond's will to fight. There was no hope of getting out of this.

Unless...unless he was pretending. Unless he really was going to help her.

Tentatively she reached out with her magic, her control only just good enough to grab at his arm, before she felt it slipping. She could do no more or that power would break free.

Nothing. No reaction at all.

Her magic dissipated like mist on the wind. With each step closer to the dais, Diamond felt her anger ebb away, hopelessness taking its place. The Queen's green eyes glittered as if she felt that creeping defeat. Diamond's stockinged feet dragged silently on the expanse of green tiles as they approached the dais.

Hugo pulled her to a stop and looked down pointedly.

Gritting her teeth, Diamond forced herself to kneel in front of her monarch, for that is who this Queen was. Diamond had been born in Avalonia. Looming above her, sitting poised on the throne was her Queen.

Hugo stood silently by Diamond's side. But now that powerful presence meant nothing, even his magic was absent. It hurt to kneel on that cold, hard floor.

"Magic wielder, I understand you are quite recovered now from your time in the forest?"

Diamond almost laughed. *Is this insane female serious? The forest?* Diamond could hardly remember the forest. Blood dripped from her wrists down between her fingers, her face throbbed and her heart had just been ripped apart by the guard at her side. In an act of defiance, she spat blood out onto the tiles at Hugo's feet and glared up hatefully at him before resting her eyes back on the Queen.

"Yes," she bit out.

"That is good," the Queen said pausing thoughtfully.

Diamond waited, trying to appear brave even as fear skittered down her spine.

"So why did you run from my hospitality this morning? That was very rude of you after I have been so kind and generously allowed you to remain in comfort in my palace," she scolded with lethal calm. Diamond tensed waiting for the axe to fall. Then suddenly a bright smile lit the Queen's face. "Never mind, I have a way for you to compensate me," she said and dismissed the subject with a flick of her hand.

Diamond blinked away her shock. The Queen's tone was now that of reasonable, benevolent leader.

"We—that is, myself and the council members here," she gestured expansively to the overdressed toads at the table, "have been discussing your future and how to ensure the safety of my people whilst you are here as my guest."

Guest? Diamond's anger flared at the injustice of that remark but held her tongue.

"As I am sure you remember, despite the comforts you have enjoyed at my expense, and let us not forget the attention you have demanded from *my* guard," Diamond tensed at the inflection on that word, "there is still a war being fought against the Wraith Lord. I expect you know Ragor is an ancient enemy of mine. What you don't know is that he has always coveted this city and now he is determined to claim it—and my other possessions."

The Queen's attention levelled on Hugo, the air becoming oppressive with magic, ancient magic tainted with a deep seething anger.

Disgusted by her Queen's hypocrisy and frightened by the sheer force of that power, Diamond ducked her head, twisting to look surreptitiously at the council toads. They too shifted uncomfortably in their chairs, rubbing their arms and faces. They were restless and edgy but clearly had no idea why.

"I don't know where that guardian came from. The last guardian I heard of was rumoured to be seen in the Fire Mountains… supposedly a servant to their imperial family. "

Diamond's heart clenched. *What does that mean? Do dragons still exist?* Maybe it was only on this side of the Rough Seas that dragons were believed extinct. The Queen did not shift her green eyes from Hugo as she spoke. "Was it hunting for you, I wonder, magic wielder, or something else entirely? Did it burn my fleet to ashes because of you? Or to try and keep what it wants from escaping across the Rough Seas?" Her voice became contemplative, a frown creasing her normally perfect brow. Cocking her head, she did not drop her attention from Hugo, almost as if he were the answer to her question. Minutes ticked by and no one made a sound.

Hugo did not react. He may as well have been made of stone.

Diamond remained on her knees. Unmoving. Trembling. Not daring to move.

The Queen slowly shifted her scrutiny to Diamond. Silence. Crushing, terrifying silence. Even the toads at the table did not dare mumble.

Against her tender skin the crystal heated, as if sensing that ancient, malevolent glare. It began to glow, clearly visible now through the sheer material of her blouse. Diamond winced, as something sharp scraped her skin, almost as if the dragon clutched the crystal tighter.

Immediately the Queen's attention dropped to Diamond's chest. Shock and elation burned through those green eyes as she beheld the glowing jewel. In fact the eyes of all those at the council table were staring at Diamond's chest. Her cheeks burned. Instinctively she clutched the crystal, bunching the sheer material of her blouse in her fist. It had been so stupid to wear such a see-through garment.

Ragor had unleashed his Seekers on Berriesford for this necklace; now everyone could see it. Dread filled Diamond's soul. The look of desire the Queen's face said she would kill for it too.

Squeezing her fist tight, Diamond winced as something sharp pierced her finger. Diamond knew every dent on the black metal chain and fierce dragon that held the clear crystal. *What is so special about it that two immortals desire it so?*

The Queen's body was graceful, her movements feline as she pushed herself out of her throne and stalked toward Diamond. A dress in shades of shimmering green gauze and lace clung to her every curve, accentuating her exquisite beauty; the perfect swell of her breasts, her slim waist and her shapely long legs. Golden hair fell in waves over one shoulder; on her head she wore a simple circlet of gold adorned with a single large emerald, and glorious golden wings glinted as she stretched them before folding them into her back.

Fingers of fear crept up Diamond's spine. *Run. Run. Run.* Screamed her instincts. But the guards who protected The Queen would catch her or loose a swift blade into her back before she had any hope of reaching the door.

The power and energy radiating from this wicked woman became more pronounced with every step closer. Her ancient and forceful power clutched at Diamond, invading her senses. It fought to suffocate her, to dominate her own pathetic ember of magic. The Queen glided closer, her hips swaying alluringly, a satisfied smirk on her face. Diamond resisted the urge to shrink into a ball on the floor. She swallowed, not daring to move.

Hugo remained frozen as his Queen approached. The thought of this female's magic touching and entwining itself with Hugo's sent a shudder of revulsion through Diamond.

It was a shock to realise Hugo could do nothing, that he was not as strong as he seemed. He was emotionally weak, weak and scarred from so many years of servitude and abuse; he had absolutely no idea how to resist the summons of this manipulative immortal.

Diamond's chest caved. She was on her own in the face of this overwhelming onslaught of grace and power. Like everyone else in this room, Hugo was just a puppet. Diamond's heart thumped against her ribs. Close enough to touch, the Queen prowled around Diamond and Hugo. A predator surveying her prey. It seemed even the room held its breath, waiting for what was to happen next.

"Stand up," ordered the Queen, her voice soft, threatening.

Challenging green eyes flicked to Hugo as Diamond scrambled to comply.

Chapter Forty-Eight

The Queen took the last step needed to reach Hugo. Not bothering to disguise her sensuality, her smile widened as she swept a derisive glance across Diamond's pale, bruised face and slowly let it travel down the young woman's body.

Diamond did not try and stem the humiliated flush that swamped her face. But for the first time in her life she forged steely determination, and controlled the panic squeezing her chest.

The council members watched silently from their table as if in a daze. Only Hugo and Diamond had an exclusive view of the Queen's beautiful, wicked face. Hugo's massive shoulders tensed minutely, a painful tug yanking at Diamond's chest as his magic flared defensively. It was hard to stifle a gasp. *Why does he do that if he worships this hateful female so?*

The air in the room thinned, and Diamond found it difficult to breathe as those icy green eyes focused on Hugo. A silent command. Hugo immediately dropped to one knee, averting his eyes to the floor. Diamond felt her heart lurch painfully. She wanted to tell him to stand, to be the proud warrior she knew and feared, but it would be a pointless exercise. He would not listen.

The Queen smiled directly at Diamond, her face and eyes full of malice and triumph. Her meaning was clear: Hugo was her property, one of her elite warriors that she could command at her whim. Placing her long elegant fingers under Hugo's chin, the Queen tipped his head back and gazed down at him.

"You may stand," she told him. Caressing his unscarred cheek, she stepped so close that when he stood, the peak of her breasts brushed his body. Long slim fingers lingered on his face, cupping his jaw. Her blonde head tilted and watching Diamond closely. She let her long elegant fingers run slowly down Hugo's neck. Diamond swallowed as she grazed the hard lines of his broad shoulder and chest and continued down his flat stomach, gliding along his weapons belt until her touch rested on the curve of his hip. A taunting smile curled the Queen's ruby mouth as she slid that same hand into the small of his back, and pushed her hips against him.

Diamond's mask nearly slipped, her stomach churning at the intimate gesture, but she held it together. This was a test. One she must pass. If the Queen knew how deep her feelings for Hugo ran, she might very well strike Diamond down where she stood. Diamond's violet eyes stayed unwaveringly on the Queen's face, unemotional and steady. The Queen chuckled and conceded a step. Diamond released a breath and looked away.

At the table a formidable-looking fae commander watched the proceedings with intense golden eyes. Feeling his regard, Diamond shifted her attention to him. He dipped his chin minutely in a nod. Taken aback by the supportive gesture from one of the Queen's own warriors, Diamond gaped at him. A frown furrowed her brow as his eyes moved to Hugo—and stayed there.

Another warrior protected the commander's back. His face was handsome in a too-perfect way, marred only by the startling arrogance glinting in his eyes. Slowly, thoroughly, he ran his eyes over Diamond, causing the fine hairs on the back of her neck to prickle. She snarled defensively. A mocking smirk curled his shapely lips before he shifted his attention to Hugo. *Who are they?* Clearly the commander was someone of importance. But that warrior....

The Queen raised her voice, the change in her demeanour incredible as she became the concerned, devoted ruler.

"Ragor will soon bring his war to Valentia. By winter solstice he will have reached the wall. If he breaches that ancient bastion of protection, he will use his dead army to seize the souls of every living thing in this city. He will turn *every* single one of you into rotting demons that will feed his power." She swept her hand expansively, encompassing all their intent faces. "All of your loved ones, your precious children, even the humans who are citizens of Avalonia—you will be left with nothing. Do you hear me? Nothing except a will to do his bidding. Ragor wants this city for himself. It is what he has always wanted."

Anxious murmurs erupted from the noble toads, the noise of their anxiety interrupting her speech. Satisfaction flashed across the Queen's face at their reaction. She stalked towards them with swishing skirts, flourished a turn and gestured back at Diamond.

"This—girl—has magic tainted by the goddess herself," she told them unnecessarily. "It is a dangerous and powerful poison that runs through her veins, one that should be eradicated. However, to keep my people—*our*—people safe, you have all agreed it is far better to have that magic fight for us, rather than risk it being unleashed against us." The Queen lifted her chin imperiously. "My council and I are benevolent in our judgment."

She gave Diamond a vicious smile that the council could not see, a smile that belied those words. Diamond held her breath in fearful anticipation. This was it—the moment she had been dreading for weeks. She grasped her own fingers, attempting to stop their shaking.

"It is the agreement of this council that rather than being executed for possessing such corruption in your blood, you shall put that goddess-cast magic to good use. You will learn to use it and you will fight to keep the Wraith Lord and his army out of my city—or you will die trying. Prince Oden and Master Commander Riddeon need a dispensable weapon. One that can be used outside this shield. That is you. You will be taught the physical skills of a warrior, and when you have become proficient enough to kill, you will learn to control and wield your magic. If you cannot learn or you try to use it to harm me or my people, I will kill you. Make no mistake, magic wielder, you belong to me as much as he does." She inclined her head at Hugo. "And when this battle is done—if you still live—you will still belong to me. Is that clear?"

Diamond's nostrils flared in horror. With her utter lack of fighting skills and magical control, she was unlikely to survive. If she did, she vowed not to return here. She would run far and fast until this despicable viper faded from her mind like a bad dream.

Suddenly the Queen was standing right in front of Diamond. Her hand shot forwards like lightening, sharp finger nails gouging Diamond's chest. A tearing sound and her blouse ripped down the front. Before Diamond knew what was happening, those long elegant fingers had grasped her necklace. Leaning in until her lips grazed Diamond's ear, the Queen's warm breath sent shivers shuddering down Diamond's neck and spine.

"You *will* learn to control your magic. You *will* fight for me, and you *will* come back to me—or I will send Lord Commander Ream to hunt you down. But I won't let him kill you. No." She placed her fingers against Diamond's cheek and gently turned her face towards Hugo. "I will have you killed by him, but not before you watch him kill your handsome prince and that pathetic human boy. Maybe I'll even get him to gut that healer you have taken a shine to. Once this battle is done and my city is safe, I will not need the mortal prince anymore than I need the locusts he calls his people. Do I make myself clear, my beautiful, young half-blood?" she asked, quiet venom in her voice.

Diamond nodded, not daring to speak. She could feel Hugo's magic surge against her, but he showed no outward sign of having heard the Queen's threats. The familiar searing heat and nip of his magic disappeared almost as soon as it touched Diamond. Hopefully the Queen hadn't noticed. Hopefully she couldn't feel Hugo's magic the way Diamond did.

Blood rushed from Diamond's head at the implications of that threat, but she willed herself to stand tall, ignoring her dizziness. This woman would kill everyone Diamond had left in the world. Perhaps dying in battle would not be such a bad thing, not if it meant they would be safe. Blood tickled her skin, running from the gouged welts between her breasts. Her torn shirt fell open revealing her skin and undergarments. Still she did not move. Not only was the Queen a depraved and manipulative adversary, she writhed with magic so powerful it stole Diamond's breath.

Hypocrites! screamed Diamond silently at the table of over-dressed toads who watched in silence. These idiots condemned or enslaved souls born with more powerful magic than their own because they feared it. Their ignorance was shameful when their Queen practically glowed with magic so omnipotent it could oppress the room and subdue any soul nearby into compliance.

"This necklace is stunning. Where did you get it?" the Queen's voice was curious. She studied the metal dragon, which seemed to clutch the crystal tighter as it lay against the Queen's palm. A curious green light pulsed from the jewel at her touch.

"My mother gave it me. Please, let go of it." Diamond managed to say, impressed by the steadiness of her voice.

"I don't think I will," said the immortal Queen, fixing her cold ancient eyes on Diamond.

The blood drained from Diamond's face completely. "W-what?" she whispered, her mask of neutrality slipping. "But this is all I have left from my home. It was my mother's. She left it to me. You can't take it.... I won't let you have it!" Panic gripped her.

"Hugo!" the Queen snapped quickly. "Relieve this prisoner of her necklace, then give it to Master Commander Riddeon."

Diamond whipped her head towards Hugo. "No," she whispered, shaking. Hugo's eyes were fathomless, endless shadow. Hopelessly Diamond swallowed her tears and closed her eyes. She could do nothing as he moved her hair gently to one side, his fingers brushing against her skin as he undid the clasp. She instinctively shrank from him.

Hugo, intent on his task, did not seem to notice. Coiling the chain into his large hand, he strode over to the golden-eyed commander, dropping the only link to Diamond's parents on the table in front of him. Master Commander Riddeon stared at the glowing crystal as if mesmerised. His guard, however, seemed more interested in Diamond, his predatory gaze fixing on her half naked torso.

"I see this necklace means a lot to you, magic wielder. Such a pity." The Queen gave a snake's smile as she taunted, "Just think how easy it will be for me to take *everything* you care about. Make no mistake, girl, if you don't do as I ask, your friends will die a horrible death."

Diamond stood mutely, gaping at her necklace. The threat and promise in those words so terribly clear. The jewel seemed so small and insignificant discarded on the table in front of the master commander's tightly-clasped hands. Sudden and unbidden, anger stirred in Diamond's belly, bursting up from her core in a torrent so deep and strong she trembled.

Across the room, the glow in the crystal flickered then went out. Hugo shifted his obsidian eyes to Diamond's face. She let all her rage and hurt burn through as she caught his gaze and held it. Before she understood what was happening, her magic surged through her blood, thrashing to escape.

Not here, not now, she beseeched it, casting her eyes down to the floor. Hugo placed his large hand on her shoulder as if to restrain his prisoner. Diamond jerked away from him. Or tried; her arms and legs were as immovable as granite. It was as if he could hold her to utter stillness with just his touch. Calm washed through her body, engulfing the raging magic until it sputtered and died. Her mind felt thick, her thoughts syrupy and slow. Diamond took a deep breath and shook her head, forcing her ravaged body to life.

She yanked her shoulder from Hugo's grasp. His only response was to glance at her impassively.

Immediately her head cleared.

Chapter Forty-Nine

The Queen continued to speak.

Gods, she's not even done yet! thought Diamond bitterly.

"You will need someone to oversee your training. A warrior who will keep you under control and ensure compliance with my wishes. A tutor who can school you in the art of weaponry and fighting—and killing," said the Queen, smiling delightedly as if that should be abhorrent to Diamond. The beautiful monarch bit her lip as if considering her options. "You will also need a warrior who is powerful enough to supervise you whilst you learn to control your magic."

The Queen turned to Hugo, who stood silently by. Diamond's heart soared with hope. Will the Queen allow us to be together? Diamond wanted it so much. That hope stuttered and recoiled into her heart. This cold guard was not the friend Diamond had come to long for.

"Commander Casimir? You will instruct Guard Attion Sarou to oversee the weapons training this girl receives."

Hugo snapped his head back to the Queen just as Diamond's stomach heaved.

"My Queen, Guard Sarou is not strong enough to contain her if her magic breaks free. She would be at risk of escaping again…or causing ruination of this palace. Having Guard Sarou train her would put you at risk." His voice remained unemotional, but Diamond knew Hugo well enough to see the dip in his brow and the minute twist to the scar upon his cheek.

The Queen cocked her head and studied Hugo, making a show of considering his words. Diamond held her breath, unable to shift her attention away from the floor. Being forced to endure Attion's attentions was unthinkable.

"So be it," the Queen conceded, giving a small satisfied smile that made Diamond wonder what game she was playing. "You will oversee Miss Gillon's training. Inform Commander Nosco of your orders and instruct him to find a suitable squadron of Prince Oden's men to attach her to. We can't have her too near my fae warriors, can we? Erebos only knows how, but she seems to bring out the baser instincts in you all." She glanced over at Fedron, who did not move his eyes off Diamond.

"Master Commander Riddeon estimates Ragor will begin his assault on the wall a week, maybe two, before winter solstice; therefore you will train this girl hard. I will expect her to attain a sufficient level of skill to be used as a weapon within ten weeks. As such, you are relieved of your duties in the palace until I tell you otherwise. Lord Commander Ream will send for you when I am ready to observe your results. And Hugo?"

"Yes, my Queen?" he answered unemotionally.

"Do not fail me in this task. It would be a shame to have to dirty your hands with her death and force me to punish you before winter solstice."

Hugo bowed low, but Diamond could feel the resentment and violence churning through the air around them. What she couldn't tell was if his ire was directed at her or the Queen. Diamond did not care. She pinned him with a hateful glare, her eyes a smouldering violet storm. Silently she vowed she would become a weapon; she had no choice if she wanted to survive or if her friends were to live. Let the Queen be fool enough to train her. The magic in Diamond's blood would bend to her will eventually.

"Master Commander Riddeon, you and your guards will take that necklace down to the palace vaults. You may choose which of the iron boxes to place the jewel in. The key will stay with the Master of the Vault," she ordered her commander. There was no doubt in her voice that he would comply with her wishes.

The golden-eyed commander stood. "Fedron! With me," he barked to his warrior, who still had his attention fixed solely on Diamond.

The warrior's hazel eyes held such predatory fae hunger it made her skin crawl. Hugo, who had already noticed the other male's attention, blasted a wave of invisible magic into the air. Diamond started, shocked by the ferocity of his response. She snarled at them both. She did not need Hugo's protection from any other fae male—not now, not ever; he had made his choice—his Queen—not her. Diamond poured wrath into her eyes and stared the other warrior down.

Amusement glinted in his eyes, and she realised he was relishing her defiance. He deliberately slid his gaze to Hugo. Challenge poured off him. It burned in his eyes and in his vicious snarl before he bowed in deference to his superior's order. As he walked away, he flashed

Diamond an insolent grin and a wink that enraged her. Hugo followed his progress with an icy gaze.

The Queen stroked her slim fingers tenderly down Hugo's cheek, bringing his attention back to her.

"Ten weeks. No longer, commander. I will expect this girl to demonstrate her new skills. If she fails, well...." That sensual smile turned cruel and she glanced at Lord Commander Ream, who stood by the throne. "My Lord Commander can have whatever is left of her. If she does succeed in her test, you will take her outside the shield. Her magic is clearly wild. With your more—practised—skills you can mould it into the weapon we all need. I want Ragor away from this city before winter solstice. After all, this will be a very important celebration for both of us, Hugo." Her voice became a sensual purr. "And we will have far more important things to occupy our time than war and inexperienced young girls."

Whilst their attention was fixed on each other, Diamond blinked and shifted her vision. Hugo's energy snapped wildly against the Queen's green confident aura. Tense seconds passed as silver serpents and sweeping green ribbons fought, but to Diamond's horror, the Queen prevailed. Slowly, like the coils of a snake her green magic curled around his torso, slithering down his thighs and along his arms. Outwardly he held his mask in place as she writhed around him. But it did not last. Disgusted, Diamond could only watch as those green ribbons touched him intimately. Hugo's jaw clenched and his eyelids flickered, his nostrils flaring. The Queen chuckled with satisfaction at his involuntary response. Stretching her neck back, she closed her eyes and shuddered with pleasure.

Seeing that magical fight made no difference to her feelings for him, or so Diamond told herself. Hugo had made his choice: he belonged to his Queen, body and soul, it seemed.

"Oh Hugo, you should not resist me so. This winter solstice is going to be the best either of us has experienced in a long while."

Hatred, and something akin to jealousy, sparked through Diamond's chest at the implied intimacy in those words. Before she could even begin to think about that, the Queen fixed Diamond with a glacial stare.

Chapter Fifty

"Now, before I let you leave, we must hold the trial."

Diamond jerked her head towards the Queen. "What trial?" she parroted automatically. Panic instantly squeezed her chest. *When would this be over?* She was already bound to servitude until she died fighting the Wraith Lord. *Will I be tortured now?*

"Lord Commander, bring in the prisoner," instructed the fae Queen with obvious relish.

Diamond twisted her head, watching Lord Commander Ream march to the double doors. Hugo turned too, the flicker of a frown between his brows. The Queen gave Diamond a calculating smile. Dread curled inside Diamond's stomach. *What in the goddess was going on now?*

A moment later General Edo was marched into the throne room between two Queen's guards. He thrashed and swore savagely, a maniacal glint in his eye. Fresh bruises marred his face and blood trickled from the corner of his mouth.

"General!" exclaimed Diamond, taking a step forward.

The general glared coldly at her, stopping her in her tracks.

"Silence!" the Queen barked. Swishing her skirts with a flourish, she walked back across the floor and sat upon her throne.

General Edo stared from her to Diamond, such hate in his face that Diamond recoiled.

"Tell me, magic wielder, do you trust this male?" she asked, narrowing her eyes on the general.

Diamond frowned and answered without hesitation, "Of course I do. I've known him all my life. He was the one who saved me from Ragor's Seekers"

"Was he indeed?" asked the Queen almost gleefully. "I wonder? How do you think Ragor's hunting dogs found you? It *was* you he was searching for, wasn't it—or at least the necklace you wore?"

Diamond gulped, not liking where this was going at all. *How does she know that?* Diamond had told no one—not even Tom—what

Cranach had said. General Edo was bucking his body with such force his captors were almost losing their grip. He bared his teeth at the Queen.

The Queen's grinned delightedly. "Oh, general. I'm so sorry but the cat's out of the bag," she purred and nodded at Lord Commander Ream, who once again disappeared, this time into a heavily reinforced wooden door behind the dais. The Queen tapped her sharp fingernails—still marred with Diamond's blood—against the arm of the throne. An irritating high pitched click.

Diamond dared a questioning glance at Hugo, but his attention was fixed on General Edo. In an almost casual move, he twisted his body slightly and placed himself between her and the general. His hand grasped the hilt of a long dagger that sat on his hip.

Minutes passed in silence. The toads at the table did not dare move, let alone talk. Diamond could almost feel their fear. *What previous horrors had they witnessed in this room of power?* Diamond wondered.

The door swung open and chains rattled. Diamond gaped, as did the toads. The Queen's guards, however, all remained stoic in their observation. Snarling and growling, a skinny Seeker was hauled before the throne. Clearly half-starved, its bones almost protruded through its skin, skin that was covered in sores and festering small wounds.

"Do you recognise him?" the Queen addressed General Edo curiously, a dangerous smile curling her lips.

"No," growled General Edo.

"Are you sure?" she asked, then turned to Diamond. "As much as it pains me, magic wielder, as much as your kind disgust me, you still belong to my kingdom, as did most of those in your town who died when his brethren attacked," she said, gesturing at the Seeker. "This creature has told me how Ragor found you and why. It seems the Wraith Lord has been hunting for you and your father for a very long time. Your father was clever enough to hide that necklace since your mother died. But alas, he wasn't clever enough to recognise the enemy and traitor that lived right on his doorstep. Was he, general?" she drawled.

Diamond stared in confusion at General Edo. His eyes held pure hate as he glared at the Queen. Slowly those icy grey eyes found Diamond. That hate did not diminish; if anything, it flared brighter. Hugo's magic pushed against her, almost as if he were trying to cocoon her in it. Diamond thrust it away.

"What does she mean?" she asked the man who had helped raise her, who had been there to pick her up when she fell, who had kissed her goodnight alongside her father.

"Nothing! She knows nothing!" he denied, his wings flaring. Diamond gasped as she noticed the small bolts that had been driven through them. Iron. So he could not armour, could not fly. "She is setting me up," he spat, panting as his wings fell uselessly behind him.

"Oh come now, general. Don't lie," simpered the Queen.

The Seeker squealed in a high pitched, decidedly human way as the chains around his neck and limbs were yanked and he fell onto his knees. Diamond flinched. It sounded disturbingly like a child in pain.

"Magic wielder, it was the general, your father's loyal *friend*," the Queen sneered, "that sold him out to our enemy. He paid this thing, and it's equally disgusting father, to take a token belonging to you to Ragor and deliver a message."

General Edo paled, his attention narrowing on the creature. As he searched the creatures face, Diamond knew with sickening certainty that the Queen was telling the truth. Diamond watched with horrified fascination as the Queen stood and prowled closer to the Seeker. She looked intently into its eyes. That ancient magic blazed, burning the air and surging like a sandstorm against Diamond's skin. She tensed as her own reacted, building along her nerves and in her blood. Hugo glanced at her, his scar twitching; once again that strange soothing feeling clouded her mind and calmed the wildness of her magic. She shook her head, trying to clear it.

The Queen's court looked on in a mixture of disgust, fear and hate.

A flash of light caused everyone to blink furiously. In its wake lay a naked child, crumpled in a heap on the floor.

Diamond gasped. Even Hugo shifted on his feet as he stared at the boy who couldn't have been more than twelve years old.

"Magic wielder, meet Simeon. He's obviously a shapeshifter. But goodness, what an ugly being to have as an alternative self, don't you think? Simeon, meet the girl whose father you helped to kill—Diamond Gillon."

Simeon peered up at her, wide-eyed but fiercely defiant. His face was as dirty as the rest of him. "I didn't kill nobody," he denied and looked hatefully at General Edo. "He paid me da. He told us he would be a king soon, and that he would pay me da more money than we 'as ever seen to run to the Dead Lord and give 'im that scrap of cloth. All them people dyin' was his an' me da's fault, not mine."

Diamond felt the weight of his words crush her heart.

"No...." she whispered, shaking her head.

"It weren't my fault!" Simeon cried in a squeaky voice, his words pouring out in a torrent. "Me da made me go with 'im. I didn't want to go, but I ain't got no ma, an' he said I 'ad to. Me da was a shifter too, but that Dead Lord, he wouldn't let us leave. He made us run back up north with them other Seekers. 'Bout nearly killed me, it did. But we 'ad no choice. They said they would tear us apart with the rest of the town if we tried to run—or you wasn't there."

Diamond could not believe what she was hearing, that the general had orchestrated the annihilation of a whole town. And he had used this *child* to do it. Diamond's mind whirled, remembering all the times he had seemed distant and cold, his insistence at leaving her father to his fate. She felt sick as she met the full force of General Edo's gaze, flinching at the deep hate and resentment in his eyes. It was far easier to look at Simeon. Before she could stop herself, she asked, "Where is your father now?"

Simeon unabashedly stood up, the state of his body ripping a gasp of dismay from Diamond. Turning to Hugo, he inclined his head at the huge warrior. "'E killed 'im. I watched from the trees." Simeon held Hugo's gaze fiercely, longer than Diamond had seen anyone else hold it. Standing naked at the mercy of his captors, she couldn't help but admire such bravery. "Then I followed yer scent back 'ere. I dodged all them dead things out in the forest, an' all them Seekers—they weren't bothered wi' me. I'm too small to threaten them—but I nicked bits of the food...they left behind." His face revealed what gruesome fare that would have been.

"Why? Why did you come here? Why didn't you run?" Diamond asked, feeling a surge of compassion for this resourceful boy.

"To kill 'im," Simeon responded, lifting his chin and glaring up at Hugo, who stared back blankly.

"Silence!" ordered the Queen.

Simeon jumped, suddenly looking like the frightened child he was. *What had they done to him in the dungeons?* Diamond thought, feeling nauseated.

"General Edo, it is clear that you conspired with Ragor, whose hunters used your token to track the magic wielder to Berriesford. You are therefore accused of wilfully causing death to my people by duplicity, and the act of treason against me by bargaining with my enemy."

Slowly she raked her imperious gaze across the council toads. "As this is an act of treason, you are not entitled to a council hearing. I therefore sentence you to death."

Chapter Fifty-One

"What?"

"*No!*"

Diamond and General Edo shouted at the same time.

"I did not kill your citizens! This boy is lying!" bellowed the general. "The only one we know died for sure was her father—and he was Rhodainian!" he thundered.

The Queen ignored him. Realising his protestations were in vain, the general began thrashing against his captors' grip, earning himself a twist of the iron bolt in his left wing. He roared.

"Now, now, it's no use fighting, general. Your fate is sealed. It's just a question of who will carry out your sentence."

Diamond fought her panic as the Queen regarded her through narrowed eyes. "Magic wielder, you will earn redemption for your attempted escape by showing me you can follow my orders." Elegantly she gestured to General Edo. "Go and end that male's life. He did, after all, cause your father's death. It shouldn't be too hard for you. Lord Commander Ream, give Commander Casimir your whip," the Queen instructed.

Diamond looked down at her feet. No. No. She couldn't. Panic tightened like a band around her chest. There was no air to breathe. The walls of the room began to press in on her, crushing her. Her chest heaved and tears burned her eyes. A sob rippled from deep in her chest, only to catch in her throat and fade to a whimper. She *couldn't* kill anyone in cold blood; she couldn't....

It was then she felt it—an unexpected blanket of reassurance and calm that descended from nowhere. Her mind and body responded immediately, totally beyond her control. Diamond felt her breathing slow of its own accord, silence filled her head and, although she didn't want to look outside that tranquil cocoon to the throne room beyond, she did.

Lord Commander Ream tore his hungry gaze from Simeon's naked body and complied with his Queen's order. Hugo took the coil of twisted leather in his big hand and curled his fingers around it. Diamond stared in horror at the three iron ends that unfurled and clattered to the floor. He wouldn't.... It was no use appealing to him. Hugo's face remained impassive, his eyes like black empty pools.

"Commander Casimir. If the magic wielder refuses her task, you are to deliver one lash to this young boy, followed by two to her. You will continue that punishment until she complies," ordered the Queen.

Simeon stared at Hugo, all his bravado now gone. Shaking visibly, he looked at Diamond with such terror, the whites of his eyes were visible.

Diamond almost stopped breathing and blanched. The Queen smirked spitefully.

"But he's only a boy. You can't," Diamond whispered, certain she was going to vomit when Hugo stepped behind her.

"I am over a thousand years old and queen of this land; I can do as I please," the Queen purred, smiling like an adder.

Simeon was led over by his chains, too frightened now to fight as he was forced to his knees, tears rolling down his face. Seeker or not he was just a scared little boy who had already suffered enough. Diamond's bladder threatened to void, blood whooshing through her ears as she felt Hugo's presence at her back. Simeon's eyes beseeched her to help, but she knew pleading for him was as useless as pleading for herself. Diamond turned to General Edo. It was an effort to look at him.

"Tell me none of this is true, general," she pleaded. "Tell me you are still the person who dried my tears and loved my father. Tell me that you did not kill your best friend?" she choked out, even as tears blurred her vision. *Was this really all his fault? Had he really been the catalyst for such heartache and pain?* "Tell me that, general!" Her voice broke, anguish tearing at her heart. The cave. The parchment. She stared in disbelief as things fell into place.

"Tell me it isn't true."

A whispered plea.

"Tell me you didn't betray my father. That all those people didn't suffer or die because of you! Gods! Please tell me you weren't going to betray Jack!" Her voice rose to fever pitch. Her attention moved to Simeon, who was trying his best not to cower despite his fear. "What did Simeon mean when he said you told his father you would soon become a king?"

General Edo leaned forward, his muscles bunching as he pulled against his captors' grip. His face twisted in a contemptuous sneer. "True? Of course it's all true! I spent the last thirteen years of my life following the final order my king gave me. He wanted me to find and protect your mother and father and not return to Stormguaard without them. When I discovered my king had gone missing—that he was presumed dead, I pleaded with Arades to return home to Stormguaard with me. I knew if King Oden truly was gone, we were meant to rule. If your bull-headed father had agreed, we could have stopped the Wraith Lord years ago, but no—he refused. That cowardly bastard chose you and your dead mother over me and his kingdom," he spat at her feet in disgust.

Diamond couldn't believe this was the same person she had grown up loving. Pain cleaved her heart.

"How could you?" she choked, tears running down her cheeks. "He was your friend...he loved you!" she cried.

General Edo snorted, "Oh, it was so easy in the end. He told me how your mother died—that the Seekers found her and almost ripped you from her belly. He even told me how they wanted that necklace, that he would not leave Berriesford and risk them finding you...or it. I begged him to return with me to Rhodainia to whip that pathetic excuse for a prince into shape. But he still refused. He foolishly believed the boy would find his own way. Ha! Look how wrong he was," he sneered.

Diamond struggled to comprehend his words. The only way to stop her sobs was to press her lips tightly together.

General Edo stood bolt upright, his strong shoulders squared, derision in his every word. "*Prince* Oden lost his heritage because he is a spoiled, weak brat who has allowed the simpering fools on his council and animals like that water leopard to influence him. He is an inadequate child who knows nothing about ruling a kingdom but everything about bringing it to its knees. His people—*my* people—are adrift like leaves on the wind, having to seek help from an evil bitch like this one. Hundreds of thousands of our people were murdered because of that boy's incompetence! Tell me, what do you think is going to happen to the survivors, Diamond? Even if any of you manage to live through Ragor's attack, Jack will always remain too weak to rule. I could have pulled what was once a magnificent army back together. *I* could have led our people back to greatness, given them back their homes. And with the decree King Oden gave me, no one would question my authority to rule once the prince was gone."

"What? Stop! What are you saying?" asked Diamond incredulously. This was not the man she had known as a child. Then she remembered that her father had hidden who he was, so it wasn't impossible that this warrior had done so too.

The Queen clapped her hands in glee, exclaiming, "Oh, this is too good. A deathbed confession. Are you hoping to go to Eternity after everything you've done, general? Do you think by explaining yourself, you will gain absolution from this child and be forgiven?" she chuckled.

"Shut up, you insane female! I don't care about forgiveness, nor absolution from a half-blood who, along with her mother and father, ruined my life!" bellowed General Edo, clearly no longer caring for the consequences of his words. His icy regard rested back on Diamond. "I needed you dead so your father would return with me to Stormguaard," he snarled. "So he had no reason to stay in the north. I knew Ragor wanted your mother and that necklace, so it stood to reason he would want her offspring with it too. Your father wasn't meant to die—you were," he hissed at her. "I saved you so I could get your necklace before that Seeker did. Once I had it I was going to throw you into that school house with your father, but one of those creatures knocked me senseless. By the time I recovered, the Queen's attack dog was too close to get you alone. Then, when I met Jack, I realised how pathetic the boy was. Gods—he was so easily distracted by you, and so weak. I knocked him out without even trying. I was hoping that damned dragon would kill you both, but no...you had to survive," he snorted with disbelief. "You even managed to save the idiot. I sent him—" he snarled at Hugo, "—after you, hoping he would find the boy dead from his injuries, and at least come to his senses and slit your throat as any self-respecting Queen's guard would, so I didn't have to get rid of you myself."

"Oh Prince Oden, how marvellous of you to join us!" the Queen exclaimed.

The general whipped his body around so fast one of his guards stumbled. But Hugo, in a lightning-quick move, unsheathed his sword and rested it against General Edo's neck. The general snarled and pushed his throat up against the blade, blood running down his neck. Hugo clutched the whip in one hand, his face turned from his Queen. Silver rage burned in his eyes. One small move and the general would be dead.

"Commander, remove your blade," ordered the Queen firmly.

Without facing his Queen, Hugo immediately complied, but he did not move from his spot between Diamond and the general.

"Guards," she ordered.

Without further prompting, the Queen's elite guard formed a large circle around them. Despite being unmanacled, there was no escape for General Edo, even if he should try.

Jack stood at the top of the throne room steps, regal and heart-wrenchingly handsome. But his face was cold, so cold Diamond shuddered. Her heart ached for her friend. Jack had lost his father well before he was ready to rule a kingdom. He must have hoped this tough, experienced warrior, once a loyal subject and friend of his father, would become his own advisor, his mentor.

Shoulders square and back rod straight, Jack looked every inch the ruler General Edo claimed he wasn't. He grasped the hilt of Dragonsblood, his fingers curled around the blood red rubies, looking far from weak or pathetic. Calm and controlled, only his eyes burned with fury. The prince ignored everyone as he paced forward, stopping only when he reached the foot of the dais. To the Queen he inclined his head regally. Not low enough to suggest subservience, only respect.

"Queen, may I ask what you are doing with General Edo in your possession?" he enquired icily.

"Prince Oden, your general has been found guilty of scheming with my enemy, of planning an attack on my lands and of causing the death of my people. You may also have heard he intended to kill you, which is an act of treason against the crown that is punishable by death, even in your kingdom—or at least it was in your father's reign."

Jack stared at her for a moment. The Queen was challenging him and he knew it. Diamond bit her bottom lip.

"Indeed you are correct," replied Jack carefully. "As a visiting monarch, we both know I have no right to interfere in your court's justice, especially for crimes against your citizens." The mortal prince turned, holding General Edo's contemptuous eyes, his handsome face remaining a forbidding mask as silent seconds passed. Jack curled his lip in disgust and nodded slightly to himself. "I have absolutely no interest in the fate of this male. As you say, Queen, he is a traitor to me and my kingdom and caused the death of General Arades Gillon, who *was* a citizen of Avalonia."

"A traitor!" spat the general. "I am no traitor to my kingdom—it was you who lost it, you who brought your people to their knees and you who leaves them now at the mercy of this scheming bitch!"

The Queen waved her hand, and Hugo slammed a forceful kick into the general's chest, bringing him to his knees and silencing his torrent of abuse. Diamond flinched at the crack of bone breaking. Unable to speak General Edo gagged and panted, holding his broken ribs.

"As you say, prince, this is my court. He will be dealt with according to his crime," the Queen informed Jack coolly.

Jack nodded then turned from the Queen and walked directly up to Diamond. His eyes softened and he gently touched her bruised cheek. Without hesitation he twisted back, "Queen, Diamond is a friend and has saved my life on more than one occasion. I agreed in our earlier meeting that training her to become a magical weapon would benefit all in this valley, but I would look on her being treated well as a sign of respect for our continued good relations," his voice was heavy with meaning. "And I'm sure it will benefit us both to maintain our current military links." He paused and let that comment sink in. The Queen smiled tightly so Jack continued. "My men are doing a good job of protecting the wall and enforcing your laws in the valley whilst your ranks are busy fighting in the forest—don't you agree? I also see you lost your armada to that guardian earlier today. I have ten ships berthed inland along the Narkus Estuary, five of which are war ships. In return for Miss Gillon's continued fair treatment, I will deploy them to protect the ocean borders of Valentia."

The Queen's mouth became a tight line. She needed those ships, Diamond realised. This city was vulnerable from the ocean even with the winter storms coming. Irritation bloomed over the Queen's face, and she waved her hand conceding to Jack's demand, "Yes, yes, of course, prince, you have my word she will be trained to grow her powers—and she will receive fair treatment." A small smile curled her lips, which Jack missed as he looked back at Diamond.

"Now, deciding the manner of this male's death is a matter for my court alone."

Jack bowed gracefully and indicated to a stoic-looking Somal and Vico, his guards, to walk to the door. General Edo had long been a legend to the Combined Army soldiers and the two Rhodainian warriors flashed the general a murderous glance before moving to await their prince by the exit. Diamond gave Jack a small smile of thanks, so relieved he had not just abandoned her, tears stung her eyes.

"I will see you soon," he promised quietly, giving her hand a squeeze before he turned away.

Hugo and Jack exchanged a glance, and the Queen's guard watched his friend leave. The door grated shut and silence settled upon the throne room. General Edo kneeled. It seemed he was having trouble breathing after Hugo's forceful kick. Diamond could not feel sorry for him. Her father was dead because of him.

Chapter Fifty-Two

"No more interruptions," the Queen ordered sharply. The guards either side of the door bowed in acquiescence. A door bar rattled loudly as it was dropped.

"Now. Kill the general, magic wielder, and you may go back to your room and start your training. Hesitate, and Commander Casimir will deliver the boy's punishment...followed by yours." The Queen smiled with delight as Diamond's face paled.

Clearly Jack's bargain meant nothing now that he was not here.

Painfully, slowly, Diamond dragged her eyes to the kneeling general. For the first time in his life he looked scared. His chin lifted and he tried to snarl, but his defiance was clearly forced. Death was staring him in the face. A tear trickled down her cheek. *How can I kill someone who has meant so much to me all these years?*

"I can't," she whispered, shaking her head, looking from Hugo to the whip in his hand.

The darkness in his eyes flickered to sapphire and his lips tightened. Simeon whimpered.

"Please—I can't," she sobbed, tears streaming down her face, dripping in tiny rivulets off her chin. Guilt seared her soul. Simeon was only a boy and had done nothing wrong.

"Oh, of course. How remiss of me," chuckled the Queen. "Lord Commander, pass the magic wielder that dagger from your belt."

Lord Commander Ream did not move his attention from Simeon's cowering form. Diamond wanted to scream and shout and warn him off the boy, but didn't know how. Here in this throne room she was helpless, utterly out of control.

"Hugo...please...." Diamond beseeched her friend, her saviour, her captor. If she murdered the general, she was no better than the Queen or the guards who served her like mindless puppets; if she didn't, Simeon would suffer.

Before Diamond could even blink, Lord Commander Ream backhanded her hard enough to rattle her brain. "You have been warned about addressing him as anything other than Commander Casimir," he responded in a flat voice.

Hugo did not move. She didn't think her bruised heart could have hurt any more, but it did. She had thought.... *What? That he felt something for me?* She stared at the dagger now resting in her palm. *His* dagger. Only hours ago this blade had meant hope and promises; now all it meant was death. General Edo stared at her, his face blanching with every second that passed. His life was at an end and he knew it.

Diamond swallowed her tears, her hand trembling violently as she lifted the blade. Hugo prowled around all three prisoners, swishing the whip threateningly. The iron tips clicked against the marble flooring. Then he stilled, his back towards his queen. A desperate sob burst from Diamond's chest.

"Please...." she cried, not caring if she sounded weak.

"You are a coward, just like your father," growled the general, but she didn't miss the slight shake in his voice.

Hugo looked directly at her. Feeling the weight of his gaze, she lifted her eyes and met silver-starred sapphires. Endless shadow devoured her mind. Gladly Diamond fell into oblivion. No matter that he had deserted her, or lied to her....

Utter concentration washed over his face, and a peculiar heat trickled from the scar on her left breast, warmth seeping out across her chest and down her arms and legs. It was not a painful sensation, but all consuming. Diamond uttered a moan that once again got stuck in her throat. This felt different to Hugo's magic. Her own did not react to its touch. Outwardly Diamond looked unchanged, still distraught, but inside that strange feeling travelled along her bones, her nerves, and out across her skin.

Paralysed now, it was impossible to escape the voice echoing in her head, demanding her compliance as the blackness cleared from her mind. Her thoughts were muffled as if she were drugged, her body and mind lost to another's control. Only conscious thought remained her own. The voice in her head commanded her to turn back towards General Edo. Silence devoured Diamond's screams. Nothing escaped her mouth. Her blood ran cold, as she approached General Edo and her hand lifted the dagger.

No, no, no! she wailed inside. No matter what he had done, she didn't want this, she was not a murderer!

'Kill him,' ordered the voice. Her mind fought and thrashed, but her body stepped forward anyway.

General Edo just looked at her as if accepting his fate. "Remember this if you live, Diamond. I loved your father very much, but in the end he let me down. You will always be let down by the ones you love. The simple answer is not to love anyone—be like him, be like me, if you want to save the innocent," he said, looking over her shoulder at Hugo. "Be able to hurt and kill anyone for what you believe. If you can, you may just survive your fate—" he grinned manically at the Queen, "—and do what she's afraid of. Save this world from darkness...."

With that he roared and lunged. Diamond could not answer, could not scream. But she did move, so fast the table of watching council toads gasped. Ducking and twisting under the general's outstretched arms, all Diamond felt was the moment the dagger sank into his flesh. It plunged between his ribs and found his heart. The strike was precise, a perfect killing blow.

The warmth of his blood on her fingers made her want to gag, but she could not. The voice did not tell her to. Sobbing and screaming inside, her shocked gaze turned to the general's face. Those beloved grey eyes met hers in a mixture of sorrow, defiance and pain. She wanted to look away but could not. Her hand withdrew the blade and a rush of hot blood covered her arm. *Will my father condemn me for this from Eternity, or rejoice in me avenging his own painful bloody death?*

This had to be the Queen's doing, no one else would have the power to control someone's mind, someone's actions. Diamond was forced to watch as General Edo collapsed to his knees before falling sideways, his life seeping onto the tiles. Blood cooled on her fingers and dripped down the blade, bright red droplets hitting her stocking feet. In front of her eyes General Edo's skin turned alabaster, stark against the deep green flooring. In seconds his breathing slowed to shallow pants.

Bile burned her throat as Diamond watched his last gasping breath. Those familiar eyes lost focus and stared unseeingly. Of their own accord, her fingers loosened and dropped the dagger. The overwhelming urge to do what the hateful echo instructed disappeared from her mind, and she collapsed on the floor. Not caring about the toads at the table or the Queen's guards—or the immortal Queen herself—Diamond crawled through the general's blood to his side, her fingers shaking she tried to stifle her sobs and gently closed his eyes.

"I'm sorry, I'm sorry," she whispered over and over.

Even though she knew what he had done, how his exile in a kingdom that was not his own had sent him to the point of desperation and insanity, all she could remember was the protection and love this fae had given her. But he had killed her father! She withdrew her hand, confused and dazed. He deserved this fate—he would have killed Jack, and her, and maybe more people to get what he wanted. Shocked, she looked at her shaking hand. Blood glistened. She had *murdered* an unarmed man. Gulping down gasps of air did not help. Promptly Diamond vomited, unable to process what she had done.

A hand reached down and hooked under her arm. Still retching, bile and saliva dripping down her chin, she was pulled to her feet. Hugo's face was empty as he turned her towards his Queen. Diamond found she could hardly stand. There was little choice but to lean into Hugo's strong grip for support, not caring what anyone thought. Simeon remained naked and kneeling nearby. She didn't know what would happen to him now. But Diamond's brain couldn't process anymore thoughts.

The Queen smiled, a thing so vicious and self-satisfied it turned her perfect face into a mask of ugliness.

"Well done, magic wielder. You have proven you can kill to save your own hide. Now all you need to do is prove that you can fight and kill to save the people of Avalonia—then I might let your friends live."

Diamond wanted vomit again—or faint or both. She had no thoughts other than collapsing. Magic caressed her skin. Unknowingly, she swayed further into Hugo, who held her firmly on her feet. Darkness fogged the edge of her vision.

"Take her back to her room, commander. You will begin her training tomorrow. Remember what I said. Do not let me down. You may release the guards from duty at her door. I doubt she will run again; but just in case, the boy will remain with me." She addressed Diamond. "He will be treated as fairly as my own trainee guards—unless you displease the commander, who will report to me as and when I desire it. I hope it is clear to you: you alone hold the fate of your friends in your hands."

Hugo bowed slightly and led Diamond, dazed and shaking, from the throne room.

Chapter Fifty-Three

Diamond could not speak as they left the throne room behind. Her torn clothes flapped open unheeded, exposing her. She could not bear to acknowledge Hugo as she staggered along the corridor. Her stomach clenched, and her eyes blurred with tears. She was a murderer. Thick, sticky blood covered her, a gruesome reminder of her sin.

Hugo had not helped her...he had stood by whilst she killed. A sudden choking rage fuelled her body, giving her strength enough to run back to her room. She screamed as rage and grief burst forth. Wanting to hit something—anything, she threw open the heavy wooden door with such force it slammed against the wall. Catching it, she slammed it back in Hugo's face.

A weapon! The Queen wanted a magical weapon! Diamond growled. Of course that was why she had been imprisoned and not killed. The hypocrisy of this kingdom—*her* kingdom, made her laugh out loud. A bitter humourless sound.

Hugo grunted as his hand collided against the swinging door with a resounding smack. The way he turned and closed it with so much care and gentleness tipped Diamond over the edge. Wild rage, grief and humiliation exploded.

"You bastard!" she yelled. "How could you just stand there whilst I was made to murder my friend? How could you do that to me?"

"He was not your friend, Diamond. He wished you harm and would have killed you if he'd had the chance," Hugo responded bluntly.

"No. No, I don't—I can't believe that!" she denied, then looked directly at him. His face was tight and pale. "I thought you said you would never leave me. You didn't even try and defend me! Gods, Hugo! Would you have done it? Would you have whipped me—or Simeon? Would you even have hesitated?" Hot tears tipped down her cheeks.

Hugo stared at the trails of wetness, conflicted emotion crossing his face. For a moment he opened and closed his mouth as if wanting to say something. Then his features hardened. "Do not judge me," he said. "You have always known what I am, who I serve. What I said this morning meant nothing. Those words—my helping you—were the actions of a fool. It was a futile gesture. My place is with my Queen, my life is hers." His voice became utterly flat. "I cannot defy an order, not even for you."

"But you are my friend. You helped me survive, and I don't just mean this morning. You fought for me so many times—with the dragon, in the forest. Hugo, you brought me back from the wraiths who would have taken my soul. You cared for me. You saved my life," she choked out, her heart aching until she had to clutch her chest. Tears flowed freely down her face, and it was such an effort to look at him. She didn't know what she wanted to do most, hit him, rage at him or just throw herself in his arms and beg him to hold her.

Instead she hugged her own body. "Did I imagine all that, Hugo? Did I imagine the things you said? Were they real or are you the best gods damned liar in the world?" she whispered, almost to herself.

Hugo cocked his head, grinding his teeth at her words, his jaw muscles tensing until his scar looked like it would rip apart. "I have never lied to you, Diamond. I warned you that very first night in the cave that you had no rights in this city, that you would be in danger. You also knew we might get caught today. I am a Queen's guard, I could not and cannot defy my Queen to help you," he rationalised again.

Diamond stormed up to him, her hands curled tightly into fists, wanting to punch that blank look off his handsome, scarred face. "How dare you!" her voice cracked. "Do you think that excuses you? You gave me hope where there was none. You might have been by my side, Hugo, but you sure as hell left me. And what of that poor, starving boy? Are you just going to leave him to the mercy of your perverted lord commander? Of course you are...." she jeered. "You brought me here knowing what your Queen would do to me, that she would use me or kill me—or both. I suppose it will ease your conscience when she orders you to slit his throat—and mine. After all, it's easy to excuse anything when you tell yourself you are only following orders."

Panting and out of breath she felt her adrenaline ebb away and—along with it—her anger. In its place was just a curious emptiness.

"I had no choice in any of it, Diamond," Hugo answered quietly. "Bringing you here was my duty, surely you know that. And the only reason I saved you, cared for you was to ensure you became what you were meant to be—a weapon for my Queen."

Diamond stared at him in abject horror.

"Oh, don't look so shocked," he stated, his voice detached and cold. "Surely you aren't naive enough to think I actually felt something for you. You were just an amusing distraction from the mundane. I would never have run from my Queen. I am an elite guard; I care for no one other than her. "

Diamond's throat was tight to the point of pain, and she was gasping for breath, "B-but this morning you were going to come with me. You...." her voice faded. No, she had been fooling herself. He was right, he had not lied. She had blinded herself to anything other than her feelings for him. Defiantly, she lifted her chin, even though her whole body shook. Her hand automatically went to the scratch marks on her chest, seeking the comfort of her necklace, only to find it gone. Anger swamped her again.

"That necklace was the only piece of my mother I have ever had. You took it away from me, Hugo, and I will never forget that. You are so honourable, aren't you?" she spat, remembering the brush of his fingers on her skin. "A petty thief as well as a trained attack dog and murderer. I would have been better taking my chances with Freddy in that forest. You are a disgusting excuse for a male," she declared, her eyes piercing his. Knowing she had been foolish with her feelings did not stop the rage in her heart. Beyond caring now, her voice rose to a fever pitch.

"And no matter what you say, you *are a lying bastard*! You did care about me, and you did save me. But you are right about everything else. You didn't leave me because you were *never* truly by my side. You *are* hers. For all your size and strength, that immortal bitch controls everything about you—even your body belongs to her!" She slapped her hands flat against his chest and shoved, utterly taken by surprise when he stumbled back. "You are her whore and a coward, Hugo. A pathetic weak coward!" she bellowed, her eyes a storm of violet lightening and hurt. "Even Simeon has more courage to stand up to her than you do."

Hugo stared at her, his eyes glittering. But Diamond ignored the warning signs: the tightness on his face, the way he clenched his fists and the growl that rose from deep in his chest.

She opened her mouth to continue her barrage of abuse.

"Shut up!" he suddenly bellowed. Savagely, he grabbed her shoulders, his face contorted with anger and self-loathing—nothing of the cold guard from seconds ago remaining. "Diamond, stop. I know my failings, both as a fae and a warrior. You are right. I am a coward. I cannot defy my Queen because I cannot protect you. I have shown you that today. Did I miss something? Because I'm sure you were listening when she threatened to make me kill you and everyone you care about! Is that what you want, for me to have to look in your eyes as I take your life? Like you did the general?" He paused and took a shaky breath.

She stared at him, shocked by his distress. His eyes were dark and swimming with regret. It had not crossed her mind to consider what that threat might do to Hugo. *But if he truly doesn't care for me, why is he bothered?* Conflicting emotions, made worse by grief and guilt over General Edo, stole Diamond's ability to think straight.

"But you treated me no better than an animal. You were going to whip me, Hugo," she accused tearfully, wondering in a moment of confusion if she had imagined his sorrow and regret as his eyes hardened and his face became cruel.

"So I was, but let's not make this all about you, magic wielder. You are dangerous, and for everyone's sake you need to learn how to control your magic. Unless I have missed something, you are no warrior; yet somehow I am expected to make you into a weapon powerful enough to subdue the immortal Wraith Lord."

The elite warrior stepped so close she had to tip her head back to look at him. Digging his fingers into her shoulders, he shook her hard enough to make her teeth rattle and gave a warning growl. "You think me a whore, a murderer, a thief...a *bastard*?" he smiled cruelly and leaned forward. Tears formed in Diamond's eyes as she watched his scar twist menacingly. "You think I shouldn't follow my Queen's orders? You think because you led me away from her with your innocence and needy glances you don't deserve the lash for trying to escape? Little girl, you have no idea how much of a bastard I can be, but you are going to find out."

Diamond felt sick at the pure ice in his eyes. He pushed her down into the armchair and squatted in front of her, his breath hot on her lips. His eyes flicked to the scrapes on her chest and a shadow flickered across his face. Just as quickly, it was gone.

"You *will* listen to me. The next few weeks are going to be hell for you. Your weak body will be beaten and likely broken, over and over, but let's be perfectly clear: I do not and will not care. You will work hard all day, every day. There will be no moaning or tears or you will hurt more. I suggest you learn quickly or be prepared to suffer the consequences."

Hugo leaned his massive frame closer until he had her pressed up against the chair back. He smiled, the tip of his nose touching hers. Warmth from his body seeped into her, and the smell of him smacked into her brain. His nearness, his scent, his impossibly beautiful eyes.... Her mind ceased to function and she could only stare at him like a cornered animal.

"And stay away from any other fae warriors—in the training ground or off it. It seems you command far too much interest from them. You are now the Queen's property—just like me. Whether you think that makes you her whore or not, I don't care; but you will keep your legs shut. You are not free to take a mate or share your body. Is that clear?"

Diamond stilled as his words sank in. The fae in the throne room.

"I will be here for you at dawn, so be ready. Wear something you can move in and fight in, or you will remove it and train in your underwear."

He smiled maliciously, his scar revealing white even teeth in a macabre way. Heat and indignation seared her cheeks as he raked his eyes over her exposed skin.

"Although, I am absolutely certain any males around will appreciate the naked sight of that beautiful body. I know I did when you begged me to undress you."

His mocking reference to the last time they had been in this room together sparked uncontainable fury in Diamond. Her hand shot out to slap him across the face. Almost lazily he caught her wrist, the hardness of his calloused skin scraping her as he squeezed. She yelped but he did not let go, he just shoved his face closer and snarled. Diamond recoiled. Moving in until his lips almost touched hers, he grinned wickedly.

"Save your anger for the training ground, little girl; you're going to need it. Every. Little. Bit. Because I'm saving mine—just for you.

Chapter Fifty-Four

Hugo slammed Diamond's door behind him, his self-control nearly in shreds. Clenching his shaking hands, he marched through the corridors, ignoring every single person that cowered against the walls. Not far now, he told himself, willing his legs to keep moving. In through the entrance to the guard's quarters, then up the winding stone stairs to his small room in the tower.

Quietly he shut the door. The silence hit just before he fell to his knees, his chest heaving. It was no good. He launched himself up, only just making it to the bathing room before vomiting in the toilet. Bile and saliva burned his throat.

Spent and emotionally wrecked, he sank onto the floor, his broad back leaning against the wall. He wearily tipped his head back. Never had he loathed himself so much. But turning Diamond into a killer had been his only choice.

He uttered a heartfelt plea to the goddess for forgiveness, trying to convince himself the hours he had spent in the palace libraries looking for old legends, and pulling out dusty old histories to research the venom bond, had paid off. What he had learned, what he now knew he could do, scared the shit out of him.

He had never wanted to control Diamond, but he *had* wanted to know how the bond worked. Selfishly, he wanted to convince himself her actions were her own when they related to him.

Was it only this morning I allowed myself to hope, to dream of an escape? He chuckled bitterly. The dog. That scruffy-looking mongrel in the temple grounds had to have been a shapeshifter, a spy for the Queen—or the general had stupidly formed a deal with the Queen before he found them. Either way, it didn't matter now. The general was gone, and he and Diamond were both trapped here.

The Queen had shown her hand. Hardly a surprising turn of events. Diamond had been allowed to live to become a weapon. Not for a moment, though, had Hugo guessed how his evil monarch was going to destroy Diamond's spirit. Hugo still didn't know if he could have whipped Diamond—or that poor pathetic boy. But he had hoped with every shred of his warped soul that he wouldn't have to. He had known Diamond would not kill the crazed general, so he had uttered a silent plea for forgiveness and grasped her mind with everything he had. The gamble had paid off.

It hadn't been Diamond who had killed her childhood protector—it had been Hugo. One day he would tell her. She did not deserve to suffer the guilt for such an action.

Sometime later, feeling calmer and in control once again, Hugo pushed himself up off the floor. Diamond was right—he was a coward; no matter his reasons, he could never undo the wickedness of his actions in that throne room, but he could try and do something good in the present.

Resolutely, he stood and walked to the window where he could watch the sun set. Patiently, determination in every line of his body, Hugo awaited the arrival of his closest friend—the darkness.

The gentle wind that fanned the two silver-haired women was neither warm nor cold. It just existed.

Diamond contemplated the woman from her vision. With arms even more emaciated and huge blue eyes that dominated her gaunt thin face, she seemed to shimmer like a spectre, coming and going with the breeze.

"Where are we?" Diamond whispered.

A snow-capped volcano smoked in the far distance, but the ground they stood on was silky soft and shifted gently. Warm blue sand squished between her bare toes. She gazed in amazement at the beautiful expanse of swirling dunes that stretched away into the distance. There was no definition between land or sky, it was all one, seamless in its making. Diamond had never seen anything like it—but she had read about it.

"This is the Sky Desert?" It was a strange and wonderful place, full of nothing yet containing everything. Diamond could feel energy burning into her magic—feeding her. Life thrived here. But one would only see it if the wizards who protected these lands deemed one worthy of entering their realm. The woman smiled but did not reply. In fact, she seemed unable to summon the energy to speak at all. She gently brushed her thin cold fingers against Diamond's chest. Her brows drew together in a frown as she touched the gouges left by the Queen's sharp finger nails. Her dull eyes were sad, questioning.

"She took it. The Queen took it," Diamond answered, feeling the wrench of that loss again. "How do I get it back?" she asked through tears that left trails of moisture down her cheeks.

The woman frowned, her eyes flashing angrily. Turbulent wind blasted across them but not a grain of blue sand shifted. Currents of air tugged fiercely at Diamond's cream silk nightgown before a bright flash of light had her squeezing her eyes shut. An answering warmth tingled along Diamond's skin, fizzling down into her bones until something tight covered her body. She gazed upon herself in astonishment, her mouth gaping open. Lifting her hands in front of her face she turned them over and over, inspecting them—inspecting her whole body in awe.

A figure hugging suit that felt like warm liquid wrapped Diamond from neck to ankles. Layered on top were beautiful iridescent scales that encased her body. Glittering and utterly indestructible, the armour wrapped around her torso like a second skin. Her boots stopped just below her knees, her legs protected by larger metallic scales that covered her thighs, forearms and shoulders. Shining and glorious, the scaled suit writhed next to her skin as though alive, fluid yet solid, an impenetrable otherworldly force.

It was impossible to do anything other than stare at herself as the outline of majestic dragons pushed through the scales before disappearing, all of them were adorned with a single jewel in their foreheads. They slithered around her body like a living shield. Diamond screeched as a huge head appeared in the scale-encrusted chest plate and endless, multifaceted eyes rolled back to meet her own. A sense of overwhelming protection filled her chest.

These are the guardians, she realised in wonderment. The everlasting deities who protected Eternity and the gods. Daggers engraved with the runes of their ancient language hung from her waist, and she felt the vicious rigidity of blades that were secreted up against her body and thighs.

The woman stepped forward and placed the flat of her hand against Diamond's forehead. Her touch was cold but the sudden images that flashed into Diamond's brain burned her mind: images of battles long past, of fighting alongside fierce winged warriors, of fire unleashed from the gaping maws of magnificent dragons, of repulsive dead-eyed monsters she had never seen the like of in any mythical books. A cloying, eternal shroud of darkness threatened to swamp her soul and suck the very life from her.

Diamond gasped for air, fighting against the swirling black veil and sudden bitter cold.

Those images abruptly disappeared, replaced by a picture of this same woman, young and strong; her eyes cerulean, bright and glowing with cold fury. She was clad in the same armour that Diamond now wore, her face feral and splattered in red and black gore. Fighting with a grace and skill that took Diamond's breath away, her movements were precise and deadly and so quick that as she turned and dipped and slashed it was hard to keep track. In one hand she held a dark metal spear, wielding it in a blur of lethal movements. Monster's loomed above her; huge beasts covered in a shell like spiky exoskeleton. Enormous jaws, tightly packed with sharp teeth, snapped at the spear as if trying to take it. Evading their claws and teeth, this woman slew monster after monster. She did not tire or give quarter to her enemy.

Magic burst from her free hand in destructive waves. But Diamond could feel the woman pulling at the energy around her, manipulating the air, the earth, the flames of dragon fire and even the moisture from the tears of the fallen. She drew it towards her until the air hummed, and she filled with a power so bright it almost burned Diamond's eyes.

The battle from a millennia ago raged inside Diamond's mind. This was the same magic she had used in the forest, except this magic obeyed the woman's command. Her energy formed a thousand swords at once, stabbing and cutting a path through her enemy. With just a thought, she thrust razor sharp ribbons outward and turned her enemies to dust. Realisation dawned, stealing Diamond's ability to breath.

This was Lunaria. This fierce woman was the goddess of creation.

She was able to manipulate the elements and magic of this world to fight her brother, Erebos. Lunaria pushed thoughts and memories into Diamond's mind. She had fought for millennia to prevent Erebos from destroying every living soul in this world. But unlike him, Lunaria had a heart and had fallen in love. That love had become her greatest weakness. The goddess had loved her fae mate, King Noan Arjuno, and their new born baby so fiercely that she had died for them.

But here, now, in this dream world, Lunaria looked like the goddess of starvation and death. Diamond swallowed, her mouth and throat bone dry as the images receded.

'Erebos is watching, he is waiting, but soon he will return. Child, it will take all your courage to fight through your grief and shadows. Even when your heart is breaking, you must remember that you are of my blood, and that only our blood can kill him.'

Lunaria's voice was but a weak echo inside Diamond's head. The bony hand lifted from Diamond's forehead. Aghast, Diamond stared at Lunaria.

"W-what do you mean? How am I of your blood? How can I beat a god? I am only a girl," she whispered, horrified that anyone would expect her to carry out such a task.

Lunaria smiled sadly. *'You must, or he will destroy everything. Not just your home but mine too. I cannot help you, not from this prison. Only you can do what needs to be done. Don't give up. Don't let death and despair win—or Chaos will reign over Eternity.'*

The goddess became more transparent, the air around them imploding. The atoms of this dream world cracked open until a gaping void yawned behind the goddess. Lunaria fought the ghastly shadow-fingers that tried to drag her into darkness. Forcing out her weak magic, the goddess drove them back before forcefully pushing her hand back on Diamond's head.

Diamond's magic flared into life, her body twitching as memories of lessons learned long ago were thrust deep into her mind, burning into her memory; a warrior's lessons: how to think; how to read her enemy; how to move, strike and kill.

'I will give you this...but you have to practice—beat him, beat death—and free me, her eyes begged Diamond.

The sands shifted, disappearing from under Diamond's feet into a huge fissure that cleaved the earth, then she was falling, falling through darkness. There was no sound, no sight, only a desperate coldness. Down she plummeted, her mouth gaping in a silent scream. Her body slammed into something solid, then there was nothing.

Chapter Fifty-Five

Hugo had not attempted to sleep or rest; guilt kept tightening his gut into painful knots. *How many times will I have to hurt her, to damage that beautiful face or body to save her from worse insult?* Now that he had calmed down, he knew he would have done it: he would have lashed her skin open to save her from Lord Commander Ream's punishments.

Hours had passed and he was still intermittently shaking, although he was at a loss to decide why. Fear. Regret. Anger. Self-disgust. He smacked a fist into the mattress and half groaned, half growled. He deserved Diamond's contempt, but that did not dull the pain of it.

Why did I have to meet her? Why does she even exist? She had become his worst nightmare and his perfect dream. She didn't know how right all her accusations had been. Hugo cared for her, to the point of losing control of his common sense. By bringing her to the palace, by guarding her room, by running after her this morning, he had broadcast his feelings.

Now she was a target for all those who wanted to get back at him.

His magic flared protectively. She was his Nexus. The implications of that almost stole his breath. Together they could stimulate and boost the other's magic. But if the books he had been devouring recently were to be believed, if he and Diamond mated, their magic would swell far beyond any the Queen could yield alone. He swallowed and squeezed his eyes shut.

If I scoop Diamond up now and run, could we escape? He slumped, his chin resting on his broad chest. Too many others would die—Jack would die. Hugo sighed; he did not want that on his conscience, and he didn't think Diamond would either. Besides, they would be hunted to the end of time by the Queen. There was no running—not for him anyway.

Hugo growled at his confused thoughts. Being ordered to kill Diamond made his soul shudder with fear, and with absolute certainty he knew he never could. Sitting on the side of his bed, he tossed his knife, catching the white-bone hilt with precision, over and over, just like he had been doing on and off for the past two hours.

The image of that possessive glare Fedron had given Diamond had sent a wave of rage bubbling through his blood. And then there was Attion. Hugo snarled, thinking about his underling. So the abused became the abuser; it was sickening to think of that cycle happening over and over in this tower, of the many hundreds of young guards subjected to unspeakable horrors at the hands of males like Ream. Hugo swallowed the bile in his throat.

First he would deal with Attion and the boy, then he would think about Fedron. Hugo had met fae like him before. Primal and debase. They were always masters of manipulation and lies, hiding their true selves to fit into society, often exploiting unwary females to get what they wanted.

The fact he had hidden his true nature enough to become one of Commander Riddeon's men showed what a good actor the bastard was. Unless....

Hugo frowned, wondering if the master commander had realised what a monster Fedron could become and was keeping him close. Fedron had been there in the forest, only obedient enough not to challenge Elexon's leadership, but not completely loyal either. Maybe Hugo would seek out Elexon and warn him about Fedron. The master commander's son struck Hugo as a solid capable warrior, he would listen—or not.

Hugo ground his teeth. Fedron had marked Diamond's scent and would come for her eventually. A wicked grin twisted his scar at the prospect of taking down a male who would threaten his mate. He sucked air in through his clenched teeth.

Hugo tossed his blade in the air, caught the bone hilt and threw it with such force the wooden doorframe split. He watched the blade wobble from side to side. That damned girl had turned his life upside down. His head was constantly filled with her. Even with that spark of spirit and defiance, that challenged him at every turn, he did not for one second believe that Diamond would be able to fight with enough skill to survive Ragor. Not after only a few weeks of training. She may not even survive the Queen's chosen test.

As for Diamond's necklace, the Queen had an ulterior motive for taking it. He had seen the greed in her eyes when she had spotted it through that ridiculous see-through blouse.

Hugo gave a frustrated growl and looked at the moon out of his small tower window. His fingers curled into the bedclothes. Every day brought him closer to the thing he dreaded most about being an elite guard: winter solstice and the Queen's bite. Hugo closed his eyes and groaned with dread, remembering the way she had run her hands down his body. He had a fool's hope she would remain satisfied with one of the other guards, but deep down he knew she would not.

No. For reasons he didn't understand she had left him alone all these years; but without a doubt, his luck had run out.

Hugo's skin crawled at the thought of letting her do to him what he had done to Diamond. Only now he wasn't sure her venom would work. His throat ached as he swallowed. He could not wipe the taste of Diamond from his mind or erase the feeling of her blood and magic raging through his body. For the first time in his life Hugo found himself uncertain how to handle the situation he was in.

Hugo dropped his head and studied the bare wooden floorboards. If he wanted to help Diamond, he had to make her into a decent fighter. Hugo needed to know she could protect herself, even if she ultimately had to protect herself against him.

The ice moon moved slowly through the glittering night. Eventually Hugo got up, yanked the knife from the door frame and studied it. Before he could attempt to get Diamond out of the city, he had to convince her and everyone else he did not care about her, not one little bit. He could not risk the Queen suspecting he had such deep feelings for another woman. The threat of her biting him before winter solstice was too high.

Hugo smiled grimly. After yesterday, making Diamond hate him enough to fight unreservedly was going to be easy. She needed to loath everything about him or she would always hold back. He swore to his empty room.

By the goddess, training her was going to test his nerves and his resolve. Hugo rubbed his hands over his face, already weary from his tumultuous thoughts. First, though, he had a debt to pay.

Attion stirred. Something had disturbed him, bringing him back from the nightmares that plagued his slumber. The exposed damp skin of his chest prickled with goose bumps. Slowly the guard turned his head, his hand sliding under his pillow to grasp the dagger he always kept there. His breathing became shallow and quiet as he listened. It had been years since the Lord Commander had visited his bed at night, but still Attion began to sweat fearfully.

Cracking his eyelids a fraction, he scanned the shadows cast by the light of Tu Lanah.

Nothing. No movement or threat. He loosed a big relieved breath and threw an arm across his face. He was being ridiculous. There was a chair wedged under the door handle; besides Ream preferred boys, not grown men.

"I can smell your fear," said a familiar voice. "Did you know you whimper for mercy in your sleep?"

Attion bolted upright, his dagger clasped in his hand. It couldn't be possible! His door was still locked, the chair still there. Unnerved, he scanned the shadows.

"If you fear your abuser so, if what he did to you disgusts you so, why did you lay your filthy hands on her?"

Before he could speak, Attion's jaw exploded in pain. His head snapped back and his lip exploded against his teeth. He hit the floor next to the bed with a resounding smack.

"Get up," ordered the disembodied voice laced with such wrath even Attion hastened to comply.

Standing naked, his mouth gaped open as Hugo materialised out of the shadows. The commander grinned at Attion's fearful expression. The scar on his face twisted and morphed until he became a demon of shadow.

"You and I have much to discuss, Attion, but I think we will not do it with words. Sometimes actions are far more eloquent—don't you think?" asked the shadow demon before he moved so quickly Attion didn't have time to formulate an answer.

Chapter Fifty-Six

Diamond awoke with a start, her heart racing and her legs entangled in the bedclothes. Loud impatient banging resounded on her door, vibrating the walls and floor. Hugo's furious voice boomed through the thick wood. Catapulting herself out of bed, her hair in disarray and her heart banging painfully against her ribs, she ran to the door, unlocking it just as he threatened to bash it down.

Hugo barged in, his face enraged, his eyes glittering like molten silver. He slammed the door shut, rattling the walls enough to shake dust into the air.

"What the hell are you still doing in bed!" he roared at her.

Speechless with fright, Diamond ran away from him, tripping over the bedclothes that were now draped on the floor.

"I-I'm sorry. I didn't sleep well..." she stammered, her face flaming with stress and embarrassment as she regained her balance.

His eyes dropped to her bare feet, then travelled slowly, deliberately, up over her bare thighs, grazing over every curve accentuated by her too short silk nightie. She felt every inch of her skin burn where his eyes rested. Magic scorched her, hitting her in an intense wave that blasted through to her bones. Immediately and against her will, her body responded, heat pulsing through her core and pooling between her legs.

Confusion rooted her to the spot. Fear told her to run from his anger, but that blast of pure lust made her want to claw every bit of clothing from that coiled muscled body.

His nostrils flared as he inhaled. For a fraction of a second his dark eyes gleamed with a feral hunger. Her breath hitched as he took one step forwards, clenching his fists. Then he stopped dead, as if hitting an invisible wall. A slow cruel smile stretched his lips and the overwhelming feeling of want receded. She released a shaky breath as he crossed his large arms over his chest and stared pointedly at the flimsy silk.

"Oh? So you've decided to entertain the troops, have you?" he drawled, his eyes resting on her bare thighs. "Nice."

The blood drained from her face, and she backed away from him.

"You wouldn't?" she whispered crossing her arms over her chest, horror driving away any remaining lust.

His footsteps thumped as he strode over the floor, shoving his face into hers. "Get. Dressed. *Now!*" he roared.

She jumped, shrieked and grabbed her clothes off the chair, running on fatigue-heavy limbs into the bathing room. Less than two minutes later she emerged, her heart banging hard in her chest. Hastily she grabbed a tunic.

"Come on!" he barked without even looking at her.

Diamond just had time to snatch a band so she could braid her hair away from her face before he was striding down the corridor to the nearest exit. Struggling to keep up with his long stride, Diamond pushed thoughts of what she had done, of the murderer she had become, deep into the recesses of her mind and locked it away. The feeling of hot sticky blood still lay heavy on her hands; rubbing them on her thighs did nothing to erase that memory.

Swearing at Hugo's back helped distract her. As soon as they were outside, without warning, he grabbed her around the waist.

Her body hit his hard, and she was forced to grab onto his armour-clad shoulders as he launched himself into the misty dawn air. She shivered as the cold penetrated her thin cotton shirt. With no time to throw it on, she was still clutching her tunic in her hands. Hugo soared gracefully through the air, his hands holding her tightly against him. If she hadn't been so terrified of what he was going to do and hadn't gripped him so tightly, it would be easy to be entranced by the glorious morning sun glinting on the silver rivulets of his armoured sapphire wings.

But she *was* terrified of Hugo, of what was going to happen today, of the nightmare in which she drowned in the general's blood—of the words of an imprisoned goddess—of so many things....

The palace towers fell away beneath them and the cityscape came in to view. Beyond it, the vista of the beautiful valley and the ancient wall were bathed in rose gold sunbeams. Diamond gritted her teeth, ignoring the shift of muscles under her fingers and the warmth of Hugo's body against hers. Hugo thought her incapable of becoming a warrior. Dream-like images burned her mind, and she defiantly lifted her chin.

He had no idea what she was capable of. Determination lit a fire through her blood. If the goddess herself believed Diamond could fight through her grief and shadows to triumph against a dark lord, then Diamond would do whatever it took to bring that belief to reality. Whatever was thrown at her, she would not cry and she would not complain, but she *would* master her magic and learn how to fight back. Never again would she be weak or helpless. Pushing against Hugo's grip, Diamond twisted her body. Defiance radiated from her as she faced forwards and readied herself to meet her future head on.

She was the daughter of General Arades Gillon, and a living blood relative of the goddess of creation; she would not be broken by anyone, least of all the warrior who had shattered her heart.

Acknowledgements

Dear reader,

Thank you so much for reading A Bond of Venom and Magic, *book one in* The Goddess and the Guardians *series. I hope you have enjoyed the journey with Diamond and Hugo so far (they still have such a long way to go!). It would be fantastic if you could find time to leave a review on Amazon and Goodreads for ABOVAM. Reviews are so important. There are millions of books out there and getting a title noticed by the right readers is increasingly difficult. It doesn't have to be an in depth review, just a few words can make all the difference to the book being visible to the right readers. Tell your friends, your family—in fact anyone you think might enjoy A Bond of Venom and Magic about the book, shout it from the roof tops if you feel like it!! That would be awesome! I am immensely grateful to you all for your interest and support and would love to connect with you. You can find me on:*

Twitter:
https://twitter.com/kytomlinson

Facebook page
https://www.facebook.com/ktomlinson.author/

Facebook Street Team
https://www.facebook.com/groups/1531458143821861/

Instagram
https://www.instagram.com/karentomlinsonauthor/

Goodreads
https://www.goodreads.com/author/show/15259538.
Karen_Tomlinson

Or Join my mailing list for information on cover reveals, Advanced Reader Copies and news about new releases at my web site http://karentomlinson.com

My heartfelt thanks,

For me the journey to publication for *A Bond of Venom and Magic* has been a huge learning curve. I have a lot of people to thank for helping me get this far, so if I miss anyone please forgive me: You are all fantastic!

Annie and Abbie: Diamond, Hugo and Jack have come a long way since they began life as a bedtime fairy story! As you have grown and changed so has this wonderful world and all the people in it. Creating characters and coming up with names for them has been so much fun, and this book would not exist without you. I love you both dearly. You inspire me (and challenge me) in so many ways. In my world you burn brighter than any shooting star. Please always be the happy, stubborn, kind, and absolutely gorgeous souls you are now. Aaron, I know you don't understand my obsession with this book or my resolve to embark on this road to being an author, but I thank you for being patient; for all the evenings I have spent in the writing cave, and the days that you have taken the girls (and poppy) out, or gone on your travels together so that I can write... I know my stubbornness and determination to achieve my goals is not always easy to live with. I'd love to say I'm done...but I'm far from finished. I have lots of stories left to tell....

So many people read the early versions of this story. A massive thank you to you all! To Natalie Sydney and Emma Cocking: you guys rock! You got the whole 250,000 words and still managed to give me feedback! To Suze Syson: Thank you for pointing out that readers do need to take a break every now and then... Shorter chapters were definitely required! You helped me think about the book from a readers perspective and I thank you for your support and feedback. Helen Samms, Patty Darranguisse, Jo Dursely, Kate Hackney and Katie (darling!) Melan. All your comments, good and painful, helped me immensely. To Wendy Hawkins: What can I say? You are a star! When I crumbled, your support and logic grounded me and put me back on track. Your in depth feedback has been amazing and ABOVAM would not be the story it is without your input.

I am very lucky to have met many kind and generous people on the journey to publication. Cassie James, I am so pleased we met. Your generosity in helping me and your support of AVOBAM has been amazing. I hope our friendship continues.

To all the wonderful people who have joined my street team: You are awesome! Thank you so much for supporting me and ABOVAM. I am grateful that you are willing to take a chance on an unknown author.

James Robert Ainsworth, you have been a wonderful supporter of this project. Your ideas and generosity have been fantastic. Though, no matter what you teach me about Photoshop, I will always be lacking in my IT skills!

Nick Kennedy: Thank you for your patience and IT assistance at any hour of the day and night! I would not look so professional without you!

To my wonderful parents: Mum, thank you for encouraging me and reading ABOVAM despite it not being your 'cup of tea'. Dad: You are the best. Your belief in me is overwhelming. I thank you both from the bottom of my heart for everything you have done for me, and Rosanne and Vivienne in every aspect of our lives; not just with this book.

Jenny Baker: You have encouraged me ever since I started this journey. I can't thank you enough for all the times you have provided me a shoulder to cry on, for bolstering me when I felt discouraged and making me believe I could do this. I still have the card you sent me! It would have been a lonely ride without you to share this with and I could not have done it without your unconditional support. You are an awesome friend and I love you dearly.

To my gorgeous 'little' sis-Zanny: I still remember hiding under the duvets to read books when we should have been sleeping! Sorry if I kept you awake but I guess all this started back then! I don't know how to thank you for reading my manuscript, with all its different titles, word counts and characters, with so much enthusiasm—so many hundreds of times! Your unwavering belief in me and ABOVAM has been amazing and your feedback invaluable. You have championed it and not let me give up on myself or my dream. You are a beautiful, kind and generous person and I love you.

Lastly thank you to everyone who has purchased and read this book. I am immensely grateful to you all. I hope you have enjoyed it and will join Diamond and Hugo on their quest to defeat the Lord of Chaos and save Eternity....

EMBERS BURN. SHADOWS GROW.

CAN BETRAYAL BE FORGIVEN WHEN
BLOOD MUST FLOW?

A Bond of Blood and Fire

The Goddess and the Guardians
Book Two

Don't miss the next book in this
outstanding series

Made in the USA
San Bernardino, CA
09 November 2016